DOMINATOR

'Professor,' Harding broke in. 'I know you've had only a few minutes to study the information. But from what you've seen, do you think the Massadas are capable of striking at principal targets on Earth?'

Horovitz looked up at the camera so that he appeared to be looking directly at the two men. 'Yes, Mr President. The design concepts are excellent.'

'What targets can the missiles threaten?'

Horovitz did some hurried calculations. 'In one hour the *Dominator*'s orbital position will provide it with a favourable window on Soviet targets lying between fifty and sixty degrees north.'

Harding's brain wrestled with his knowledge of Eastern hemisphere geography. 'What cities does that include?'

'Leningrad, Kazan, Gorki, Moscow –'

By the same author
**available in Mandarin Paperbacks*

The Doomsday Ultimatum
Crown Court
*Ice
*U-700
*Churchill's Gold
The Tip-Toe Boys (*filmed as* Who Dares Wins)
Earthsearch
Earthsearch – Deathship
*Mirage
*Swift
*A Cage of Eagles

DOMINATOR

James Follett

Mandarin

A Mandarin Paperback

DOMINATOR

First published in Great Britain 1984
by Methuen London Ltd
This edition published 1989
Reprinted 1990 (twice)
Reissued 1991
by Mandarin Paperbacks
Michelin House, 81 Fulham Road, London SW3 6RB

Mandarin is an imprint of the Octopus Publishing Group

Copyright © James Follett 1984

ISBN 0 7493 0262 3

A CIP catalogue for this title
is available from the British Library

Reproduced, printed and bound in Great Britain by
BPCC Hazell Books
Aylesbury, Bucks, England
Member of BPCC Ltd.

1   The MiG-35 was the world's fastest combat aircraft.
      It hurtled in from the west – boring silently through
      the Mediterranean haze at six times the speed of sound,
at a height of fifty feet, with the roar from its two Tumansky
engines trailing a hundred miles behind.

The strike aircraft's titanium alloy skin was beginning to glow as
a result of its colossal speed. Its wings were tucked into its
shark-like fuselage because at that speed it did not need them.

There was little for the pilot to do. Armon Habet sat in a cocoon
of silence and electronics. On-board computers controlled every
aspect of the flight, translating the signals from the terrain-hugging
radar into impulses that maintained the aircraft's course and height
with a deadly precision that was beyond the capability of any
human.

Armon kept an anxious eye on the hazard monitors that would
warn him when they had detected an approaching missile. He had a
healthy respect for the Israeli coastal defences. A surface-to-air
Mishmar missile had chased him for two minutes on the last raid.
Luckily the MiG-35 had the speed to outstrip the Mishmar but it
had been a close thing and there was always the chance that a
Mishmar well-placed for an intercept would score.

The target proximity warning tone chimed. Armon thumbed the
attack status touch key causing the MiG to climb automatically to
five hundred feet.

Suddenly the hotel and apartment blocks were on the horizon.
And then they were streaking towards Armon at one mile per
second.

A jolt. A changed digital reading. And his AS-20 missile was
away.

Armon never saw the attack he had launched; his MiG had
penetrated ten miles into Israeli airspace and was climbing to clear
the Golan Heights by the time the missile had identified and locked
on to its target.

The AS-20 was a hundred yards from the hotel when its on-board radar detonated the warhead so that it spewed forward a cluster of three hundred anti-personnel bombs.

The hotel's guests had no time to comprehend the hellish weapon that had been unleashed on them. Nor did they have time to panic. The baseball-sized bombs smashed through the hotel's façade at the same moment that the shockwave from the MiG's passage rocked the building and the surrounding apartment blocks.

The bombs exploded in bedrooms and bathrooms. They exploded in lifts. They exploded in the restaurant and bar and in the sauna. They exploded in the hairdressing salon; in the lobby and in the gift shops. Some even exploded in the crowded swimming-pool. Nine out of ten of the detonating bombs sprayed their surroundings with hundreds of tiny plastic barbs that embedded deeply in flesh. For those victims that survived, the barbs would be virtually impossible to find on X-ray plates. And the toxin they released as they dissolved into the bloodstream ensured that the victims would eventually die anyway after having drained the enemy's medical resources. Every tenth bomb was an incendiary that splattered globules of sticky, white-hot magnesium in all directions.

Armon and his MiG – emblazoned with Palestinian markings – were over Nazareth and streaking towards Syria by the time the first panic-stricken screams of the victims were heard in the Mediterranean holiday resort.

Hendrik Rymann, Israel's tenth Prime Minister, was taking his customary one-hour afternoon sleep in the bedroom on the top floor of his official residence in Jerusalem's Smolenskin Street when the green bedside phone warbled softly.

His thoughts were organized by the time his groping hand found the handset. Only one man could call him on the green encryptophone – his close friend and lifelong confidant, Dr Michael Greer, the donnish civilian head of the Institute. Better known as Mossad – the Israeli Secret Service.

It had to be bad news. Serious bad news. There was no such thing as good news any more.

'Good afternoon, Michael,' said Rymann with contrived crispness, while rubbing his eyes.

Greer didn't bother with an apology for disturbing Rymann

because he knew that it would be cut short. 'Hendrik – there's been another MiG-35 rhubarb,' he stated without preamble.

Rymann was suddenly wide awake. 'Where?'

'Netanya. The Dan Hotel.'

'Casualties?' asked Rymann, voicing his first concern.

There was a pause at the other end of the line. 'In excess of two hundred killed. Another forty-plus injured.'

Anyone who did not know the Israeli Prime Minister well would have assumed from his good-humoured expression that he was unaffected by the news. The truth was that Hendrik Rymann suddenly felt sick in his stomach. He ran his fingers through his close-cropped hair while mentally composing the letter that he would be sending to all the victims' families. He made a point of setting aside an hour of every working day to send personal letters to all the close relatives of those men and women who had died in the conflict. It was to his credit that the year of the sustained and bloody war with the PLO had not desensitized him against casualty figures. 'Thank you for calling me, Michael,' he said at length. 'We'll discuss it at this evening's meeting.'

Rymann replaced the receiver without waiting for a reply. He lay back on his bed staring up at the ceiling.

His predecessor would have called the *Chel Ha'Avir* High Command and ordered an immediate retaliatory air strike. But that was why the emotional Hari Ritz was no longer Prime Minister of Israel and Hendrik Rymann was. Twelve months previously a section of the Wailing Wall had been destroyed by a PLO suicide pilot. Incensed at this attack on the holiest of Jewish shrines, Ritz had ordered an air strike against the Kaarba at Mecca. He had issued the order without consulting his advisors or the Cabinet. Nearly five thousand Moslem pilgrims gathered around the sacred black stone had been killed in the raid on the Grand Mosque.

It had been a lunatic move that had cost Israel dear and had triggered the Second War of Attrition. Oil-rich Saudi Arabia abandoned its moderate policy towards Israel and came down firmly on the side of the PLO. Egypt scrapped its peace treaties with Israel and followed suit, and then the rest of the Arab world followed Egypt. The Soviet Union, sensing which way the wind was blowing, had immediately offered the PLO an interim homeland at Bakal on the Black Sea, which the PLO's charismatic leader, Joseph Maken, had accepted.

Hari Ritz had resigned his office and his Knesset seat, forcing the political parties of the ruling DMC Alliance to find another leader – and quickly.

Hendrik Rymann, the good-humoured, plain-speaking Minister of Defence, with his unashamed taste for a steady procession of beautiful women, had not been the obvious choice, whereas the austere Jacob Kasser of the Herut party most certainly was.

The feeling was that Rymann's candour and easy-going humour would count against him. Journalists who did not know Rymann well had argued that it was impossible to take seriously a man who had once told a CBS reporter that the only thing wrong with Israel was its scarcity of blondes.

When the fierce party lobbying had started, many had been astonished at Rymann's popularity. Over forty Haver Knessets out of one hundred and thirty members had expressed their support for Rymann's nomination. Even more surprising was that the influential Rabbi Val Nassim of the ultra-orthodox Agudat Israel party, one of Rymann's main enemies and a man with direct access to the ailing President Kammat, should have come down on Rymann's side saying that it was better to have an honest man as Prime Minister than a hypocrite. And as for Rymann's sense of humour – well – he was going to need that in the months to come.

And so it was, at the age of forty-nine, that Hendrik Rymann had become Prime Minister of Israel during the first year of the eighteenth Knesset.

Rymann's mind turned to the phone call he had just received. It was not hard to see why Joseph Maken had picked the Dan Hotel for yet another of his lightning raids. The beachfront hotel was considered one of the finest in Israel and had often been used for the signing of peace treaties with neighbouring hostile countries in the days of Israeli military supremacy. As a young army officer in 1983, Rymann had attended the initialling of a treaty in the Dan Hotel between Israel and the Lebanon. Over the intervening years the hotel had become identified in Arab eyes as the scene of repeated humiliations. It was inevitable that the PLO would seek to destroy it once they had the ability to do so.

Rymann glanced at his watch. He had twenty-five precious minutes of solitude before his secretary called him. He considered sending for Semona to share them but decided against it. *Rav-Turai* (Sergeant) Semona Lucca was the most stunningly beautiful

8

chauffeur in the Israeli army. Her greatest asset, after her magnificent body, was that she didn't have to be smuggled in and out of his residence; she was already on the staff. The trouble was that he was getting much too fond of her.

As Rymann dozed off to sleep, he had a strange premonition that another major shock, far worse than the Dan Hotel attack, was awaiting him.

2 There was nothing to suggest that a very sudden and very horrible death lay thirty minutes in the future for one member of the crew of the space shuttle Orbital Vehicle OV-141 – *Dominator*.

Neil O'Hara's thirty-one shuttle missions had failed to make him blasé about the awesome spectacle of the Earth viewed from space. The astronaut reckoned that even when he had flown a hundred missions, he would still be grabbing every quiet moment during a flight to feast his eyes on the tranquil, aquamarine planet that was home.

Like many of his colleagues who flew the shuttles, working in space had had a profound effect on the fair-haired young astronaut. Seeing Earth as a finite entity in the cosmos had instilled in him a cynical disregard of national boundaries and national differences. From a height of two hundred miles, the petty squabbles of mankind seemed futile and destructive. Even the question of his deteriorating marriage rarely intruded on his thoughts when he was in orbit. Helen was a being on, literally, another planet – someone he visited on his trips to Earth. Space was his rightful environment – nothing else made sense. For Neil, space travel had become a drug, and the splendour of the remote Earth was the hallucination.

Antarctica was slipping past two hundred miles below his port window and the east coast of the African continent had appeared straight ahead as a steadily darkening smear on the massive crescent of the horizon.

Poised above the coasting orbiter was the huge bulk of KARMA II, one of the three television relay Direct Broadcasting Satellites owned by the United Arabic Broadcasting Commission. With its two mighty wings – solar panels spread to trap energy from the

9

sun – KARMA II resembled a giant bird of prey about to devour the fly-like *Dominator*.

Two weeks before the five hundred million-dollar satellite had suffered a total failure which was why Neil and his close friend, Al Benyon, were flying their tenth orbiter mission together. As Al had cynically observed before lift-off: 'Who would've thought that a mission would be paid for by a bunch of Bedouin tribesmen who've been deprived of their daily dose of camel operas and quiz shows?'

It was one of Al's typical over-simplifications. The truth was more complicated; KARMA II, together with its two sister satellites, carried over two hundred simultaneous TV and radio programmes in all Arabic dialects covering subjects ranging from farming to computer programming. During their five years' service, the three DBS satellites had become the most powerful unifying force in the Arab world after Islam. The ten most popular channels among the hundred million audience were those beamed up by the Palestine Liberation Organization from their new temporary homeland on the Black Sea.

Neil lolled in the shuttle commander's seat while listening absently to the exchanges between Al and Kellinah Assad, the third member of *Dominator*'s crew.

Assad was standing with his back to Neil at the flight deck's aft crew station where the observation windows looked out on *Dominator*'s yawning chasm of a cargo bay. He was a senior engineer employed by the United Arabic Broadcasting Commission and had received minimal training to enable him to fly on shuttle missions as a payload specialist. A reserved, soft-spoken Jordanian in his mid-thirties, he was particularly skilled at operating the fifty-foot-long, crane-like manipulator arm of the remote-controlled Canada robot, used to recover satellites for servicing or for placing new satellites in orbit.

Assad was prevented from drifting around the flight deck in the weightless condition by his Velcro overshoes that gripped the platform he was standing on. He craned his head up and peered through the overhead observation windows at the spacesuited figure of Al Benyon who was working on KARMA II. The astronaut was wearing one of the new low-bulk spacesuits – extra-vehicular mobility units in NASA jargon – that enabled him to reach into awkward corners when servicing an in-orbit satellite that was too large to haul into the cargo bay.

Neil had not been happy about Al's extra-vehicular activity. It had not been scheduled but Kennedy Space Center ground control had decided that a close eyeball examination of the giant satellite was the quickest and therefore the cheapest way of finding out what was wrong with it.

'Guess I've found the trouble, Kell,' said Al's voice over the speaker. 'Get the Canada to eyeball the Goddamn PDUs. A meteoroid's taken them out.'

'All three?' Assad queried.

'Sure looks that way.'

Assad operated the pistol-grip control that worked the manipulator. The Canada was provided with close-circuit TV cameras on its elbow and wrist that turned the arm into a useful inspection instrument. Assad positioned the articulated arm well clear of Al and zoomed the wrist-mounted camera in on KARMA's power distribution units. He muttered an expletive in Arabic when the close-up picture on his monitor revealed the extent of the damage. A chance in a million meteoroid had hit the plug-in modules at an angle, wrecking all three of the twelve-inch-square instruments.

Al chuckled throatily over the speaker. 'Reckon your bosses might put it down to Allah's will, Kell?'

'Only if he's sent another meteor to wreck the spare units in the cargo bay,' Assad countered good-humouredly. He glanced over his shoulder at Neil. 'Commander.' He always addressed Neil by rank because he was not at ease with the easy-going first-name familiarity of the NASA astronauts.

Neil dragged his attention away from the thousand-mile-long stretch of silver that marked Africa's Lake Malawi and Lake Tanganyika. He twisted around in his seat. 'What's the problem, Kell?'

'I'm sorry, Commander, but we have to replace all three of the satellite's power distribution modules. And then they'll have to be calibrated. That's before we can proceed to the routine servicing schedule.'

Neil nodded and pulled on his headset. 'How much extra time will you need?'

Assad considered: fifteen minutes to replace the modules; an hour for the servicing; and another two hours to boost the satellite back to its operational orbit. 'At least an extra three hours, Commander.'

Neil nodded. 'Okay, Kell. But that'll have to be another two orbits on the mission profile. It's going to cost your outfit an extra million dollars. Plus the cost of Al's EVA.'

'I believe UABC can afford it,' Assad replied stiffly.

Neil grinned to himself and set the control unit on his belt to external communication. 'Control, this is *Dominator*.'

'Go ahead, *Dominator*,' answered Earl Hackett's voice from the Kennedy Space Center.

'Clients require an additional two orbits to effect repairs.'

Jason Pelham, NASA's humourless Director of the Kennedy Space Center, smiled thinly to himself in his office when he heard the news that *Dominator* had requested an extension to the mission. He rose from his desk and stared out across Merritt Island's alligator-infested lagoons towards the giant Vehicle Assembly Building that had been built for the assembly of *Apollo/Saturn V*s spacecraft during an earlier age when there had been a money-no-object race to land men on the moon. Since the halcyon days of *Apollo*, Americans had not returned to the moon. Pelham intended to change that.

For the moment he was well pleased. He did not need to refer to files to know that the extra two orbits requested by OV-141 added up to another one million-dollar brick in the solid wall of profit for the Shuttle Applications Program that he had promised a congressional committee at the beginning of that fiscal year.

Despite his job, Jason Pelham had no burning interest in the spiritual adventure of aeronautics and space research, just as he had had little interest in trains when he had been chief executive of Amtrak. With Amtrak he had pulled off the impossible and trebled its profits within seven years. He was committed to doing the same thing for the shuttle. There had been an academic furore within NASA following his appointment five years previously but the combination of his brilliant administrative ability and a thick political hide had enabled him to weather the storm and deal with the subsequent plotting of his downfall.

Upon taking office he had recruited a team of top management scientists and tasked them with the streamlining of the entire shuttle programme.

'We've got a fleet of fifty operational orbiters,' he told his team. 'That's more vehicles than Pan Am's and TWA's supersonic airplane fleet put together. I want the launching of a shuttle to be as straightforward as sending a Pan Am SST from New York to London. Everything about a launch should be routine because routine is the mother of expenditure reduction.'

That was what Jason Pelham wanted and that was what he got. Gone were the countdown decision committees; gone was the time-consuming travel between the Johnson Space Center at Houston because Pelham insisted that all shuttle operations, including astronaut training, should be based at Kennedy. His most controversial decision was to scrap development of the new shuttle that could make a powered landing. His argument had been: 'Why spend money to produce a system that gravity does for free?'

Nothing escaped his cost-cutting eye. Research programmes into larger shuttles were slashed, expansion of the shuttle-handling facilities at Vandenberg Air Force Base in California was suspended, and the five-million visitors a year that the Kennedy Space Center attracted had to pay for admission.

There were screams of anguish – especially over the research cutbacks into larger shuttles – but in many ways Pelham was right: the shuttle was a reliable and proven design; several congressional committee members had endorsed his view that there was little point in spending vast sums on larger shuttles to achieve with one flight what the existing shuttles could manage with two flights.

Pelham turned away from the window and toyed with the model space station on his desk. It was in the form of four wheel-like structures, each one connected to a common hub by a series of spokes. The elegant model was the symbol of his current obsession. It represented the result of a secret study by the Shuttle Applications Team to build in orbit a huge two hundred billion-dollar space station hotel that would provide NASA with a staging post for routine, low-cost trips to the moon. To make such a project as near self-financing as possible, Pelham had held a series of top secret meetings with an international consortium made up of hotel, leisure and travel interests that included Hilton, Pan Am, TWA, Holiday Inns, Disney, Sheraton, and Trust Houses Forte.

Each member of the consortium was in possession of a confidential discussion document detailing plans of a fifteen

13

hundred-foot-diameter space station hotel which would turn at two revolutions per minute to provide a comfortable artificial gravity for the guests staying in the hotel's four thousand bedrooms.

Pelham's plan was for the consortium to pay seventy-five per cent of the cost of the space station hotel's construction. In return NASA would retain use of the station's docking facilities and crew accommodation for nothing and lease to Pan Am and TWA a fleet of fifty two-hundred-seater, passenger-carrying shuttles which would be used to ferry guests, scientists and technicians up to the hotel. NASA would also have a twenty-five per cent stake in the hotel. He had worked out a similar package with the world's major research oganizations to build a giant observatory adjoining the hotel. Visiting astronomers would, of course, have to pay for their trip and for their stay.

It was a bold and imaginative scheme that had fired the enthusiasm of the hard-nosed men and women on the consortium – especially as their market research had shown that there were plenty of rich people and scientific institutions throughout the world who would clamour for reservations in the orbital hotel.

After weeks of tough bargaining the consortium was on the brink of initialling an interim agreement but it was still concerned about public confidence in the shuttle. Admittedly over a thousand people had journeyed in shuttles – including severe burn-case patients who required treatment in weightless conditions aboard NASA's space hospital – but the safety and practicality of the shuttle for carrying passengers on scheduled flights was a question that was worrying the majority of the consortium's members.

Pelham had given the consortium another six months to come to a decision. That was the maximum period of time that Rockwell and Rocketdyne were prepared to wait for the go-ahead to build another fifty orbiters. After that they would have to start running down their workforces.

Pelham was determined that nothing would happen during that six months that might shake the confidence of the consortium in the shuttle.

Jason Pelham's ability as an administrator was matched only by his ruthlessness.

All Benyon hinged the first and second power distribution modules from their housings in the KARMA satellite without difficulty. He

14

held them up so that Assad could catch hold of them with the manipulator arm and stow them in the shuttle's cargo bay for examination on return to Earth. Al gripped the bow handle on the third unit with a gauntleted hand and twisted.

Nothing happened.

He planted his spaceboots firmly on the side of the satellite and heaved. The plug-in module refused to swivel outwards.

'Christ, Kell,' Al muttered into his helmet microphones. 'The impact must've buckled the hinges. I need a prybar. The small one.'

Assad swung the Canada's arm and dipped its head into the shuttle's gaping cargo hold. Like a heron's bill seeking fish, the robot arm's head located the toolbox and deftly removed a prybar. Satisfied that the tool was gripped firmly in the arm's mechanical fingers, Assad swung the arm towards Al. Assad was careful – the movements he permitted the arm were unhurried. Sharp tools and spacesuits did not mix.

'Hurry it up!' pleaded Al.

Neil smiled to himself. After nearly an hour's work in a muggy, sweat-soaked extra-vehicular mobility unit, Neil knew exactly how Al was feeling.

'Maybe I could use the Canada to swing the module out?' Assad suggested.

'It'll tear the handle off,' Al answered brusquely. 'It's gotta be prised out – a degree at a time. I'll try it from a different position. Hey! We're diverging – you'd better close up a tickle.'

'Commander,' Assad called out. 'Aft pitch up five.'

Neil reached for the central Digital Autopilot (DAP) console with his right hand and switched the orbiter's reaction control system jets to manual. A few pulses from the tiny thrusters that controlled the shuttle's orientation were enough to nudge its tail nearer the satellite. The other DAP controls were for altering the shuttle's yaw – for swinging the spacecraft to the left or right.

'OK – that's fine,' said Al's voice.

'I could work the DAP controls from this station,' Assad volunteered over his shoulder.

Neil shook his head. 'Sorry, Kell. Not while an astronaut's on an EVA.'

Assad accepted Neil's decision. He peered up at Al who was using both hands to ease KARMA's stubborn module gradually

15

from its housing. Occasionally Al would request Assad to pass him up various tools from the shuttle's cargo bay.

Neil settled back in his seat to watch the Earth rolling past. Immediately below were the Suid marshlands of the upper Nile. Further north was the barren crown of the Sahara Desert, and beyond that, clearly visible on the curving horizon, was the azure sweep of the Mediterranean. War-torn Israel, most of Italy and Greece, and Spain as far as the Pyrenees, was cloud-free. Neil could even see the molten thread of the River Jordan that linked the Sea of Galilee with the Dead Sea. During his thirty-one shuttle missions, he had never known such breathtakingly perfect visibility.

Neil was so captivated by the spectacle that he hardly heard Al's voice say: 'OK – she's coming free.'

A tiny point of brilliant white light suddenly flared in the Negev Desert about fifty miles due south of the Dead Sea. Neil blinked and wondered if the phenomenon might have been due to a slight optical fault in the window.

'You know these gizmos, Kell,' said Al, relaxing for a moment and returning the prybar to the manipulator arm's metal fingers. 'Reckon she's come free about ten degrees?'

Assad moved the manipulator arm closer to Al and operated the TV camera's zoom control.

Neil knew that there could be nothing wrong with the orbiter's windows. Something had happened in the Negev Desert.

Something stupendous to be visible from a height of two hundred miles.

'You're right,' said Assad, agreeing with Al while studying his TV monitor. 'Ten degrees.'

To Neil's distracted ears, Assad had said: 'Yaw right – ten degrees.' He immediately reached for the yaw trim toggle and flicked it to the right. The orientation thrusters fired, slewing the shuttle to the right.

'Cancel!' screamed Assad.

His warning came too late.

The manipulator arm swung.

The long prybar slashed deep into Al just above the hip and across his stomach. The tool ripped through his spacesuit as though the layers of Terylene, polyurethane and Spandex mesh were tissue paper. Air erupted through the gash from the spacesuit's pressure bladder, taking with it a cloud of cooling fluid and blood droplets that splattered the aft crew station windows. The force of the air venting from the spacesuit sent Al's body tumbling at right angles away from the shuttle.

Neil was at Assad's side, staring wide-eyed at Al's receding form. There was a single, strangled cry from Al over the speaker and then a series of croaking gasps.

'For mercy's sake!' Assad almost shouted. 'Why in the name of –'

'Al!' said Neil urgently, cutting Assad short with an angry gesture. 'Al – do you copy?'

The answer was the soft hiss of white noise from the speaker punctuated by another shuddering croak as the dying astronaut's lungs sucked at the last remnants of air that were voiding from his spacesuit. Al's gauntleted hands, staining red with blood, were pressed over his stomach as if in a desperate attempt to minimize the effect of the terrible wound. There was a final choking gasp and then Al's hands fell lifelessly away.

'Al!' Neil repeated, staring fixedly at the diminishing form. 'Do you copy? Do you copy?'

'We've got to go after him,' said Assad huskily, breaking the stunned silence that followed after Neil had tried calling Al several more times.

It was two seconds before Neil replied. He forced himself not to allow a despairing note to creep into his voice. 'We don't have the fuel for that sort of translation burn.'

'We use the manned manoeuvring unit backpack!' Assad snapped.

Neil shook his head while continuing to stare out of the window at Al. He estimated that his buddy was now over two miles from the shuttle. 'It would take me thirty minutes to suit-up and go after him. And even if I caught up with him and didn't get the bends, the MMU doesn't carry enough propellant to bring myself back, let alone Al's mass as well.'

'So we do nothing?'

Without looking at Assad, Neil said in flat, unemotional voice: 'Take a close look at him. Al's dead.'

Assad stared hard for a moment and then realized that the loops of pallid substance spilling from the ripped spacesuit and slowly wreathing themselves around the astronaut's twisting body were not cooling fluid tubes as he had first thought.

Suddenly Assad wanted to be violently sick.

3 The only sign of life visible from one thousand feet were a few soldiers milling around a large marquee the size of a circus big top. They were too busy even to look up at the approaching helicopter. Parked by the marquee's entrance were two armoured personnel carriers and a communications truck. Nearby was a large black cross that the army had marked out on the desert floor as a helicopter landing pad.

Rymann and Greer stared down from the Solomon helicopter at the appalling devastation below.

There was hardly anything left of the Negev Guided Weapons Research Establishment. The concrete blockhouses, laboratory buildings, test chambers, administrative offices and the accommodation village had been blasted out of existence by a single, cataclysmic explosion. By a quirk of fate only the school was still standing.

Only six weeks had elapsed since Rymann had last visited the top-secret rocket station deep in the trackless hills of the Negev Desert thirty miles south of the *Chel Ha'Avir* airbase at Ramon. Then there had been congratulatory speeches from Rymann following the successful test-firing of the first pre-production Massada booster from an Israeli merchant ship in the Southern Ocean. Afterwards he had toured the establishment. All the facilities had been cleverly disguised as the buildings of a desert agricultural research station. There were even fields terraced into the surrounding hills for genuine experiments into new crop strains.

Rymann had chatted to each of the two hundred and fifty engineers, scientists and designers involved with the Massada booster development. He had shaken hands with every man and kissed every woman.

After visiting the school and spending an enjoyable fifteen minutes with the children, Rymann had stood beside the giant twenty-wheel launcher/transporter and watched the second pre-production Massada booster, with its Massada missile in position, being craned into place.

The ten-metre-long Massada booster was the result of two years' intensive development on a crash-programme that had absorbed sixty per cent of Israel's defence budget – a programme that Rymann had bulldozed through when he had been Minister of Defence. Nearly all of the tiny state's top scientists and technicians who had designed the successful Massada missile had been attached to the booster programme. The result of their efforts was the world's first mobile-launched intercontinental missile. The Massada missile, together with its new booster, was a brilliant concept. It didn't require large and vulnerable fixed bases, and its range of ten thousand miles, together with its precision celestial/inertial navigation computer, meant that it could hit any target in the Arab and black African world. Two would be capable of wiping out the PLO base at Bakal on the Black Sea.

A celebratory luncheon held in the air-conditioned booster assembly block had marked the end of Rymann's visit. He had delivered a short speech during which he had stressed what his uncritical audience was already profoundly aware of: that the survival of the State of Israel now depended wholly on the Massada booster. Without it Israel's enemies could and were waging a merciless war with impunity from behind their screens of deadly surface-to-air SAM-50A missile batteries. The Soviet-built missiles could pick Israeli fighters out of the sky with such infallible accuracy that the *Chel Ha'Avir* had lost half its operational aircraft in the first six months of the war. With the Massada and its booster Israel would have the means of delivering a nuclear warhead to any point on the globe where her enemies were hiding.

That speech had been delivered six weeks ago.

The men and women who had listened to it were now dead.

All that was left intact of the Negev Rocket Establishment was the school building and the fields of experimental crops, and even some of those had been obliterated by the appalling explosion.

The helicopter settled on the black cross. The airforce pilot cut his engines. As soon as the dust thrown up by the slowing rotors had settled, a man in army uniform left the marquee.

He was Lieutenant-General Daniel Kazaar, the GOC of the *Zahal* Southern Command. A tough, thickset man aged about forty-five. He was wearing a green paratrooper's beret. Above the right pocket of his battledress blouse were the ribbons of the *Ot Haoz* – Israel's second highest military award. During his thirty years as a professional soldier he had witnessed the bloodiest

19

fighting imaginable, and yet that had not prepared him for the ordeal of the clear-up in the aftermath of the explosion. He stood to attention under the blazing desert sun, his face haggard and drawn.

The heat hit Rymann and Greer like a wall as they stepped down from the helicopter. General Kazaar saluted and shook hands with his visitors.

'I'm sorry there's no proper welcoming committee, sir,' said the general as he led the way to the marquee. 'But I'm the only senior officer present.'

Rymann dismissed the apology. He entered the giant tent and surveyed the interior with a single glance. A number of reservists were working at field desks. A roped-off area in the centre of the marquee was piled high with twisted and blackened pieces of unrecognizable ironmongery that two civilians were picking over. On the far side of the tent was the fat, cylindrical bulk of an air-conditioned cargo pod resting on a wooden cradle.

'It contains the bodies, sir,' said General Kazaar in answer to Rymann's question.

'All of them?'

'Yes, sir.'

'How many?'

'Two hundred and ninety-one, sir.' The general shot a glance at Rymann and noted that for once the politician's usual good-humoured expression was absent. He continued: 'There's a reserve Chinook on its way to airlift the pod to Tel Aviv.'

'How many survivors?' asked Greer, speaking for the first time.

General Kazaar turned to face the head of the Mossad. 'Thirty-one,' he replied. 'They were all children. For some reason or other, the schoolhouse escaped the worst of the blast. They've been flown direct to the military hospital at Hatzor.'

Rymann made a mental note to visit the children as soon as possible. 'Do you have any idea as to the cause of the explosion?' he asked.

The senior officer shook his head and indicated the civilians who were examining bits of wreckage. 'That's what those two hope to find out. So far they're certain that it wasn't sabotage.'

'Do you have a list of the victims, General?' Greer enquired.

'Yes, sir,' Kazaar answered stiffly. He didn't care for Greer and had been one of those who had opposed the appointment of a civilian as the *Memuneh* – father – of Mossad. Even so, the officer

20

had been the first to admit in private that the scholarly Greer was probably the best chief that Mossad had known. In common with all the members of Rymann's Cabinet, what General Kazaar really disliked about Greer was his closeness to and influence over the Prime Minister.

'We'll need a copy now, please,' Greer requested. 'And a desk.'

4   There were some names on the list that Rymann remembered from his last visit. Alan Delmante – one of Israel's top rocket designers – appeared on the first page, but most of the names were meaningless to him. He could not bring himself to read the list to the end. 'Why no rank or positions?' he asked Greer.

'No personnel records were kept here.'

'Does the Institute have records?'

'No. They're in Ab Yaranski's office. They're the only set in existence. My orders.'

Rymann picked up the encryptophone that General Kazaar had provided. 'Get me Ab Yaranski at the Rafael Armament Development Authority,' he ordered the girl corporal in the communications truck. He looked up at Greer while waiting for the connection to be made. 'We're going straight from here to see those kids.'

'There are other, more pressing matters, Hendrik.'

Rymann scowled. 'So let's deal with them now. How long will it take to assemble a new Massada team?'

Greer looked uncomfortable. 'I'm sorry, Hendrik. I can't give an exact answer until we have a clearer idea of the talent that's been lost and whether such talent is duplicated elsewhere. Yaranski could give you an answer off the top of his head. I can't.'

Rymann's expression hardened. 'For once, Michael. Just for once, stick that scrawny neck of yours out and risk a guess. I guarantee that you'll find the operation painless.'

The phone rang. 'I'm sorry, sir,' said the communications girl. 'But General Kazaar says that Ab Yaranski is on the casualty list.'

'What!' Rymann exploded. 'What was he doing here?'

General Kazaar came on the line just as Greer located Yaranski's name on the last sheet of the list. 'We don't know, sir,' said the army officer. 'But we found a reservist ID bracelet with his name on it.' The general decided against adding that the ID bracelet had been found on what was left of a human arm.

'Thank you, General,' said Rymann. 'Contact Yaranski's deputy and find out what he was doing here.'

Greer looked up from the list. His gaunt face was suddenly even more haggard than usual. Rymann saw his expression, made a hasty apology to General Kazaar and replaced the handset. 'What's the matter, Michael?'

For a moment Greer seemed lost for words. 'These names,' he muttered, indicating the list. 'At first I thought they were coincidental. But they're not. Harriman, George Kingsley. That can only be *the* George Harriman.'

Rymann stared at his friend in horror. George Harriman was Israel's brilliant aircraft designer and the technical director of Israel Aircraft Industries, the state-owned aerospace giant. In the late 1960's, following President de Gaulle's suspension of arms sales to Israel by France, Harriman had been a junior designer on the team that had built a Mirage fighter based on drawings obtained by Mossad agents from Switzerland. That early fighter led to the production of the Kfir, Israel's first home-produced supersonic combat aircraft. After that, Harriman's promotion had been rapid. Within fifteen years his brilliant mind had conceived the Sharav – Desert Wind – multiple-role combat aircraft that could out-perform the MiG-25 Foxbat. Five hundred operational Sharav IVs now formed the backbone of the *Chel Ha'Avir*.

During the next five minutes a stunned Greer picked out from the list several more names of Israel's top scientists.

The phone rang again. It was General Kazaar. 'I've been in touch with Yaranski's office, sir,' the army officer told Rymann. 'He was here because a top-level meeting had been called to resolve a number of pre-production problems.'

Rymann listened to General Kazaar for a few more minutes and thanked him. 'My God!' he muttered to Greer. 'They were all here. Every top rocket engineer in the country.'

There was a silence before Greer spoke. His lined face was grey. 'In that case this explosion may have cost us the war,' he said at length. 'Without the booster for the Massad –'

'Let us not be defeatist, Michael,' said Rymann mildly.

22

'And let us not be blind,' Greer countered. He pointed to the mounting piles of debris that the civilian experts were sorting out into marked squares. 'Look at that lot, Hendrik. Jigs, press tools, dies. A thousand and one specialized tools that were needed to put the booster into production. Two years' work and now there's nothing left.'

'So we start again,' said Rymann quietly. 'We've done it once. We can do it again.'

Greer leaned forward on the desk and confronted his friend. 'Hendrik – listen. Two years ago when we set up the Massada booster project we had a ready-made team of our best brains that had already produced the main missile. Today we have nothing.' He waved the list under Rymann's nose. 'Designers; scientists; technicians; fuel chemists; production engineers. They're all dead, Hendrik. Every last one of them.'

One of the civilians approached the desk where the two men were sitting. He was balding and overweight. He nervously cleared his throat.

'Sirs – General Kazaar told me to report directly to you as soon as we knew something,' he began. 'We can't be one hundred per cent certain jus yet, but we think we now know what caused the explosion.'

'You'd better sit down,' said Rymann, nodding to an empty chair.

The civilian did as he was told and placed on the table a shapeless mass of grey plastic that had some wires hanging from it. 'This was a remote-controlled gate valve,' the civilian explained. 'It metered the flow of liquid rocket fuel oxidizer from the main underground storage tank to the fuel solidifying facility.' He mopped his forehead with a handkerchief and glanced at the two men in turn. 'We now know for certain that the explosion took place near the storage tanks.'

'So?' Greer prompted.

'We've found the remains of another valve identical to this one. American. The two valves worked in tandem as a fail-safe device so that the fuel couldn't reach the oxidizer when the tanks were closed down.' The civilian pointed to the valve. 'It has a serious design fault that can cause it to jam open when it has been switched off. This one is open now although it should be in the closed position when there's no current flowing through it. If both valves remained

23

jammed open at the same time . . . ' the civilian left the sentence unfinished. The silence from the two men made him uncomfortable. 'Of course – we can't be certain just yet.'

'So it wasn't sabotage?' Rymann demanded.

The civilian shook his head. 'We don't think so, sir.'

Rymann picked up the faulty valve and regarded it thoughtfully.

'How much do these things cost?'

The civilian looked uncertain. 'I'd say no more than five hundred dollars each, sir.'

Rymann caught Greer's eye. The two men knew each other well enough to know what the other was thinking: nearly three hundred men and women had died and the State of Israel was in grave peril because of two faulty pieces of hardware that had cost less than five hundred dollars apiece.

5   Normally Neil enjoyed driving. The sensation of being luxuriously cocooned from his fellow humans in a high-tech womb of vinyl, steel and glass was the nearest he could get to the strange feeling of detachment from worldly problems that he relished when in space.

But this time the twenty-mile drive from the Kennedy Space Center to Melbourne was a nightmare.

It was Al's car. The two astronauts had always shared a car when they were flying on a mission together. Everything about the vehicle screamed Al: the selection of tapes; the sunglasses; the hunting magazines on the back seat.

Neil turned off Highway A1A – Florida's Atlantic coast road – and slowed as he approached the two high gates that guarded the entrance to the Indialantic Gardens Estate. He punched out his pass number on the dashboard keypad and the gates opened automatically. He drove slowly along the palm-lined roads of the elegant estate. Bud Allison's two teenage sons broke off their chatter with two girls to stare at him as he went past. The open hostility in their gaze forced upon him the realization that the combination of Al's death and living on the lush Melbourne estate was going to raise a whole set of problems that he hadn't even thought about. Indialantic Gardens was refered to locally as 'Astronaut Alley' because several orbiter crews had moved there from Houston when NASA had decided to concentrate most of its shuttle activities at Kennedy. It was a small, close-knit community of Philishaved lawns, high-security fences and low-security marriages, whose houses fetched a third of a million dollars apiece for the alimony lawyers to fight over.

Neil and Helen had been among the first to move on to the new development three years previously when he had first landed his job with NASA after he had quit flying for Pan Am. They had picked a house that fronted on to the ocean. After having lived in Texas all their lives, there was magic in lying in bed in the morning and watching the panorama of the Atlantic emerge as the wall-to-ceiling windows depolarized. Also there had been magic in their ten-year marriage, but that had been yesterday.

Neil parked the car in the drive beside his Winnebago camper and cut the engine. He was exhausted and miserable. Landing the *Dominator* without A1 had not been too bad. It was what had followed: the intensive debriefing; the searching questions over what had gone wrong. Even Jason Pelham had showed up – smooth-talking the press – no statements until there had been the fullest inquiry into the accident. Shit-scared that adverse publicity might damage the reputation of his precious dollar-spinning orbiter fleet.

Neil waited. The kids didn't come racing out of the house as they usually did when he returned from a mission. No Pippa rushing out with a racous, 'Hi, Pa!' and flinging herself at him as he stepped from the car. No Andrew standing shyly in the background. Helen never came out any more.

He went into the house. Helen was watching a movie on the new big flat-screen television that had been installed the month before. The windows were polarized to maximum darkness, shutting out the view of the Atlantic. She was wearing the shapeless trouser suit that she used for messing about in the house. She knew he hated her in it. He guessed that she didn't care any more. She didn't even care for herself. Thirty-two years old and she looked forty. Once she had reached thirty she had given up trying. She wasn't so careful about her diet. The weekly trip to the hairdresser became fortnightly, then monthly, and after that only on the rare occasions when they were going out.

Helen cut the television's sound but didn't look up when he

entered the room. He remembered the times when he had dropped Al off after a mission. Jane had always thrown her arms around her husband and literally smothered him with kisses. All he usually got the moment he showed himself was a catalogue of minor domestic crises that had arisen during his absence: 'Pippa's got another tooth coming'; 'Andy caught a baby rattler in the yard'; 'the cat's shed all over the new Persian rug in the Florida room' . . . . It was the sort of trivia that he could only steel himself to face after three days following a return to Earth, but this time he would have been glad of even that instead of the icy silence as he sat down.

'Hi.' He tried to sound cheerful and failed. He could see that she had been crying.

Her reply was a flat, unemotional, 'Hallo', like he had just got back from a ten-minute drive for a take-away meal rather than been into space.

He poured himself a drink, his first since the landing that morning. The whisky scalded the back of his throat. He began to feel better. He poured a drink for Helen and set it down before her. She ignored it and him.

'Where are the kids?' he asked.

'Staying at mother's for tonight.'

'Why?'

'Because I didn't want them to see me looking like this – that's why.'

'You know I like to see them when I get back.'

'Well it won't hurt for you to consider my feelings for once,' Helen retorted.

Neil needed all his self-control to keep his temper in check. Helen had a knack of blaming him for her irrational behaviour. Christ – she could've asked after him – knowing what he'd been through – instead of being so wrapped up in her own emotions.

'OK,' he said evenly. 'So you've been crying. So what? It's nothing to be ashamed of.'

'I don't care. I didn't want them to see me.'

'Have the press been calling?'

'Two landed on the beach,' said Helen savagely. 'Walked across the lawn like they owned the place and sat outside. I had to call security to throw them out. What's the point of paying out twenty-five grand a year –'

'How's Jane?' Neil interrupted, sensing he was about to lose the battle of keeping his anger under control.

Helen looked at him for the first time. 'I got back an hour ago from seeing her. I thought maybe she was under sedation but she wasn't. She was suddenly finding jobs to do. Cleaning the pool. Clearing out the garage. She talked about everything under the sun except Al. Don't you think that's strange?'

Neil didn't think it strange but he went along with Helen because he suddenly felt too drained for an argument. 'Any calls?'

'No. But Jane wants you to go see her.'

Hell. 'When?'

Helen shrugged without taking her eyes off the television. 'She said as soon as you'd got back and had eaten. But not to bother if you were tired. Do you want me to fix you something?'

Neil drained a third whisky. 'No. Guess I'd better drop the car back.'

Without saying another word to Helen, he showered and drove slowly to Al's house on the other side of the estate. What was he going to say to Jane? What could he say? 'Sorry, Jane – I made a mistake that killed your husband?'

He parked Al's Pontiac in the drive. Jane came out to meet him as soon as she heard the car. Cool, elegant Jane with her long ash-blonde hair blowing in the breeze. She was wearing shorts, very short – very tight – and a loose halter top. Neil's mouth went dry. She even managed a wan smile which she followed up with a light kiss on the cheek as he got out of the car.

'Hallo, Neil. I'm glad you came.'

He forced a smile. 'Nice to see you again.'

'Helen looked in. I expect she told you?'

'Yes.'

The conversation was all so unreal. Like he had dropped by for a drink.

He followed Jane through the house and on to the terrace by the swimming-pool. A light breeze had sprung up and was draining the late afternoon of its heat and energy-sapping humidity. Al and Jane didn't have children so the place was usually neat and tidy. This time the terrace was a mess. Bags of peat and plantpots strewn everywhere.

'Sorry about the mess,' Jane apologized. 'I thought it was time I started on repotting the plants.'

She cleared some magazines off the aluminium chairs. Neil had a perfect view of her breasts as she bent over. Small and perfect. Guiltily he tore his eyes away.

'Al keeps saying he'll do it but . . . .' Jane's voice trailed away. She gave Neil an embarrassed smile. 'You'd better sit on Al's chair – it's stronger.'

'Jane,' Neil began, marshalling his courage as he sat down. 'I want to tell you how desperately sorry –'

'You look hungry,' Jane interrupted. 'I bet you had nothing to eat when you got home?'

Neil was bewildered by the abrupt change of subject. 'What?'

'You haven't eaten, have you?'

'Er – no.'

Neil knew that Jane had a low opinion of Helen. He was sure she was thinking: 'I bet that lazy wife of yours didn't bother to fix you a meal when you got home.' Oh God – her husband had just been killed. How the hell could he know what was going on in her mind? The realization that he hadn't eaten since leaving Kennedy shouldered aside his thoughts about the strangeness of the conversation. He gave Jane a crooked smile. 'Last meal I ate was something reconstituted on the orbiter.'

Too late – he had mentioned the shuttle – the one subject he had decided not to bring up unless Jane mentioned it first.

But it was as if she hadn't heard him. She stood, brushed her hair away from her face and gave Neil an enigmatic smile. 'I've fixed you a Madras curry. Not too hot – just the way you like it.'

She was gone before Neil could protest.

Madras curry? Sure he didn't mind a curry. Jane often did them for her dinner parties because she did them well. Madras curry was a dish Al was crazy about. Provided it wasn't too hot.

Christ . . . . He began to feel even more uneasy.

Jane was back five minutes later with a tray that she set in front of Neil. She ladled the curry from a casserole dish on to two plates of fluffy boiled rice and pulled up her chair.

'This is fantastic,' said Neil appreciatively. He had to stop himself from wolfing the meal down.

Jane toyed with her food and gave Neil another of her enigmatic smiles. 'Shall we finish off the last bottle of Graves?'

'Why not?' said Neil, puzzled. Surely she hadn't forgotten that he hated wine? It was something she often made jokes about.

He drank one glass of wine while Jane finished off the bottle. She stood unsteadily. 'Let's have coffee in the lounge,' she said. 'It's getting chilly out here.'

Jane's idea of coffee was strong and black, liberally laced with rum. They sat together on the davenport. Neil worked through the coffee pot while Jane concentrated on the rum bottle.

They made small talk. The garden. The new houses at the northern end of the estate. The planning row over a new condominium. It was as if they had entered into a binding agreement not to mention Al. Jane's speech was becoming slurred. Her halter top had loosened even more.

'What will you do now?' asked Neil tentatively, using a lull in the conversation to change the subject. He avoided looking at her.

Jane lolled back and regarded Neil. 'Whaddayermean?' She gave a little hiccup, giggled and apologized.

Neil decided against reverting to the small talk. He turned towards her and took hold of her hand. 'Jane – have you thought about what you're going to do now that Al's . . . Now that Al's . . . '

She went rigid, staring at Neil, her eyes wide with shock. 'Al?' she echoed blankly.

'What will you do now?' Neil repeated gently. Her knuckles were white where she was crushing his hand.

It was as if he had ruptured a dam. Suddenly the tears were streaming down her cheeks. She threw herself across the davenport and buried her face in his lap. Her sobs were uncontrolled paroxysms that wracked her entire body.

He lost count of the minutes that slipped by as he sat holding her. It was getting dark in the room by the time her weeping had subsided. She was still clinging to his hand – her grip tightening automatically whenever he tried to disengage his fingers.

After a while Jane's regular breathing told him that she was asleep. To avoid waking her, he gently eased her weight to one side and stood up. He gratefully stretched the cramp from his body and looked down uncertainly at the sleeping girl. Her long, graceful legs were doubled up awkwardly under herself. He straightened them carefully. She stirred and moaned something to herself but did not wake up. He considered creeping out of the house. He would have to walk home but that didn't matter. Then he realized that she would feel terrible when she woke up – especially as the meal hadn't

29

been cleared away. If he took her into the bedroom, he would be able to clear up without waking her. He slipped his arms under her and lifted her without difficulty. She did not stir. Carrying her up the short flight of steps of the split-level house was no trouble but he wished he'd thought to turn on the bedroom lights first.

He found the bed in the semi-darkness and gently laid her down. He slipped off her sandals and stood for a moment looking at her. Her halter had come unfastened, exposing her pale breasts. He tried to retie the halter, gave up, and bent over her to kiss her lightly on the cheek. Suddenly her arms snaked around him with surprising strength and pulled him down on the bed. Before he could recover from his surprise, her mouth had fastened on to his. He shifted his hand to steady himself and his fingers brushed against her nipples. They hardened to his touch. And then he was responding to her mouth – probing her tongue with his tongue in one long kiss that silenced that part of his subconsciousness that was yelling *'No! No! No!'*

It wasn't him sliding his hand across the smooth skin of her stomach, frantically unfastening her shorts and yanking them away from her long legs. It wasn't him slipping his fingers into her moistness. It wasn't him easing his weight over her as she moved her legs apart. It wasn't him listening to her soft moans as he entered her.

It wasn't him!
It wasn't him!

At the moment of her climax, when she cried out 'Al! Al!' and he felt her spasms gripping him as she arched her pelvis off the bed, he realized with terrifying clarity that it wasn't him she was making such desperate love to.

It was the ghost of a dead man whose corpse was drifting far away in space.

Neil woke with a start and groped for the bedside light. It was 4 a.m. He sat on the edge of the bed, tried to sort out his thoughts, and gave up. Jane was sprawled naked on her back, breathing deeply. Moving quietly so as not to wake her, he got dressed and pulled a sheet over her because it seemed the decent thing to do.

Decent? That was a joke coming from someone who'd spent an hour making love to his best friend's wife.

Five minutes later he was walking through the broad avenues of the sleeping estate, hoping that a security patrol didn't spot him. He tried to push what had happened out of his mind while he concentrated on what he would tell Helen. But it was useless: his thoughts kept returning to Jane and the raw excitement he had experienced as her magnificently erotic body squirmed deliciously beneath him.

6   The Suntree Golf Club was one of the best and most exclusive on Brevard County's Space Coast and was the one place where Jason Pelham could usually be found when he wasn't behind his desk.

He lifted a hand to his lined forehead and shaded his eyes against the setting sun. He studied the fairway for some seconds and placed his ball on the tee.

Earl Hackett, Director of the Shuttle Exploitation Program, looked on while Pelham stared first at the ball and then down the fairway. Hackett loved golf, but not partnering Pelham. Not so much because Pelham took the whole business too seriously – as if there was a $1 million dollar bet riding on every game – but because one couldn't relax with Pelham. When the senses of humour had been handed out, Pelham had been overlooked.

'Most unfortunate about Al Benyon,' Pelham observed, question-marking his lanky frame over his bag to select a club.

Hackett was relieved that the embargo on discussing the subject had finally been lifted. It had taken six holes. He agreed with Pelham, adding: 'We're going to ban the use of the word "yaw".'

'Oh?' said Pelham mildly, scratching a speck of almost invisible mud off the face of the club with a fingernail. 'Won't that reflect on us?'

Hackett was puzzled. 'How do you mean?'

'This accident must be seen for what it was – human error. Not an operational error.'

'You're saying that the accident was Neil O'Hara's fault?'

Pelham squatted and squinted down the fairway. 'I'm not saying that. But you will be saying that to the review board.'

'It wasn't O'Hara's fault,' said Hackett quietly. 'The word

31

"yaw" should've been banned twenty years ago. OK – so maybe he should've verified what was said. But –'

'Precisely. He should have done something and he failed to do so.'

'The cause of the accident goes back to the early days of manned space flights –'

'There's only one thing about the past that interests me,' said Pelham icily, fixing Hackett with a bleak gaze.

'What's that?'

There was no humour in Pelham's eyes when he smiled. He was a sound judge of character. Hackett was a coward who would do exactly as he said. 'Do you know how much business we lost to Arianespace in the last decade?'

Hackett knew that the West European space agency had grabbed a sizeable chunk of the world's small payload market but he did not have the exact figures. Pelham would have them and they would be very exact. He played safe and shook his head.

'Twelve billion dollars,' Pelham stated.

'In terms of percentage of our turnover, that's nothing,' said Hackett uncomfortably.

'It's still twelve billion dollars that Europe got their hands on and we didn't,' Pelham remarked curtly. 'And they'll try to grab even more when the Euroshuttle enters service. Then, in a few years, the Soviets will have their shuttle operating. We can only stay ahead by maintaining the reputation of our shuttles as the safest and cheapest carrier fleet in the world.' He paused. 'And then there's the orbital hotel . . . .'

Now we're really getting down to it, thought Hackett.

'Any weakening of public confidence in the shuttle at this stage and the consortium might pull out before the contract's signed. That would be three years' work wasted and the wrecking of our chances of getting back to the moon on a self-financing basis.' Pelham swung his club experimentally. 'Do you support me on that?'

'On that point I do,' said Hackett. 'But shifting the blame on to O'Hara –'

'Who is to blame anyway.'

'The accident was nothing like one hundred per cent his fault.'

'That's for the review board to decide.' Pelham deftly flicked a dead leaf from in front of the tee. 'You were acting capcom at the time of the accident, therefore you will be a principal witness. Whether you give your evidence as a former NASA administrator or as someone on my payroll is entirely up to you. Do I make myself clear?'

Hackett wanted to throw his job in Pelham's face there and then. But there was his new house at Indialantic, the kids at college, three cars. A life-style. Instead he nodded and said: 'I guess so.'

Pelham settled his grip on the club and shuffled his feet until he was correctly balanced. 'Excellent. That means I shall be happy to renew your contract next month for another three years. With a raise in salary, of course.'

'You realize that it will destroy O'Hara?'

'A substantial pay-off never destroyed anyone with any sense,' Pelham remarked casually. He took a deep breath and drove. The club connected neatly but he sliced the shot. He watched the ball swinging towards the palm trees that lined the fairway. 'Damn,' he muttered. 'Damn.'

7   A crack of a sniper's rifle. A neat hole torn in the grille over the driver's visor, and *Rav-Turai* Dessouter was dead.

Lieutenant David Heinlein threw his powerful bulk across the cab and tried to grab the wheel as his corporal slumped forward but he was too late. The Datsun armoured personnel carrier careered across the Nazareth street, overturned and crashed into an Arab-owned TV shop just as Heinlein broke the seal on the tiny radio beacon that was sewn into his drill shirt. The continuous sideband signal from the miniature transmitter would summon immediate reinforcements. He pushed Dessouter's body clear of the emergency door and scrambled out of the vehicle.

The crash had taken place near the Church of the Annunciation on the Haifa–Afula road. There were more Arab youths than usual hanging about. The overturning army vehicle acted as a signal for the riot to begin.

The other six paratroopers in Heinlein's patrol piled out of the back of the carrier and took up defensive positions behind its metallic bulk as the stones from the yelling mob rained down. The shop-owner was screaming hysterically at them in a mixture of Arabic and Hebrew. A petrol bomb shattered with a loud *Whummph!* against the side of the overturned carrier and engulfed it in a ball of fire.

'Get clear!' Heinlein yelled at his men.

The six men stumbled across the debris from the wrecked shop. Heinlein ignored the Arab mob and the searing heat from the blazing vehicle. He scanned the tops of the buildings from which he was certain the sniper had fired.

It was imperative to catch the sniper. The sniper would be one of Joseph Maken's agents infiltrated back into the township from the PLO base on the Black Sea. The sniper would be the organizer of this trouble: a man or woman trained in sabotage techniques, whose opening shots were the signal to the Arab populace for the riot to start. It didn't matter about the mob – it wasn't important, there would always be Arab mobs – but the sniper was important. Get the sniper and you smashed the cell. And if you caught him alive, you might get some useful intelligence. That's what the staff training colleges were preaching now.

'OK! Follow me!' Heinlein yelled, straightening up. He was tall and powerfully-built, yet the force of the grenade that exploded fifty yards away was enough to lift him off his feet and hurl him backwards, winding him for precious seconds. He staggered groggily to his feet, made sure his assault rifle was undamaged and raced down the side street towards the apartment block. Blinds were being hoisted and faces were appearing at the building's windows with the exception of one on the top floor where the blind was already up despite the fact that the room would be receiving direct sunlight. It made him suspicious. But he had to get nearer. He signalled to his men to flatten themselves against the wall and suddenly realized that he was alone. There was the sound of small arms fire but it was too late to go back. He had to get the sniper.

Heinlein moved swiftly along the narrow street. Some young Arabs heading towards the sound of the riot gave him puzzled glances as he pounded by. He ignored them. At the end of the street he swerved into an alleyway and threw his considerable weight into a doorway with such force that the timber frame nearly collapsed inwards. He now had a clear view of the block's façade. He yanked his fieldglasses from their case and focused them on the suspect window. The sunlight reflected from the half-open sash made it difficult to pick out any details but he was certain he could see the head and shoulders of a man, and what could have been sunlight glinting on a rifle barrel.

He counted the levels. The seventh floor. It was all he needed. A minute later he was running down the litter-strewn street towards the apartment block's main entrance.

An army staff car, its turbine howling, shot out of the crossroads in front of him and disappeared. There was the sound of screeching brakes, the harsh whine of a gearbox in reverse, and the car reappeared. It slewed to a standstill in his path. Heinlein dodged around it. He was within fifty yards of the block's main entrance when he heard a familiar voice from behind.

'Lieutenant Heinlein!'

Heinlein kept running.

'Lieutenant Heinlein!' The voice barked.

Heinlein's army boots kicked sparks as he skidded and turned.

Segan-Aluf Sharon was sitting in the back seat of the car. He was regarding Heinlein with an expression that was even more unfriendly than usual.

'The disturbance is in the other direction, Lieutenant.'

'Yes, sir,' Heinlein acknowledged. He jerked his thumb at the apartment block. 'I think the sniper that started it is holed-up in there. With your permission, I –'

'Sniper?' said Lieutenant-Colonel Sharon mildly. 'I've received no reports of a sniper operating in this area.'

'Well you're receiving one now, sir.'

Sharon's eyes narrowed. 'Where are your men, Lieutenant?'

'I was separated from them, sir. I thought they'd heard my order to follow me.'

'You *thought*?'

'Yes, sir,' Heinlein replied. He gave up all hope of catching the sniper. *Segan-Aluf* Sharon was in one of his all too frequent bloody-minded moods.

The senior officer held the rear car door open. 'I think, Lieutenant Heinlein,' he said slowly and deliberately, 'that it might be a good idea if you accompanied me.'

8   Helen O'Hara sat bolt upright on her sunbed and stared at her husband in rank disbelief.

'You did what?'

Neil glanced anxiously at Pippa and Andrew who were swimming happily in the pool. 'Neither of us knew what we were doing,' he explained. 'I'd had too much to drink and Jane was in a state of shock –'

'So you took advantage of her?' Helen's voice was hard, her eyes glittering dangerously.

'It wasn't like that.'

'OK – so you tell me what it was like.'

'That's what I'm trying to do, Goddamn it. And keep your voice down.'

'Why should I?' Helen sneered. 'I've done nothing to be ashamed of.'

'The children –'

Helen scowled angrily. 'If you're so worried about the kids, maybe you should have thought of that before you screwed your best friend's wife.'

Neil was not a man given to violence. In the ten years they had been married, he had never even threatened Helen, but in that instant he had to suppress a desire to hit her. So intense was the urge that it frightened him.

There was a sudden loud scream from Pippa, complaining that Andrew was splashing her. Glad of the distraction, Neil dived into the pool and pretended to be an ogre rising from the depths to exact a fearful revenge on Pippa's behalf. The children shrieked with delight. Pippa laughingly scrambled on to Neil's shoulders and steered him towards Andrew. The seven-year-old was like Neil in many ways: the same fair hair and blue eyes, and the same deceptive shyness that could erupt with great suddenness into positive action. The boy laughed uncertainly as his father and sister approached, and suddenly dived below the surface where he knocked Neil's legs from under him. As usual, Neil was caught unawares by the seven-year-old's strength.

As Neil played with his children, he was uncomfortably aware of

36

Helen's smouldering eyes on him. He hated deceit and felt that a great burden had lifted from his shoulders now that he had confessed. Originally he had had no idea how Helen would react and had been surprised with himself when he had realized that he didn't really care. Anyway, he reflected, caring was a two-way thing; Helen had never once asked him how he felt about Al's death, therefore he hadn't told her about the living nightmare that had returned to haunt him on each of the four nights since he had returned home. She would never have understood.

Neil hoisted Andrew out of the water and sat him on the springboard. The boy gazed at his father with large, serious eyes.

'Pa – is it true what the other kids are saying about you and Uncle Al?'

A stiletto twisted in Neil's guts. 'Is what true, Andy?'

'That you killed him. It's not true, it is, Pa?'

Neil chucked Andrew under the chin. 'Just crazy kids' talk, young feller,' he said dismissively. 'You don't want to take no notice of what they say.'

Helen came over. 'What's the matter?'

'Nothing, Ma,' said Andrew, sliding into the water. 'Nothing.'

Helen made no more reference to the affair that day. She hardly spoke to Neil until they were preparing for bed when she suddenly said: 'I think we should sell up.' She said it casually, as though she were deciding on a restaurant for an evening out.

Neil stopped unbuttoning his shirt. 'You're kidding? Why?'

Helen sat at the dresser and toyed absently with her face. 'You know how much I hate it here.'

'Forget it,' Neil said curtly. 'We can't afford to move to Delray Beach. And they get hurricanes down there.'

Helen scowled and turned to face him. 'The kids around here have been giving Andy a bad time. Did he tell you?'

'That's just kids' talk.'

'And adults. I was in the mall bookshop this morning. I overheard Donna Williams and Maddie Lake. They were saying that they didn't think we'd have the nerve to go on living here.'

'For Chrissake!' Neil exploded. 'No one has the right to judge me until the review board has reported!'

'Maybe,' said Helen cynically. 'But that isn't going to stop the creeps around here making life hell for us if they've a mind to.'

'Don't take any notice of them.'

'It's easy for you to say that!' Helen flared. 'You've got your own little world to live in. We have to live in the real world. Maybe you don't care about the kids getting hurt but I do.'

That night the gap between them in the kingsize bed was wider than usual.

The following morning's post brought a formal letter from Earl Hackett telling Neil that he was suspended from operational duties pending the findings of the review board set up to investigate the cause of Al Benyon's death. The letter concluded with:

> You will, of course, continue to draw full pay until the review board have published their findings. In the meantime, you are not required to report to the KSC for duty until you are called upon to give evidence to the board.

'So now what do we do?' demanded Helen when she had read the letter. 'How do I explain why you're at home to the kids and neighbours?'

'How about telling them the truth!' Neil snarled.

9 Thirty tonnes of laser-guided bombs rained down on Ben Gurion International Airport with pinpoint accuracy from a height of one hundred and sixty thousand feet.

The concrete-piercing bombs destroyed the airport's runways, underground fuel tanks, the El Al hangers and the control tower. Both Sharav assembly lines at the adjoining Israel Aircraft Industries factory were wiped out together with the main drawing office. Thirty-one designers and draughtsmen were killed.

Six Sharav IV fighters from the *Chel Ha'Avir*'s 101 Squadron had climbed to their maximum ceiling of one hundred thousand feet to intercept the raider. The pilots launched their air-to-air Wolvereens at the solitary Tupolev V-G long-range bomber and had to watch in angry impotence as the American-built missiles burned out at one hundred and fifty thousand feet. The missiles self-destructed and their debris spiralled back to earth.

The Tupolev flew on its way, serene and unconcerned.

A voice broke through on the UHF channel that the Sharav fighters used to communicate with each other.

'Tupolev bomber to Sharav Leader. Do you read?' enquired the voice. It was an educated voice speaking good Hebrew.

The *Chel Ha'Avir* squadron leader refused to acknowledge the call.

'I think perhaps you do read me,' continued the voice. 'This is Joseph Maken speaking from the Tupolev bomber.'

All six Israeli pilots switched on their flight voice recorders but none of them answered Maken.

'The raid on Ben Gurion Airport is regretted,' said Maken smoothly. 'But it is also the home of Israel Aircraft Industries and therefore a legitimate military target as far as the PLO is concerned. Soon we shall be deciding whether or not all of Israel can be considered a military target. I shall be sorry if that happens but remember that this war is not of our making.'

The dull crump of the exploding bombs could be heard thirty miles away in Jerusalem.

A report on the raid reached Rymann fifteen minutes later as he was about to open the morning meeting of the Emergency Defence Council. The council's full strength was six although it was rare for more than five to attend. This morning there were three: Ben Irving, Commander-in-Chief of the *Chel Ha'Avir*; Samuel Kuttner, the Foreign Minister; and Michael Greer. Like his Cabinet, Rymann prefered his executive groups to be of a minimum size coupled to maximum power.

The report was short and sharp – one side of a sheet of paper – the way Rymann liked them. He read it out to the three men who were seated around the oval olivewood table in his private conference room on the fourth floor of the Prime Minister's building. The western side of the rectangular parliamentary building was festooned with scaffolding following a bombing raid the previous month.

'So,' said Rymann when he had finished reading out the report. 'We now have Joseph Maken overflying Israel to justify his selection of targets.'

'An act of bravura,' Ben Irving commented sourly. He was a large, powerfully-built man, accustomed to saying exactly what he thought. His bluntness earned him plenty of enemies but it was a characteristic that Rymann liked. He knew exactly where he stood with Ben Irving.

'Possibly,' Rymann agreed cautiously while running an appreciative eye over the girl taking minutes. 'But an act that will certainly look good on Arab television. You can be sure that a video recordist went along with him. Now we know why that last raid was shown live on their networks. A dress rehearsal.'

One of Rymann's strengths was his ability to place himself in the enemies' shoes and see things from their point of view.

'All tyrants are power-mad publicity seekers,' Irving grunted. 'He's revealed an Achilles' heel.'

Rymann caught Greer's eye for a moment and switched his gaze out of the window across the President Park and the gardens of the Hakyria Government Centre. 'Well he's certainly found one of ours if we can't shoot him down from one hundred and sixty thousand feet,' he gently reminded Irving. 'Sam – you have some information from Washington for us?'

Foreign Minister Samuel Kuttner cleared his throat and shuffled a large number of papers that Rymann looked at in alarm. He was a small, florid man. Always very correct in manner and speech, apart from his ability to drone on for hours without actually saying anything. Rymann found him a useful bore.

'The informal talks on the renewal of the arms supply agreement with Secretary of State Hallam ended yesterday,' Kuttner began. 'As you know, the current agreement expires at the end of next month.'

'Quite right,' Rymann agreed patiently. 'We do know. The conclusions in a nutshell, please, Sam.'

'President Marshall will renew the agreement as it stands. Renegotiation of the present level of materials quantities and weapon sophistication is out of the question.'

Irving muttered a one-word expletive under his breath. 'More of their surplus junk from the last decade. That agreement was based on our peacetime supply needs.'

Rymann steepled his fingers. 'I can see Marshall's point of view,' he murmured while eyeing the outline of the girl's breasts. 'He's facing an election this year. He can't afford to make the supply of arms to Israel an election issue – which is exactly what would happen if the agreement is renegotiated. This isn't the mid-twentieth century. The Jewish vote is a declining factor in US politics. We can thank Ritz for that.'

'What are Marshall's chances of being re-elected?' asked Irving, who rarely followed American politics.

'Slim,' said Greer, speaking for the first time. 'Most of the opinion polls are predicting a ten per cent win for Harding. And Senator Harding, as we know, is not over-friendly towards Israel. If he does get into the White House, it will be the black vote that puts him there.' He ran his long fingers through his mop of grizzled hair. 'From our own survey of Jewish organizations in the US, it seems unlikely that he'll pick up more than five per cent of the traditional Jewish vote.'

Ben Irving leaned forward, his hands clasped together and his eyes hard. 'Rymann. As I see it, we've now got nothing to lose by launching a Massada attack against Maken's base as soon as the missiles can be made ready. I don't give a shit if such an attack is interpreted as a violation of Soviet sovereignty. A one-off attack. That's all we need. Right now we've got nothing to lose.'

Rymann shook his head. Army security was especially good if news of the Negev explosion hadn't filtered through to Irving. 'That won't be possible.'

Irving stuck out his granite jaw. 'Why not? Development on that damn booster's finished isn't it?'

Originally Irving had been no friend of the Massada programme because it had siphoned funds from the *Chel Ha'Avir*'s budget. It was the appalling aircraft losses to Soviet SAM-50As missile batteries during the early stages of the war that had forced him to accept the need for the Massada.

Provided it and its bloody booster worked.

'I have some bad news about the Massada booster,' said Rymann. He went on to outline the details of the Negev explosion. Irving's weathered face seemed to pale as the truth sank in. When Rymann had finished speaking, he burst out:

'You mean that there's *nothing* left?'

Rymann nodded unhappily.

Kuttner gazed at Rymann with a stunned expression and slumped back in his chair.

For a moment it looked as if the mercurial Irving was going to lose his temper but he succeeded in maintaining his self-control. 'Not even a pre-production model?'

Rymann shook his head. 'All we've got are the drawings and

41

test specifications. We've lost all the jigs, the specialist machine tools – and worse – the brains that created them.'

'Holy shit.'

Kuttner broke the brief silence that followed. 'We've still got the basic Massadas,' he pointed out.

Irving rounded on him. 'What bloody use are they? What's the use of an accurate short-range missile if we can't get close enough to the enemy to launch the bloody thing? The whole point of the Massada booster is that it's a delivery system to give the Massada the kick it needs for an intercontinental capability.'

'*Was* a delivery system,' Rymann corrected mildly, wondering if the girl was minuting Irving's expletives as accurately as the previous secretary used to. He hoped so.

'How long will it take us to produce the boosters now?' Irving growled.

'Michael?' asked Rymann.

'Probably three years,' Greer replied promptly, without consulting his notes.

'What!'

'We lost all our top rocket scientists and technicians in the explosion,' said Greer. 'They can't be replaced overnight. The Hebrew University have given me the names of twenty promising graduates who will form the nucleus of a new team. The most brilliant was about to join the Gas Turbine Research Establishment at Sedom – Professor Yarikon. She is looking into the problem and will give an accurate timescale as quickly as possible. My institute's operational research department has come up with three years.'

'Three years!' Irving exploded. 'Do you know what will happen to our country within one year at the current attrition rate? Do you?'

'I think we all know the answer to that,' said Rymann unemotionally.

The *Chel Ha'Avir* chief glowered at his Prime Minister. 'Does the President know?'

I saw him this morning.'

'May I ask what he said?'

Rymann stared levelly at Irving. 'He said that I was to buy time. I was to buy three years – no matter what the cost.'

The meeting ended twenty minutes later. The only decision taken was that the Cabinet would have to approve the establishment and funding of a new booster development team as a matter of top priority.

Greer remained behind with Rymann after Irving, Kuttner and the secretary had left. Rymann stood for some moments, staring to his right across at the Hebrew University sprawling across Mount Scopus. Within the magnificent white buildings were the twenty young men and women upon whom the future of Israel depended.

'Have all the students we've approached agreed?' asked Rymann.

'Every one of them,' Greer replied.

There was a long silence while Rymann continued to gaze out of the window. He returned to his chair and regarded Greer thoughtfully. 'The President's right, isn't he? We've got to buy three years – no matter what the cost.'

Greer nodded.

'Any ideas?'

'Not offhand.'

Rymann grinned impishly. 'But you'll think of something, Michael.'

'Is that an order?'

'Yes.'

'In that case I'll think of something,' Greer promised.

He was a man who kept his promises.

10 Even at a distance of ten miles the sustained thunder of the *Dominator* lifting off from Launch Pad A at Complex 39 was enough to shake the plate-glass windows of the Titusville coastal-strip diner. The shuttle was on her way to continue the repairs to the KARMA II satellite that had been abandoned the week before.

A shuttle launch was a familiar enough sight in Titusville. The regulars in the diner didn't even turn round on their stools but a New York family rushed to the door to gaze excitedly across the Indian River and Merritt Island lagoons at the spectacle of the shuttle climbing into the clear Florida sky astride a column of roaring flame and smoke.

'Which one's she, Neil?' asked Harry, the diner's owner, placing a beer in front of the astronaut.

'One-four-one.'

'Isn't that your bird?'

Neil took his gaze away from the windows and nodded.

'You know,' said Harry affably, 'I've been watching those birds fly for close on twenty years now and it still gets me.'

Neil closed his eyes and heard the calm, matter-of-fact voice of the capcom in his ears. The yearning to be back in space, to be away from the banal, everyday problems of life on Earth had become an insidious cancer eating away at his reason.

The family returned noisily to their table.

'Hey, mister,' their small son called out to Harry. 'What's the name of that shuttle?'

Harry nodded to Neil. 'He's the guy to ask, sonny.'

Neil opened his eyes and saw a boy aged about eleven looking questioningly at him. 'She's Oscar Victor 141,' he obliged. Seeing the lad's puzzled expression he added: 'Orbital Vehicle 141. *Dominator*.'

The boy was impressed. 'Do you work at the space center, mister?'

'You could say that.'

Harry chuckled. 'He's an astronaut, sonny.'

The boy's eyes lit up. 'Hey that's great. Could I have your autograph, sir?'

'Sure.' Neil obliged by signing across a blank page in the autograph book that the boy pulled from his pocket.

'Neil O'Hara?' the boy questioned.

'That's me.'

'Weren't you on TV a few days back?'

Harry grasped the boy by the shoulders and gave him a friendly push towards his family. 'You've seen a shuttle go up and you've met an astronaut. Guess you've done pretty well for today, huh, young feller?'

The boy sat down with his parents. Neil watched as the father glanced at the autograph and opened a copy of the *New York Times*.

'Another beer, Harry.'

'Th.. t'll be seven.'

Neil groaned. 'Don't you start. I only came out because Helen gets on my back when I have a couple of drinks.'

44

'Better that than the law on your back,' Harry commented, sliding Neil a full glass. 'If you want me to call Mary to run you home –'

'I'm OK, for God's sake!'

The boy's father glanced up from his newspaper and read from it in low tones to his wife and son.

Harry sat opposite Neil and looked at him in concern. 'You go right ahead and tell me to keep my nose out if you want, but when's this inquiry or whatever it is you have?'

Neil drank half the glass in one swallow. 'Tomorrow.'

'Just want you to know we'll be thinking of you.'

'Thanks, Harry.'

'How long does it go on for?'

'About two days. They'll be publishing their findings next week.'

'Fast.'

'They want it out of the way and under the carpet.'

The family paid their bill and left. Harry cleaned their table and fished a ball of coloured paper out of the ashtray. He smoothed it out.

'My autograph?' Neil queried.

Harry nodded. 'Kids,' he commented in disgust.

Neil ordered another drink.

11 Heinlein was inwardly seething with rage. He knew what the verdict of the court martial was as soon as he was ushered back into the courtroom. Gideon Tal, his useless defending officer, avoided his eye. *Segan-Aluf* Sharon did nothing to disguise his smirk of triumph.

President of the court martial tribunal was *Aluf-Mishne* Leonaida of the Tenth Armoured Brigade. A distinguished-looking man who had gone to considerable lengths to ensure that Heinlein had received a fair hearing. He sat in a high-backed chair, flanked by two junior officers who had not spoken a word during the three-day hearing. The Star of David flag was pinned to the wall behind him.

'We have considered all the evidence most carefully, Lieutenant Heinlein,' said Leonaida, glancing down at his notebook. 'In particular, we have studied most carefully the findings of Dr

45

Karolski who could find no evidence of death from a sniper's bullet when he examined the remains of your driver.'

Of course not! His body had been burnt to a frazzle!

'Then there is the evidence of the men in your company. All of them have said under oath that they did not hear you shout at them to follow you.'

Leonaida paused and studied the tall, dark-haired young man standing before him. In his heart he did not believe that Heinlein was a coward. For three days the young officer had stood rigidly to attention. Saying nothing. His craggy features a mask; his eyes two unblinking black pools burning into the wall. The only time he had nearly opened his mouth to speak was when Sharon had given evidence. There had been moments when Leonaida would have given his commission to know what Heinlein had been thinking.

Leonaida continued: 'We have also heard the evidence of your commanding officer. *Segan-Aluf* Sharon stated that he has never received reports of a PLO agent or sniper operating in Nazareth. In view of these facts, we have no choice but to find you guilty of the charges laid against you. Will you please place your firearm on the table before you.'

Heinlein dragged his eyes away from the wall and stared at Leonaida with dark, unseeing eyes. The request was repeated. Heinlein stirred himself. Like a man in a trance, he unbuckled his Luger. For a moment it looked as though he was about to slam the weapon down but he seemed to think better of it and laid it carefully on the table.

'Lieutenant David Heinlein,' said Leonaida. 'In view of your excellent service record in the Special Parachute Brigade, we have decided to deal leniently with you. On the charge of desertion under fire, you will serve a sentence of ten years. On the charge of showing cowardice in the face of the enemy, you will serve a sentence of ten years. Both sentences to run concurrently.'

Not a flicker betrayed Heinlein's innermost fury.

'You may retain your rank of *segan*. Do you have anything to say?'

There was only the slightest hesitation before Heinlein replied. 'No, sir.'

Gideon Tal rose to request leave to appeal to the President of the Military Court. The request was granted. Leonaida stood. The court martial was over. The NCO guarding Heinlein touched his elbow.

Tal was standing by the military police car that was waiting outside. He stopped talking to the driver when Heinlein appeared with his escort. Heinlein pointedly ignored him.

'Don't worry, Lieutenant,' said Tal, unperturbed by Heinlein's slight. 'I'm sure we can get the sentence reduced on appeal.'

'Or increased?' countered Heinlein sarcastically.

'There is always that risk,' the officer admitted.

A thought occurred to Heinlein as he was about to get into the car. He said to the officer. 'Do you know how old I'll be when I'm released?'

Tal looked nonplussed. 'Er . . . Well . . . thirty-three? Thirty-four?'

Heinlein regarded him with unconcealed contempt. 'Bastard!' he snarled. 'You didn't even bother to read my file properly. I'll be forty.' He climbed into the back seat beside the NCO. 'Come on. Let's get out of here.'

The car swept out of the Central Command barracks and merged with the stream of traffic heading into Tel Aviv.

12 Five thousand miles away in Florida, Neil O'Hara was facing a similar ordeal to that suffered by Heinlein.

Opposite him at a long table were the seven members of Congressman Edward Williams' review board. Sharing the row of tables with Neil were Kellinah Assad, the payload specialist on the shuttle mission, and Earl Hackett. Jason Pelham was sitting at the side tables occupied by senior NASA officials. Moving among them like an inquisitive, one-eyed bird was a WESH cameraman. Jane Benyon had entered the room when Neil had first started answering Williams' questions an hour earlier. It was the first time he had seen her since the day of Al's death.

'OK, Mr O'Hara,' said Williams, addressing the conference room's ceiling. 'If you find our phraseology hard to follow, let us put that question to you in another way. Would or would you not consider it reasonable for a shuttle commander to verify any potentially ambiguous statement made by a member of his crew?'

The WESH cameraman kept his lens aimed steadily at Neil.

'Yes – if he knew it to be ambiguous at the time,' Neil replied.

Congressman Williams had the unnerving habit of staring in a bored manner at the ceiling when putting questions to Neil – as if he expected the answers to be fabrications – and then allowing his gaze to wander around the conference room during Neil's replies as though those expectations were being confirmed. Being a former NASA administrator – a lawyer – he tended to give his questions a certain authority, although most of the time he was reading from a list of questions set by the expert members of his review board.

It was the first day of the board's sitting. Their first witness had been Assad. He had answered Williams' questions with the same degree of politeness with which they had been put. He had stuck to the plain facts and had refused to be coerced into making comments or enlarging unnecessarily on his answers.

'OK,' said Williams after a whispered conference with his colleagues. He gave Neil a contemptuous glance. 'It looks like we're getting somewhere at last so we'll stick with this line of questioning. If a shuttle commander fails to verify an ambiguous statement, would you say that that commander was being negligent?'

'That's a hypothetical question,' Neil retorted.

'There was nothing hypothetical about Al Benyon's death,' Williams observed.

'You ask me hypothetical questions, Mr Chairman, and you must expect hypothetical answers.'

'It seems a reasonable question to us, Mr O'Hara.'

'Are you implying that I was negligent?'

Congressman Williams' eyes opened wide in an expression of injured innocence. 'This board is not competent to offer implications, Mr O'Hara. All we have to do is establish the cause of Al Benyon's death – not apportion blame. At least – not yet. However, our questions concerning possible negligence appear to be touching a raw spot so we'll move on to something else.'

Neil made no reply. He glanced across at Jane Benyon who looked quickly away. Jason Pelham returned Neil's gaze without blinking.

Williams conferred briefly with the other four members of the review board before turning his attention back to Neil.

48

'Mr O'Hara. We have here your statement. Correction – your report on what took place on OV-141 last week. You have a copy in front of you?'

'Yes, sir.'

'Are there any amendments that you wish to make to that report? Any minor additions or deletions?'

'No, Mr Chairman.'

Williams nodded and looked at his watch. 'Thank you, Mr O'Hara. We have no more questions for you at the moment. You may sit. Mr Earl Hackett.'

Earl Hackett stood. 'Mr Chairman?'

'We understand that you are chief of shuttle operations and that you were capcom during OV-141's mission?'

'That is correct, Mr Chairman.'

'OK,' said Williams. 'We'll break for sixty minutes now and reconvene at a quarter after one when we will be questioning you.'

A nice warning, thought Neil.

During the lunchbreak Neil spotted Earl Hackett and Jason Pelham in the coffee lounge deep in earnest conversation. He guessed that they were going over Earl Hackett's evidence.

The video recorder rolled, forcing Neil to relive the moments before Al's death. The cameras and microphones aboard the shuttle had missed nothing. The shots showed Al's spacesuited figure struggling to release the damaged satellite power units.

'You know these gizmos, Kell,' said Al's recorded voice. 'Reckon she's come free about ten degrees?'

A long pause and then Assad's fatal words of reply were heard in the still conference room: 'You're right. Ten degrees.'

The closing shot was taken from the camera mounted on the manipulator arm. In horrific detail it showed the prybar slashing into Al's spacesuit.

'Cancel!' screamed Assad's voice from the speaker. 'For mercy's sake!'

Neil tried desperately to deafen himself to the rest of the torture but he could hear his voice calling out to Al and the hideous croaks of the dying astronaut.

'OK. That's enough,' said Williams.

The recording stopped.

Williams nodded to a security guard. 'Tell Mrs Benyon that she may return now if she wishes.' He looked up at Earl Hackett who had been answering his questions for fifteen minutes. 'How many times have you played those tapes, Mr Hackett?'

'I've lost count, Mr Chairman.'

Williams grunted. 'In the seconds leading up to the accident, did either of the three men say anything that was out of the ordinary when compared with other orbiter flights?'

'No. Nothing.'

'You are also familiar with Mr O'Hara's report in which he claims the accident was due to ambiguity over the two words "yaw" spelled y-a-w, and "you're" spelled y-o-u apostrophe r-e.?'

'Yes, Mr Chairman.'

'In your expert opinion, would you agree with Mr O'Hara? The pronounciation of the two words is identical.'

Without hesitation, Hackett said: 'There was no ambiguity, Mr Chairman. I have played the tapes many times.' He picked up a sheaf of documents. 'And I've studied the mission transcript. It is perfectly clear from the dialogue continuity that Assad's phrase "You're right. Ten degrees" was in answer to a query by Al Benyon. Had it been an instruction to Mr O'Hara, the phrase would have been prefixed with the word "Commander". If you turn to page twenty-three, line seven; page twenty-eight, line twenty, and thirty-three other entries for which we've prepared a list, you will observe that Assad always prefixed his instructions to Mr O'Hara by addressing him as "Commander".'

Jane Benyon entered the room and sat in a chair at the side. She was careful not to look at Neil.

'But the pronounciation of the two words is identical,' Williams persisted. 'Is there a case for reviewing your terminology to ensure that such a misunderstanding does not arise again?'

'No,' Hackett replied emphatically. 'Many words in the English language have the same pronounciation but different meanings. It's not NASA's task to rewrite the English language.'

Williams gave a sudden grin. 'When I was at NASA I remember a hatch being called an ingress/egress facility. That's a pretty good attempt at rewriting the English language I would've thought.'

There was some quickly suppressed laughter from the back of the conference hall.

'Ingress and egress are perfectly normal English words,' Hackett countered. 'For example – the words t-o-o and t-w-o sound exactly the same. We use both with great frequency and have never encountered problems. I said that it was not NASA's task to rewrite the English language. To qualify that, I should add that it is not possible for us to rewrite the English language to compensate for unforeseeable instances arising out of negligence.'

Williams raised his eyebrows. 'Are you saying that Mr O'Hara was negligent on the *Dominator* mission?'

'I was talking generally,' said Hackett blandly.

'OK. So let's talk specifically. Is it your opinion – your expert opinion I must add because you are an experienced astronaut – that Neil O'Hara was negligent on the *Dominator* mission?'

Hackett considered his reply for a moment. 'Yes,' he said at length. 'Having examined all the data, there is no doubt whatsoever in my mind that Astronaut O'Hara's negligence was the direct cause of Al Benyon's death.'

13 Heinlein had been in Tel Aviv's military prison for two days when his father visited him.

'Five minutes,' said the corporal, withdrawing from the austere room that Heinlein had been assigned.

The two men regarded each other with mutual suspicion. It was their first meeting since Yom Kippur the previous year. The autocratic Avram Heinlein was a millionaire diamond merchant, a licensed bullion dealer, and a leading member of the ultra-Jewish Orthodox Satmar sect of the Hasidic movement. He wore an immaculate black suit and untrimmed Hasidic sidelocks.

'Your case was reported in all the papers,' he said to his son. 'This is the first time I'm glad that your mother isn't alive.' He spoke in English. Hebrew was a sacred language to be used only for prayer.

Heinlein looked cynical. 'You said that at my Bar Mitzvah, and you said something similar when I took my army commission when I told you that I wasn't interested in religion.'

'I didn't come here to open old wounds,' said Avram stiffly.

'No. And you didn't come here to heal them. So why did you come?'

Avram took a deep breath. 'You misjudge me, David. Whatever

51

I may have said, I've always loved you.' It was the nearest Avram could get to an apology.

Heinlein looked faintly incredulous. 'You cursed me the day I took my commission.'

'The founding of the State of Israel is a blasphemy,' said Avram with sudden vehemence. 'Only the Messiah can perform that sacred duty. By joining the armed forces, you were helping to perpetuate that blasphemy.'

'The way I feel now, I agree with you,' said Heinlein bitterly. 'Personally I wouldn't give a toss if the Palestinians wiped the place out tomorrow.'

'You included?'

Heinlein shrugged indifferently.

There was an awkward silence. Avram glanced around the plainly furnished room. There was a small television set screwed to the wall, and a shower and toilet facilities in one corner. There was even a plain writing desk and an empty bookcase.

'This place isn't as bad as I thought it would be.'

Heinlein gave a wry chuckle. 'It used to be a British Army HQ. They jailed members of the Haganah here. As an officer, I'm entitled to a room on the northern side of the building. I suppose you really came here to gloat?'

Avram stiffened. He decided to ignore the insult by changing the subject. 'Moshe and Uri send their regards.'

Heinlein looked bored at the mention of his brothers.

'The business is doing well,' Avram continued. 'We've opened new offices here in Tel Aviv, near the Diamond Exchange. Moshe has taken over in Amsterdam, and Uri is running the London office.'

Heinlein looked uninterested. 'You can hardly say that my case has brought ruin and disgrace upon the family.'

'I've had to put up with the whispers and innuendoes!' Avram snapped angrily.

'That's your problem,' Heinlein replied. 'I've got to put up with ten years in this hole.'

'I never did understand why you signed on for so long,' said Avram.

'Simple,' said Heinlein. 'I found army life more exciting than peddling diamonds around the world for you.'

'You were good at your job.'

'I was an even better soldier.'

52

Avram glanced around the sparsely furnished room. 'You think so? David . . . if your appeal is successful, I want you to come back into the business. I need you.'

Heinlein raised his eyebrows. 'I thought Uri and Moshe were doing so well?'

Avram gave an impatient gesture. 'They're both too soft. They let people trample them. You were tough. Remember that deal you pulled off in New York? I don't think Uri or Moshe could do that.'

'Thanks for the offer, Father,' said Heinlein. 'But if I ever get out of here, the last thing I'll want to do is work for you.'

For once Avram was unsure of himself. He was sorely tempted to condemn his son but realized that he had no stomach for such a task. 'I'm not far from here, David. I can call in any time. If there is anything you need . . . .'

If Heinlein was touched by his father's offer of friendship, he did not show it. 'Thank you, no, Father. For the next ten years I'm the guest of the blasphemous State of Israel. The bastards will be seeing to most of my needs.'

'But you will contact me if there's anything you need,' Avram insisted.

Heinlein stared his father straight in the eye. 'The only thing I need right now is justice. I never did expect it from you when I was a kid, so I certainly don't expect or want it from you now. And as for getting it from this lousy country of ours – I might as well go and piss into the wind.'

14 Two miles from where Heinlein was imprisoned, Michael Greer was working late in his top-floor office on Rothschild Boulevard.

There was a stack of intelligence reports and memos on his desk for him to speed-read, digest and initial. Most of them were routine reports from Mossad agents throughout the world. All would eventually end up in the appropriate agent's 'volume' computer record on the building's third floor.

As Greer ploughed through the paperwork, he wished that there were reports from Joseph Maken's base at Bakal on the Black Sea. The last agent to be successfully infiltrated into the PLO base had

had his cover 'blown' within ten days. The agent didn't even have the chance to use his satellite link radio transmitter. What information Mossad had on the base had been collated by the cell in Istanbul – and that was little enough. The most recent report was that Leon Dranski, the Soviet Premier, was planning a visit to Bakal within the next few weeks.

Greer read a report on an army lieutenant who had been court-martialled for desertion and cowardice. The officer's defence had been that he had left his unit to chase a suspected PLO agent in Nazareth, a sniper. The prosecution had maintained that no agents were operating in Nazareth.

Greer wondered why the report had been funnelled through to him. Then he read that the officer in question was a member of the Special Parachute Brigade and had once served on the army security staff of a 'government establishment in the Negev'. That explained why the report was on Greer's desk; as soon as he had heard about the explosion, he had issued a standing order that any mention of government establishments in the Negev Desert should be referred to him.

The court martial report was of no interest. He initialled it, tossed it in his 'out' tray, and turned his mind back to the promise he had made Rymann: that somehow he would find a way of buying Israel a three-year breathing space to enable the new development team to produce the Massada booster.

A bizarre plan was already taking shape in his mind. Bizarre was hardly an appropriate word. It was a lunatic idea and one that Rymann would be certain to turn down out of hand unless he was handled carefully.

Also it needed a lot more thought.

Greer skimmed through the next three reports with only half his customary attention until he came to a 'low-grade' report from a Mossad agent who had infiltrated the dissident Arab community in Nazareth. The agent was commenting on a rumour rather than supplying 'hard' intelligence. The rumour was that a trained PLO operative had been sent into Nazareth. The agent concluded by stressing the 'soft' nature of the information and that he would try to obtain more reliable data as quickly as possible.

Nazareth?

Greer frowned and riffled through the papers he had just initialled. He pulled out the report on the court martial and read it through twice. The prosecution did not have access to this latest intelligence on the possibility of an agent operating in Nazareth, therefore there was a possibility, a faint possibility, that this Lieutenant David Heinlein had been the victim of a miscarriage of justice.

Greer considered the matter for a few moments. He could hardly present the army authorities with flimsy, unsubstantiated evidence from an unnamed undercover agent for airing before a court martial appeal hearing.

Anyway, the case was nothing to do with him. Best forget it.

15 Neil was refuelling the big Winnebago camper at a Melbourne filling station when Jane drove past in her car. He quickly paid his bill and followed her to the car park outside Melbourne's main shopping mall. He pulled the Winnebago alongside her Datsun as she was locking the doors.

'Hi there, Jane.' He smiled uncertainly down at her. As always, she looked stunning. It was the first time he had spoken to her since Al's memorial service and even then she had only muttered a cursory 'good morning' in response to his greeting.

Jane looked up at the camper's driver's cab and dropped her keys into her purse. It was obvious from the indifferent look in her eyes that she had no wish to talk to Neil.

'We thought you'd moved for good,' said Neil, adopting a cheery tone.

'I have,' Jane replied coldly. 'I've come back to fix the furniture sale and see the realtor.'

Neil opened the Winnebago's door. 'How about coffee?' he invited. 'I've got everything on board.'

'I don't think that would be a good idea.'

'Please, Jane. I must talk to you.'

Jane hesitated. She sighed and entered the motor home. She sat in the front swivel chair and turned to face Neil who was busying himself at the galley.

'Well?'

'How's everything?' he enquired, unable to think of anything more sensible to say for the moment.

Jane shrugged and unfolded the dashboard table so that Neil could set out the cups and saucers. 'So. So.'

'Jane – about the other night –'

'I don't want to talk about it.'

'It's just that I don't want you to think –' The words stumbled out but Jane cut him short.

'Didn't I make myself clear just now?'

Neil sensed that he was red with embarrassment. He busied himself with the cups and saucers. 'Jane – about the review board hearing . . . .'

'What about it?'

Christ, he thought, she's determined to make it difficult for me. 'They made it out to be my fault. It wasn't like that.'

'The review board's report isn't published until tomorrow,' said Jane abruptly. 'And I don't think there's much point in this topic either.' She reached for the door but Neil restrained her.

'Please, Jane. Hear me out.'

She relaxed and brushed a strand of her ash-blonde hair away from her eyes. 'OK. I'm listening. But if you try to make it out that what happened to Al wasn't your fault, then it won't wash. I've read the mission transcript. Even to me it was perfectly obvious that Assad was talking to Al.'

'I've been wanting to speak to you and now I hardly know what to say. I know how useless saying sorry is. But I am sorry for what happened to Al. Desperately sorry. Every night I find myself praying for the chance to relive those moments so that Al . . . .' His voice trailed into an awkward silence. He cursed his inability to express himself coherently.

Jane opened the door. This time Neil made no move to stop her. 'Goodbye, Neil,' she said. 'Give my love to Helen.'

'Shall we keep in touch?'

'I don't think that would be a good idea,' Jane replied. She turned her back on Neil and walked towards the mall's main entrance.

16 The ten-man inflatable boat, propelled by muffled paddles, crept towards the beach under the cover of darkness.

The eight Palestinians crouching low in the boat were lightly armed. They all wore combat dress that would provide effective camouflage against the sand. Their cargo included several pieces of electronic equipment of which the most sophisticated was a Soviet-built millimetric radar jammer. It was unlikely to be needed because the team had selected a night when the waves were higher than their boat. The chances of them being detected by Israeli coastal radar was slim.

The spot they had selected to go ashore was a windswept stretch of beach halfway between Tel Aviv and Netanya where the sand-duned coastline ran virtually dead straight for twenty miles. It was also free of the many reefs that guarded this particular part of the coast.

As soon as the boat grounded, they scrambled out, quickly hauled it clear of the surf and hid it in the shadows afforded by piles of stacked beach beds.

They froze when a heavy transport aircraft from the nearby *Chel Ha'Avir* base at Herzlia took off and flew over them, its landing lights blazing. The aircraft faded into the darkness. On a signal from their leader the men set to work.

They worked swiftly and methodically without getting in each other's way, each man concentrating on his allotted task. The three weeks of hard training were paying off.

It would have been easy enough for them to plant landmines under the sand that would wreak havoc when the holidaymakers flocked on to the beach. Instead they scooped sand and shingle samples into marked plastic containers and took a number of measurements with a nightsight gunnery rangefinder. They even used a clinometer to check the angle of the beach while two of their number carried out a brief survey of the low dunes. One man, armed with a miniature three-D video camcorder fitted with a image intensifier, moved across the dunes towards the nearby main highway and spent some time making a series of recordings of the surrounding terrain.

Ten minutes later the men were paddling silently out to sea with their precious samples and recordings stowed in waterproof bags. After three hours' sweated labour in the humid night they shipped their paddles and started up the fifty-horsepower Mercury outboard.

It took them another hour to reach the nondescript motor yacht that was waiting for them. They climbed aboard, their faces wreathed in broad grins, and trooped down to the stateroom. The tall, dark-haired man who had been waiting anxiously for their return, clapped them warmly on the back and pumped their hands.

Joseph Maken was delighted with the results of the night's work.

17   'Piss off,' said Heinlein shortly.

The little man looked shocked. He blinked in alarm.

'But I'm from the *Hava'ad Lema'an Hahayal* welfare committee. I'm the military prison visitor. I've got a selection of books, magazines, video discs –'

'I don't care if you're a reincarnation of Moses with a second Ark of the Covenant. I told you to piss off.'

The little man backed off towards Heinlein's door. 'You don't even have a copy of the Torah in –'

'I don't want a copy of the bloody Torah!' Heinlein shouted. 'Now get out and leave me alone!'

The little man hurriedly abandoned Heinlein's room.

'Told you,' said the corporal who was waiting outside in the corridor, propped up against the wall chewing gum.

'He appears to have a chip on his shoulder,' the little man commented.

'Chip? It's the whole bloody tree.'

'Is he always like that?'

The corporal shook his head. 'No. He's in a good mood today.'

18   Greer was worried. For reasons he could not immediately identify, the case of Lieutenant David Heinlein kept preying on his mind.

He had spent the morning in his office, grappling with the problem of his promise to Rymann to buy three years for the new booster development team, but whenever he concentrated on the problem, the name Heinlein would intrude on his thoughts. Perhaps it was the thought that his country would be losing the services of a good officer. There was no doubt that Heinlein was a good officer. His record showed that. If there had been a sniper in Nazareth on that fateful day, then Heinlein had been right to forget everything else and go after him.

Greer pursed his lips and decided to do something positive about Lieutenant David Heinlein. He picked up his telephone and made three calls. It was during the third call that he suddenly realized why the question of Lieutenant David Heinlein had been dominating his thoughts.

19 Like an oversized croquet ball rolling through a hoop Leon Dranski eased his bulky frame out of the helicopter's doorway.

He waved his plump arms at the batteries of TV cameras, at the members of the Supreme Council of the PLO, and at the cheering Palestinians crowded six-deep behind the crash barriers lining the airbase. His aides assisted him down the aluminium steps on to the red carpet where he embraced Joseph Maken like a long-lost brother.

'Comrade Chairman,' said Maken warmly. 'On behalf of all the peoples of Palestine, welcome to Bakal.'

The second man to leave the helicopter was Marshal Ustinov, Chief of the Red Army General Staff: a hatchet-faced, unsmiling man who shook hands with Maken without saying a word.

Dranski's jovial smile never left his cherubic face for an instant as he mounted the rostrum. The platform was decked out with the flags of the Soviet Union and the PLO. The hammer and sickles were larger and higher than the Palestinian flags because this was Soviet territory.

The speeches that blared out of the speakers were brief but enthusiastic. Dranski responded to Maken's welcome by saying that the struggle of the Palestinian people was the struggle of the Soviet people. Shoulder to shoulder they were fighting the same glorious revolution. Shoulder to shoulder they would be victorious. Together they were walking down the socialist path that would lead ultimately to world peace and prosperity.

The wily chairman ended his party piece by holding his arms

59

aloft and declaring in well-rehearsed Arabic that the Soviet Union would not rest until the Palestinians had their rightful heritage restored to them.

The crowd went wild. The cheering and yelling lasted for several minutes and only subsided when Dranski laid a wreath on the recently erected memorial to the PLO's fallen heroes.

Five minutes later a cavalcade of armoured Mercedes swept out of the airbase, whisking Leon Dranski and his retinue away on the first stage of their one-day tour of the PLO base at Bakal.

'Incredible, Joseph,' said Dranski jovially, cramming his mouth full of cold roast chicken. 'We lease you three hundred square kilometres of wilderness and you turn it into a miniature state, complete with an air force, an army, and a navy. Schools. Farms. Villages. Television and radio studios. An amazing achievement in such a short time.'

Maken gave a wry smile. 'We have no navy apart from a few rubber boats and my yacht, Comrade Chairman,' he corrected politely.

'Ah. You're complaining?'

'Not at all, Comrade Chairman. You have been more than generous. Without you we could have achieved nothing.'

Dranski shoved some more chicken in his mouth and grinned amiably at Maken. 'True, Joseph. True. But we're used to pouring aid into countries that fail to seize the opportunities that such aid offers. I took many political risks persuading my colleagues to let you have Bakal. It is good to see that I was right and they were wrong.'

Maken smiled and remarked drily, 'I should imagine that the only political risks involved were those taken by your colleagues who opposed you.'

Dranski looked surprised. Then he threw back his head and laughed, splattering the table with bits of half-chewed chicken. 'Their argument was that by allowing the PLO on to our soil, we'd be nursing a viper to our breast.'

'We've learned many lessons over the years, Comrade Chairman,' said Maken gravely. 'The most important being how to distinguish one's friends from one's enemies.'

Dranski nodded emphatically. 'Precisely.'

Maken was silent for a moment. The chains of SAM-50A missile batteries that the Soviets had built around the Crimea Peninsular to defend Bakal against air attack could be turned against the PLO at any time if ever the guests seemed in danger of becoming vipers. Also Bakal had only a limited supply of fresh water – most of the homeland's water needs were met by a Soviet-controlled pipeline.

'Some more salad, Comrade Chairman?'

'Thank you, no.'

The two men were sitting in the dining room of Maken's bungalow eating a cold lunch. Maken had requested that they eat alone. Dranski had readily agreed and had overruled Marshal Ustinov who had been opposed to the idea.

The two leaders made a strange pair. The florid Leon Dranski was fifty-nine years old. What he lacked in the way of formal education he made up with peasant cunning – enough to have taken him to the top of the Kremlin heap. That and his renowned streak of arrogant ruthlessness was sufficient to ensure that he would remain king of that heap for many years to come.

By contrast, Joseph Maken was tall and sophisticated. He was forty. The son of a successful Paris lawyer. His mother was a Palestinian whom his father had first met when handling a case for the PLO's Paris office where she had worked as a secretary.

Joseph was their only child. His father had died while Joseph was still at the Sorbonne. His mother, finding herself with a substantial fortune on her hands for which she had no real need, gave a third of it to the PLO and spent the rest on packing Joseph off around the world to develop his gift for languages.

Joseph emerged from ten years' study in Moscow, Beruit and New York with a remarkable fluency in Russian, Arabic, Hebrew and English. He was working in New York as a United Nations Russian to French interpreter when his mother fell ill with cancer.

After her death he decided to carry on her work for the PLO. George Kahn, the PLO leader who had rebuilt the organization after its near destruction in the early 1980s, immediately recognized the value of the personable young Joseph Maken and sent him to Moscow as the PLO's special emissary to the Kremlin. Maken had spent three years building a close working relationship between the PLO and the Soviets.

For their part the Russians had never learned to trust Maken completely, but at least they knew him. Dranski was shrewd enough to realize that the charismatic Maken was a potential leader of the PLO movement – a pro-Soviet leader at that. Maybe not a puppet, but one couldn't have everything.

When George Kahn was assassinated in New York – supposedly by Mossad agents – the Soviets dropped hints in influential PLO ears suggesting that if Maken was made the new leader of the PLO, then the Soviet Union would consider substantial increases in military and economic aid to the movement.

After a protracted power struggle within the PLO and its twenty-nine rival factions, Maken emerged as the movement's new leader. Suddenly he was a public figure. An immaculately dressed, soft-spoken, educated man who didn't fit the popular image of PLO leaders that looked like guerilla fighters. His skilfully worded speeches to the United Nations, his lecture tours of the United States, and audiences with the Pope, quickly won him and the PLO friends and established him as a new and unexpected force in the turbulent waters of Arabic politics. His crowded daily schedule left him with little time for women.

Whether or not he was a force for good, no one was sure at first – especially the Israelis. But one thing was certain: Joseph Maken was very different.

Just how different emerged soon after the fateful Israeli air attack on the Grand Mosque in Mecca. Leon Dranski announced that the Soviet Union had agreed to Joseph Maken's request to provide the Palestinians with a temporary homeland on Soviet soil. That homeland would be at Bakal on the Crimea Peninsula on the Black Sea. Even more astonishing to the outside world was the decision that the Soviet Union should provide the PLO with a squadron of ten MiG-35s.

It took four days for an advance party of Palestinians to clear an airstrip. Within six days the first MiG-35 'rhubarb' sortie was flown against Israel – an attack that had destroyed the fusion reactor complex at Yavne.

The war had begun and had now dragged on for a year.

Leon Dranski mopped his plate clean with a piece of bread and swallowed his cup of black coffee in one gulp. He belched and beamed expectantly at Maken. 'Shall we continue with our tour, Joseph?'

As a former infantryman, the Soviet leader was more than impressed by the brilliant tank-handling tactics of the PLO's 3rd

Armoured Brigade. He spent thirty minutes with his retinue, watching the T-100s exercising in the difficult terrain of northern Bakal. Not only had the smartly uniformed PLO soldiers learned well from their Red Army instructors, but there was a lot about unorthodox battle tactics that the Red Army could learn from the PLO.

It was impossible to tell if the impassive Marshal Ustinov was impressed. On one occasion Maken noticed him whispering something in Dranski's ear and the Soviet leader nodding in agreement.

Afterwards two hours were spent touring the administrative centre. All the buildings were prefabricated – supplied courtesy of the Soviet Army Support Directorate.

Maken's guests saw the rooms where immigrant Palestinians were screened against computer files to weed out potential Israeli infiltrators. They visited the PLO Army Staff College and even tried out the Arafat three-millimetre sub-machine gun, a tiny but highly effective firearm that was being developed by the Palestine Weapons Research Authority.

'I'm very sorry, gentlemen,' Maken apologized to his guests towards the end of the afternoon. 'But there's a change to the last item on the itinerary. It's a surprise.'

Dranski chuckled. 'Another surprise, Joseph? I think we're immune to them by now.'

The party followed Maken into a large room whose walls were covered in large-scale maps of Israel. The centre of the room was dominated by a giant tabletop model of a stretch of beach. The top of the beach was fringed with sand dunes and beyond them was a four-lane highway that ran parallel to the coast. The scrubland adjoining the beach was flat and uninteresting.

'This is a two-kilometre-wide stretch of coastline between Tel Aviv and Haifa,' said Maken as the party gathered around the table. He used a long pointer to indicate salient features of the model. 'The beach consists of fine shingle and sand in equal proportions – and it's firm. Very firm. And so are these dunes. Beach gradient at its steepest point, near the dunes, is no more than five degrees. Also the beach is a designated recreation area and is therefore unmined.'

Maken swung the pointer seawards. 'The approaches are good: a shelving sea floor – the same angle as the beach out to the two

63

hundred-metre line – and the sea bed is free of the rocky outcrops and reefs that are common along this part of the coast.'

Maken paused and smiled benignly at his guests. 'Any questions, gentlemen?'

'Just one, Joseph,' said Dranski, not smiling for once. 'A question I believe I know the answer to.' He waved a pudgy hand at the model. 'What is the purpose of all this?'

'Simple, Comrade Chairman,' Maken replied smoothly. 'This is the landing spot and beachhead for our invasion of Israel.'

20 Maken's bombshell stirred Marshal Ustinov into words.

'A lunatic scheme,' he observed cryptically.

'Why, Comrade Marshal?' Maken enquired.

'What men and materials are you proposing to land?'

'The force of the first wave will consist of twenty thousand assault troops, one hundred T-100 tanks, twenty RGD self-propelled guns – and ten SAM-30 anti-aircraft missile batteries.'

Ustinov snorted. 'We don't have a seaborne version of SAM-30 yet, therefore the Israelis will blast your landing craft out of the water before they've got within a hundred kilometres of the coast.'

'We're not proposing to use landing craft,' said Maken evenly.

For once Marshal Ustinov managed to look interested. 'Then what are you proposing to use?'

The moment had come for Maken to tread very carefully. He glanced at Dranski and Ustinov in the hope of gauging their moods. Their expressions were not encouraging. A lesser man would have taken a deep breath. Maken plunged right in.

'I have a confession to make, comrades. Within the past three months a PLO sympathizer who works in the Pentagon has sent us an outline of an intelligence report that he thought might be useful to us. The report was prepared by the US naval attaché in Istanbul. It suggested that three Soviet Kosygin Class cruisers based at Sevastopol had been converted to carry a novel type of very large submarine in their holds. The report said that the submarine represented an entirely new concept in marine

64

warfare. It was a one-trip disposable assault submarine that could run into shallow water, beach itself, and disembark up to twenty thousand troops and over one hundred tanks and supporting equipment.'

Maken paused. Not a muscle moved on his guests' faces.

'Such a mother ship and submarine would be able to pass through the Bosphorus without arousing undue comment,' Maken continued. 'And the submarine itself is certain to be equipped with silent running gear and the latest DWF foxers that could fool the Israeli sonar buoy chain.'

Maken decided that he had said enough for the time being. He had dropped a very large and very dangerous ball in the Soviet court and he wondered what they would do with it.

Dranski gave one of his deep chuckles. Maken knew that it meant nothing. The Soviet leader was probably chuckling at the method he had decided on to have him 'deactivated'.

'Interesting, Joseph,' said Dranski thoughtfully. 'Very interesting. Assuming that such a submarine exists, and assuming that you had the use of one, surely you don't think that you could overrun Israel with only twenty thousand troops and one hundred tanks?'

Maken sensed that the worst was over. 'Of course not, Comrade Chairman. Once the SAM-30 batteries are in place, we would cut off the highway and use it as a landing strip to operate a continuous airlift of heavy transports to bring in more men and artillery. Timing is vital of course. In fact the first transports would be landing within thirty minutes after our beach landing. As you know, the Israelis have never taken the idea of a seaborne invasion seriously – all their armour is concentrated in positions where they can easily reach their western, northern and southern borders. It will take them three hours to deploy units to engage us. By that time we will have landed one hundred thousand men and it will be too late.'

'How do you know that the highway can take heavy transports?' Ustinov demanded.

'Simple. We've measured it.'

Dranski's eyes opened wide in surprise. 'Really? How?'

'Twice we have landed survey parties on the beach who have recorded every aspect of the coastline,' Maken replied smoothly.

Dranski looked at Maken with renewed respect. 'Have you?' he said thoughtfully. 'Have you indeed?'

Maken nodded. 'We believe in detailed planning, Comrade Chairman. If I may quote Winston Churchill: "Give us the tools and we'll finish the job."'

The Soviet leader was lost in thought for a moment. He suddenly gave Maken a beaming smile. 'Joseph – there is much that I have to discuss with the Defence Ministers and the Chiefs of Staff. We may have to summon you to Moscow within the next few days to answer a number of questions. Can you hold yourself in readiness?'

Maken felt that a massive weight had been lifted from his shoulders. He shook Dranski warmly by the hand. 'I shall consider it a great honour, Comrade Chairman.'

21 Rymann was busy, or rather his chauffeur was, when his bedside phone rang.

'Damn,' he muttered to Semona, rolling her off him and reaching for the handset. 'That'll be Michael.'

Sergeant Semona Lucca pushed her full lips into a sulky pout and pulled the sheet across her breasts.

'Hendrik?' There was an urgent note in Greer's voice. 'I'm sorry to disturb you.'

'Not as sorry as I am,' said Rymann wearily.

'We must talk.'

Semona smiled mischievously at Rymann and walked her talented fingers sensually down his stomach and set them to work.

'When?'

'Now,' said Greer.

Rymann grabbed hold of Semona's hand and held it still so that he could concentrate. 'You realize that this time in the afternoon is sacred to me?'

Greer knew all about Rymann's afternoons. 'Time is what I want to talk to you about,' he remarked drily.

Rymann was at a loss. 'Time?'

'Three years.'

Rymann was suddenly alert. Semona forgotten.

'I've cancelled this evening's meeting so that we can go for a drive,' said Greer.

'Where to?'

When Greer told him, Rymann sat up and nearly tipped Semona on to the floor. 'Why there, for God's sake?'

'I'll be ready in fifteen minutes,' said Greer.

The line went dead. Rymann replaced the handset and stared at the far wall.

Semona waved a hand before his eyes as if to catch his attention jokingly. 'Hallo? Is anyone there?'

Rymann smiled and cradled her lovely face in his hands.

'Sergeant Lucca. It's time you earned your keep by doing what the state pays you to do.'

Semona laughed, jumped off the bed and started wriggling her glorious olive-coloured body into her uniform. 'And where does my lord and master wish me to drive him?'

'Massada,' said Rymann.

22 Massada.
The Judean Desert. The lowest point on the Earth's surface. Blistering heat. A sun-bleached, moonscape mountain plateau where Herod had built his lair: a fortress summer palace overlooking the haze-layered toe of the Dead Sea. A five-minute cable car ride up the precipitous barren slopes that had taken a Roman army three years to conquer.

Massada.

The last stronghold of the Jewish Revolt of AD70 where nine hundred and sixty men, women and children, under the leadership of Ben Ya'ir, had held out for three years against the tyranny of Roman rule.

Rymann and Greer strolled across the remains of the marbled terraces of the Northern Palace while soldiers kept a watchful eye on them. Semona followed the two men at a discreet distance, her black hair blowing in the pleasant breeze, her eyes alert, her hand resting on an Uzi sub-machine gun slung from her left shoulder.

The few visitors the soldiers had cleared from the historic mountain had been Jewish pilgrims. Israel was no longer popular with tourists.

Rymann and Greer reached the balustrade and stood in silence, each wrapped in his own thoughts – Rymann turning over in his mind the incredible plan that Greer had outlined to him during the one-hour drive from Jerusalem.

Together they gazed down at the threatening lines of the Roman siege dykes – huge stone walls surrounding the mountain that had been designed to prevent the Jews of Massada escaping the terrible end that the Romans had in store for them. To the left of the two men, clawing its way up the northern slopes, was the mighty earthen ramp that the Romans had painstakingly built in their grim determination to breech the ramparts of the mountain fortress.

As Rymann stared down at the ramp he could well imagine the feelings of Ben Ya'ir as he watched it being built. Month by month, inching inexorably towards him. Each day a little higher. Each day bringing him and his people a day nearer the inevitable end.

The same was happening to Israel today. Each day brought fresh jabs at the wound that was slowly bleeding his beloved country to death. Aircraft destroyed faster than they could be replaced; tanks and mobile guns wiped out; factories bombed. And always the deaths; the funerals; the weeping relatives. A horrific bloodshed that seemed unending. And yet, from the grim daily reports Rymann knew that it could not be unending – just as Ben Ya'ir knew that one day the ramp would be completed.

Unless Israel could buy time. Three years.

Ben Ya'ir had bought time for his people.

He had bought them eternity.

The Romans had dragged their mighty siege engines up the huge ramp and were ready to batter down the walls of Massada the following day.

Ben Ya'ir summoned all the heads of the families into the main square where they decided what to do. At midnight the dreadful decision was taken. The nightmare that followed was chronicled thus:

> They then chose ten men by lot from their number to slay the rest, every one of whom lay himself down on the ground by his wife and children and threw his arms about them. They then offered their necks to the stroke of the sword from the ten who courageously carried out their melancholy office.

> And when the ten were done, they drew lots again, leaving one man to kill the other nine. And when this was done, the last man killed himself.

*The Romans entered the fortress and came upon the slain that
numbered nine hundred and sixty. They took no pleasure from what
they beheld, even though the fallen were their enemies. They could
only wonder at the courage and resolution and contempt for death
which so great a multitude had shown.*

A sound disturbed Rymann's thoughts. He and Greer looked
down at the lower terrace where a party of army conscripts were
lining up to take their oath. Originally only paratroopers took the
Massada Oath. Now all conscripts journeyed to the desert fortress
to swear that 'Massada shall never fall again.'

'Can you remember the day you took your oath, Hendrik?' asked
Greer, speaking very quietly.

Rymann turned to face his friend. Greer was staring fixedly at
him. He nodded. 'It was a torchlight ceremony. The sort of thing
one never forgets.'

'We are still bound by that oath, Hendrik. More so than any
soldier because God has given us more power than any soldier.'

'Has he, Michael? I sometimes wonder.'

Greer looked sharply at his friend and saw a tiredness that he had
never seen before. 'Massada must never fall again,' he stated with
uncharacteristic vehemence. 'It would be better to destroy Israel
and the whole world rather than allow an enemy ever to set foot on
this mountain again.'

'The whole world?'

'The whole world,' Greer affirmed without hesitation. 'If the
whole world is prepared to stand by and see Israel destroyed then
we shall have the right to exact an ultimate eye for an ultimate
tooth.' He mopped his lined face with a handkerchief.

'It's an incredible plan.'

'It'll give us the three years we need.'

Rymann gazed across the Dead Sea at the Mountains of Moab.
'The whole world?' he repeated softly to himself.

'My plan is our only hope. But it needs your approval.'

Rymann remained lost in thought for several seconds. Eventually
he came to a decision. 'Very well then, Michael. But we'll keep it to
ourselves – in case it doesn't work.'

'It will work,' Greer promised, a note of triumph in his voice.

'I hope so, Michael. I pray to God that it will. But we'll keep it to
ourselves for the time being. Just the two of us.'

23 I've been what?' Heinlein almost shouted.

'Pardoned,' Gideon Tal repeated, grinning from ear to ear.

'I don't believe you.'

'Take a look at your release papers.'

Heinlein's powerful fingers reached out and snatched the documents from Tal. He scanned through them. 'New evidence? What new evidence?'

Tal looked uncertain. 'I don't know.'

'Then *you* didn't pull this off?'

'Er – well not exactly. I received a phone call two hours ago summoning me to Central Command HQ to collect some papers. One set for the prison commandant, which I've delivered. And one set for you.'

'And no explanation?'

Tal produced an unmarked envelope from his briefcase and handed it to Heinlein. 'Maybe this is it. It's for your eyes only. I'm to ensure that it's destroyed after you've read it.'

Heinlein ripped the envelope open. There was another, better quality envelope inside. The seal surprised him. The contents of the inner envelope's letter surprised him even more. He read it through twice more as if committing it to memory and suddenly laughed out loud.

'May I ask what it's about?' Tal enquired curiously. He had noticed that Heinlein's name on the inner envelope had been inexpertly typed.

'Compensation. No wonder the miserable bastards want this letter destroyed. They're offering me an extra month's pay as compensation. A month's pay for what I've been through!'

'You could get much more,' said Tal. 'I could fight that for you.'

Heinlein fixed his dark eyes on Tal. 'You? You couldn't fight a dead sparrow.'

'Thanks.'

'Anyway – I don't want their bloody compensation.'

Heinlein took a lighter from Tal, burned both envelopes and

70

the letter in an ashtray and ground the blackened flakes to powder.

'Now what?' asked Heinlein.

'You can get your things and walk out of here – a free man to return to your unit without a blemish on your record. You will receive full back pay and there will be no loss of seniority or promotion.'

'Let's get my things,' said Heinlein indifferently.

'Glad everything turned out OK, sir,' said the corporal, checking Heinlein's personal effects against a clipboard and putting them in a suitcase.

'I'll miss your cheerful winning ways, Corporal,' said Heinlein sourly. 'Like you bellowing in my ear at six every morning.'

The corporal grinned and closed the briefcase. 'If you'd just sign here, sir . . . . Thank you, sir. You know – I always said there was something not right about your case. Read about it in *Ma'arakhot* I did.'

'Oh yes,' said Tal to Heinlein. 'I've been told to remind you that as an officer, you're still under army regulations. You must not discuss your case with the press or anyone. An official press release will be issued by the Ministry of Defence tomorrow.'

'I'll talk about it to whoever I please,' said Heinlein curtly.

'But you can't. Army regulations –'

'Fuck the army regulations. They won't apply to me if I'm not in the army.'

Tal stared aghast at Heinlein. He had a feeling that everything was beginning to go horribly wrong. His instructions had been to accompany Heinlein back to Central Command Headquarters. 'But you're returning to your unit, aren't you?'

'Yes – to resign my commission and collect my back pay.'

'But you can't!'

'Try and stop me,' said Heinlein, snatching up his suitcase and moving towards the door.

'Oh, God,' muttered Tal, distraught. 'Listen, Lieutenant. Even if you quit, you can't go shooting your mouth off to the press. You're still subject to the laws of this country.'

Heinlein turned round slowly to face Tal. 'Who said I wanted to stay in this bloody awful fucking country?'

Tal went pale.

Heinlein yanked the door open and strode out into the sunlight and freedom.

'Hell,' Tal muttered.

'Funny one him,' the corporal remarked. 'Never did show any gratitude.'

Tal had a suspicion that precious little gratitude was going to be shown him when he returned to Central Command Headquarters.

'You'll keep quiet about this,' he warned the corporal.

'Oh – of course, sir,' assured the corporal who couldn't wait to relate the scene to his comrades.

Heinlein suddenly reappeared.

'Someone lend me five hundred shekels for a cab.'

24 A Barbie Doll secretary showed Neil into Earl Hackett's office in the administrative block at the Kennedy Space Center.

'Good to see you, Neil,' said Hackett genially, shaking his visitor's hand and waving him to a chair. 'You'll be pleased to know that Bud Wilson and Lewis Markstein have just fixed the KARMA II comsat.'

'That's good news, Earl.'

Hackett looked rueful. 'Trouble is that we can't charge Bud's and Lewis' mission against the satellite owner's account.'

'That must've kept Pelham awake at night,' Neil observed acidly.

Hackett chuckled. His face became serious. He glanced at his watch. 'The review board's report will be published in two hours. I thought it fair that you saw a copy before the press embargo is lifted.' He opened a drawer and handed Neil a plastic binder containing a document that ran to several hundred pages.

Neil weighed the report in his hand without speaking. It was much larger than he had anticipated.

'Part One is an outline of the mission profile,' Hackett explained. 'Part Two is a transcript from 141's voice recorder.' He hesitated. 'The section that affects you is in the review board's conclusions. Part Six – pages fourteen through sixteen.'

Neil turned to Part Six and read through the numbered

paragraphs. There was a verbose closing passage printed in bold face that jumped off the page:

> In the final analysis we conclude that the commander of OV-141 was not paying full attention to the voice exchanges between the payload specialist and Al Benyon during the latter's EVA. A study of the appropriate section of the voice recorder transcript (see Part 2 pages 8 through 20) clearly demonstrates that the payload specialist's exchanges had been directed at Al Benyon and not the orbiter's commander. This, taken in conjunction with the commander's statement in his written report on the mission (see Appendix B) that he was distracted by an optical phenomenon in the Negev Desert, means that we have no hesitation in attributing the tragic death of Al Benyon to this failure of concentration by the commander of OV-141.
>
> No blame can be attached to any of NASA's shuttle hardware or operational procedures which we have examined in detail and found to be satisfactory (see Part 5).

Neil turned to an appendix that listed all the individuals who had given evidence to the review board. He was shaken by what he found.

'They were tough on you,' said Hackett apologetically, avoiding Neil's eye. 'I'm sorry.'

Neil angrily tossed the report on Hackett's desk. 'Why didn't the review board call the other astronauts to give evidence?'

Hackett looked puzzled. 'What other astronauts?'

'I submitted a list to your office of four astronauts who've told me that they are worried about the use of the word "yaw". What happened to it?'

'It wasn't part of your report –' Hackett began.

'But it was part of my evidence!' Neil protested.

'Congressman Williams said that he was only prepared to call evidence from those who were directly involved in your mission. The review board's terms of reference are spelled out –'

'I'm not talking about terms of reference. I'm talking about four astronauts who I thought were going to be interviewed.'

'I'm sorry, Neil. But it wasn't possible to call them.'

'Did you submit the list to Williams?'

'What would've been the point? He would've refused to consider –'

Neil came close to bringing his fist down on the desk. 'Did you submit it to him?'

'I wanted to. But –'

'So who stopped you?'

'It was a senior administrative decision.'

'Meaning a Jason Pelham decision?'

'Your list was considered irrelevant.'

'So that my scalp could be nailed to a post?'

Hackett's face hardened. 'Don't try swinging the blame for what happened on to us, Neil. We've known all along that you weren't paying attention during that phase of the mission. And you as good as admitted in your report that you were momentarily distracted by a light in the Negev Desert. Another thing – I advised you to be legally represented at the hearing and to attend on .he other two days. You decided to ignore that advice.'

Neil wanted to argue but deep down he knew that Hackett was right on every point. He realized that sooner or later he was going to have to accept that a measure of the blame for Al's death would have to be laid on his doorstep. Suddenly he no longer wanted to squabble. He was gripped by the familiar lethargy that was forever trying to separate him from the trivial, day-to-day problems of living on Earth. 'OK,' he said uninterestedly. 'What happens now?'

'Your suspension remains in force until you've been transferred. There can be no question of you being allowed to return to shuttle operational duties.'

It was a blow that Neil knew was inevitable and yet he was wholly unprepared for the fateful words. He stared at Hackett, who was gazing out of his window at the Vehicle Assembly Building. 'You can't. I gave up everything to work with NASA.'

'I'm sorry, Neil.'

'Do you know what this will do to me?'

Hackett met Neil's eye without flinching. 'I think perhaps I do. That's why I believe it would be in your interest if you were taken off shuttle operations.'

'My medical reports –'

'I never mentioned your medical reports,' said Hackett harshly. 'Maybe there's something I should know, yes?' His tone became conciliatory. 'Listen, Neil. We need you to continue working for us. We can't afford to lose people with your experience and qualifications. There's a vacancy coming up next month for a

74

manager to look after the ground support facilities for the Gulfstream STA fleet. You'd be ideal for the job.'

Neil could hardly credit what he was hearing. The Gulfstreams were four ageing twin-engine jet trainers that had been rebuilt to give them the handling characteristics of an orbiter. What Hackett was offering him wasn't even a flying post. He heard himself say: 'I joined NASA to work in space. I want nothing more, and nothing less.'

'I'm sorry, Neil,' said Hackett with genuine sympathy. 'But you have to settle for less.'

'And if I'm not prepared to accept that?'

'Then you'll have to accept nothing. We're prepared to release you from your contract. It has two years to run. If you leave your resignation with my secretary, she'll arrange for you to be paid the balance of your salary and grounding insurance in a lump sum and you can drive off KSC right now and never come back.' Hackett met Neil's hard stare. 'Is that what you want?'

'Yes,' said Neil unemotionally. 'That's exactly what I want.'

Helen flew into a rage when Neil broke the news to her. She sent Andrew and Pippa on to the beach and turned to confront Neil.

'So now what do we do?' she demanded.

'How do you mean?'

'We can't afford to keep this place up.'

'I'll get two years' pay.'

Helen snorted. 'Which will just about pay off the mortgage. You'll have to fight them. You'll have to hire a lawyer and get that review board reconvened or whatever.'

'What would be the point?'

'Our future – that's the point. You call Mike Maguire right now and get –'

'Helen – you don't understand – I don't want to fight them. I walked out. I quit.'

Helen regarded him with contempt. 'That's typical of you. You let people walk on you. You never stand up and fight for your rights. You've got grounds to have that board reopened –'

Neil suddenly flared up. 'Don't you understand, woman? Whatever I say, or whatever I get a whole battery of lawyers to say, nothing can change the fact that it was my negligence that

75

caused Al's death. Today I saw it spelled out in black and white and I realized that it was time that I faced up to the truth.'

Helen appeared to calm down. 'All right, Neil,' she said, speaking quietly. 'If you're not prepared to fight to keep your job and self-respect, then you can't expect to keep me and the children.'

25 The Aeroflot Ilyushin touched down at Moscow at 10.30 a.m.

Maken and his party of aides, security men and secretaries, were met on the tarmac by a first deputy minister from the Military Council.

Rain was gusting horizontally across the airport – driven by a biting North wind. There were no welcoming speeches and no crowds.

'We don't even rate a minister,' Maken observed cynically in Arabic to one of his aides as the cavalcade of cars hissed through the bleak streets, ferrying the PLO leader and his party to their hotel.

Even the motorcycle outriders escorting the vehicles seemed to lose interest; they peeled away at a junction and disappeared.

Three hours later, having washed, shaved and eaten, Maken went alone to the Kremlin, as requested, and was shown into Dranski's palatial office.

Dranski was his usual exuberant self; a beaming smile of welcome; outstretched arms followed by a crushing bear hug that Maken considered highly appropriate.

'My dear, Joseph. How good of you to come so promptly. Please. Please. Sit down. You had a good flight?'

The inane small talk continued for five minutes and ended when Dranski suddenly said: 'Ah, Marshal – please come and sit down.'

Maken stood to shake hands with Marshal Ustinov and was surprised to see five men in sober charcoal-grey suits filing silently into the room. The five strangers looked so alike that they could have been clones. Neither Dranski or Ustinov made a move to introduce them to Maken. They dotted themselves around the office like predatory penguins and said nothing.

'To business,' said Dranski briskly, rubbing his fat little hands together. 'Joseph – you wouldn't believe the long meetings we've held in here discussing your request. Sometimes I've not got to bed before four in the morning.'

'I do hope you haven't tired yourself on our account, Comrade Chairman,' said Maken. He was a good diplomat and knew how to inject what sounded like genuine concern into his voice.

Dranski grinned wolfishly. 'Thank you, Joseph.' He unwrapped a boiled sweet and popped it in his mouth. He sucked on it while regarding his visitor. 'You're right about the Kosygin cruisers. Except that only two have been converted to carry assault submarines – not three.'

It was a surprising admission. It gave Maken hope. If the cunning little Russian was going to turn down the PLO request, he had only to deny that the submarines existed.

'We're interested in the sources of your intelligence on the cruisers – the name of your Pentagon informant,' Dranski continued. 'You will recall that the terms of our little treaty specified a free and frank exchange of intelligence on matters of mutual interest.'

'Full details will be on their way to you tomorrow, Comrade Chairman,' Maken assured him.

Dranski sucked contentedly on his sweet. 'Marshal?'

Ustinov cleared his throat. 'Comrade Maken, our combined operations staff have looked at your plans for the invasion of Israel and they are of the opinion that you are not ready to undertake such an operation.'

'They are quite right . . . .' Maken agreed smoothly.

Ustinov looked surprised.

' . . . The operation will require at least a year's planning and training.'

'We estimate two years,' said Ustinov evenly.

In that moment Maken knew what he had suspected all along: he was going to be turned down. A little humour was called for to cloak his disappointment. 'In two years I believe we will be ready to invade the United States, Comrade Marshal.'

Dranski laughed and nearly swallowed his sweet. Even one of the clones managed a chuckle.

'But we don't wish to invade the United States,' Maken continued, pleased at Ustinov's frosty expression. 'Only Israel.'

Dranski crunched down on his sweet. 'The marshal hates coming to the point. I'm sorry, Joseph – but we don't want an escalation of the War of Attrition.' He nodded to the clones. 'Our experts say that you're winning it anyway. In a year you will force Israel to negotiate. In two years you will have licked them.'

Maken knew better than to argue with the Soviet leader. 'If that is your verdict, then I accept it, Comrade Chairman.'

'Spoken like a diplomat,' said Dranski genially. 'But we're friends, so let's hear your views.'

'Israel will never negotiate with us,' said Maken emphatically, noticing Dranski give one of the clones an almost imperceptible nod.

'Rymann won't but his successor is certain to,' said the clone. 'We do not believe he will survive in office when the Israeli public realizes that their days are numbered. Also the Israelis' great military weakness is that they do not have a phlegmatic attitude towards human life. Minor losses cause them excessive grief. Even if their present casualty rate is not likely to bring about a population imbalance – that is by reducing their numbers of young people – the time is not far off when the Israeli public will believe that it is. When enough mothers have lost enough sons and daughters – then they will sue for peace.'

'On our terms?' queried Maken, impressed by the clinical coldbloodedness of the clone's analysis.

The clone nodded. 'The other point in your favour is that Senator Harding is likely to win this year's presidential election, which means that there won't be a change in US policy towards Israel. If anything, the American attitude towards Israel will harden.'

The fruitless discussion dragged on for another thirty minutes and involved the other four clones. It ended with Dranski standing and shaking Maken's hand. 'You see, Joseph, you're doing such a fine job that there's no need for the terrible casualties that you'd be certain to suffer if you invaded Israel. We will, of course, maintain our present level of support. In fact, as you're making such excellent use of the MiG-35s, we're flying you in another six, and some more trainers.' Dranski winked. 'So that your political enemies can't accuse you of returning empty-handed.'

Maken bowed. At least the Soviets wanted him to remain the PLO leader, which was something. 'That is most generous of you, Comrade Chairman.' He paused. 'There is one more thing,

Comrade Chairman. Regarding the exchange of intelligence – we would be most grateful if you would pass anything on to us relating to a new Israeli weapon code-named Massada.'

Dranski frowned and glanced enquiringly at his arms advisor clone. The clone considered and shook his head.

'Sorry, Joseph,' Dranski apologized. 'We've never heard of it. What have you heard?'

'Only that it's an intercontinental-range missile that the Israelis have developed. Obtaining hard information has proved impossible.'

'Highly unlikely,' said the clone confidently. 'The Israelis have developed a number of intermediate-range weapons of course. But they have neither the resources nor the firing-range facilities to test the necessary booster rocket that an intercontinental missile would require.'

'If we hear anything, we'll let you know,' said Dranski cheerfully. 'I understand you're flying on to New York?'

'I have a number of matters to attend to at our office there,' Maken replied.

Dranski gave a sly smile. 'I believe Senator Harding will be in New York. Give him our best wishes if you happen to bump into him.'

Once he was alone in the back of the limousine returning him to his hotel, Maken allowed himself the luxury of a heartfelt expletive in his native French.

To hell with any concealed radio transmitters.

26   Heinlein completed his local telephone call to a Tel Aviv number and hailed a taxi to take him to his bank. Within five minutes he was certain that his taxi was being followed.

White Ford saloons were common enough in Tel Aviv but this one had been following a few cars back for several streets and he was sure he had seen the driver's lips move, as though he were talking to a hidden, voice-activated microphone.

The Ford nosed into a parking space. A battered, neglected van swung out of a side street and tucked in behind the taxi as it cruised down Allenby Street. It closed up behind the taxi at the David Square traffic lights so that Heinlein could hear its motor – finely tuned – running sweet as a sewing machine. He glanced down at the tyres. New Michelins. Gleaming, well-maintained suspension. The van only looked a wreck.

He was definitely being followed.

He could guess why – he had once been posted to their Massada development plant and had worked at the station in the Negev where the Massada booster had been developed. He knew a lot about their plans – a helluva lot. It was, therefore, understandable that they wanted to keep an eye on him.

Heinlein sat back in the seat and relaxed. What could they do to him? He was out of the army. For the first time in eight years he was free to do as he pleased, go where he pleased. He would not miss the comradeship because he had always been a loner. Even so, having been a regular soldier since he was twenty-two, he accepted that civilian life was certain to take some getting used to.

The taxi dropped him outside the tower block of the Bank Leumi. The fingerprint recognition pad on the bank's customer service terminal accepted him as David Heinlein and provided him with a printout of his balance. With his back pay and severance gratuity he had enough money to last him six months provided he was careful. He would have to find a job. He considered going back to work for his father and immediately rejected the idea. Diamond trading was not to his taste. No – a job could wait. He was going to buy himself some new clothes, find himself a smart hotel and relax for two weeks.

A girl would come in useful.

It was nearly midnight. The floodlit Namir Square was crowded with young people enjoying the open air bars, the blaring televisions and the cool Mediterranean breeze. The square was a large, split-level, traffic-free concourse sandwiched between the coast road and the beach. It was overlooked by the towering five-star edifice of Tel Aviv's Plaza Hotel.

Heinlein was sitting at an outside table drinking a beer when a smartly dressed girl in a mini-skirt scurried by and tripped over his outstretched legs. She gave a cry of alarm and went sprawling across a vacant table, drenching herself with the contents of half-empty glasses that she had sent bouncing over the flagstones.

80

'I'm very sorry,' said Heinlein, helping the girl to her feet. 'Are you OK?'

She seemed dazed. 'Oh – yes. I think so.'

She looked about twenty-five. Very dark. Very pretty. And trembling.

'You'd better sit down a minute.'

'I'm all right,' the girl protested.

'No you are not all right – you're shaking. It was careless of me. I should look where I put my big feet.'

A waiter armed with tissues and a cloth came hurrying to the table.

'I think the lady will be OK,' said Heinlein, using the tissues to mop up the drink that had splattered the girl's skirt, arms and legs. 'What do you drink?'

'I must be going.'

'You'll have a drink,' Heinlein ordered. 'You're still shaking.'

She met his hard, dark eyes and hesitated. The man was unusually tall for an Israeli. Nearly two metres she guessed. She was also uncomfortably aware of his powerful fingers digging into her forearm. 'A small screwdriver, please.'

'A large screwdriver,' Heinlein instructed the waiter. 'With plenty of vodka. What's your name?'

'Esther.'

'Mine's David. You'd better sit down.'

The incident was observed by a young man in faded jeans and a grubby T-shirt. He was idly swinging his legs over the balustrade on the square's upper level. Occasionally he took a swig from a can of Coke. He looked indifferent to the bustle around him but his eyes were alert – missing nothing. He had admired the way Echo Oscar had 'siamesed' with her target. A copybook operation. Brilliant in fact. Her instructor at Mossad's central training school would have been proud of her. For several minutes he watched Heinlein and Echo Oscar drinking and lifted the Coke can to his lips.

'Four-Double-One – on.'

'Go ahead Four-Double-One,' answered a familiar voice in his ear.

'Echo Oscar is siamesed.'

'Nicely?'

'Very nicely.'

'Acknowledged, Four-Double-One. QSY to her channel. Out.'

The young man touched a control in the Coke can's base and listened to the conversation from the table below where they were on their third round of drinks.

'So,' Heinlein concluded, 'I'm going to do nothing but laze about for two weeks.'

Esther smiled and crossed her long, slender legs. Her white mini-skirt set off her tanned thighs. A bit on the thin side, thought Heinlein, but she would do. He had told her a little about himself to keep the conversation rolling. In return he had learned that she worked in a travel bureau and that she lived with her parents in a rundown apartment block on Ben Gurion Street.

'I've got the next few days off too,' said Esther.

'Maybe I'll see you on the beach?'

'Oh – yes. I love swimming. Isn't the Plaza very expensive?'

Heinlein glanced up at the hotel and shook his head. 'They can't fill them since the Netanya attack. And I'm on the tenth floor. It's cheaper.'

'Why?'

'Further from the air-raid shelters.'

Esther giggled, hiccupped and tried to focus her eyes on her watch. 'Oh – stupid thing.'

'Just after midnight,' said Heinlein.

She looked dismayed. 'Damn. I'm locked out. Mum and Dad always assume I'm staying with friends if I'm not back by midnight.'

'Surely they'd answer the door?'

'I hate disturbing them.' She gathered up her purse. 'Well – if that hotel is as cheap and as empty as you say, I could –'

'Save your money. There's a spare bed in my room.'

Esther stared sombrely at Heinlein and then giggled. 'I couldn't.'

'You won't have to,' said Heinlein drily. 'But after staring at those fantastic legs of yours for the past fifteen minutes, I know damn well that I could.'

Esther giggled again and stood. She swayed and steadied herself on the back of her chair. 'OK, David. Let's take you up on that.'

Heinlein was woken in the morning by Esther shaking his shoulder.

'Wassermatter?'

She was kneeling on the bed, wrapped in a sheet, her eyes large and serious.

'I must've been drunk last night. I don't normally do this with strange –'

'You were and you did,' said Heinlein unsympathetically. 'And what's more – you screwed like it was about to be made illegal.'

She pouted and then giggled. 'You're crude.'

'Just honest. I'm going back to sleep.'

Esther threw the sheet aside and hopped astride Heinlein before he had a chance to roll on to his side. He groaned as her weight crushed his balls.

'What the hell are you playing at?'

'Let's pretend.'

'Pretend what?' On arrival in the room, they had tumbled on to the bed and made love in the dark. Heinlein was now able to appreciate her lithe, olive-skinned body and pert little breasts.

Esther looked at her watch. 'Let's pretend that it's about to be made illegal in thirty minutes.'

Heinlein toyed with the heavy pendant that was hanging between her breasts. A hundred yards away in a nondescript van, a Mossad agent hurriedly turned down the volume on his radio receiver to prevent the heavy rustling in his headphones from blasting his eardrums.

'I'm incapable of doing anything at the moment,' Heinlein confessed.

Esther wriggled seductively, grinding herself against him and grinning impishly. 'Oh, but I've got this feeling that you're becoming very capable.'

Esther took the ice-cold lager from the poolside waiter and sipped. She stretched luxuriously on her bed. 'What a life. A pity it can't last.'

Heinlein grunted. 'When I've made it – this is what I'm going to do – live in the best hotels.'

'No house? Wife? Family?'

'No. Just me and my money. Independent.'

'I know why you want to make money,' said Esther.

'Why?'

'To prove to your father that you can make it in the world without his help. Right?'

'Wrong.'

Esther drained her glass. 'I don't think so.'

Heinlein shook his head. 'I just want to make money. I've had eight years of earning next to nothing. I've got a lot of catching up to do.'

'Do you know anything about your father's business?'

Heinlein turned his dark eyes on her. 'A little. He taught me to classify and value diamonds. And I know a little about the international diamond market.' He laughed as a thought occurred. 'It's funny but I'm a diamond merchant according to my passport. I put it down on my first passport because that's what I thought I was going to do – and it's stuck ever since.'

'Well there you are,' said Esther. 'Become a diamond merchant.'

'Too late. I've wasted eight years.'

'Why did you quit the army?'

'I thought I told you last night?'

'No. You just said that you'd quit.'

Heinlein told her about the riot at Nazareth, his court martial, imprisonment and subsequent pardon.

Esther propped herself on her elbow and regarded him. 'Are you bitter about it?'

Heinlein laughed. '*That* is the understatement of the year.'

'Why? If there was a mistake –'

'Because the miserable bastards wouldn't even give me the benefit of the doubt in the first place. Eight years in the army counted for nothing. If the new evidence hadn't come up, I'd be rotting in a military prison, and would be for the next ten years. If the system can do that, then it's corrupt – right through.'

'At least they admitted that there'd been a mistake. A lot of countries wouldn't have done that.'

Heinlein scowled. 'A lot of countries wouldn't brand a man a coward and then offer him a month's pay as compensation. If that's what being an Israeli means, then I want out. As soon as possible.'

The following morning Heinlein was sitting on the bedroom balcony reading the *Jerusalem Post* when he spotted a news item on an inside page. He debated with himself what to do. He eventually made up his mind. His passport and birth certificate were in order.

He might as well act now. He showered, dressed and quickly packed his few possessions. Esther was stretched naked across the bed like a drugged sex kitten, sound asleep. Hardly surprising – the way she made love. He scribbled a brief note to her on the hotel's stationery and left it beside her. She didn't stir when he left the room, closing the door silently behind him.

He settled his bill, paid for Esther to use the room for another two days, and walked the half mile to the United States Embassy on Hayarkon Street. He was certain that he wasn't followed.

After three hours of queuing, form-filling, answering questions and producing documents, followed by an hour's wait, he walked out of the embassy with a neatly stamped visa in his passport to replace his earlier visa that had expired.

A taxi took him to the Pan Am office on Frishman Street. A large notice outside stated that, owing to the deteriorating war situation, the airline was suspending its Israeli operations the following week.

'There's a cancelled seat available on this evening's seven o'clock flight to New York, sir,' said the girl, looking up from her computer terminal.

'Nothing earlier?'

The girl shook her head. 'Sorry, sir. The afternoon flight is fully booked. You'll find it much the same with the other airlines. What with the airport being closed for a week and the number of people quitting the country –'

'OK. I'll take it.'

He made a long phone call from a public call box and, to avoid running into Esther, spent the rest of the day killing time at Ben Gurion Airport. He felt no twinge of guilt at the way he had run out on her. She had been an easy pick-up – almost too easy – and a day's energetic fun. Nothing else. Anyway, she had used him as much as he had used her.

At 19.15, he and five hundred and thirty other passengers were airborne in an SST Boeing, climbing over the Mediterranean and turning westwards towards the blood-red sun that was setting on Israel.

27   Although the conversations between Esther and Heinlein and the sound effects they had created had been recorded by the Mossad communications vehicle parked near the Plaza Hotel, Ether was still required to give a full report to her section leader. The transcripts were before him but they were no substitute for the personal contact that Esther had maintained for thirty hours. She was one of Mossad's best shallow cover agents. On a number of occasions she had proved her remarkable ability to turn the pages of a man's mind and read his innermost thoughts.

'Do you think he's going to defect?' the section leader enquired.

Esther considered her reply carefully. 'I don't honestly know. He wants to make money and he hates Israel like poison at the moment. In his present state of his mind he could do anything. But if I was going over to the Palestinians, I wouldn't go to the expense of flying to New York. He was short of money and I'm sure he wouldn't turn to his father for help.'

'Joseph Maken has arrived in New York,' said the section leader. 'It was in the morning papers.'

Esther met his eyes. 'In that case, I'd say he's defecting.'

The section leader nodded.

'What will happen now?' asked Esther.

'I don't know.'

The section leader did know but it was not Esther's concern. The New York station chief had been instructed to keep Heinlein under observation and report direct to Greer on his movements.

28   The satellite management director at Bell's Daytona Research Center studied Neil's résumé, even though he had already made his decision the previous evening.

'Neil,' he said, speaking slowly and carefully. 'It would be easy for me to tell you that we'll be in touch in a few days. But your honesty deserves the same. It's true that we need a shuttle payload specialist of your experience but we can't offer you the job just yet.'

It was as Neil had expected. 'Can you say why?'

'I think you're intelligent enough to work that out for yourself. If I hear of anything going. I'll be in touch. That's a promise.'

Neil shook hands with the director and walked out into the steamy afternoon heat. He sat in the Winnebago's driver's seat with the engine running to keep the camper's interior cool and consulted his list. He noticed that the camper was vibrating, probably due to an unbalanced turbine blade. Worrying about it would have to wait – he had an appointment at 2 p.m. and another at 4 p.m. After three days spent working his way through the companies that had mushroomed along Florida's space coast with the growth of the shuttle programme, he had no illusions about the outcome of the applications. No one wanted to employ an astronaut who had been cited as responsible for the death of a fellow astronaut. His chances of getting back into space now seemed even more remote than ever and deepened the black depression that was falling about him like a suffocating cloak.

29 Eight years had passed since Heinlein's last visit to New York during his globetrotting days representing his father. Apart from the cars, which were smaller and even quieter, he was surprised to discover how little the city had changed. The twin, monolithic towers of the World Trade Center had acquired another thirty floors, restoring its title as the world's tallest building, and there was a new bridge across the Hudson River carrying the Washington–New York monorail. Everything else seemed much the same and, as the cab lurched along Broadway, Heinlein couldn't help wondering if the potholes had been subjected to conservation orders.

After a night at a cheap hotel in Greenwich Village, he had opted for the Hilton at the Rockerfeller Center where, according to the garrulous taxi driver who picked him up, 'the Palestinians always holed-up'.

He glanced out of the cab's rear window and told the taxi driver to make a couple of back doubles.

'Anything for a customer,' said the taxi driver, obliging.

Once back on the Avenue of the Americas, Heinlein's suspicions were confirmed. 'We're being followed,' he announced.

'Yeah,' agreed the taxi driver. 'I noticed. Buick.'

'Can you lose it?'

'Cost yah extra fifty.'

'Done.'

Hardly was the word out of Heinlein's mouth when he was nearly pitched on to the floor as the cab made an unexpected, tyre-squealing right turn.

'Great doing this,' the taxi driver observed laconically, hooking his car down 50th Street and accelerating. 'Always wanted to drive stunts for the movies.'

There was a sudden succession of violent turns that had Heinlein hanging grimly on to the passenger handles. Blaring horns. Shrieking brakes. The smell of burning rubber. And then the cab slowed to a more moderate speed.

'Yeah – we shook him off OK,' said the taxi driver cheerfully, sliding on to the Hilton's covered forecourt. 'Could've done it quicker but too many cops about.'

The taxi driver was right about the Palestinians using the Hilton. A video screen in the lobby proclaimed: THE NEW YORK HILTON EXTENDS A WARM WELCOME TO THE DELEGATION FROM THE PALESTINE LIBERATION ORGANIZATION.

The hotel lobby was riddled with security men in various guises. The reception clerk did his best to conceal his discomfort when he saw Heinlein's passport. 'Ah – you're an Israeli citizen, Mr Heinlein?'

'You can read?' said Heinlein admiringly.

A man in a brown suit and horn-rimmed glasses appeared at Heinlein's side. 'Any problems?'

'This gentleman is an Israeli citizen,' said the clerk.

'Don't worry,' said Heinlein. 'It's not catching.'

The sarcasm was lost on horn-rimmed glasses. He flipped through Heinlein's passport. 'How long are you staying for, sir?' He was very polite.

'I don't know yet.'

Horn-rimmed glasses nodded to the video screen. 'It's just that you may be more comfortable at another hotel, sir.'

'I'm not interested in politics,' assured Heinlein. 'Only diamonds.'

Horn-rimmed glasses came to a decision. 'OK – a room on the tenth floor,' he told the clerk. He returned Heinlein's passport. 'I hope you enjoy your stay in New York, sir.'

As Heinlein accompanied the bellboy to the elevators, he noticed that one of the sliding doors had a man posted on each side. He guessed that the PLO had taken over an entire floor of the hotel which could only be reached by that particular elevator. After unpacking and taking a shower, he sat on his bed and wrote a brief letter on the hotel's headed notepaper.

Room 1015

Dear Mr Maken,
I know about Massada. Also I am looking forward to meeting you.
Yours sincerely,
David Heinlein.

He wondered if the note was too bald but decided that it said everything he wanted to say. He sealed it in an airmail envelope so that there was no danger of it being treated as a potential letter-bomb.

He addressed the envelope, took it down to the lobby and handed it to the clerk.

'Can that be sent to Mr Maken's suite now, please?'

The clerk examined the envelope and signalled to one of the hovering security men. 'I don't see why not, sir.'

As Heinlein stepped into the elevator to return to his room and await events he noticed that two men were examining his envelope.

His bedside phone rang fifteen minutes later.

'Mr Heinlein?' A woman's voice.

'Yes?'

'Mr Heinlein – we'd be most grateful if you would come down to the assistant manager's desk in the lobby.'

'Sure. What's it about?'

'There's a hotel guest who wishes to meet you.'

30 The macabre list of precedents that had established assassination as a Mossad tool against Palestinian terrorism was long and not particularly distinguished.

It had all started with Ghassan Kanafani, a member of the PFLP Central Command who had planned the Lod Airport massacre of May 1972. Two days after the atrocity, his car was blown up, killing him and a teenage girl passenger. Next there had been the systematic assassination of those Palestinians who had planned the Munich Olympic Games kidnapping in which nine Israeli athletes had died. Occasionally things went wrong – such as the time when a Mossad deep-cover team operating in Norway had murdered an innocent man. Most of the Israeli team had subsequently been arrested by the Norwegian authorities.

The carefully planned assassinations went on through the 1970s. The targets were invariably Palestinian intellectuals – the staff planners – the men and women with no taste for military combat but who had been trying to shape international terrorism into a deadly political weapon. Suddenly they found themselves victims of the tactics they had devised: Mossad had killed them with letter-bombs in their post and with bombs planted in their cars. Sometimes they had died from a single bullet in a deserted street. Sometimes it was from a hail of bullets in a full-blown commando-style raid.

Whatever method the planners had used against Israel, so Israel had replied in kind.

During the late 1970s the forces of evolutionary change within the PLO had led to a decline in the influence of the Marxist intellectuals who believed that society had to be destroyed before it could be changed. The PLO had eventually discarded international terrorism in favour of methods aimed at achieving long-term political objectives.

By the early 1980s assassination had virtually ceased to be used by Mossad and it was never employed against successive PLO leaders. Nevertheless, Israel's killing machine was kept in a permanent state of readiness: Mossad still employed a number of operatives who kept themselves well-versed in the theories and

90

practice of clandestine murder, which was why Rymann and Greer were discussing the use of such staff when they were alone after the evening meeting of the Emergency Defence Council.

'There's no doubt that Heinlein is about to contact the PLO?' asked Rymann.

Greer nodded to the decoded signal he had just received from the Mossad station chief in New York. 'No doubt whatsoever. He's checked in at the Hilton Hotel. What further proof do you need?'

'Michael – it's much too dangerous. If Heinlein were to –'

'We have no chance,' Greer interrupted.

Rymann looked curiously at his friend. 'Do you have a man in mind?'

'A woman, actually. One of our best marksmen. And she's met Heinlein. She would have no trouble recognizing him.'

'He's elusive. He was in the Special Parachute Brigade. He's trained. Look at the times he's given your agents the slip.'

'She will find him,' Greer murmured confidently.

'She's got to be a damn good shot.'

'She is.'

Rymann gave a dry, humourless laugh. 'I doubt if anyone has ever been given such a strange order before. The question is, will she do it?'

'Without question,' Greer replied impassively.

'It's a hell of a price to pay.'

'One that's worth the prize.'

Rymann walked to the window of his private office and stared out across the Hakirya, his hands thrust into his pockets. He remained deep in thought for a while and then spun round to face Greer. 'All right then, Michael – go ahead.'

31   Two armed Secret Service men accompanied Heinlein in the elevator from the lobby to the top floor of the Hilton. The doors slid open and he was handed over to two cheerful Palestinians in business suits who showed him along a heavily guarded corridor to a bedroom where he was carefully searched. He was then taken by an aide to a penthouse suite that the Hilton management reserved for their VIP guests: double-thickness, bullet-proof windows; twice-daily sweeps for bugging devices; and antennae dishes on the roof that provided conference-secure microwave links via communication satellites with any country in the world.

Joseph Maken was dictating to a secretary when Heinlein was shown into the room.

'Mr Heinlein,' said the aide, and withdrew.

'Ah, Heinlein,' said Maken, waving to a chair. 'I hope you don't mind if my secretary takes notes?'

'No,' said Heinlein indifferently. He sat down and studied Maken with interest. This sleek, well-groomed man had succeeded where other PLO leaders had failed: he had united all the warring factions of the PLO; won for them a secure if temporary homeland where the *Chel Ha'Avir* couldn't get at them, and was striking at Israel with impunity with the world's smallest air force – albeit an air force equipped with MiG-35s.

'You're the author of this strange letter?' asked Maken.

'That's right.'

'How is it that you know about Massada?'

'Until last week I was a lieutenant in the *Zahal*. The Special Parachute Brigade. I've had several postings to various Ta'as weapons research centres.'

Mention of the crack regiment failed to impress Maken. Instead he regarded Heinlein with stony inscrutability. 'I am a busy man, Heinlein. If you're another bungling attempt by Mossad or the Aman to plant an agent in my organization, I'll have a car deliver you to the Israeli Embassy within the next thirty minutes.'

Heinlein briefly outlined the circumstances that led to him being in New York.

'All right,' said Maken coldly. 'So you're a disillusioned Israeli soldier who wants to make some money. I know nothing about Massada other than that it is a new weapon. Therefore I have no way of verifying the accuracy of whatever information you try to sell me.'

'I never said that I was here to sell you information,' said Heinlein calmly, suspecting that Maken was deliberately trying to annoy him. 'I'm here to *give* you information. *And* I've got a plan that will enable you to defeat Israel within eighteen months.'

'Really?' said Maken uninterestedly.

'I have two ambitions. I want to hit back at Israel and I want to make money. A lot of money. My plan will enable me to do both.'

Maken was puzzled. When Heinlein had first walked into his suite, he had been convinced that this was another Israeli agent. Now he had serious doubts. Mossad didn't operate in such a clumsy manner. The methods they were using in their attempts to penetrate Bakal, although futile, were clever; they did not send agents into the field armed with flimsy covers that could be blown by a few simple checks. He decided to change tactics.

'Do you support the PLO cause, Heinlein?'

Heinlein looked contemptuous. 'Personally I don't give a monkey's fuck about your cause. I just want to hit Israel where it hurts and make some money at the same time.'

'You want to use us?'

'If you wish to put it like that – yes.'

Maken was still suspicious although he found Heinlein's straightforwardness a refreshing change. He was not the first Israeli to offer his services to the PLO. There had been those who had sensed which way the wind was blowing and had been anxious to ensure that their comfortable life-style would continue should the Palestinian cause succeed. Other offers of help had come from a small number of Israelis who were genuinely sympathetic towards the PLO. Then there were the Marxist and Trotskyist idealists who wanted to overthrow Israel by any means available.

Maken was a cynical realist: he used such people when it suited him although he didn't trust the Israeli volunteers and he had little confidence in the idealists. Some bitter lessons had taught him that it was relatively easy to stimulate such people into a fervent support of revolutionary principles, but they didn't have the stomach for playing an active part in a bloody guerilla war.

Heinlein was different. Just how different the dark, unsmiling young man sitting opposite him was would be interesting to find out.

'Tell me about Massada,' invited Maken.

'How do I know I can trust you?' Heinlein enquired.

'You don't. You tell me about Massada and then we'll see how much mutual trust we can scrape together between us.'

Heinlein smiled. He was beginning to see why Maken was such a successful leader. 'Massada is a new missile.'

'That much I had guessed.'

'The basic Massada is a single-stage, solid-fuel rocket that can be armed with a nuclear warhead. It's equipped with a new type of combined inertial and celestial guidance system that gives it pinpoint accuracy. It's advantage from the Israeli point of view is its versatility. With a conventional warhead it can serve as a surface-to-air missile or a sea-to-air missile. Also it's small enough to have an air-to-ground capability. Over a hundred have been built but it hasn't gone into operational service.'

'Why not?'

'Because it has only an intermediate range, therefore it doesn't give Israel a tactical advantage over her enemies. Over the past few years most of Israel's effort has been ploughed into developing a booster for the Massada that gives it a range of five thousand miles-plus.'

Maken raised his eyebrows. 'You're talking about an intercontinental missile.'

'Correct. A Massada lifted into space by a booster can separate from the booster and use its motor as a sustainer to bring it down on any target within a range of five thousand miles at a speed of Mach 15 – eleven thousand miles per hour.' Heinlein stopped and regarded Maken's deadpan expression. 'They'd be on their target before a SAM missile was clear of its launcher. Two Massadas with nuclear warheads would be enough to take out Bakal. In fact Bakal is the number one target.'

'How big is the Massada?'

'About thirty feet long and it weighs twenty thousand pounds.'

Heinlein spent the next five minutes answering Maken's searching questions as accurately as he could. He even marked on a map the exact location of the Negev Guided Weapons Research Establishment where the Massada booster was being developed, and he explained how the base had been disguised as an agricultural research station.

'How near completion is this booster?' asked Maken, glancing up at the girl taking shorthand to make sure she was getting everything down.

'The prototype was nearing completion when I was there six months ago,' Heinlein replied. 'After the firing of the prototype, the plan was to build two pre-production models and test-fire them from a cargo ship in a remote area.'

'When will the production boosters be ready?'

'Within a year. I don't know the exact time.'

There was nothing in Maken's expression to indicate the alarm he was experiencing. 'Is Massada to be fired from fixed sites?'

'No. Mobile.'

Maken doodled on a pad. 'All right, Mr Heinlein. If you have been frank with me – I thank you. One of my assistants will ask you more detailed questions. Turning to your motives for your telling me this, it will not be difficult for us to check your story about your court martial.'

Heinlein shrugged indifferently.

Maken continued: 'As for your other motive – greed. How do you expect to make money out of my organization?'

'By supplying it with weapons.'

Maken raised an eyebrow. 'Most arms' dealers are well aware that we have existing sources.'

Heinlein snorted. 'I'm not talking about the toy soldier gear the Soviets give you. I'm talking about real weaponry – the sort of armament that you're going to need if you want to smash the Israelis.'

'Our suppliers meet all our requirements,' Maken observed.

'Really? OK – so they've given you some MiG-35 hit-and-run aircraft. But where're your heavy transports? Where're your anti-aircraft missile batteries? Where's your navy? Your submarines? Your assault craft? Because that's what you're going to need at the end of the day to beat the Israelis. And don't kid me the Soviets are prepared to supply you with that sort of material because they won't – just as they won't supply their own Warsaw Pact countries with weapons that could be used against them.'

Maken did not allow his face to betray the fact that Heinlein had touched a nerve. Instead he said pleasantly: 'And you can supply us with a navy and an air force?'

'No. But with something much better.'

'Such as?'

'Four Massada missiles fitted with nuclear warheads.'

Maken would have dismissed anyone else as a crackpot but not someone as deadly serious as Heinlein. 'At what sort of price?'

'The plan I have in mind means that the missiles won't cost you a penny.'

'A fascinating plan, no doubt,' said Maken drily. 'But the Massada needs a booster. Surely you are not claiming to be able to supply us with Massada boosters as well? Difficult I would've thought, especially if the Israelis haven't completed them yet.'

Heinlein smiled coldly. 'I have a much better delivery system for the Massadas in mind.'

The former Israeli officer then spent five minutes outlining a plan aimed at restoring Palestine. The operation was so daring, so audacious, so carefully thought out, that Maken's initial instinctive reaction was that it stood a crazy, impossible chance of succeeding. It was the sort of plan that could have come only from an Israeli.

As Heinlein talked, Maken's mind raced ahead, weighing up the plan's chances. The more he thought about it, the more he realized what a stupendous concept it was. Its most attractive feature, apart from the certain capitulation of Israel, was that it did not require any assistance from the Soviet Union.

Despite the careful façade that Joseph Maken adopted for the benefit of his Soviet allies, he was not a committed Communist and nor were his closest followers. To Maken, there were aspects of Communism that were as distasteful as violence but he was prepared to embrace both doctrines to achieve his ambition of overthrowing Israel. Communism and guns were tools to be discarded once they had served their purpose. The same applied to mercenaries like Heinlein. But before using Heinlein, he had to be certain that the tool was genuine.

He brought the meeting to a close by promising that he would discuss the matter with his advisors. Heinlein agreed to Maken's request to stay at the Hilton Hotel until further notice.

32 'What will you do now,' asked Helen.

Neil stopped at a set of lights. He shrugged. 'I'll find a job. Don't worry about me.'

'I wasn't. For the first time in ten years, you're the last person I'm gonna have to worry about.'

'Let's take that counsellor's advice and not try to hurt each other, Helen. We've got an amicable separation. Let's leave it at that.'

The lights changed. The Winnebago surged forward.

'So where will you sleep tonight?' Helen enquired.

It was a question Neil hadn't thought about. 'In this. Or a motel. I don't know yet.'

'You can't sleep at the house.'

'I know that.'

They were five miles further north along US1 before Helen spoke again. 'I was talking to Mother this morning. She wants to move back to Houston. With what she'll get for her house, and the two-thirds I get from ours, we should be able to buy a really nice place between us.'

Neil's stomach turned over. 'You never said anything about that before.'

'I hadn't made up my mind until now.'

'We agreed that I could have unlimited access to the kids.'

'Who said I was going back on that?'

'For Chrissake, Helen – it's a thousand miles to Houston!'

'Two days' drive in this thing. Two hours flying from Orlando. So?'

'If I land a job, how in the world am I going to get to see them?'

Helen laughed cynically. 'Do you really expect to land a job?'

Neil glanced at her and said nothing. The change in her since they had decided on a separation had been dramatic. She had tidied herself up, gone on a strict diet that she was sticking to for once, and she now made regular trips to the hairdresser. All he had done was step up his drinking.

It would be some time before Neil realized that they had swapped roles: he had started going downhill while Helen was looking forward to a new life.

33 Esther spent her first forty-eight hours in New York City familiarizing herself with its geography, particularly Midtown Manhattan where the Hilton Hotel was located. She had never visited New York before. At first she found the city overbearing and confusing. After the first day she began to feel more comfortable despite the awesome nature of the assignment that was hanging over her.

According to her passport she was Tessa Oliveria, a courier for a Tel Aviv travel agency. She had excellent references, several thousand dollars in traveller's cheques, and had no difficulty finding herself a medium-priced apartment off First Avenue near the Jewish Center.

On her third day in New York – a Monday – she purchased a copy of *Guns and Ammo* and spent two hours combing through the mail order advertisements. She decided on a Remington recoilless 'Spotlight' .22-calibre rifle with Leupold gas-laser sights because it was the closest weapon to the small-bore lightweight rifles she had trained with.

'Automatic, ultrasonic rangefinding and fully automated sighting,' boasted the mail order company's blurb. 'You pull the trigger and the computer built into the stock does the rest. One hundred rounds free with all orders received by the end of the month.'

Esther wired the company her order and a credit card number.

She spent the next day keeping the Hilton under observation from the vantage point of a snack bar. She sat by the window, pretending to pore through travel brochures, while drinking endless cups of coffee. She was rewarded in the afternoon when Heinlein emerged from the hotel's main entrance.

Following him was easy. He headed north towards Central Park and spent an hour wandering around the zoo. He entered a bar for twenty minutes before returning to the hotel.

His movements were much the same on Wednesday and Thursday and included a visit to a theatre. It was as if he was killing time. She wondered what he was waiting for.

On Friday she purchased a clipboard and a pocket computer and entered the Museum of American Folk Art, rehoused in its original building opposite the Hilton. No one challenged her when she took an elevator up to the top floor. The corridor was empty. A short flight of stairs took her up to what had to be the roof, judging by the daylight visible under the bottom of the locked door.

She tried out the various acid-resistant plastic keys from a large assortment on a bunch and found one that fitted neatly into the lock although it would not turn. She removed the key, took an acid ampoule from her purse and pushed it carefully into the lock without breaking it. She reinserted the key in the lock and pushed hard. The ampoule broke. Vapour curled from the lock as the powerful acid went to work on the lock's moving parts. After a few seconds she found that she could turn the key a few degrees. She waited patiently. Timing was critical. Allowing the acid to attack the lock for too long would result in it being welded into one

98

immovable mass of metal. A minute went by and she tried the key again. This time it turned. It was stiff but at least she could feel the lock's tongue sliding out of the striker plate. She pushed the door open, removed the key and halted the action of the acid with an ampoule of neutralizing fluid.

With her clipboard tucked under her arm she marched boldly on to the roof as if she had every right to be there and pretended to examine the window cleaner's cradle rails. To anyone watching from an office window in one of the neighbouring buildings that overlooked the roof, she was a safety inspector checking the window-cleaning gantry equipment. 'Clipboard and pocket computers are invaluable,' a Mossad instructor had once told her. 'They can get you into unauthorized areas and make you look as though you belong there.'

The roof was ideal. It had a commanding view of the Hilton's covered main entrance and there was a low parapet on which she could rest the rifle.

She finished her examination. The lock was so stiff when she tried to turn it after closing the door behind her that she was afraid the key was going to break. Eventually it turned. Fortunately the lock bore no external signs of the damage caused by the acid.

When she arrived back at her apartment, the janitor produced a parcel that was addressed to her. Her rifle had arrived.

34 Heinlein was no stranger to boredom. The long hours spent as duty officer at the Negev Guided Weapons Research Establishment had seen to that. But after four days waiting for Maken to call him, he was getting impatient. He never left the hotel for more than three hours at a time and he always checked upon his return to see if there were any messages for him.

After returning from yet another interminable walk along Broadway and a visit to a bar, he left a curt note for Maken telling the PLO leader that he was considering returning to Israel.

35 Esther lay on her stomach in the clearing and aimed the rifle at the Coke can that she had wedged in the branch of a tree. The can was three hundred yards away and yet it loomed bright red in the rifle's sights as though it were only two yards away.

She steadied her aim until the dancing spot of light from the laser beam shining out of the optical sights was centred on the letter 'C' in the word 'Coca'. There was an almost inaudible whirr from the rifle's computer-controlled servomotors as they made the necessary sighting corrections based on information received from the rifle's ultrasonic rangefinder. A green light winked in the sights, indicating that all was ready. She squeezed the trigger.

The report was louder than she expected but, as the makers had claimed, there was hardly any recoil. She peered through the sights. The letter 'C' had a neat round hole punched through its centre. She squeezed off four more rounds that stitched a row of perfectly placed holes around the outside of the letter.

Esther was delighted with the rifle. Apart from allowances for wind-deflection that still called upon the traditional skills of a marksman, the rifle was about as foolproof as one could get. She dismantled it and thrust it into a voluminous shoulder bag before trudging back through the trees to her hire car.

36 It was a hot afternoon. The air-conditioning in Maken's suite was working hard.

'We've checked your story, Heinlein,' said Maken. 'And I'm pleased to say that it stands up.'

'There's no reason why it shouldn't. It happens to be the truth.'

Maken toyed with a detailed report that was lying in front of him. The incident that had led to Heinlein's court martial had been well documented by his agents. It stated that there had been a PLO sniper who had started operating in Nazareth on that day and that several Arabs had reported seeing a soldier answering Heinlein's description escaping from the overturned personnel carrier and running away from the disturbance. The report also stated that all the details Heinlein had supplied on his background were correct. The PLO agents had been thorough – the report even included a summary of Heinlein's court martial transcript.

'I've discussed your plan with a few of my very close colleagues,' said Maken, watching Heinlein carefully. 'Naturally, they are astounded.'

'Naturally,' agreed Heinlein indifferently.

'And very worried by your proposals.'

'Why?'

Maken looked sharply at Heinlein. 'That should be obvious. What you're proposing to do has never been done before.'

Heinlein gave a lazy smile. 'Which is a good reason for doing it.'

'Precisely. You and I think alike.'

'Good. When do I start?'

'You don't. At least not yet.'

'Now look,' said Heinlein in some irritation. 'I've had a week –'

'The four thousand dollars expenses you require is no problem,' said Maken smoothly. 'But you say that you need a PLO cell – a trained team – for the first phase of the operation.'

'Correct.'

'That is a problem.'

'Why?'

'My colleagues are not prepared to give you one,' Maken answered bluntly. He raised a hand to cut short Heinlein's objections. 'If you want a team, you will have to return to Israel and build your own.'

Heinlein controlled himself with an effort. 'In that case, the deal's off. I can't –'

'It was never on in the first place. There are plenty of Palestinians in Narbus and Jerusalem who are itching for action. You could recruit them.'

Heinlein resisted the temptation to laugh in Maken's face. 'Are you kidding? You expect me – an Israeli – to be accepted by the Arabs as a PLO recruiting officer?'

'You're a man of ingenuity, Heinlein.'

'I'll need a damn sight more than ingenuity to put a team together. I need at least two trained agents with Israeli passports. I can't possibly carry out a series of major robberies in Israel within

101

three months if I've got to start from scratch. I need experienced men that can outshoot *Zahal*-trained guards. If you can't provide them then the operation's off.'

Maken thought for a moment. 'There's no reason why you shouldn't return to Israel now. Stay at the Plaza Hotel in Tel Aviv until one of my men contacts you. He'll give you our final decision.'

'Meaning that you still don't trust me?'

Maken gave Heinlein a disarming smile. 'Meaning that a little mutual mistrust might be in both our interests for the time being.'

37 Patrolman Sean Lewis of the New York City police was destined to go a long way in his chosen career because he had an unusual gift of observation. There was very little going on in the streets of Midtown Manhattan that escaped his attention. He had seen the beautiful, dark-haired girl before.

Four times to be exact.

Either she had been sitting in a snack bar or she had been wandering up and down the Avenue of the Americas. She didn't behave like a hooker; she never picked up a client and yet a girl with her looks would have to fight them off. So what in the world was she up to?

Patrolman Lewis watched her walk jauntily across the street, a bag slung over her shoulder, and enter the Museum of American Folk Art. Maybe she wanted an air-conditioned bolthole to escape the suffocating heat; maybe she was a genuine student of American culture just as Patrolman Lewis was a student of human behaviour – especially criminal behaviour. He decided that it would do no harm to keep an eye on the building to see how long she remained inside.

Esther had difficulty opening the door on to the roof. Perhaps some traces of acid had continued eating away at the lock's mechanism. She was running with perspiration by the time she persuaded the key to turn. She stepped on to the roof and stood luxuriating in the strong breeze blowing off the Hudson River while trying to ignore her quickening pulse.

She knelt down near the parapet and glanced across at the

Hilton's main entrance. If Heinlein stuck to his pattern, he would be leaving the hotel for his afternoon walk in ten minutes. She hoped he would not be late because someone at an overlooking window was certain to notice her presence. It was then that she realized that the blazing sun provided just the cover she needed. She stripped off down to her bra and panties and stretched out on her skirt. She was just another office girl taking advantage of the fine weather.

She rolled on to her stomach and rested her chin on her hands so that she could see over the edge of the parapet.

Once settled, she drew her bag nearer and opened the flap so that she could quickly grab the Remington when Heinlein appeared.

Heinlein sat brooding in his hotel room. Training a cell in Israel was going to be dangerous in the extreme. He inwardly cursed Maken's over-cautiousness in refusing to supply him with a ready-made team.

'You'll stay at the Plaza Hotel in Tel Aviv and we'll be in touch,' a PLO aide had instructed Heinlein after the meeting with Maken. The aide also handed Heinlein four thousand dollars in cash and made him sign a receipt.

The phone rang. It was the travel desk confirming that he had a reservation on an El Al evening flight to Tel Aviv. He thanked the girl and glanced at his watch. He had been stuck in the hotel all day. There was plenty of time to go out for a drink.

The museum security guard looked doubtful. 'Bag slung over her shoulder? Yeah – there was a girl – dark hair. Took an elevator a few minutes back. Could be in any of the offices.'

Patrolman Lewis thanked him. Another characteristic that was going to take him a long way as a police officer was his sixth sense. That sixth sense was telling him to check the roof. He touched the elevator call button.

Esther saw Heinlein emerge from the hotel. Her movements were methodical. Unhurried. But her hands were shaking.

Crazy, a corner of her mind said. The videos depicted assassins as cool and calculating, yet here she was – her hands trembling and her heart pounding.

She slipped the Remington from her bag, rested it on the parapet and squinted through the sights. It took her a few seconds to pick out Heinlein. He was walking away from her. His back completely filled her field of view. She flipped the switch that activated the laser beam and watched the spot of light dancing all over Heinlein's back. Gradually her trembling eased and the point of light steadied. He was walking slowly as though deep in thought. The wind caught at her hair and blew it across her face.

You must allow for the wind!

The point of light became still as Esther forced herself to gain total control of her body. Sometimes pedestrians passed between her and her target. And then Heinlein was strolling along a stretch of sidewalk outside Burlington House where the passers-by had thinned out. She made a final aim correction. The tiny computer-controlled servomotors whirred briefly as they compensated for the increasing distance as Heinlein moved further away from Esther. And then the green, light-emitting diode glowed brightly in the sights. Esther pulled the trigger. Once. Twice. Three times.

The first bullet struck the sidewalk within six inches of Heinlein's foot and ricocheted through a Burlington House window. He recognized the sharp crack of a high-velocity round and dived for cover behind a raised flowerbed. The second round unleashed a cloud of dust as it chewed a chunk out of the flowerbed's brick surround.

A woman screamed as the third round whined past her ear and embeded itself in a wall.

Patrolman Lewis kicked open the door just as Ether was about to fire a fourth shot.

'Drop it!' he snarled.

Esther turned her head and stared blankly at him. The policeman was facing her, both arms outstretched, clutching a .38 that was pointing straight at her head.

'I said drop it!'

Esther released her grip on the Remington. It clattered on to the parapet and would have gone over the edge had she not made a sudden grab at it.

Two things happened in that instant. The first was the posing of a question in the mind of Patrolman Lewis that was to haunt him for the rest of his life: had the girl grabbed instinctively at the rifle to stop it falling or had she intended to use it against him?

The second thing that happened was that he shot her in the left eye, killing her instantly.

38 Heinlein gazed down at Esther's body and nodded to the man in the horn-rimmed glasses.

'Yes. I knew her. I ran out on her in Israel. She used to drive me crazy. If I as much as looked at another woman, she'd threaten to scratch my eyes out. She really was crazy. To have followed me from Tel Aviv to New York. Can you imagine that?' He shook his head in disbelief.

The man in the horn-rimmed glasses was an FBI agent, the man who had interviewed Heinlein in the lobby of the Hilton Hotel. He gave an almost audible sigh of relief. He was one of the team responsible for the security of the PLO delegation. On the face of it, one Israeli shooting at another Israeli outside the hotel where Joseph Maken was staying didn't look too good. And yet the farewell note in Heinlein's handwriting that had been found in the dead girl's apartment, plus Heinlein's story, all added up to one of those curious coincidences that the FBI man was all too familiar with. Also the rest of Heinlein's story checked out: the former Israeli army officer was the son of Israel's leading diamond and bullion merchant and he had visited the United States before on business.

The two men left the mortuary on Tenth Avenue. The FBI man hailed a cab and told the driver to take them to the Hilton Hotel.

'Do you want me for any more questioning?' Heinlein asked.

'Just one. Why did you see Joseph Maken?'

Heinlein smiled. 'Altruistic motives. He's a Marxist. I merely wanted to know if Tel Aviv would continue as a major bullion and diamond centre should he ever take over. Like I told you before, I'm interested in business, not politics.'

'When do you plan on returning to Israel?'

'This afternoon. I missed yesterday's flight because of this business.'

The FBI man gazed uninterestedly at the passing traffic. 'No more questions, Mr Heinlein. But if you do run out on any more jealous chicks, don't let them chase you to New York. OK?'

'I'll try not to,' Heinlein promised.

'Something else,' said the agent.

'Yes?'

The agent regarded Heinlein steadily. 'We might just take a fatherly interest in your well-being once you're back in Israel.'

'She was definitely a Mossad agent,' Maken declared

Heinlein gave a languid smile. 'You think so?'

'I know so.'

'Oh? How?'

'Let's just say that we know.'

Earlier that morning Maken and his aides had sifted through the photographs of employees of known Mossad front organizations in Israel. The photograph of Esther matched the photograph of an employee of a travel agency-cum-souvenir shop near Namir Square in Tel Aviv.

Heinlein grinned. 'I thought Mossad trained their operatives to shoot straight?'

'With that wind and lay-off angle? She was lucky to have got a shot within six inches of you. The attempt on your life answers one question about you but poses another. Just how useful can you be to us if Mossad are after you?'

'*If* she was a Mossad agent, my guess is that they'll now leave me alone.'

Maken was intrigued. 'Why?'

'Because the matter is closed as far as the FBI is concerned – a case of a jealous woman who tried to bump off her lover. If anything happens to me, the Israelis can't afford an international row blowing up if the Americans decide to delve too deeply into who the girl was. Accusations of attempted political assassinations in New York won't do much for Israeli/US relations in the present climate.'

Maken toyed with his gold pen. 'You could be right. Which brings me to another question. We're prepared to accept that you're genuine, therefore we've decided to provide you with an operational unit. They'll work closely with you, Heinlein. So close in fact, that if anything goes seriously wrong, you'll be their last target. I hope I make myself clear?'

39 'Sorry – we've got all the payload specialists we need,' said Intelsat.

'Payload specialists?' questioned ITT. 'We've got a team of ten – all electronics engineers. Are you an electronics engineer, Mr O'Hara?'

Twenty appointments and three days later, after a trip that had taken him as far south as Miami, Neil returned to Melbourne in his camper to an echoing, empty house. Helen had gone, most of the furniture had gone, and all that was left to remind him of the children was their float cushion drifting aimlessly around the swimming-pool. She had even taken the hologram discs he made of them growing up.

He spent most of the following day at Harry's place getting slowly drunk. The day after that he took the Beeline Expressway to Orlando to pick up a repair kit for the Winnebago's troublesome turbine. He was an expert mechanic and enjoyed keeping the big camper in good shape. He figured that a day spent fixing it would take his mind off Helen and the kids.

It didn't work out like that. When he opened the garage doors he found it piled high with old toys that Helen didn't think worth taking to Houston. Neil surveyed the jumble of broken bicycles and toy cars and decided that it would be easier to spend the day drinking at Harry's.

That evening he sat in the Winnebago, parked in the drive, and ate a meal of beans straight from the can while reading the General Motors workshop manual for the camper's turbine. He was engrossed in the procedure for removing the turbine from the chassis when Jason Pelham's face appeared on the television. Until then he had paid scant attention to the news programme.

'I believe that the orbital hotel project is an even greater concept than the Apollo moon exploration programme,' Pelham said in answer to the interviewer's question. 'With Apollo it was only possible to land two men at a time on the moon at a considerable cost. The outcome of the orbital hotel project will give thousands of men and women from all walks of life the opportunity to share the spiritual adventure of going into space, and at the same time reopen the moon frontier at a fraction of the sixties/seventies cost –'

Neil hit the television's one-minute buffer store button to pick up the beginning of the story:

'Today NASA announced the signing of an agreement with a consortium of major hotel and leisure interests for the joint financing of a giant orbital hotel,' stated the newscaster. 'Not only will the four thousand-room hotel provide accommodation for up to eight thousand guests, but it will also serve as a staging post for regular, low-cost moon voyages.'

The picture cut to the news conference room at the Kennedy Space Center. Jason Pelham was sitting at a long table flanked by various worthies who included Theo Kahn, head of WED (Walter E. Disney) Enterprises, and Caroline Shultz, the president of Hilton Hotels. All the men and women at the table had smiles as wide as the wheel-shaped model space station in front of them. Facing them was a horde of newsmen and batteries of TV cameras.

Jason Pelham spent a few minutes going over the salient features of the proposed orbital hotel laying special emphasis on 'the opportunity for ordinary men and women from all walks of life to share the spiritual adventure of journeying into space.'

As Neil stared at the television an eel of suspicion wriggled in his mind. He had heard rumours about a secret feasibility study into the construction of a giant orbital space station but had no idea that commercial interests were involved.

When Pelham finished speaking, the abrasive Steve Hudson of CBS News was on his feet firing questions:

'Mr Pelham – can you say how much a week's stay at the hotel will cost?'

Pelham smiled blandly. 'As yet, detailed costings are not finalized.'

'You must have some idea,' Hudson insisted. 'No one sinks two hundred billion dollars into a project without some idea of the return.'

Caroline Shultz took up the challenge. 'A preliminary figure is around seven thousand dollars a week for a room,' she replied.

'So the ordinary men and women who will share the spiritual adventure of going into space will have to be pretty well-heeled men and women?'

'That should come as no surprise to anyone,' Pelham intervened. 'Of course, many of the guests will be students from
108

universities and research organizations who will be staying free. That's part of the deal.'

'Will ordinary men and women be able to withstand the G-forces of a lift-off?'

'Those forces are only slightly more than those experienced during the take-off of a conventional SST aeroplane,' Pelham replied. 'Many of our customers' payload specialists have required only elementary training before a shuttle flight, and we've sent many sick people into orbit for specialized treatment in the space hospital.'

Hudson's questioning was relentless. 'Is the present shuttle fleet big enough to handle your estimated numbers of passengers?'

'A new orbiter fleet will be built, Mr Hudson,' Pelham answered.

'Would you agree that the shuttle is an old design?'

'It's a proven design.'

'But it *is* an old design,' Hudson persisted.

Pelham gave the journalist a bland smile. 'There have been many improvements to the original design over the years, Mr Hudson. They can now uplift nearly double the payload of the first shuttles. The design of your microphone is very old, Mr Hudson, but it's reliable and safe, otherwise you wouldn't be holding it. Reliability and safety is what comes first when we passenger-rate the new shuttle fleet.'

There was some laughter from the other journalists. Hudson was unperturbed. 'There was a shuttle fatality last month,' he pointed out.

Pelham nodded. 'The review board's report attributed the accident to human error.'

'Negligence by the commander,' Hudson agreed. 'That's something we never hear when there's been an airplane crash. How can we be sure that it's something we won't hear again when you've got a shuttle fleet operating that's carrying eight thousand passengers each week?'

'By a significant raising of the standards we'll be looking for in our shuttle crews,' Pelham replied.

'Meaning that your standards haven't been high enough so far?'

It was a tricky question but Pelham handled it with his customary adroitness. 'No – I don't mean that they haven't been high enough. Improvement in the quality of the men and women who will crew the shuttles is essentially an evolutionary process –

109

we freely admit that we're still on the learning curve when it comes to determining all the qualities that make the best shuttle crewmen and women. Allowing a man of Neil O'Hara's incompetence to become a shuttle commander was a mistake. One that can't and won't happen again.'

Neil could hardly credit his senses. The General Motors manual slipped from his fingers and he gaped disbelievingly at the television press conference. He reached for the buffer store button again and watched Jason Pelham castigate him for a second time. The suspicion as to why Pelham had suppressed evidence about Al's death suddenly hardened into the bitter realization that he had been a victim of Pelham's ambition. The NASA chief wanted to be certain that nothing reflected on the shuttle's operating procedures before the consortium signed the agreement.

Neil was normally a placid, easy-going man whose Irish blood permitted him occasional but quickly forgotten losses of temper. But in those moments spent watching the NASA press conference, his mounting anger gave way to a lasting blind rage.

40 A bombing raid on Ben Gurion Airport forced Heinlein's Boeing to divert to the *Chel Ha'Avir*'s Etzion airbase in the Sinai Desert. Internal passenger flights had been suspended in Israel and the passengers had to await the arrival of coaches to ferry them to Ben Gurion for customs and immigration clearance.

As expected Heinlein encountered no problems with the immigration girl who scrutinized his passport. He was hot, tired and hungry by the time he checked in at the Plaza Hotel.

He spent the following morning sleeping off his jet lag and emerged in the late afternoon. Sun Tours opposite the hotel rented him a Ford. He drove into the centre of Tel Aviv and spent an hour touring various hardware stores purchasing a number of small tools, a moneybelt, some electrical items and even an aerosol can of shaving cream. After that he went to Berners on Rothschild Boulevard and bought a Polaroid document camera equipped with an electronic flashgun. His last visit was to a men's outfitters where he purchased a pair of trousers, a lightweight sweatshirt, gloves, socks and a pair of soft shoes. All the garments were black.

He spent a few minutes in his hotel room fitting a small-bore flexible plastic pipe to the shaving cream aerosol in place of the ordinary nozzle and whiled away the rest of the evening drinking coffee at the outdoor bar in Namir Square where he had first met Esther. He paid his bill at midnight and drove ten miles north along the coast to where his father had a house on the select Jaffa Gardens Estate. He concealed the car in some undergrowth half a mile from the estate's guardhouse and changed into the black clothes. The tools went into various pouches in the moneybelt and he slung the Polaroid camera from his shoulder.

He left the car's driver's door ajar and placed the ignition key on the floor where he could find it easily in a hurry. His Special Parachute Brigade training had laid as much emphasis on escape from the scene of a clandestine operation as on going in in the first place. 'It's no good messing about with half a dozen keys on a bunch or trying to drag keys from your pocket when you're sitting behind a wheel,' an instructor had once drilled into him. 'And don't leave the key in the ignition because that's asking to have your getaway vehicle stolen.'

That same training enabled him to move cat-like through the dense undergrowth surrounding the estate. He scaled several walls and crossed a number of gardens belonging to his father's neighbours. Before darting across lawns or open ground where he might be seen, he spent several minutes crouching in the shadow of shrubs, listening for the slightest sound indicating that his presence was known. His greatest worry was detection by the infra-red surveillance monitors and closed-circuit TV cameras although from his knowledge of the estate he knew that such devices were mostly arranged to cover the drives and front gates of the houses.

Heinlein climbed the familiar wall surrounding his father's mansion and circled cautiously around the building. There were no lights on in any of the rooms and the hum of wall-mounted air-conditioning units from his father's and brothers' bedrooms told their own story: Avram Heinlein was cost-conscious and only permitted the air-conditioners to be run in those rooms that were occupied.

He climbed nimbly on to the roof of the double garage and

located the steel shroud that covered the external burglar alarm bell. It took him less than a minute to inject the entire contents of the shaving cream aerosol through the plastic pipe and under the alarm bell's cover. The mass of white foam effectively jammed the alarm's relays, preventing them from triggering their circuits when he unscrewed the cover. He reached into the alarm and deftly unplugged all the connectors from the main printed circuit board.

The next obstacle was the patio door leading to his father's study. Boring a tiny hole in the aluminium surround was relatively easy. The trick was boring the hole in the right place. Heinlein was lucky with his first attempt and his probing efforts with a long slender screwdriver through the hole to release the internal catch were rewarded with a satisfying click. He slid the door open and slipped into the study. A quick examination with a penlight showed that the layout of the book-lined room was unchanged. As always, his father's diary lay open on the desk, displaying his appointments and movements for the following day.

Heinlein dumped his tools and camera on the desk and turned his attention to the Tom Keating watercolour hanging on the wall that his father had paid a hundred thousand dollars for at a New York auction. Behind the painting was a small but extremely robust wall safe protected by a formidable six-digit combination lock. Praying that his father had not changed the combination, Heinlein set the handwheel to the first two digits of the year of his father's birth, and the third and fourth digits to the year of his mother's birth. He dialled his own year of birth for the last two settings.

He offered a silent prayer and gave a gentle pull. The safe opened. Inside he found a bag of uncut diamonds and a leatherbound notebook. It was the book he was interested in because it was a diamond merchant's 'traffic' register containing details of forthcoming diamond and bullion transactions and shipments. He glanced quickly through the columns – all in his father's rounded handwriting – and was relieved to see that his father had not changed his code. Like many leading diamond merchants, Avram Heinlein used a coding system that he had devised himself. Heinlein propped the book open on his father's desk and used the Polaroid document camera to photograph the last twenty pages. The operation took less than five minutes. He returned the book and bag to the safe, closed it and reset the handwheel to its original position. He left the room, sliding the

112

patio door closed. He plugged the hole he had drilled in the door with a headless rivet. It was a far from perfect disguise yet it was unlikely to be noticed for some time, nor would the shaving cream under the alarm shroud be discovered until the system was subjected to its six-monthly inspection. He returned to his car without incident and spent two minutes relaxing in the driver's seat while his heartbeat gradually returned to normal.

In the privacy of his hotel room Heinlein laid out the Polaroid prints on the desk and studied them through a magnifying glass. The automatic sonic focusing device on the camera had done its job well – the images on the photographs were pin sharp. With the aid of a calculator, he divided all the numbers in the first column for each entry by Pi – 3.142 – and arrived at the reversed Julian date for each shipment. His father prefered the Julian date notation because most people would naturally assume that a Hassid would opt for the Mosiac system of dates.

Heinlein decoded all the dates and wrote them down on a separate list. Out of over two thousand entries there was one date for two weeks hence that occurred against four hundred and forty-five entries. The unusually high number of shipments on one day aroused his curiosity. Also the number in the second column was the same for each consignment – 1,042. That meant uncut diamonds. Most of the numbers in the third column were meaningless to Heinlein because they were assigned to those clients who owned the diamonds, but he had no difficulty deciphering the fourth column – the weight of each consignment in metric carats All four hundred and forty-five entries added up to a staggering quarter of a million carats – in weight alone that was fifty kilograms. Certain that he had made a mistake, he added up the figures again. There was no mistake.

Fifty kilograms of uncut diamonds!

Such a vast quantity represented one year's production of all the world's diamond mines. Furthermore they were all being moved on the same day in the same consignment to the same destination: Eliat Airport on the Red Sea.

Heinlein sat back and debated with himself as to why his father was moving such a fortune out of the country. The state of Israel's economy as a result of the War of Attrition meant that clandestine funds were probably leaving the country every day. There was no

113

doubt that the massive shipment was illegal, but Avram Heinlein was no great lover of the State of Israel and he would have no qualms about undertaking such a risky operation on behalf of his clients.

The following morning Heinlein made a number of phone calls and established that on the date of the consignment a party of fifty Jerusalem Hassidim had chartered a flight from Eliat to Warsaw, the spiritual home of their sect, with a stopover at Amsterdam.

Eliat made sense; it was one of the few airports not subject to PLO air attacks, and Amsterdam was certain to be the destination for the diamonds.

The more Heinlein thought about that fifty kilograms of diamonds, the more attractive the operation appeared. Only one raid would be required instead of the series he had envisaged, nor would he require much assistance from Maken's agents. All he had to do now was discover how the party of Hassidim and their baggage would be travelling to Eliat.

A single telephone call to a special number would answer that question.

41 Jason Pelham drove across the virtually deserted car park and parked in the shade cast by a Winnebago camper. He wondered what the large, unsightly vehicle was doing at the Suntree Golf Club and noted, with a flash of annoyance, that Earl Hackett's car hadn't arrived. Pelham liked his Sunday game of golf to start at 7.30 a.m. precisely, before Florida's appalling heat and ninety per cent humidity made concentration difficult.

He was lifting his golf club trolley out of the car's boot when a shadow fell across him. He turned around and came face to face with Neil O'Hara. The former astronaut was staring at him with an expression of abject loathing.

Rarely lost for words, Pelham said smoothly: 'Good morning, Mr O'Hara. I had no idea that you were a member of this club.'

'I'm not, Pelham. I wouldn't belong to any organization that you belong to, which is why I'm glad to be out of NASA.'

Pelham nodded. If he was alarmed at Neil's threatening stance – legs slightly apart, fists clenched at his sides – it did not show on his

114

face. 'In that case,' said the NASA chief uninterestedly, 'your departure suits both of us. Now if you will excuse me—'

Neil's fist slamming into Pelham's stomach prevented him from finishing the sentence. He gave a loud gasp and doubled up just as Neil followed through with an upper cut to the jaw. Pelham staggered back and clutched blindly at his car for support, blood streaming from a deep cut on his chin. Neil was tempted to step forward and hit the NASA administrator again but the cold fury that had been gnawing at his reason for the past two days suddenly evaporated. The invective he had prepared to use against Pelham was unaccountably no longer there. He stepped back from Pelham and stared at him dispassionately.

For all his faults Pelham was no coward. As soon as he got his breath back, he choked out: 'You're a generation younger than me, O'Hara. What you've just done reinforces my contempt for people like you who settle grievances with their fists instead of their brains.'

Pelham straightened up and held a handkerchief to his jaw. He even managed a crooked smile. 'Also your actions have assuaged whatever worries I had about getting rid of you, whereas you will have to live for the rest of your life with the knowledge that you were directly responsible for Al Benyon's death. Now get out of my sight before I call the police.'

42 A blow in the small of the back caused Heinlein to choke on his beer.

'David!' boomed a foghorn English-accented voice. 'David Heinlein, well I do declare! If it isn't the old rogue himself.'

Before Heinlein could react, a rotund little man aged about forty and with several chins plonked himself down at Heinlein's table in Namir Square and beamed at him. The midday sun had pricked out beads of sweat on the stranger's forehead which he mopped with a well-used handkerchief.

'Who the hell are you?' growled Heinlein.

The little man looked crestfallen. 'David – surely you remember that party in London? When your father let you off the leash for a

115

couple of days before you became a regular? By God, that was some party, eh? How many girls did we get through?'

Heinlein gaped at the little man in astonishment. Maken's aide in New York had told him that the name of the agent who would be contacting him in Tel Aviv was Sarcha and that he would introduce himself by talking about a party in London.

'I'm sorry. I don't remember you.'

'Oh, David – really.' The portly little stranger beamed and patted his belly. 'Well, maybe I have put on a bit. But nothing to stop me earning a dishonest crust. Sarcha – Peter Sarcha.' He gave Heinlein a knowing wink. 'There – I expect that name's aroused a lot of guilty memories, eh?'

Heinlein glanced around the square. As usual it was crowded with youngsters. 'I think,' he said carefully, 'that we ought to go somewhere where we can talk.'

'Good idea,' Sarcha agreed. 'Fancy a spot of fishing?'

The two men hired an outboard boat from the marina together with some fishing gear. They cut the engine a mile from the beach and allowed the boat to drift.

'Much better,' said Sarcha grinning broadly. 'I like boats a long way offshore. Our Mossad friends employ some of the best lipreaders in the world. And they've got some beefy binoculars. But it's useless trying to train them on two blokes bobbing about in a boat.'

Heinlein looked at Sarcha in grudging respect. Obviously the little fat man was a lot shrewder than he looked. 'OK, Sarcha. Who exactly are you?'

Sarcha beamed and outlined his background. He was a former Special Air Service sergeant in the British army. Upon leaving the army he had set up a military bookshop in London and made frequent trips to the United States buying up books on guerilla warfare.

'Not books that were actually illegal in the UK,' he explained to Heinlein. 'But hard to get hold of. You know the sort of thing – how to blow yourself up with homemade bombs. The business didn't do too well – not with the law walking in every few weeks and making off with my stock. Anyway, some of my customers pointed me in the right direction and I started a little sideline working for the PLO.'

'What sort of work?'

Sarcha waved his hand airily. 'Oh, the odd little bumping off here and there. Right up my street, what with my SAS training and that. Funny thing though – those bumped weren't Israelis. In those days half the factions in the PLO seemed intent on rubbing out the other half. Then Maken took over and all that ended. I still work for the guy now and then because I admire what he's doing. Right now I'm here on one of my regular business trips, buying up books on Jewish military history. Only this time I was told to make contact with you to help you out. I've also looked up a few old friends while I'm here.'

Heinlein looked curiously at Sarcha and wondered what use the improbable little fat man could possibly be to him. His weight would be against him for one thing. What Heinlein needed was agile young men.

'You're a mercenary?'

'Got it in one.'

'I see. So if you're offered more money, you'd change sides?'

Sarcha looked faintly alarmed 'And upset Joseph Maken and all his works? Good grief, no. I'm also a shocking coward.'

'Is Sarcha your real name?'

Sarcha grinned. 'Oh, yes. Peter Sarcna.'

'Do you have any idea of what I might be planning?'

Sarcha's grin remained fixed. 'Let me guess. Something to do with diamonds? Lots of diamonds?'

The remark triggered about a thousand of Heinlein's built-in alarm systems. He looked sharply at the Englishman. 'Why should you think that?'

'That was a neat little job you pulled on your father's house the other day.'

Heinlein's pulse hammered. 'Job?' he questioned, his mind racing ahead.

Sarcha nodded complacently. 'I followed you. All those bloody walls you made me climb over. And, David, my lad – you weren't that professional. We always reckoned that the Special Parachute Brigade relied more on luck than judgment. If it had been me, I would've drawn the study curtains properly so that no one could've peeped through the windows and seen me working on the safe. And the flashes from your camera bloody nearly lit up the whole garden.' Sarcha broke off and laughed at Heinlein's stunned expression. 'So it *is* a diamond job. Right, David?'

Dumbfounded, Heinlein could only nod.

'A big one?'

Heinlein hesitated and then realized that it was pointless hiding anything from the cunning little Englishman. 'A very big one,' he confirmed.

'How many men will we need?'

'*I* will need at least six men including myself,' said Heinlein pointedly.

Sarcha started the outboard motor. 'OK, David, my boy,' he said breezily. 'Our friends said that you would be planning something, but they didn't know what. They also said I could include myself in for one per cent.'

Heinlein regarded the Englishman steadily. 'Is that so?'

Sarcha chuckled. 'But that you were to take your ten per cent first. So what say you and me buckle down to a bit of the jolly old planning?'

Heinlein spotted the distant anomaly from his observation point overlooking the Arava Highway – one of the loneliest roads in the world – which crossed the Wilderness of Zin from Beer Sheva to Eliat.

He steadied his binoculars against a rock and focused them on the distorted image that was twisting and dancing like a demon in the blood heat haze that layered the burning hills. The gyrating image gradually hardened into the vague outline of a touring bus towing a cloud of dust. He unclipped the children's two-way radio from his army belt and barked in the microphone: 'They're coming.'

'Roger,' Sarcha acknowledged.

The fifty-milliwatt children's radios, with their piano-wire antennae, were ideal for the operation because their range was less than a half a mile and therefore there was little chance of their signals being picked up by any of the army's desert monitoring stations.

Heinlein scrambled down the barren hillside and helped Sarcha, Alef and the three other Palestinian recruits drag the military roadblock signs into position and park the two jeeps on each side of the road. All six men were wearing suitably scruffy *Zahal* combat fatigues with soft-vizored desert caps and MK.20 Galil assault rifles. Every item of their uniforms was genuine, right down to the identification bracelets that each man wore on his right wrist. Heinlein was wearing his own uniform which

118

bore the two stripes of a *segan* – lieutenant – on his shoulder straps.

On a word from Heinlein the five men took up their positions and waited for the approaching coach to round the bend.

'Jesus,' Sarcha muttered, wiping away the sweat that was coursing into his eyes. 'Another hour in this bloody heat and a new, slimmer me will emerge.'

'Give me a chance to get used to the old one first,' Heinlein retorted.

The whine of the bus's engine swelled. The vehicle hurtled around the bend and braked to a standstill when the driver spotted the roadblock. As expected, the vehicle was an Egged Tours charter bus. Heinlein went aboard as soon as the door hissed open.

'Everything OK?' queried the driver. He was a fresh-faced man aged about twenty-five.

'Your licence and SC permit please,' Heinlein requested. He glanced at the passengers. Two rows of dark suits, sombre beards and sidelocks, and uninterested expressions from the fifty Hassidim stared right through him.

The driver handed Heinlein a document wallet.

'There's no stamp on your SC permit,' said Heinlein, glancing through the papers and noting the driver's name. 'Didn't you check through the Beer Sheva control point?'

The driver looked puzzled. 'Well – no, sir. There wasn't one.'

Heinlein nodded. 'You must've passed through before it was set up. Follow the jeep to the marquee please.'

One of the passengers in a front seat stood up. 'I'm Rabbi Sharrat. I'm the leader of this group. We're on a pilgrimage to Warsaw –'

'I'm sorry, Rabbi,' Heinlein interrupted. 'But we have to search this bus. We've had reports that arms are being smuggled to Eliat. The sooner we –'

'Surely you don't think we would smuggle arms!' the rabbi protested.

Heinlein smiled and noticed the flicker of alarm that appeared on a number of faces. 'Of course not, Rabbi. But there is the possibility that arms have been planted on the bus without your knowledge.' He turned to the driver. 'Are you a reservist?'

'Yes, sir. A corporal.'

'Right now, Corporal Mishan, you're under my command. Follow the first jeep and maintain radio silence.'

Heinlein jumped down from the bus and hopped on the tailgate of the first jeep driven by Alef as it moved off. The tour bus obediently followed. The second jeep, with Sarcha driving, took up the rear position.

The convoy turned off the main road and bumped along a rough track for about half a mile to where a marquee had been pitched on a patch of level ground. Heinlein's two privates dragged the tent's flaps aside and waved the bus into the hot interior.

'This is disgraceful!' Rabbi Sharrat shouted as he stepped down from the coach and spotted the long row of trestle tables. 'You have no right to delay us like this!'

'We're acting on the authority of the GOC Southern Command, Rabbi,' said Heinlein calmly. 'I want everyone in your party to remove their baggage from the bus's stowage bays and place their cases on the table. Any locked bags must be unlocked. Anyone making a suspicious move is liable to be shot. The sooner we get this over, the sooner you'll be on your way.'

The rabbi decided against further argument. He muttered in Yiddish to his companions. One by one the sullen Hassidim dumped their suitcases on the table and unlocked them. They looked on impassively as two of the privates rummaged through the bags while Sarcha searched the bus's interior. Alef crawled under the bus armed with a mirror and a powerful flashlight.

After thirty minutes nothing had been found.

'Body searches,' ordered Heinlein.

There was a renewed wave of protests from all the passengers when they were ordered to turn out all their pockets and undress. One brought down a particularly vitriolic curse on Sarcha but the nature of any intervention from above that the fat little Englishman was worried about was more likely to be mechanical than divine.

'Another hour and an army chopper's certain to spot this tent,' he muttered to Heinlein. 'What the hell's gone wrong?'

'Corporal Mishan!' Heinlein called out.

'Sir?'

'Did you pick this party up in Jerusalem?'

'Yes, sir.'

'Where?'

'Outside their library in Mea Shearim, sir.'

'Did they place their baggage in the stowage bays or did you load it for them?'

120

The young bus driver looked puzzled. 'Well – I suppose they loaded it.'

'What do you mean "you suppose"? Don't you know?'

'No sir. They've had possession of the bus from last night for cleaning by their wives.' Mishan lowered his voice. 'You know how nutty those guys can be. Non-kosher litter, that sort of thing. They were all seated and ready to go when I arrived at the library.'

Sarcha muttered a curse.

'Do you always drive the same bus?' Heinlein fired at the driver.

'Nearly always – yes.'

'So you know it inside out?'

'Pretty well – yes.'

'Right,' said Heinlein with finality. 'You and I are going over every inch of it – inside out and from front to back.'

After thirty minutes' meticulous examination, Mishan poked his head around the door of the bus's toilet compartment and said to Heinlein: 'There's something wrong here, sir. It's not flushing as fast as it should.'

'Where's the tank?' Heinlein demanded when he had flushed the toilet and witnessed the meagre trickle of water for himself.

'In the roof, sir.'

'Did you fill it?'

'No, sir. They must've done.'

The faces of the Hassidim remained inscrutable as Alef and his brother scrambled on to the bus's roof and removed the water tank's access panel. Alef shouted down for some wrenches which were passed up to him. The Palestinians worked for five minutes while Sarcha and Heinlein listened anxiously for the approach of an army helicopter. Rabbi Sharrat opened his mouth to say something but changed his mind. He and his fellow Hassidim watched in sullen silence as the bus's bulky hundred-gallon water tank was lowered on ropes to the ground. Sarcha squatted down and examined the tank's saucer-sized inspection and cleaning cover.

'It's been taken off recently,' he announced, removing the thumbscrews that enabled him to slide the cover to one side. He thrust his arm into the hole and groped around. A broad, triumphant grin lit up his face. He withdrew his arm. Clutched in his fingers was a plastic bag that bore a numbered tag. 'Feels like hundreds more bags in there too,' he said to Heinlein, handing him the bag.

121

Heinlein opened the bag and tipped its contents into the palm of his hand. The sixty or so uncut diamonds surprised him by their size and variety. They were mostly cleavages, maccles and flats ranging from half a carat to about eight carats. The eight-carat stone had already been bruted – the first stage in the polishing of a diamond. That alone was a clear indication of the panic within the Tel Aviv Diamond Exchange that had precipitated this particular clandestine flight of stones from the country.

'How much are they worth?' asked Sarcha.

'This little handful? About thirty thousand dollars. OK – get the rest of the bags out.' Heinlein took the diamonds across to Rabbi Sharrat and held them under his nose. 'I'm sure you and the members of your little flock must know about Emergency Defence Regulation 131, Rabbi?'

The rabbi returned Heinlein's stony gaze and said nothing.

'Regulation 131 covers the illicit export of bullion and precious and semi-precious stones,' said Heinlein casually. 'It stipulates an automatic sentence of twenty years' imprisonment for any person convicted, and there is no right of appeal. Also the state has the right to impound the stones.' He jerked a thumb at the bags Sarcha was lifting out of the water tank and smiled. 'If you can't produce export licences for that little lot, perhaps you'd like a receipt before we allow you to continue your journey?'

Suddenly Sarcha forgot the seasickness brought on by the five-hour journey in the inflatable boat.

'Over there,' he said, pointing and breathing a great sigh of relief. 'Four one-second flashes and a five-second pause. A close thing, eh, David, my lad?'

Heinlein saw the light winking across the oil-black sea and swung the outboard's tiller. He steered the inflatable cautiously in the direction of the light. The five hours' punching into the teeth of a brisk sou'westerly had left them dangerously low on fuel. He kept the outboard idling and only opened the throttle when he had satisfied himself that the cycle of flashing lights was correct.

Between the two men, securely lashed down, were three rope-handled ammunition boxes that contained the most priceless cargo that had ever put to sea.

A black shape eclipsed the stars low down on the horizon and a

122

few minutes later the two men heard the surge of the Mediterranean's swell slapping against a ship's hull. Heinlein removed the children's two-way radio from a waterproof bag and pressed the talk key.

'This is Delta Hotel standing by.'

'Roger, Delta Hotel. We copy you,' squawked the radio's tinny speaker. 'Welcome aboard.'

At that moment the rubber boat bumped against the hard chine flank of Joseph Maken's motor yacht.

Maken and his aides gathered around the open ammunition boxes and gazed in awe at their contents. The PLO leader knelt on the plush state-room carpet, scooped up a handful of the uncut, lustreless diamonds and allowed them to trickle through his manicured fingers.

'I've taken my ten per cent,' said Heinlein curtly.

'And I've taken my one per cent,' Sarcha chimed in.

Maken smiled and nodded. 'You've helped yourselves to some good stones, no doubt?'

'Pretty good,' said Heinlein evenly.

Maken stood. 'A well-earned percentage if I may say so.' He gestured to the boxes. 'How much is all this worth?'

Heinlein shrugged. 'It's impossible to say. I did a rough valuation on a handful as a typical sample. The whole lot, released over a period of a year, will realize in the region of three hundred million dollars.'

The only sound in the state-room for some seconds was the muffled thud of the motor yacht's diesels. Maken's customary sang-froid seemed to desert him momentarily. He allowed his gaze to return to the fabulous prize at his feet. '*Three hundred million dollars?*' he repeated numbly.

'I could be out by a factor of fifty million either way,' Heinlein replied casually as though he were a builder submitting an estimate to repoint a chimney. 'But it would be about that. They'll need careful handling – especially some of the larger stones. De Beers make a hologram recording and catalogue every diamond they release that's over twenty carats. But I estimate that ninety per cent of these are under ten carats – the best international currency in the world.'

'And there'll be no come-back?' asked an aide.

Heinlein gave a cold smile. 'Not immediately. But the truth's bound to leak out eventually. When it does, the scream will be heard around the world. Not that that need worry you. You won't have any trouble laundering them. There's plenty of buyers in Amsterdam, London and New York who treat the holder of uncuts as the owner in return for a ten per cent markdown on their trade value.'

Maken was unable to resist touching the gems again. He trickled another handful through his fingers. 'Three hundred million dollars,' he breathed in wonder.

'More than the GNP of some countries,' Sarcha commented.

'And enough to finance a nuclear war,' Maken added jokingly. 'Correct, Mr Heinlein?'

'Correct, Mr Maken.'

43 Neil's week-long visit to Houston to see Helen and the children had gone badly. The two-day camping trip with Pippa and Andrew had been great fun but Helen had soured everything on their return by producing a new lawyer who had insisted that Neil pay for the children's education in advance – a fifty thousand-dollar lump sum – instead of the quarterly payments Helen had originally agreed to.

'It will be in your own interests in the long run,' Mr O'Hara,' the lawyer had said. 'You have the money as your share from the sale of the house. But you no longer have a job, therefore you may have a struggle in the future finding the payments. This route releases you from the worry of becoming entangled in lawsuits.'

The bitter argument had dragged on all day. Neil had eventually been worn down by the lawyer with the result that he was returning to Melbourne fifty thousand dollars poorer. He didn't begrudge the children one cent. What annoyed him was that Helen, having grabbed most of the money from the sale of the house, had then set out to extract the last of his capital.

Once back in Florida he stopped at a rest area on Highway 1 near St Augustine and checked his bank balance on the Winnebago's built-in computer. A column of glowing figures appeared on the screen once the bank's satellite had matched his personal number against the Winnebago's transmitter 'fingerprint'. Neil's black depression deepened as he studied the screen. The lawyer had wasted no time clearing the cheque. His account was now less than ten thousand dollars in credit. It meant the end of his plan to sell the Winnebago and buy a small house on a new condominium at Edgewater.

He continued his journey and was five miles south of Daytona Beach when the camper's troublesome turbine decided that it had had enough. There was a loud scream from the motor followed by the sound of impeller blades breaking up. A melody of other noises suggested that the camper had dumped a high percentage of its entrails on the highway. The combustion chamber pressure indicator dropped to zero.

'Major turbine failure,' announced the synthesized voice of the camper's computer.

Neil's self-control nearly snapped. 'I know that!' he snarled back at the computer. He uttered several heartfelt expletives and swung the Winnebago on to the shoulder. He touched the keypad to switch in the fuel cells and the emergency electric motors. The computer informed him that the camper had a range of twenty miles – enough to get him off Highway 1. Cautiously he applied power, eased the camper back on to the highway and accelerated to the maximum speed possible on emergency power.

The next intersection took him on to a lonely, little-used road between De Land and Edgewater. With the air-conditioning closed down, the afternoon sun began cooking its way into the camper's interior. He nursed the vehicle towards De Land. There was nothing but swampland either side of the road. He was beginning to despair of finding any human habitation when he spotted a derelict-looking filling station adjoining an ancient frame house. The grizzled Negro reading a paper on the porch looked up and watched Neil turn the big camper on to his forecourt and stop.

'Can't help you, mister,' the man said when Neil approached him.

'What's that?'

The man lowered his paper. 'You come creeping in like a ghost so I figure you're running on your electrics. Turbine gone?'

'You've got it.'

The old man scratched his crinkled grey hair. 'Never did understand 'em.' He grinned, exposing an impressive collection of

125

rotting teeth. 'Never did understand piston jobs much neither. All Lena and me do is sell gas. Not much of that since the new beeline opened.'

'You've got a workshop,' Neil pointed out.

The old man rose stiffly to his feet and shuffled unsteadily down the porch steps. He was wearing shabby dungarees. His stoop was so pronounced that he almost walked bent double. 'Sure I've got a workshop. But no mechanic since my boy quit. You'll need Smithers to come out from Daytona with a wrecker.' He nodded to the filling station's pay booth. 'Phone in there. Or they listen out on channel 19 if you've got a CB.'

'You rent me your workshop for a coupla days and I'll fix the turbine myself. I've got all the parts.'

'Hundred a day,' the old man answered promptly.

'Ninety.'

'It's yours, mister. You gonna sleep in that thing?'

'Yes.'

'That's ten a night for camping up.'

'For Chrissake –!' Neil began.

'Includes hooking up to my power,' said the old man quickly. 'I can't sleep if you have a generator running all night. Hundred in advance.'

Neil decided that it would be pointless to argue. He counted out five twenty-dollar bills into the grimy, outstretched hand.

'Name's Jackson – Jacko.'

'Neil O'Hara.'

'OK, Neil. You go right ahead and help yourself. There's a tit left of the workshop doors that opens them.' With that the old man shuffled back to his porch.

Neil had a pleasant surprise when the ramshackle double doors slid open. Not only was the workshop big enough to house the camper, but it was clean and well-equipped with hoists, lifting gear, and electronic tuning equipment. Along one wall was an aluminium-topped workbench and the wall itself was covered with neat rows of various handtools and wrenches. There was even a modern lathe standing in one corner beside an industrial air-conditioning plant. The ninety dollars a day rental was good value. It was the sort of workshop he had always dreamed of owning himself.

He cooked himself a meal, cleared it away and changed into his
126

coveralls. An hour later, with the Winnebago parked in the centre of the workshop, his problems were forgotten as he set about jacking the camper on to axle stands and removing its front grille.

By 7 p.m. he had completed all the stripping down that gave him access to the turbine. He was a methodical worker: as he removed a part, so he would clean it and lay it out on the workbench. His careless handling of a heavy wrench that he nearly dropped on his foot made him realize how tired he was. He decided it was a sensible time to stop work. It seemed like a good idea to shower, have a light meal, and maybe watch a video before turning in for an early night. He was pulling on a dressing gown when there was a tap on the door.

'Who's there?'

A bright voice answered: 'Hi, there. I'm Lena. I thought maybe you could use some coffee.'

Neil opened the door and goggled at the stunning black girl who was holding a coffee pot. She gave him a friendly smile.

'Can I come in, Mr O'Hara?'

'Er – yes.'

Lena entered the camper and set the coffee pot down on the table. Neil decided that she had to be the most beautiful girl he had ever seen. She was aged about twenty-five. She was wearing jeans that could have been two coats of blue lacquer on her legs, and a T-shirt that looked like one coat. Looking at her was like having cocaine injected straight into an artery near the brain.

'I didn't trouble you before because you were so busy,' she said, wiping clean two cups that were lying in the sink. 'I peeked around just now and saw you'd finished so I figured you could use some coffee.' She smiled mischievously. 'Was I right?'

'You've never been more right in your life,' Neil asserted, returning her dazzling smile. 'It smells good. But would you think it rude of me if I ask who you are?'

'Lena – Jacko's daughter – God help me. Aren't you going to ask me to sit down?'

There was an infectious quality about Lena's easy-going nature that stimulated the good-humoured side of Neil's character. 'Sure – help yourself. Hey, before you do, how do I know that a jealous husband isn't going to bust in? This heap's in no state for quick getaways.'

127

Lena laughed throatily. A lovely laugh, Neil decided. And sexy enough to be illegal in Salt Lake City.

'I promise you, there's no husband, or even a boyfriend. Let's have some coffee before it gets cold and I'll bore you with my past.'

Lena told Neil that she was twenty-six, single, and that Jackson was her father. She had a degree in business administration from Florida Institute of Technology. 'Ma died ten years back,' she said. 'And George – that's my brother who used to run the workshop – he's now got a Borg Warner repair franchise in Miami.'

'Have you got a job?' Neil asked.

'Not a go-to-an office job. I've got an IBM terminal in the house and a satellite link. I look after the accounts and stock control for about twenty stores in Edgewater. I'm saving up to rent an office in one of the malls on the coast. OK – that's enough about me. How about you?'

'There's nothing much to tell,' said Neil. 'You carry on talking. I could listen to your voice all night.'

'Well I sure as hell couldn't look at your knees all night. You've got a Kennedy pass on the windshield so you work for NASA. Yes?'

'Used to.'

'What happened?'

Neil told her the whole sorry story from Al's death to the break-up of his marriage. Lena was silent for a few moments after he finished talking. 'You really have been through it,' she said softly.

'Honey – the last thing I want is sympathy.'

Lena grinned. 'I wasn't going to give you any.' She stood up and, to Neil's alarm, kicked off her shoes. 'I can offer you something much more practical,' she went on, removing her watch and placing it on the table. 'I can get Pa to cut the rent he's charging you on the workshop. OK if I use your shower? Only our's isn't working.' She wriggled out of her jeans, revealing first a pair of white running shorts followed by a pair of fantastic running legs.

Neil decided that the black vision before him couldn't possibly be real. 'Go right ahead,' he said weakly. 'There's soap –'

But the shower door slammed shut before he could finish the sentence.

44 The sixteen members of the Supreme Council of the Palestine Liberation Organization had flown in to Bakal from all over the world for their regular quarterly meeting. Instead of using the conference room, they were shown into the fifty-seat preview theatre that was normally used by the executives and staff of the PLO Broadcasting Commission.

Joseph Maken shook hands and chatted briefly with each member of the council as they entered the theatre.

Heinlein sat at the back of the theatre behind the control panel. Sarcha was at his side, wondering what was on the slide that Heinlein had in front of him. He turned his attention to the Palestinians taking their seats. He recognized none of them; they were sixteen faceless men and women, not necessarily loyal to Maken, but who had nevertheless been picked up by him because of their administrative abilities which qualified them to run PLO centres throughout the principal capital cities of the world.

Sarcha leaned across to Heinlein and whispered: 'Jesus – if our friends were to raid this place now.'

'They'd never get past the SAM-50As,' was Heinlein's curt reply.

Sarcha lapsed into silence. A week had passed since they had arrived in Bakal on Maken's yacht. Sarcha's astonishment at what his Palestinian friends had achieved in their temporary homeland had been largely negated by his discovery that the place was dry.

Maken stepped on to a dais at the side of the theatre's screen. 'Good morning, comrades. We have a long agenda to work through during the next six days. Item One – "Future Military Strategies" – is the most important which we shall discuss and decide on now. Afterwards we shall adjourn to the conference room for the rest of the business. Our guests at the back are two of my most valued aides who will, with your approval, be carrying out the most daring military operation in our history. An operation whose objective is an overwhelming victory for us within six months.'

There was a stir. Sixteen faces turned round to stare curiously at Heinlein and Sarcha.

Sarcha gave a low groan. 'What have you let me in for?' he

129

muttered under his breath to Heinlein. 'Have you no regard for my cowardice?'

Heinlein hissed at him to keep quiet.

'As you are aware,' Maken continued, 'the War of Attrition has become virtually a stalemate with the refusal of Chairman Dranski to support our invasion plan. Although we can strike at will at Israel with the MiG-35s and the Tupolevs, causing major disruptions of the Israeli industrial machine, we lack the armament to strike a decisive blow. Also there is evidence that Israel is dispersing her production facilities in much the same way that the Allies and the Germans did during the Second World War. This will make the destruction of the enemy's war machine even more difficult. Such a difficulty may tempt us to strike at soft civilian targets and thereby make the same mistake that Hermann Goering made during the Battle of Britain and the Americans made in Vietnam.' Maken paused to look at each of his audience in turn. 'I make no apologies for the history lesson. There is an old saying that those who forget the past are condemned to relive it.

'At the moment the Israelis do not have the ability to strike a decisive blow against us. The *Chel Ha'Avir*'s severe losses have led them to abandon attempts to penetrate the SAM-50A screen around Bakal. We are vulnerable to missile attack but the Israelis do not have a long-range weapon. However, from our latest intelligence reports we know that they have developed and perfected an easily transported and fired intermediate-range missile – the Massada – that can carry a nuclear warhead. Moreover, the Massada has been in production for a year, so we can safely assume that the Israelis have amassed a considerable stockpile of them, probably in excess of one hundred missiles. What is most alarming is that reliable reports reveal they have been working on a first-stage, solid-fuel booster that turns the Massada into an intercontinental missile. If that is so, then we are in grave danger.'

Maken anticipated the outburst of questions by holding up his hand and calling for the slides. Heinlein fingered a touch control on the console. Three aerial photographs appeared on the screen which showed a cluster of wrecked buildings surrounded by the barren, eroded hills of a desert.

'The Israelis' Negev Guided Weapons Research Establishment thirty miles south of Ramon,' Maken explained. 'Or rather, what's left of it following a major explosion. The pictures were taken at

130

different times by MiG-35s flying on photo-reconnaissance sorties. That is where the Israelis built the Massada boosters. The photographs suggest that the explosion must have caused considerable loss of life. What we don't know is the effect the explosion had on the development of the Massada booster. The fact that they have made no attempt to rebuild the place suggests two things to our operational research team. Firstly – the explosion wrecked the entire booster development programme to such an extent that the Israelis have been forced to start again from scratch at a different site. Or secondly – that the development on the booster was finished anyway and that production is now under way at various plants.'

Maken sipped from a glass of water. He was a clear, fluent speaker. There was no sound from the members of the Supreme Council as they waited for their leader to resume.

'For our own safety,' Maken continued, 'I am sure you will agree that it is essential we assume the latter to be the case. Obviously, an intercontinental booster has to be subjected to many tests before it can become operational. We have identified the merchant ship that the Israelis use for missile testing in the Southern Ocean. At the moment it is lying at Haifa. We will continue to keep it under constant observation but its idleness and the complexity of a testing programme is a definite indication that we have several months' leeway in which to plan and execute appropriate counter-measures.'

'Gentlemen – the planning of such an operation is completed. We will be stealing four Massada missiles armed with nuclear warheads and fitted with celestial/inertial guidance systems. These will be loaded into the cargo bay of a space shuttle that will be launched from the United States' Kennedy Space Center. A shuttle in a ten-degree-inclined equatorial orbit at a height of one hundred and fifty to two hundred miles is an ideal launch platform for intermediate-range missiles – especially the Massada which is designed for atmospheric entry. A space shuttle in the right orbit will be capable of launching a Massada against any target in Israel every two hours and there would be nothing that the Israelis could do about it. A nuclear strike against a selected suburb of Tel Aviv on a Sunday morning . . . . And then another on Haifa at lunchtime . . . . Jerusalem at teatime . . . .' Maken smiled thinly. 'I doubt if there would be an Israeli government by suppertime.'

He stopped speaking. There was an incredulous silence for a few

131

seconds and then everyone starting talking at once, firing questions at Maken. What about the loss of Palestinian life? What about the cost? How accurate were the missiles? How would they be obtained. Some members of the council jumped to their feet and came near to shouting to make themselves heard.

Sarcha's face was ashen. He nudged Heinlein in the ribs. 'Is this your lunatic scheme?'

'More or less. Why?'

'Because it's the craziest, most crackpot idea I've ever heard. You're mad. Absolutely and ravingly out of your tiny. Have you any idea of –'

Heinlein put his fingers to his lips to silence the Englishman while Maken held up his hand, refusing to speak until order was restored.

'Let us take the questions one at a time,' said Maken when all was quiet. 'First – the cost. As the result of a daring preparatory operation in Israel, we have the necessary funds to finance the operation.' He smiled and added: 'Israeli funds at that. On the question of accuracy, the Massada is equipped with a precision celestial/inertial navigation system – an on-board computer that will steer the missile to any pre-selected target no matter where it is launched from provided it is launched within range of the target. The other questions on obtaining the Massadas and access to a shuttle relate to operational details which it is not appropriate to discuss at this stage. What we must now consider are the consequences of going ahead or not going ahead with the operation. I would be grateful if the two aides would now kindly leave the theatre.'

Heinlein stood. Sarcha appeared to be suffering from temporary paralysis, obliging Heinlein to kick him on the shin.

'Operational details!' Sarcha expostulated once he and Heinlein were in the corridor. 'Did you hear him? He said that getting hold of the Massadas and grabbing a shuttle were operational details!'

'Shut up,' growled Heinlein, striding along the corridor. 'I've never known a mercenary who did so much complaining before.'

'I've never been involved with megalomaniacs who wanted to chuck nuclear warheads about before.'

Heinlein stopped and spun round to face Sarcha. 'Do you want to be in on this operation or not?'

'Will you be running it?'

'Yes.'

'After that cock-up you made of busting into your dad's house?'

132

Heinlein began to get angry. 'That wasn't a cock-up. I got the information didn't I?'

'It was a cock-up. I followed you. And for all you know, the entire Mossad field team could have been following me.'

'OK – if you want out –'

'Of course I want out. An important quality in any leader of a dodgy operation is the ability to recognize internal weaknesses. Your particular blindspot is your failure to appreciate just how startlingly brilliant I am and how much you need me.'

'Oh yes?' Heinlein queried cynically. 'And what about your renowned cowardice? Do I need that as well?'

'Of course you do. If anything smells a bit dodgy, I'd be the first one to say.'

Heinlein studied the plump little Englishman with unconcealed distaste. 'Against my better judgement, I'd like to have you along. That body of yours might come in handy for absorbing lead when it starts flying about.'

'You see? You need me.'

'And there are two other reasons why you'd better join me,' Heinlein continued. 'Firstly, you'd be in the line-up for another one per cent of the diamond haul. And secondly, if you decide not to join me, you will have to stay here in Bakal until the operation's over. That could be as long as six months.'

Sarcha blinked in alarm. 'But this place is dry!'

'Precisely.'

Sarcha groaned. 'OK. Include me in.'

That afternoon Heinlein and Sarcha were summoned to Maken's office.

'The Supreme Council has debated the plan at some length,' Maken opened without preliminaries. 'The voting was eight for and eight against. Those who voted against felt that we should not initiate a major operation until after next month's US presidential election which Senator Harding is certain to win. He is no lover of Israel, therefore some of my colleagues believe that he may take prompt action to end the war. Personally, I have no such hope. I've met the senator from Wyoming on a number of occasions. He's a careful man who does nothing in a hurry, and even then only after the fullest consultations. When he does decide to raise his hand against Israel, it may be too late. I used my casting vote, therefore the operation goes ahead.'

Heinlein looked relieved. 'In that case there's no reason why we shouldn't start right away.'

'There's one thing all the members of the council insisted on,' said Maken. 'You can't use any of our overseas offices or their services.'

Sarcha's eyes popped in surprise. 'We can't carry out the operation alone!'

'You'll have to. It could go wrong. I'm not saying it will, but it could. If it was linked to the PLO before those missiles are in orbit, then our European and United States offices would be finished and we'd be kicked out of the United Nations. We can't afford that, therefore you've got to operate alone. What we can do is provide you with plenty of contacts before you leave – organizations whose services you can buy.' Maken chuckled. 'After all, you won't exactly be short of money and Sarcha has plenty of Palestinian contacts in Israel.'

Sarcha opened his mouth to protest but Heinlein cut him short. 'OK, Maken. We'll manage by ourselves.'

The PLO leader looked pleased. He unlocked a drawer in his desk. 'Excellent. That leaves only one small matter to deal with. One that must be kept a closely guarded secret between the three of us.'

Heinlein raised questioning eyebrows. Maken placed a bottle of whisky and three glasses on his desk and said: 'I think we ought to drink a toast to the success of our little plan.'

Sarcha beamed and decided that maybe life wasn't so bad after all.

45 Lena entered the workshop clutching a handful of twenty-dollar bills. The sight of a pair of unsuspecting legs sticking from under the Winnebago implanted evil thoughts in her mind. With a mischievous light in her eye, she crept quietly forward and deftly plucked a hair from one of the shins. The owner of the violated shin emitted a loud yell and foolishly straightened up while he was lying under the camper. His yell became even more pronounced as he cracked his head on something metallic and unyielding. Neil wriggled out and glared up at Lena who was looking down at him with laughing eyes. The sight of her was enough to evaporate his indignation. 'Miss Lena,' he drawled in a miserable imitation of a Southern accent. 'Them legs o' yours look like a million of them dollars you's holdin'. Guess they're jest about the most fabulous legs I aver did feast ma tired ol' eyes on.'

Lena fluttered her eyelashes. 'Why, Mr O'Hara, you do know how to flatter a girl so.'

Neil gingerly rubbed his temple. 'And you know how to flatten a man's head,' he said with mock severity as he climbed to his feet. 'I think a little tender massage is called for.'

'Why, Mr O'Hara. How can I touch a gentleman like you with hands like this from pickin' cotton all day?'

They stared at each other and then burst out laughing.

'So where did this money come from?' Lena asked, holding the dollars under Neil's nose.

'An election motorcade came through on their way to De Land. About twenty cars. You and Jacko were shopping. They wanted gas so I sold them gas.'

'That was very good of you, Neil. Democrats I hope?'

'Oh definitely.'

'I hope Harding wins.'

'So do I,' said Neil grinning. 'But I didn't give them a discount.'

Jacko shuffled into the workshop while they were laughing. 'How's it goin', Neil?'

Neil started cleaning grease off the tools and returning them to their hooks. 'Oh – another coupla days will see me through, Jacko.'

Jacko chuckled. 'Takin' longer than you reckoned. Them jobs always do.'

'Neil sold some gas while we were out, Pa.'

'Guessed that's what happened,' said Jacko. 'Just seemed like a lot o' cash seeing we were only gone three hour or so.'

'And I fixed a flat for a lady.'

'Pretty?' asked Lena.

'Oh, very. Only charged her three dollars.'

'OK. And how much did you charge for fixing her flat?' said Lena, keeping her expression deadpan.

All three burst out laughing. As Neil wiped the tears from his eyes, he realized just how happy he was when in Jacko's and Lena's company. Especially Lena's.

46 Heinlein and Sarcha changed flights at Moscow and arrived at London's Heathrow Airport eighteen hours after setting out from Bakal.

They checked into a pre-booked suite at the Savoy Hotel at 3 a.m. and spent the rest of the morning sleeping off the exhausting journey before embarking on their hectic schedule.

'We'll spend tomorrow buying ourselves decent clothes,' said Heinlein over a magnificent lunch that was served in their room. 'Then we must buy or lease a large country house within a couple of hours' drive from London.'

'As a safe house?' asked Sarcha, talking with a mouth full of smoked salmon.

'Yes. One with a large barn.'

'Presumably it would be too risky for me to visit my flat? Just to see who's threatening to sue me for unpaid bills?'

'You'd best stay away,' Heinlein agreed.

Sarcha tucked into some more smoked salmon and downed a gulp of champagne. 'I suppose I shall just have to rough it like this then. A country mansion is going to cost a small fortune.'

'Don't worry about it. We've got a large one to get through.'

The plump little Englishman grinned. 'It's going to be hell.'

'It's going to be Goddamn hard work,' said Heinlein curtly.

Sarcha helped himself to a generous portion of out-of-season strawberries that the Savoy flew in from South Africa. As he smothered them with cream, he reflected that his companion was not over-endowed with a sense of humour.

The following day the two men went to Harrods and spent over a thousand pounds each on clothes and half as much again on two sets of the finest hide luggage. Their purchases were delivered by chauffeur-driven car to the Savoy.

Upon their return to the hotel, Heinlein combed through a document provided by the PLO Foreign Intelligence Service that listed the names and addresses of prominent British scientists and the projects they were involved with.

'Sarcha. Go out and buy me a copy of *Who's Who*.'

136

As soon as he was alone, Heinlein made a long-distance telephone call. He drummed his fingers impatiently while the person he was calling was summoned to the phone. He spoke for five minutes and hurriedly finished the conversation when Sarcha returned from his trip to Foyles and dumped the massive tome beside Heinlein.

'How about some feminine company tonight?' enquired Sarcha.

'Sleep's more important,' Heinlein grunted as he concentrated on checking the PLO's list of scientists against entries in *Who's Who*.

'OK then – so we sleep with feminine company.' Sarcha waited and then sighed. Life was tough. 'Found anyone?'

'I think so,' said Heinlein, glancing up from the *Who's Who*. 'Sir Max Flinders, Fellow of the Royal Society and Vice-Chancellor of the University of Surrey. He's a leading authority on satellite communications and space technology . . . . This is interesting – he personally headed a team that designed a giant satellite called *Cyclops* that was intended to search for blue shift pulsars and other astronomical oddities.'

Sarcha chuckled. 'Looking for stars with no dress sense?'

Heinlein ignored the feeble joke. '*Cyclops* was intended to be launched by the shuttle. But it was axed by the British government because of the launch cost. It was so large, it would have required its own shuttle mission.'

Sarcha whistled. 'Sounds like exactly what we're looking for.'

'That's what I thought,' said Heinlein. 'But we've got to double-check this first. Another job for you, Sarcha. I want you to find out everything you can about the University of Surrey, their vice-chancellor, and *Cyclops*.'

Anyone opening a bank account with a draft from the Bank of Liechtenstein for ten million dollars is worthy of respect. Heinlein was treated with great respect by the director of the London branch of the Florida-based Brevard County Bank.

'I'm delighted Mr Stavolos named us in his will, Mr Heinlein,' said the director, pouring his visitor a sherry. 'We're a young bank but our policy of providing specialized banking facilities for scientific institutions has proved a great success. We will, of course, be pleased to attend to all the legal formalities in setting up the trust. I will need a copy of Mr Stavolos' will and the Liechtenstein abatement certificate from his bank, plus–'

'You will find all the documents you need in there,' said Heinlein, handing the director a folder.

The director skimmed through the photocopied will with a practised eye. 'He names you as chief executive of the trust. Why not chairman?'

It was a question Heinlein was ready for. 'Mr Stavolos said that it would be a good way of his continuing to employ me after his death.'

'A most generous employer if I may say so,' the director commented when he spotted the emoluments' table. 'Isn't the sponsorship of space research projects a curious trust for a shipping magnate to set up?'

Another question Heinlein was prepared for. 'Mr Stavolos was always fascinated by space research. Also he was a keen amateur astronomer. As his personal secretary, I can vouch for the many space research projects he helped finance through his various companies. He was a man of great vision.'

'I see that you have power of attorney and that all grants have to be authorized by you. Under British law that means that you will also have to be a trustee. There are other complications–'

'I'm not interested in the details just yet,' Heinlein interrupted. 'You set the trust up and deduct your charges from the account.'

'Ten million dollars is an awesome responsibility, Mr Heinlein.'

Heinlein met the banker's level gaze. 'Mr Stavolos' total bequest to the trust is nearer three hundred million dollars,' he replied acidly. 'Funds will be transferred from Liechtenstein as they are required.'

The director thought that it would be interesting to find out more about Julius Stavolos but he knew that attempts to extract information from Liechtenstein's bankers or authorities would run smack into a stone wall. Anyway, one did not argue with clients placing ten million dollars on central deposit.

'Very well, Mr Heinlein, I will instruct our legal department to set up the European Space Research Trust just as soon as you furnish me with the names and addresses of the trustees.'

'I have an appointment for tomorrow with Sir Max Flinders to ask him to serve as chairman of the board,' said Heinlein.

The director nodded his approval. This Heinlein, whoever he

was, knew exactly what he was doing. 'We know Sir Max very well. An excellent choice, if he'll agree. Would you like a letter of introduction?'

'Thank you,' said Heinlein graciously. 'That will be most helpful.'

He left the bank a few minutes later. Everything was going exceptionally smoothly. A taxi drew up alongside the kerb. Sarcha's moonlike face appeared at the open rear window.

'How did it go, David?'

'So, so,' said Heinlein noncommitally as he sat beside Sarcha and ordered the driver to take them to the Savoy.

'We're in luck with the University of Surrey,' Sarcha commented, closing the driver's glass partition. 'The PLO info checks out. Surrey University have been up to their necks in space research since the late seventies. They've built umpteen satellites which have been launched by Arianespace and the US shuttle.'

'And *Cyclops*?'

'The row over its cancellation was monumental. Flinders nearly resigned. The satellite definitely still exists. I found an article about it in a recent back number of the *New Scientist*.'

Heinlein looked impressed. 'You've done very well, Sarcha. We'll hire a car and go down to Surrey this afternoon.'

'What for? Your appointment with Flinders isn't until tomorrow.'

'We have to find a suitable country house near the university,' Heinlein pointed out.

Sarcha frowned. 'But you don't know if Flinders will accept.'

'He will,' said Heinlein confidently. 'He's got to. And we don't have a great deal of time to waste on house-hunting. The sooner we start looking, the better.'

'I've arranged for two delightful young ladies to entertain us in our suite tonight,' said Sarcha sorrowfully.

'Well you'll have to unarrange them,' was Heinlein's unsympathetic reply.

The third mansion the estate agent showed them was ten miles south of Guildford, tucked away in the Surrey hills near the picturesque little village of Thursley.

'Thursley Hall is one of the finest houses in Surrey, Mr Heinlein,' said the estate agent, opening the double doors of the

139

huge barn. 'Hopefully this is large enough to house your collection of cars?'

Heinlein and Sarcha entered the spacious barn. It was big enough for three fire engines.

'About eighty feet,' Sarcha murmured when he had finished pacing the length of the barn. 'Just the job.'

'So it would seem,' Heinlein murmured.

The estate agent was only twenty-two but he knew enough about the business to sense when a quick sale was in the offing. These two potential customers had turned up at his Godalming office in a Rolls-Royce and left it parked on double yellow lines in the narrow high street, much to the fury of two traffic wardens. The darker man, Heinlein, was obviously the boss. He had enquired about secluded mansions for sale. The first two properties the estate agent had shown Heinlein were of no interest to him because they lacked storage facilities for his collection of vintage cars.

'OK,' said Heinlein, looking up at the barn's roof. 'This will do. I want possession from Friday. We'll return to your office and I'll call my bank for them to pay you direct.'

The estate agent swallowed. 'Er . . . . You can't have immediate possession, Mr Heinlein. There is the conveyancing –'

'How long will the legal formalities take?'

'For a cash sale – we could push everything through in about two weeks. There's a solicitor in Godalming –'

Heinlein cut the young man short. 'I like the house and I like the furnishings and fixtures, and I like the housekeeper,' he said briskly. 'I have to leave the country on urgent business very soon and I want this business cleared up first. I suggest I take out a two-month lease to cover the changeover period. I shall pay in advance with enough to cover the housekeeper's wages. I'm an extremely busy man so shall we return to your office now and complete the initial formalities?'

Sir Max Flinders was a large, overpowering man with a rich, booming voice. He listened carefully to Heinlein's proposition, threw back his head and roared with laughter.

'I like you, Heinlein. You're different. It's not everyone who walks in here with such offers. Four meetings a year for a retainer of fifteen grand per annum? How can I refuse?'

The two men were sitting in Flinders' office on the top floor of

Senate House overlooking the laboratories and landscaped campus of the University of Surrey on the outskirts of Guildford.

'I'm very pleased, Sir Max,' said Heinlein.

'Why did you decide on me?'

'Mr Stavolos had read your British Association papers on satellites and admired your work. Also our bankers considered you an excellent choice.' Heinlein noticed Flinders' smile broaden and guessed that the scientist loved having his ego massaged. 'Also, of course, your name does carry a great deal of weight.'

Flinders' laughter rumbled around the office. 'It's not my name that carries weight around here – it's my voice.'

Heinlein smiled politely. 'We need a board of trustees of ten.'

'Seems reasonable. How much do they get each?'

'Five thousand pounds per annum. I shall be happy to leave the selection of trustees to you . . . .'

'Jobs for the boys, eh?'

'. . . For my approval, but I need their names and addresses by Friday. They should all be prominent in the field of space research – that was Mr Stavolos' great interest. As the trust's chief executive, I have an automatic seat on the board.'

'You'll have the names by tomorrow,' Flinders promised. He stood. 'Now – how about that tour of our space research facilities? Used to call them labs but we've gone all American now.'

'Yes, I'd be most interested to see them,' said Heinlein politely.

The two men took the lift down to the ground floor. Sarcha was waiting outside in the Rolls-Royce. Heinlein went over to the car.

'I'll be about an hour. Go and see the estate agent. Make sure everything's going OK with the lease on Thursley Hall.'

Sarcha acknowledged. The car slid away and Heinlein accompanied Flinders to a recently built laboratory complex. For the next thirty minutes, he was genuinely absorbed by his conducted tour of the various laboratories where a wide variety of prototype satellites were being tested.

'This is the last port of call,' said Flinders. He ushered Heinlein into an observation room. The room on the far side of a plate-glass screen resembled an operating theatre.

'This is our "clean" room,' Flinders explained. 'Where satellites are finally assembled, sterilized and checked out.'

The two men watched a team of gowned and masked technicians working on a satellite that looked absurdly small in comparison with the attention it was receiving.

'And that's it,' said Flinders when he finished outlining the satellite's purpose. Well? What do you think of our little set-up?'

'Very impressive, Sir Max. But why are all the satellites so small?'

'Have to be. We can't afford to hog an entire Ariane payload. And she's not like the shuttle. That thing can put a fifty-six-seater bus into orbit.'

'But what about your *Cyclops* satellite?'

Flinders stiffened. He gave Heinlein a searching look. 'What about it?'

'I used to prepare the weekly press-cuttings for Mr Stavolos on subjects that I thought would interest him. I remember reading that *Cyclops* was an extremely large satellite.'

Flinders hesitated for a moment and then came to a decision. 'Come with me,' he said abruptly. With that, the scientist turned on his heel and strode towards a windowless building that resembled an aircraft hangar. Heinlein nearly had to break into a trot to keep up with the scientist.

Flinders unlocked a side door and pushed it open. They entered a tiny cubicle.

'An airlock,' said Flinders savagely. 'Not that there's much point in it now because we couldn't afford to keep the bloody air-conditioning going.' He threw open an inner door. Heinlein followed him into the vast interior.

'*That*,' said Flinders pointing, 'is *Cyclops*. The finest multi-spectrum orbital observatory ever built. X-ray, infra-red and optical. If it wasn't for an ignorant bunch of bloody-minded cretins, it would be in orbit right now – sending back a priceless motherlode of data on the Universe instead of rotting here.'

Heinlein gaped in astonishment at the spectacle that confronted him. Supported on massive trestles in the centre of the floor was a monstrous, bug-eyed creation as big as a bus, with huge outstretched black wings that spanned the entire width of the building. The entire mind-numbing contraption looked like something out of a billion-dollar science-fiction movie. 'Hell,' he breathed, and could not help adding, 'Jesus bloody Christ.'

142

47 Heinlein walked slowly around the giant satellite and returned to where Flinders was standing. 'I can see why it required its own special shuttle mission,' he observed.

Flinders pointed to a huge cylindrical container that was bigger than the carriage of an underground train. It was resting on blocks beside the satellite. 'That thing is a dummy of a NASA shuttle cargo pallet – the largest size in the range because it's near enough a dead fit into a shuttle's cargo bay. We used that to ensure that the satellite would fit.' He indicated the outstretched wings. 'They're the solar panels that collect the sun's energy to power the thing. They fold up and the entire satellite fits inside the pallet. The plan was for us to stow the satellite here and ship it to Kennedy with our own payload specialist. Once the shuttle was in orbit, the pallet would have been lifted out of the shuttle's cargo bay and opened to release the satellite.' Flinders' anger gave way to bitterness. 'I put six years of my life into the *Cyclops* project. It destroyed my marriage and the marriage of my chief designer. And now look at it . . .' his voice trailed into silence.

For a few moments the two men regarded the colossal satellite without speaking.

'Why not make the launching of *Cyclops* the first project of our Stavolos European Space Research Foundation?' Heinlein suggested.

Flinders had been about to say something. Instead he turned to stare at Heinlein. 'What the hell are you talking about?'

Heinlein repeated his suggestion and added: 'It's just the sort of project that would have appealed to Mr Stavolos.'

Flinders seemed unable to credit his senses. 'Have you any idea of the cost of financing a shuttle mission?'

'One hundred and fifty million dollars,' Heinlein replied without hesitation. 'That's well within our first year's budget.'

Flinders seemed unable to reply for a moment so that Heinlein had to prompt him. The scientist shook himself from his daze. 'But there'd be another fifty million needed to restore *Cyclops* to launch readiness. She'd have to be stripped right down and –'

'How long will that take?'

'Now look – you can't be serious –'

'How long will it take? A crash programme.'

'About six months. It's a huge operation – almost as big as building her in the first place.'

'Do it in five months and we'll launch her.'

Flinders recovered his composure. 'Are you kidding me or what, Heinlein? I don't know you from Adam. You walk into my office. And now –'

'Sir Max, this project is exactly what would've fired Mr Stavolos' imagination. He liked to think big and so do I. OK – so it'll cost upwards of two-fifty million. So let's get down to some hard talking.'

'Keeping me waiting all that time,' Sarcha complained as he filtered the Rolls-Royce off the campus and on to the A3. He headed south towards Thursley.

'Anyway, it's all in the bag,' said Heinlein, sinking back into the car's soft cushions. 'He's over the moon at the prospect of getting his *Cyclops* into orbit.'

'Any problems?'

'He was a bit worried about the sniping he might get from his contemporaries as chairman of a trust that votes his own pet project a two-fifty million-dollar budget. I told him, what was the point of power if one didn't use it now and again? And it's a cost-effective project because the Goddamn satellite is already built.'

'Stroke of luck.'

'One hell of a stroke of luck,' Heinlein agreed. He pulled a sheet of paper from his pocket. 'He was so excited, he rang up some colleagues immediately. The board of trustees of the Stavolos European Space Research Foundation now boasts two Nobel prizewinners, three Fellows of the Royal Society, a former Astronomer Royal, and the chairman of the British Association for the Advancement of Science.'

Sarcha whistled. 'Not bad.'

'Not bad at all,' Heinlein agreed. 'Their names will look slightly impressive on our stationery. I think we can now say that we're ultra-respectable.'

'So what's next?'

'Florida.'

'Bit early, isn't it?'

144

'We've got to set up a project coordination office at or near the Kennedy Space Center. Flinders said that there's a lot of paperwork involved, and that we'll need an experienced payload specialist – preferably an astronaut. Flinders reckons that NASA will provide us with an astronaut at a price. He said that opening a full-sized pallet needs an experienced astronaut as the payload specialist in case he has to go EVA.'

'EVA?'

'Extra-vehicular activity. Spacewalking.'

Sarcha accelerated to pass a dawdling Ford. 'I don't like the sound of that. I mean – a NASA guy's not going to arm and deploy four missiles for us.'

'Precisely.'

The florid little Englishman suddenly looked very worried. 'And don't you dare ask me to go spacewalking. I suffer from agoraphobia and cowardice.'

Heinlein looked thoughtful. 'There's too much at stake to entrust anything too difficult to you anyway . . . .'

'Nice to be appreciated.'

' . . . So it looks as if we've got to find our own astronaut. Someone who's retired or who has set up his own space consultancy business. Just so long as he's on our payroll.'

'That's not going to be easy.'

'Everything's been a piece of cake so far.'

'I know,' Sarcha remarked. 'That's what's worrying me. We've still got to get hold of those missiles, *and* ship them to this country.'

'One problem at a time, Sarcha – that's going to be the secret of this operation's success. One problem at a time – one solution at a time.'

48   A warm breeze from the Atlantic instead of the cloying furnace-like heat of summer was bringing Florida a welcome taste of winter.

Neil ducked out from under the yawning bonnet of the stranded woman's elderly Jaguar and slammed it shut. He massaged his aching back muscles through his coveralls.

'That's it, Mrs Simmons. She's done.'

145

'I'm so grateful, I just don't know what to say,' Mrs Simmons exclaimed.

'Just count yourself lucky we had the parts in stock,' said Neil, wiping his greasy fingerprints off the car's chromework.

'I never thought I'd be so lucky to find somewhere on a Sunday,' said Mrs Simmons. 'I'll tell all my friends to come here for their petrol.' She was a very large, very refined Englishwoman. 'I told Peter it was silly importing the wretched thing but he insisted. How much do I owe you?'

'See Mr Jackson over there.' Neil nodded to the veranda where Jacko was watching TV pundits sounding off about Senator Harding's chances in the presidential election the following week.

Neil watched Mrs Simmons bearing down on Jacko like a Spanish galleon under a full spread of canvas, and he entered the Winnebago for a shower. His two weeks' work on the camper were virtually finished. He had moved it out of the workshop and parked it on some wasteland at the side of the filling station. He was awaiting delivery of a new turbine mounting from Daytona following his discovery that the old one was cracked.

Jacko shambled across to see him a few minutes later when he was making coffee. The old Negro could smell coffee even before the jar was opened.

'Nice timing, Jacko. Large or small?'

'Large please, Neil,' said Jacko, easing his creaking back gratefully into the driver's swivel seat.

'How much did you charge her?' asked Neil.

'Two hundred.'

'Crook.'

Jacko cackled and cupped his gnarled old hands around the mug that Neil gave him. 'Took you three hours. And it's a hundred off your rent.'

Neil sat opposite Jacko and sipped. They remained silent for a few moments.

'What's Lena doing?' Neil asked.

'Working.'

'Does she work every Sunday?'

'Every day. She wants to get on. I was took back when she went off with you to Titusville last Sunday. Never known her do that before.'

'It's just that I hadn't seen a launch for some days,' said Neil absently.

Jacko shook his head sadly. 'You'd best forget all that, son.'

'Now don't you start, Jacko.'

'S'true. What's done is done. No good trying to turn back the clock.'

Something Jacko had said earlier had aroused Neil's curiosity. 'You've never known Lena do what before?'

Jacko gave one of his toothy grins. 'Drop some urgent work to go out with a feller. Reckon she must think something of you.'

Neil laughed abruptly. 'Every time I try to be serious, she goes into that cotton-picking voice routine of hers like she's putting up one big "off limits" sign.'

'Give her time.'

'I don't have time. That turbine mounting will be through tomorrow. Then I'll have to head north, looking for a job.'

'You could always stay,' said Jacko, draining his mug.

Neil stared at him. 'How do you mean?'

'You turned over four hundred dollars last week on them casual repairs. Set it all up proper and that four hundred dollars could be double. Maybe even triple.'

Neil gaped at Jacko in astonishment. 'Me? Become a car mechanic?'

'Why not? You got hands, you got brains, and you gotta workshop.'

'Correction – you've got the workshop.'

'OK – so I rent you the repair franchise. Business is gonna climb through the roof with all them new condos popping up. You ever fix a shuttle on all them flights?'

'How do you mean?'

'You ever go spacewalking with a wrench?'

'Sure. I've lost count.'

'OK – so there's your sign to put up – big photograph of a spaceman and underneath: "I've fixed spacebirds so your car won't be no problem."'

Neil suddenly burst out laughing. 'Jacko – you're crazy.'

The old Negro climbed unsteadily to his feet and hobbled to the doorway. As he lowered himself down the camper's steps, he turned and said to Neil, 'You think I'm crazy if you like, but you think on what I've said.'

'Yes – but what would Lena say?'

'Was her idea.'

With that Jacko shuffled back to his veranda and portable TV set leaving Neil lost in thought.

49 In Jerusalem the first item on the agenda of Rymann's morning Cabinet meeting was not the first night-time bombing raids made by the PLO when they had attacked and destroyed the oil pumping stations at Herzlia and Haifa, but the previous day's victory of Senator Harding during the US presidential election.

The disappointing but expected result was reviewed by a group that was hardened to dealing with gloomy news. But the success of Senator Harding meant a certain end of Israel's already slim hope of obtaining a desperately needed massive increase in US military aid. Throughout the whole convoluted process of the American presidential election campaign, the only reference the Wyoming senator had made to the conflict in the Middle East was in answer to a question fired by a Jerusalem journalist who wanted to know if the senator had any plans to help Israel. Harding had brushed the question aside by saying that he, in common with the American people, had enough confidence in Israel's military prowess to appreciate that additional US interference would be an unwarranted incursion into Israel's affairs.

'OK,' said Rymann, winding-up the item. 'I favour a low-key approach to Harding for the time being.' He turned to Foreign Minister Samuel Kuttner. 'Harding named his administration before the election, didn't he? Who's going to be his Secretary of State?'

'Walter Swift – New Jersey.'

'Sum him up in a few words,' Rymann ordered, mindful of Kuttner's ability to ramble.

'Devious and dangerous,' Kuttner obliged.

'Friendly, hostile, or neutral?'

'I don't know.'

Rymann resisted saying, well you damn well should know. As a student of history, he knew that such attacks invariably led to leaders being fed inaccurate or optimistic information by their ministers. Rymann knew the value of hearing honest answers rather

148

than what his ministers and advisors thought he wanted to hear. He thought for a moment. 'Right now everyone will be beating a path to Swift's door. Nevertheless, get our embassy to make the necessary approaches immediately to fix up a meeting as soon as possible between you and Swift. Meanwhile we'll keep Harding off our Cabinet agendas until you've reported back.'

The meeting moved on to a discussion on the worsening situation, in particular the ugly turn of events suggested by the PLO's sudden switch to night bombing.

'What worries me,' said Rymann, 'is that the raid was a success. For their first attempt, one would have expected something to go wrong. And why weren't the air-raid sirens sounded?'

'Like everyone else the *Chel Ha'Avir* was caught unawares,' Ben Irving freely admitted. 'For the past seven nights a flight of three Tupolevs have approached us from the east. We've always monitored them warming up their engines at Bakal and we've always sent up six Sharavs to intercept them when they were within a hundred miles of the coast. The Sharavs can't reach the Tupolev's ceiling but at least we've always let them know that we were there. Until now the Tupolevs have always turned back for home within fifty miles of the coast. This time they didn't. Our ground and airborne search radar is useless against the Tupolevs because their ECM jamming wipes it out. Our pilots used their infra-red heat-seeking equipment to look for the raiders where they thought they'd be. It's a mistake that one can't blame them for.'

'I agree,' said Rymann. 'But it must not happen again.'

'Unless we can get hold of the new US micro-millimetre radar, it *will* happen again,' was Irving's candid reply. 'We haven't a cat in hell's chance of countering the Soviet broad-band ECM equipment.'

'Do you have any suggestions?'

'Yes. We arm our Massadas with low-yield warheads and use them as airburst weapons against those bastards next time they come in from the Med.'

There was a complete hush in the room. Greer removed his glasses and polished them.

'You know my views on using the Massada, Ben,' said Rymann, breaking the silence.

'And you know mine, Prime Minister. The view that Israel should not be the first to introduce nuclear weapons into the

149

Middle East was one that I agreed with. Someone once said that a wise man changes his mind and a fool never. Well I've changed my mind about using the Massadas. I'm talking about clean, one-kilotonne airbursts at a height of thirty miles – that's the altitude those Tupolevs come in at, and that's a height the Massada can reach easily. No one will even hear them detonating. And I am only talking about the attacks from the Med. Deploying the Massada has a number of advantages. Firstly, we hit those bloody bombers – so far they've been getting away unscathed. Secondly, using the Massadas in this way entails no danger to civilians. Thirdly, our use of them will bring home to the Americans just how desperate our situation is. There'll be an outburst of world criticism –'

'That's an understatement,' Greer cut in.

Ben Irving turned his granite features on the head of Mossad. 'OK. What if there is an outcry? We can point out with more than enough justification that our options are being eroded. That'll frighten a few governments who are supposed to be our so-called bloody friends.'

Rymann glanced across at Greer and wondered if he was behind Ben Irving's sudden about-face on the use of nuclear weapons, even on a limited tactical scale such as he was now proposing. Greer caught Rymann's look. As if guessing exactly what his Prime Minister was thinking, he gave an almost imperceptible shake of his head.

Kuttner started waffling about the use of nuclear weapons making the position of his diplomatic staffs around the world untenable.

'Right now the PLO are making our position untenable,' Rymann observed drily. 'I believe we should give serious consideration to the Commander-in-Chief's proposals.'

'I'm opposed to any large-scale mobilization of the Massadas,' said Irving. 'As they come on their own launch platforms in units of four, I suggest that we deploy one transporter with four missiles for the time being.'

The meeting dispersed a few minutes before midday leaving Rymann and Greer alone in the Cabinet office. Rymann let out a long sigh.

'I had no part in it, Hendrik,' said Greer. 'I was as surprised as you.'

Rymann chuckled. 'To think I thought we'd have a major battle on our hands convincing him. Great minds think alike.'

'But not always for the same reasons,' Greer pointed out.

'True, Michael. Very true.'

50 The project office that the University of Surrey had leased to the Stavolos European Space Research Foundation overlooked the clean room where a party of technicians were dismantling the *Cyclops* satellite.

Sir Max Flinders watched the huge solar panels being carefully lowered to the ground by an electric hoist. Heinlein was explaining the duties required of a secretary sent that morning by a Guildford employment agency. The office was strewn with the packaging materials from a new word processor that had just been delivered.

'Know something, Heinlein?' Flinders boomed. 'I have to keep pinching myself to tell myself that it's not a dream. I just can't believe that it's really happening.'

Heinlein left the secretary to experiment with the word processor and stood beside the scientist's bulk and watched the activity taking place below. The technicians had been working for three days, carefully removing all the observatory's system modules for cleaning, testing and recalibration in various laboratories. The work was proceeding in accordance with a schedule that Flinders had drawn-up during a sleepless forty-eight-hour period. There was another three weeks' dismantling work still to be carried out, but preliminary reports indicated that the huge satellite was in good shape.

'When do you leave for Kennedy?' asked Flinders.

'That depends on NASA's reactions to our initial approach,' Heinlein replied.

Flinders gave a throaty chuckle. 'With the sort of money we're going to spend? They're sure to be slightly enthusiastic.'

'That's what I thought. I think it best if you sign the first letter to the director of the Kennedy Space Center.'

'It'll make Jason Pelham's day. It's not often that someone buys up an entire mission.'

The two men watched the men working below.

'What are the chances of bringing the satellite's readiness date forward?' Heinlein ventured. 'Does it really need another three months' work?'

Flinders grunted. 'We're lucky it's only three months. If the Newtonian mirror had become pitted in this damp atmosphere, it would've taken six months to have it stripped and repolished. Anyway, I don't suppose you'd be able to book a shuttle flight much before April – another five months. That's assuming that this new American president doesn't change everything.'

'Harding is unlikely to interfere with the space programme,' Heinlein replied, no longer surprised by the scientist's political naïvety. He had discovered that Sir Max Flinders lived an insular life that was totally devoted to his university to the exclusion of all else. The only politics Sir Max ever concerned himself with were those of the academic jungle in which he was the master of survival.

Sarcha entered the office carrying a heavy box. 'The stationery,' he announced.

Flinders made his excuse and left.

Heinlein examined one of the sheets of notepaper. It was headed: THE STAVOLOS EUROPEAN SPACE RESEARCH FOUNDATION, University of Surrey, Stag Hill, Guildford, Surrey. Chairman: Sir Max Flinders, Vice-Chancellor, University of Surrey. At the foot of the page were nine of the most prestigious names in the field of science together with Heinlein's name as chief executive.

'Impressive, eh?' said Sarcha, grinning.

'Very,' said Heinlein. He turned to the secretary. 'Is the word processor working?'

The girl's cheeks dimpled. 'Yes, sir.'

'Then there's no reason why we shouldn't start work now.'

51 Ten days later Heinlein and Sarcha flew into Miami Airport at noon. After a wearisome hour being processed through US immigration and customs controls, they identified themselves at the information desk where a NASA driver was waiting for them.

'We've booked you into a suite at the Oceanfront Holiday Inn at Cocoa Beach,' the driver explained as he loaded their baggage into

152

the boot of a Cadillac. 'It's on the ocean, just south of the space centre. Mr Pelham will be pleased to meet you tomorrow morning.'

'That'll be fine,' said Heinlein.

A few minutes later they were speeding northwards out of Miami on the five-lane US 1. Sarcha opened a window and immediately closed it again as the hot air hit him like a blast of dragon's breath.

'Hell,' he muttered accusingly to Heinlein. 'You didn't say it could be like this in December.'

'I didn't know myself,' said Heinlein curtly. He opened his briefcase and starting reading various booklets and papers on NASA's shuttle operations. They were the same documents that he had studied during most of the four-hour flight from London.

After a long and monotonous drive the car turned into the palm-fringed forecourt of the Oceanfront Holiday Inn. NASA had seen to it that Heinlein and Sarcha received VIP treatment: they were shown into a magnificent third-floor double suite with adjoining doors that had a panoramic view of the Atlantic.

'Nice,' Sarcha commented, eyeing naked female flesh strewn temptingly about the beach. 'What must it be like in the summer I ask myself? So, what's the schedule for the rest of the day?'

Heinlein picked up the telephone and dialled room service. 'We eat. A drink at the bar. And then we sleep.'

'No nightspots?'

'No nightspots.'

'But it's early.'

'It's late. Your body clock is five hours ahead of local time. We've a busy day tomorrow, so get plenty of sleep.'

'But my body clock can cope with anything if it's well-oiled,' Sarcha protested.

'I say we rest. Understand?'

'Yes, chief,' said Sarcha sadly.

His gloom was interrupted by a deep, reverberating roar that sounded like distant thunder. Both men stared at each other and raced for the balcony. Heinlein yanked the sliding door open and the sound hit them like a solid wall. To the north a huge tongue of brilliant crimson-gold fire of an intensity that almost hurt the eyes was lancing into the sky.

'A shuttle!' Sarcha shouted, his eyes popping in wonder. 'Dear God – are there men on top of that?'

The apex of the monstrous expanding pyramid of smoke and

153

flame arrowed into the cloudbase and disappeared. The skull-oscillating thunder continued and the clouds themselves glowed with a strange light from the fragment of mobile hell they were hosting. Gradually the fire and thunder faded. A flock of pelicans drifted past the balcony as if nothing had happened. The girls on the beach returned to their posturing for the benefit of the men, and the men returned to their surfing and ball games for the benefit of the girls.

'Will you be going up?' asked Sarcha.

Heinlein continued staring for some moments at the point in the sky where the shuttle had vanished. 'It's more than likely,' he said.

The next day NASA laid on the red carpet treatment for Heinlein. The car called for him at 10 a.m. and whisked him north through Port Canaveral and across the causeways that traversed the flat, reclaimed swamplands of the Kennedy Space Center's sprawling three hundred square miles on Merritt Island. Rising above the wilderness of lagoons and citrus groves were numerous launch pad gantries. Some were in use but most of them were ancient structures – relics of a bygone, high-spending era – and were being allowed to rust away in the humid Florida atmosphere. Dominating the skyline was the box-like shape of Complex 39's Vehicle Assembly Building. The literature that Heinlein had read about NASA on the flight the day before said that the VAB was one of the largest buildings in the world: a statement that was hard to believe until, in answer to a query, the driver pointed out that it was still five miles away.

A small deputation led by Jason Pelham was waiting for Heinlein outside the administrative offices in the industrial complex. He shook hands all round and was introduced to Earl Hackett.

'Earl is Director of the Shuttle Exploitation Program,' Pelham explained once they were seated in a conference room. 'He'll be dealing with the processing of this remarkable application of yours.' Pelham smiled broadly. For the benefit of major paying customers, he had the ability to conjure up a charm that was otherwise non-existent. 'We've fixed up an itinerary for you. A two-hour tour of the centre followed by lunch when we can get down to some detailed discussions.'

Despite his impatience to get started, Heinlein could hardly fail to enjoy his tour of the Kennedy Space Center. He was particularly

154

interested in the vast Vehicle Assembly Building where two shuttles were being assembled on the gigantic land crawlers that would transport them to their respective launch pads. The building was mind-bending in its vastness. It was so large that, during its early days, before the air-conditioning was working, clouds forming inside had led to miniature rainstorms. Heinlein paused on one level within the building to watch NASA technicians loading small cargo pallets into the open cargo bay of an orbiter.

'Supplies for the orbital hospital,' Hackett explained in answer to Heinlein's question.

'Who packs the commercial pallets? You or the satellite owners?'

'We do now,' said Hackett. 'We've had a number of instances when lift-off acceleration has caused a pallet's contents to jam up. On one occasion an astronaut going EVA was unable to free several instrument packages from inside a pallet. He couldn't close the pallet which meant that it had to be abandoned in orbit.'

The three men left the VAB in an electric car. Lying on its side outside, like a felled colossus, was a complete Apollo-Saturn V space vehicle.

'That's one exhibit we wouldn't have if the last moon missions in the Apollo programme hadn't been axed,' Hackett observed as the party paused to study the corroding behemoth.

The tour ended and the three men adjourned to Alma's Italian restaurant on Cocoa Beach for lunch.

'I take it you took advantage of our authorization to Brevard County Bank to disclose our financial status to you?' enquired Heinlein, spiralling spaghetti on to his fork.

'Of course,' Pelham replied.

'So how much is a dedicated mission going to cost our trust?'

Pelham stirred his soup and considered. 'We did some preliminary estimating when we received Sir Max's letter. It will be in the region of one hundred and sixty million dollars. The exact figure will be agreed between us when we draw up the contract, but we will require a one per cent returnable deposit from you – say, one decimal five million dollars – so that we can proceed with the preliminary work.'

'The amount being credited against the final bill?' Heinlein queried.

'Of course.'

The waiter cleared the table of the first course dishes.

'I've studied all your general terms in some detail,' said Heinlein. 'They seem reasonable. But there's one thing the trust insists on. We shall require to load *Cyclops* into the pallet ourselves, at the University of Surrey. That means the sections of your largest cargo pallet will have to be flown to England.'

'I'm sorry,' said Hackett, shaking his head. 'But that won't be possible. We have to load the pallet.'

'Why can't we do it?'

'For the reasons we gave you in the VAB,' said Pelham frostily.

'We don't mean any disrespect,' said Hackett hastily. 'But those full-sized cargo pallets distort easily if they're incorrectly packed. If it jammed in the orbiter's hold during the mission, we'd be placing the crew at risk. The orbiter won't be able to re-enter and land with a payload of *Cyclops*' weight. The payload has to be left in orbit.'

'In that case,' said Heinlein with finality, 'there can be no deal. Sir Max is insisting that the University of Surrey undertakes the stowing of *Cyclops* into its pallet.'

'Mr Heinlein – we've put thousands of payloads into orbit –'

'Not many the size of *Cyclops*.'

'Maybe not. But we've had no problems with the various spacelabs. And the orbital hospital consisted of twenty sections that required twenty missions –'

'Hold on. Hold on,' Pelham intervened. 'Maybe we can work out a compromise here . . . . David, supposing we fly a team of our technicians to the UK with the pallet sections to advise on the *Cyclops*' stowing? How does that grab you?'

Heinlein allowed a decent interval to elapse during which he pretended to contemplate Pelham's suggestion. He was secretly delighted because it was exactly what he had been about to suggest himself.'

'I think that's an excellent idea, Jason,' said Heinlein, reverting to the American custom of using first names from the beginning of an acquaintanceship.

'At your expense, of course,' Pelham added.

'Of course,' Heinlein agreed.

Pelham nodded complacently. One hundred and sixty million dollars was safely in the bag. He raised his glass of wine. 'That's great, David. Just great.'

52 Heinlein arrived back at the Holiday Inn before Sarcha. He spent some minutes catching up on the news on the television. The major story was the resignation of President Marshall following a heart attack and the bringing forward of President-elect Harding's inauguration. His reflection on how the news would be received in Israel reminded him to make another of his long-distance phone calls. He emerged from the bathroom with a towel around his middle just as Sarcha entered the suite and flopped sweating into a chair. The news item on the television had switched to President-elect Harding outlining the policies of his new administration to a team of newsmen. It was a broadcast that the station's programme planners decided not to break up with interminable commercials for children's Christmas presents.

Heinlein opened two cans of beer from the refrigerator and gave one to Sarcha. 'Well?' he enquired.

'What an absolutely bloody climate this is. Give me Israel any day.'

'I'll give you something extremely painful in a minute if you don't stop wingeing,' Heinlein warned.

Sarcha pulled a sheaf of papers from his pocket and tossed it on the table. 'The names and addresses of thirty payload specialist companies. I used a Cocoa Beach private detective, Matt Connors. It's not complete. He's promised to stop by with the full list tomorrow morning.'

Heinlein skimmed through the list and turned to a tenancy agreement on an office suite in Titusville.

'I've looked at about twenty places,' said Sarcha, toeing his shoes off while sipping his beer. 'The Titusville one is the best. Ground floor. Parking. A bar next door. We've taken out a one-year lease. I've purchased a load of office equipment that arrives tomorrow. I've found a signwriter, called the phone company and bought some model space hardware to pretty-up the window display.'

'Excellent, Sarcha. So we now have a Florida base.'

'We need someone to run it. I've not had time to get round to advertising for staff. What sort of day have you had?'

157

Heinlein outlined his meeting with Jason Pelham and Earl Hackett concluding with: 'All we need now is a payload specialist.'

'What? Right away?'

'Apparently so. He or she will have to liase with NASA on all day-to-day technical matters right from the word go. NASA say that it's essential with a payload the size and complexity of *Cyclops* that we use an experienced astronaut. They've given me a list of specialist astronauts on their books that they've got on tap. I'd sooner find someone for ourselves. We don't want a company and we don't want someone who's on NASA's payroll.' Heinlein paused and looked at his watch. 'Is your investigator working now?'

'He said he'd work through the night for the expenses we're paying him.'

'OK. Call him up now and tell him we want a retired astronaut – something like that. Someone who could use some extra money. Someone whose first loyalty will be to us.'

Heinlein spent the next few days locked in contractual negotiations with NASA while Sarcha concentrated on getting the liaison office at Titusville organized. Once the office equipment was installed, he interviewed several girls for the post of secretary. None was suitable although he did hire a word processor operator to handle the correspondence that Heinlein was generating.

He was filing copies of letters when Matt Connors, the private investigator, looked in with his latest list of astronauts.

'Three possibles for you there, Sarcha,' said Connors, dropping the list on a desk and his lanky frame into a chair, 'William Zabranski – forty-five. Runs a small plant in Cocoa that turns out experimental clothing for NASA. Not doing too well because his wife's drinking her way through his profits. Alaric Silkin – thirty-nine. Threw in his job when NASA axed the work he was doing on the runway take-off and powered landing shuttle. Runs a door-to-door video tape service in Orlando. Works thirty hours a day paying off a loan to cover a fine for handling tapes you wouldn't want your kids to see.'

'They all look as useless as ever,' Sarcha observed caustically.

Connors shrugged. 'Down-and-out ex-astronauts aren't that thick on the ground.'

158

'I didn't say we wanted a down-and-out ex-astronaut. Just one who could do with some extra income.'

'So what's the difference?'

Sarcha studied a press cutting clipped to the list beside the last name. 'Neil O'Hara,' he read out. 'Blamed by a review board for the death of another astronaut. For Chrissake, Matt – you do find them.'

The private investigator grinned. 'Had more trouble finding him than any of the others. He might be what you're looking for. His house at Melbourne has been sold because his marriage broke up. His wife and kids went back to Houston. She left an address with a former neighbour. I contacted her in Houston and she told me that her husband was running the auto repair franchise at a filling station somewhere between Daytona and Orlando. That's all she knew because he hadn't given her a number when he called her. Took me all yesterday to track him down. He fixed a window motor on my car. Made a good job of it too. He's smart. Good with his hands. Got a lot of business coming in, he told me. Thirty-two shuttle missions. Ten spacewalks. He's the youngest ex-astronaut I've found but he's one of the most experienced – and he's only been out of NASA a few weeks.'

'Yes, but NASA are going to howl if we propose a payload specialist that was crucified by a review board,' Sarcha pointed out.

Connors looked indifferent. 'Maybe. Maybe not. But I did come across a rumour that O'Hara wasn't entirely to blame for the accident. There was talk of a cover-up but I didn't delve too deep.'

'Why not?'

'You paid me to find names and addresses – not go chasing rumours.'

'We're paying you now,' said Sarcha, making an uncharacteristic snap decision. 'Find out all you can about Neil O'Hara.'

53 Deep underground in the audio monitoring room at the *Chel Ha'Avir* airbase at Herzlia, Sergeant Alana Bader heard a new sound in her headphones. The noise print was duplicated as a glowing pattern on her visual display unit. She reached for two control knobs and made some minor adjustments.

At Gaza and Acre, batteries of highly sensitive directional microphones shifted their positions in response to her commands so that their converging 'area of interest' intersected even more precisely on the PLO's base eight hundred miles to the north at Bakal. All Alana's telemetry data was transmitted by fibre-optic landline or microwave links; there were no spurious radio frequency emissions from Israeli military signals traffic to be picked up by eavesdropping satellites.

A computer had analysed the industrial uproar from both microphone arrays – trains, ships, traffic – and had filtered them all out with the exception of one sound within a specified pattern that was being received simultaneously by both microphone arrays. That sound was the shrill whine of jet engines warming up.

Alana's fingers danced over her keyboard, instructing the computer to match the sound with the 'fingerprint' recordings in its memory. Alana identified the sound a split second before the computer. It was exactly the same sound that she had heard at the same time on previous nights. An 'option' appeared at the bottom right-hand corner of her screen:

ORIGIN: BAKAL

SOURCE: SOVIET KUZNETSOV NK-201 JET ENGINES
   AT 25 PER CENT POWER

QUANTITY: 6

AIRCRAFT: PROBABILITY 90 PER CENT 3 TUPOLEV
   V-G LONG-RANGE BOMBERS

As Alana watched the screen, the curiously compressed whining noise rose in frequency and the figure that showed the engines' power output changed to thirty per cent. She pressed her red talk key, the priority key that alerted the operations room.

'AMR Monitor Bader,' she reported. 'I have three Tupolevs warming up their engines at Bakal.'

Rymann rolled Semona's left nipple between his teeth and made her squeal in delight. His lips then proceeded to track determinedly across her olive skin and got as far as her naval when the telephone rang. He groaned and pretended not to hear it.

'Phone,' Semona giggled.

'Did I ever tell you that just touching you makes bells ring?'

Semona laughed and reached for the handset. Rymann panicked

160

and snatched it up before she touched it. He listened for a moment and became very tense. 'Right. I'll be down in two minutes.'

He slammed down the handset, gave Semona a quick peck and battled his way into his tangled pyjama trousers.

'Don't be long,' said Semona as he headed for the door, still thrusting his arms into a dressing-gown.

Rymann paused at the door and looked back at the impossibly beautiful girl decorating his bed. His eyes were alive and gleaming with the light of battle. 'I won't be,' he promised. 'Tonight we're going to nail the bastards. And then we'll celebrate.'

As soon as the lift reached ground level, the driver gunned his engine and sent the Massada transporter roaring out of the bunker. He drove through the gap in the anti-blast embankment and on to the tarmac, parking near the airbase's perimeter fence, facing the sea. Four men scrambled out of the vehicle and aimed the microwave control dish on the cab roof at a similar dish on the airbase's flight control blockhouse. With communications established and checked, the servicemen waited for further orders.

Two minutes later Hendrik Rymann's voice said in their headphones: 'You are cleared to arm weapon.'

'Prime Minister's voice confirmed,' stated the synthesized voice of a computer in the men's headphones once Rymann's voice had been voiceprint analysed.

One of the Massada technicians set to work. Arming the nuclear warhead was a straightforward operation; it merely involved opening a panel and setting a four-digit combination. The Massada had been designed for the utmost simplicity of operation. Improvements in communications, especially voiceprint analysis technology which enabled the missile crew to be certain that their instructions were being issued by the Prime Minister, made obsolete many of the complex and sometimes counter-productive failsafe arming procedures of earlier decades. More complicated was the procedure for setting the Massada's celestial/inertial navigation computer. That could not be undertaken until more information was available on the target. The technician closed the panel. He and his colleagues returned to the missile transporter's cab and pressed the button that elevated the heatshield that would protect them from the Massada's blast when it was fired. They

161

waited, listening to the messages flowing back and forth between the operations block-house and the Combat Control Centre at Tel Aviv.

'They're following their usual pattern,' Irving told Rymann as the two men watched the three blips on the giant liquid-crystal wall-screen map that displayed all aircraft movements in the eastern Mediterranean. 'They'll head south-west across the Black Sea, skirt Turkish airspace and then swing eastwards towards us. Once they've reached their operational altitude east of Crete, they'll switch on their ECM equipment and we'll lose them. That's what usually happens.'

Rymann switched off his headset microphone so that his voice would not be picked up and asked Irving what speed the raiders were travelling at.

'Mach two and increasing,' the *Chel Ha'Avir* Commander-in-Chief replied.

'Massada armed and standing by,' a staff officer reported.

The two men watched intently as the menacing blips traversed the Aegean Sea. Behind them, in the softly lit communications room, men and women were sitting at consoles, monitoring the signals traffic between all the command centres and the Combat Control Centre. A digital display at the foot of the liquid-crystal screen indicated that the targets had reached a hundred and fifty thousand feet. The order went out to 101 Squadron to scramble six Sharav fighters.

'Our response pattern is the same as for the previous attacks,' Irving explained. 'We don't want our friends to think that tonight might be different from any other night.'

The blips cleared the Aegean Sea and turned eastwards towards Israel. They remained on the screen for a couple of minutes, edging purposefully towards their target, and then disappeared.

'Contact lost. They've activated their ECM systems,' a voice reported from the back of the room. 'At last fix targets were bearing two-seven-five, flight level one-six-four-zero. Range six-two-nine kilometres.'

'CCC state they have enough data for way-point loading,' another voice reported.

'Go for way-point loading and detonation altitude setting,' Irving ordered.

162

The setting commands for the Massada's guidance system were signalled to the technicians in the missile's transporter cab. Keying in the way points on to a portable console that would guide the Massada and determine the height at which its nuclear warhead would explode took a matter of seconds.

'Missile loaded and ready,' one of the technicians reported.

From now on it was up to the computers. Working on data that was subject to 'decay' – that is, the last-known height, course and speed of the raiders – they took over the Massada's launch countdown.

'What are the chances of the Tupolevs altering course?' Rymann asked.

'Low,' Irving growled. 'The cocky bastards have always come in dead straight when we've optically-tracked them on daylight raids.'

'LT minus fifty seconds,' advised a computer voice.

The seconds ticked by.

'LT minus forty seconds.'

Rymann switched his microphone to active. His voice alone was now the only one that the fire-control computers would recognize. All he had to do was utter the single word 'abort' and the Massada launch would be cancelled. He remained silent, his eyes riveted on the digital display that was winking through the passing seconds.

'LT minus twenty seconds.'

Rymann realized that the palms of his hands were sweating. He wiped them on his dressing-gown. It was too late to re-examine the philosophy of the attack they were about to launch. The endless Cabinet and Emergency Defence Committee debates had worn everyone down. If the attack was successful, the international political storm that was certain to break as a result of Israel's use of nuclear weapons would outweigh the military advantage of three enemy bombers destroyed. But as Rymann glanced around at the silent, expectant faces, he realized that after the long catalogue of defeats, Israel's ever-willing armed services badly needed this one small victory. If there was to be one, that is.

'LT minus ten seconds.'

Irving shot a quick look at Rymann to see if there was any weakening of his Prime Minister's resolution. What he saw was reassuring – Rymann's features were a hard, expressionless mask.

'LT minus five seconds. Four . . . . Three . . . .

The missile crew in the transporter pulled on their ear defenders and braced themselves. One of them misquoted a line in Hebrew from Isaiah: 'For Zion's sake I will not hold my peace.'

'Two . . . . One . . . .'

The Massada's rocket motor suddenly vented its pent-up energies against the shield. It sprang into life with a suddenness that caused the entire transporter to shudder. Despite the ear defenders the missile crew were wearing, the mighty thunder pummelled their senses. There was a mighty jolt from the transporter's suspension caused by its abrupt relief from the load it had been supporting.

'Missile away!'

The crew piled out of the cab. For a moment there was nothing to see in the midst of the dense, swirling clouds of acrid fumes from the missile's solid-fuel rocket motor. And then they saw it: a brilliant comet boring a trail of fiery, rapidly diminishing light and thunder into the night sky.

Rymann, Irving and everyone else in the room watched the infra-red trail from the Massada's exhaust gases track across the liquid-crystal screen. A voice intoned the weapon's rapidly changing height and range but no one was listening – all were watching for the sudden burst of heat and light that signified the warhead's detonation.

The sun that flared briefly that night thirty miles above the Mediterranean was seen by fishermen. It was witnessed in Cyprus and as far south as Alexandria. Satellites also saw it. But those instruments saw far more than the visible light spectrum; they saw the radiation of a nuclear airburst and they obediently radioed their findings back to their masters.

'We've got them!' a jubilant voice yelled. 'Their ECM's gone dead!'

It was true. The giant liquid-crystal screen was suddenly showing a scattering of curious radar echoes.

'Debris,' breathed Irving. 'By the prophets! We've done it!'

Rymann's hand was suddenly seized and pumped furiously by a triumphant Ben Irving. Normally phlegmatic operations personnel were on their feet, cheering and clapping each other on the back.

Meanwhile, a silent rain of wreckage – wings, engines, bits of fuselage – and people, was drifting down towards an unmarked grave beneath the moonlit sheen of the Mediterranean thirty miles below.

54 'Could we see Mr O'Hara please?' Heinlein asked Lena.

The black girl glanced at the dark-haired man and his chubby companion sitting in the Cadillac and decided that they looked reasonably respectable. 'Sure,' she said. 'Won't be a minute.'

'Wow,' and Sarcha appreciatively, watching Lena's thigh muscles rippling provocatively as she disappeared into the filling station's workshop. 'Bloody hell, it must take her an hour to get into those shorts. If O'Hara's in the habit of sitting on that nest, a million dollars won't drag him off.'

'I suspect it will,' said Heinlein acidly. 'She must be Lena Jackson. If Connors is right, she's got business ability. We could always buy her as well. After all, we need someone to run the office here.'

'A brilliant piece of thinking,' Sarcha congratulated.

'I'm incapable of anything else.'

Neil emerged from the workshop. 'Good morning,' he said suspiciously, eyeing the Cadillac and wondering if the strangers were more of Helen's lawyers hounding him for yet more blood.

'Mr O'Hara?'

'That's me.'

'Can we talk in private?'

Once settled in the Winnebago Heinlein came straight to the point. 'Mr O'Hara,' he said, sliding a business card across the table to Neil. 'I'm the chief executive of the Stavolos European Space Research Foundation and this is my general manager. We're planning a shuttle launch for next year of an astronomical research satellite and we need a payload specialist.'

Heinlein talked for five minutes, outlining the nature of the trust and the purpose of the satellite. Neil sat in silence, the colour draining from his face as the full import of Heinlein's offer sank in.

'Well, Mr O'Hara? Are you interested?'

Neil looked bewildered. 'Well – yes. But I don't know anything about you or your organization.'

Heinlein snapped open his briefcase and handed Neil a

pamphlet on the Stavolos trust. Neil was reading it when Lena's voice suddenly broke through the squelch on the camper's CB radio.

'Do you folks require coffee?'

Neil stopped reading and pulled down the microphone. 'Yes please, Lena.'

'We're prepared to offer you a one-year contract,' Heinlein continued when Neil released the microphone. 'Twenty-five thousand dollars per month plus expenses. The job will involve a good deal of travelling between Kennedy and Surrey University in the UK. Are you interested?'

Neil was about to say something and dried up.

'Well?' Heinlein prompted.

'A month ago I would've jumped at the chance. But now . . . . Well – right now I'm going through an expensive divorce and most of what I've got left I've sunk into buying this repair franchise.'

'We'll put a first-class mechanic in here to keep the business ticking over,' Heinlein offered. 'And we'll pay you three months' salary in advance.'

Neil was again at a loss for words. It was an unbelievably tempting offer. He shook his head sadly. 'There's something you should know. I left NASA under a cloud. I don't think they'd let me near an orbiter, even as a payload –'

'We know all about it,' said Heinlein smoothly. 'We also know that some astronauts are saying that the accident wasn't your fault – that there was a cover-up because Jason Pelham didn't want to shake the confidence of the group involved in the orbital hotel project.'

'Yes – but if NASA –'

There was a rap on the Winnebago's door. Lena entered bearing coffee.

'You must be Lena Jackson,' said Heinlein pleasantly, unable to avoid the temptation of allowing his gaze to take in the girl's long, bare legs.

'That's right,' said Lena, assuming that Neil had mentioned her. 'Do you all want cream?'

'Miss Jackson,' said Heinlein earnestly. 'We represent the Stavolos European Space Research Foundation.' He pushed the pamphlet across the table to Lena. 'I'd like you to read that please.'

Neil returned Lena's questioning glance with a shrug. She sat
166

down, read quickly through the leaflet and looked up at Heinlein. 'What's this got to do with me?'

'We're here to offer Neil a job, but we've heard about the accounts you look after for various stores, and we're wondering if you would like to take on the management of our NASA bureau.'

'How did you find out about us? About me?'

'We used an investigator.'

Lena's eyes burned. 'You used a private eye on me! Well of all the Goddamn nerve!' She jumped to her feet. 'Christ – I could sue you for invasion of privacy –'

'Please, Lena,' said Neil catching hold of her wrist. 'Hear them out. Please.'

'Why in hell should I? I don't like people –'

'*Please*, Lena.'

Lena hesitated and then relented. She sat down and glared at Heinlein.

'Firstly,' said Heinlein smoothly, 'we'll be spending several hundred million dollars over the next few years and therefore we have to vet our staff carefully. Secondly, all the investigator did was phone you when he saw your accountancy advert and you told him the sort of work you did and who your main clients were. And that's all. We want you to work for us and we want Neil to work for us. Now, do we have a sensible business discussion or don't we?'

'Smooth,' Sarcha commented on the drive back to Titusville. 'Two birds with one stone.'

'Do you think there's anything between them?' queried Heinlein, driving at a steady fifty-five in the centre lane.

'I don't know. But if there isn't, I wouldn't mind jumping in.'

'It would suit us if there *was*. Or if something develops.'

'Oh? Why?'

Heinlein sighed. 'You're a good operator, Sarcha, but sometimes you don't think. Consider the advantages of a situation in which he's up there with me, and you're down here with her.'

Sarcha considered and then chuckled. 'Good planning, David, me lad.'

'I'm incapable of anything else.'

55 Walter Swift's first task upon taking office as US Secretary of State in the Harding administration was to summon the Israeli ambassador to the State Department. Yaarcov Efrat knew the reason for the summons to C Street and was well prepared for the encounter.

'Excellency,' said Swift with deceptive mildness after the formal introductions. 'We have positive evidence that Israel has detonated a thermonuclear device in the ionosphere within the past forty-eight hours.'

'That is perfectly correct, Mr Secretary.'

'Why?'

'I'm sure what I have to say will merely confirm your own intelligence reports, but we took action to destroy enemy bombers that were about to attack our homeland. Israel is no longer prepared to be a sitting duck for Soviet and PLO aggression. We took the decision to use a low-yield tactical nuclear warhead against the raiders only after a painstaking investigation by our physicists. Their conclusion that levels of radioactivity produced would be harmless have been borne out by measurements we have made since the detonation. We are sure that the United States has made similar measurements and has reached the same conclusions.'

The Israeli's statement was true but Swift was not prepared to confirm it. 'Israel gave an undertaking that it would not be the first country to introduce nuclear weapons into the Middle East,' he pointed out.

'That was before we were subjected to almost daily raids by PLO bombers,' Efrat replied. 'Mr Secretary, we did not want to use such weapons – we have been pushed into it. We have no other means of countering these savage assaults on our people. The United States has refused to supply us with high-altitude interceptors, therefore we have been forced to use what resources we have.'

Swift looked displeased. 'Mr Efrat, if what you're saying is an attempt to push us into reviewing our arms' supply agreements, it won't work.'

The insinuation failed to rattle the experienced Israeli diplomat. He met Swift's bleak gaze and said simply: 'It was never intended

168

as such. The move has been forced upon us. Over two thousand civilians have been killed in the raids. No government can stand by and witness the slaughter of innocent men, women and children if it has the means to prevent such atrocities happening. We do have the means. We have used them. And we will use them again.'

And then Efrat followed with a statement that chilled Swift's blood. 'Mr Secretary, we are being driven into a dark, friendless corner. If our actions lead to a global holocaust, then so be it. The Children of Israel have nothing to lose.'

For the moment Swift had no answer ready.

'I believe,' said Efrat slowly, 'that a meeting between President Harding and my Prime Minister would be useful.'

It was starting to snow as Efrat left the Department of State in the company of his three bodyguards. They were US marines in plainclothes, their eyes everywhere except on their charge. 'Merry Christmas, sir,' said one of them, holding open the rear door of Efrat's Rolls-Royce.

Efrat stared blankly at him.

'It's Christmas Eve,' the marine explained.

56 'I'm opposed to their choice of O'Hara,' Jason Pelham declared emphatically to Earl Hackett. 'There's a clause in the contract that gives us the right to veto the client's choice of payload specialist. I want that clause exercised.'

As usual, Hackett was about to agree when he suddenly decided to stand his ground. This time he was not going to give in to Pelham. 'There is no valid reason why we should turn O'Hara down,' he answered.

Pelham's features tightened at this challenge to his authority from an unexpected quarter but his voice remained calm and matter-of-fact. 'If being found to be the cause of an astronaut's death isn't a valid reason, then I should like to know what is.'

Hackett did not flinch from the hard stare. 'There's a number of things I admire in you, Jason, and a lot of things I dislike. But I never thought that you had the ability to start believing your own distortions. We both know the truth about O'Hara. God knows, I've lost enough sleep as it is over his crucifixion. Well, now that he's got himself a decent job, I'm not going to be a party to kicking him down again.'

Not a muscle moved in Pelham's face. 'I've heard the rumours that have been circulating about O'Hara. Having him back working within the astronauts' office could be dangerous. If you're not prepared to veto him, then I shall find a shuttle exploitation director who is.'

The threat left Hackett unmoved. He had a new three-year contract under his belt. 'You do that, Jason, and not only will you have a grand-daddy of a lawsuit on your hands, but I'll be telling every pressman in the centre the full story about O'Hara. And I wouldn't like to stand too close to the fan when Congressman Williams discovers that evidence was deliberately withheld from his review board.'

Pelham's tone became even more icy but what he said amounted to a climbdown. 'Your feeble attempt at blackmail doesn't cut ice with me, Earl. But before we both lose our tempers, I think it would be best if we reviewed the situation within the next three days.'

As Earl Hackett returned to his office, he suddenly realized that he had won a round against Pelham. If he could win one round, there was no reason why he couldn't win the battle. His step became noticeably jaunty.

57 Immediately after Christmas, Lena threw herself enthusiastically into her new job. She organized the filing system, hired a competent stenographer, obtained Heinlein's authority to sign cheques up to a thousand dollars and settled the rapidly accumulating bills. She worked her way efficiently through the mountain of unanswered videotext messages and letters from the University of Surrey and she even pinned Heinlein down on his promise to hire a mechanic to look after Neil's automobile repair franchise. He agreed and she started advertising for candidates and interviewing applicants.

Neil's return to the Kennedy Space Center was marked by a warm handshake and a hearty backslap from Earl Hackett.

'Good to have you back, Neil. I expect you've got all the details
170

on the payload. We'll be sending a team over to the UK to advise on the satellite's palletization. Paul Quincy's eyeballed some hologram tapes of it but if you're going over there soon, maybe you could brief him in advance on any likely bugs?'

Neil spent the rest of the day going around the various facilities and renewing old friendships. Everyone he met – astronauts, ground crew, technicians – was pleased to see him again. No one mentioned Al's death and there was certainly no trace of rancour over the affair from anyone. He sensed that the undercurrent of contempt for Jason Pelham was still there – perhaps stronger than before – but tongues were guarded because Pelham had pulled off the orbital hotel coup that would guarantee many jobs for some years to come.

Neil returned to Titusville that afternoon at 3 p.m. and parked the Winnebago just as Lena was locking up the office. Gone were the tight jeans and T-shirt. Since taking over the office she had splashed out on a new wardrobe. Today it was a cashmere skirt and a white silk blouse.

'Did you know,' he observed as she turned around and nearly cannoned into him, 'that black is especially beautiful in silk? And extra specially beautiful in white silk. Did Tweedledum and Tweedledee get their flight?'

Lena giggled as she always did at Neil's use of his nicknames for Heinlein and Sarcha. 'They'll be in London by now. And I've booked for you to go next week. How did the black sheep's return to the fold go?'

'All it needs is for you to let me take you out tonight and I'll be able to say that it's been a perfect day.'

'OK. But I'd like to go home and freshen up first.'

Neil could hardly believe his luck. With the exception of their one trip together to watch a shuttle launch, all his previous overtures had met with refusals. Joking, lighthearted refusals but still refusals. Her excuse had always been her pressing workload. He jerked his thumb at the camper.

'Why drive all the way home? You could use that.'

'If you're planning on doing some of your cooking, forget it.'

'I was thinking of an expensive restaurant,' was Neil's lofty response. 'Anywhere you like. Tonight you're the boss.'

Lena gave an impish smile. 'OK. Vero's.'

He goggled at her in mock alarm. 'Vero's! What are you trying to do to me?'

'I'm the boss tonight,' Lena reminded him.

'Vero's it is,' said Neil resignedly, opening the camper's door for Lena. He patted her playfully as she sat in the passenger seat – the first time he had ever touched her in that manner. 'I figure you're worth the investment of one course – but no side salad, mind.'

Lena gave no indication that she objected to the pat. 'OK,' she said as Neil started the turbine. 'That's fine. I only want a double plate of lobster claws.'

'You're out to ruin me.'

'Why not, sugar?' Lena queried, lapsing into the phoney accent that Neil was beginning to find irritating. 'Ain't you out to a ruin me too?'

'What would you like to do first, boss?'

Lena thought. 'Well. It'll be dark soon. I've heard that EPCOT is fabulous at night. I've never been there. Have you?'

'I took the kids there once.' Neil broke off guiltily with the sudden realization that he had hardly thought about Andrew and Pippa for the past week. He hadn't even called Helen.

Lena sensed that something was wrong. 'What's the matter, Neil?'

He merged the camper into the traffic heading south. 'Nothing.' The reply was almost snapped out.

She decided not to press the matter. It wasn't until they were heading east on the Beeline Expressway that Neil spoke. He apologized for his abrupt answer.

'Forget it,' said Lena cheerfully.

Their conversation drifted around to Heinlein and Sarcha.

'An odd couple,' Neil agreed. 'Hey, you don't suppose the pair of them are gay?'

Lena laughed. 'Not the way Sarcha ogles me when he thinks I'm not looking. But he's strange. Really strange.'

'Tweedledee? How's that?'

'How much would you say he weighs?'

Neil thought. 'He's fat. About two hundred. Two-twenty.'

'That's right. And yet that fat little man can move like a ghost.'

Neil gave Lena a sidelong glance. 'He can what?'

'He can come into the office without making a sound. And the stairs up to the storeroom creak. Anyone goes up them and you know it. But not with Sarcha. He goes up and they don't make a sound. Don't you think that's weird?'

'I've known plenty of big men who were quiet on their feet,' Neil

172

replied sounding bored, not particularly interested in Lena's views on Sarcha. 'Watch out for the right to EPCOT.'

By the time they had spent three hours exploring the delights of Walt Disney's EPCOT complex, Neil's black mood had lifted.

It was a warm, balmy night and not too humid, so they ignored open-sided buses and the passenger boats and walked hand in hand around the lagoon, visiting shops in all the various miniature countries of the World Showcase that Disney's imaginers had created out of the swampland. Neil bought Lena a necklace in the English village and they drank draught beer at the Rose and Crown in the company of a crowd of noisy British tourists who had homed-in on the pub like moths to a lantern. Later they paused outside the pavement restaurant in Paris.

'As I'm the boss, I say we forget Vero's and eat here,' Lena declared excitedly.

They laughingly struggled with the menu and ate a meal that consisted of several delicious but unidentified dishes.

It was 10 p.m. when they neared the glowing giant geosphere of Bell System's Spaceship Earth that had dominated the entrance plaza to EPCOT for over a quarter of a century. Most of the queues waiting to visit the various pavilions had thinned out. Lena dragged Neil towards the shining edifice of the giant NASA pavilion.

'We haven't been in any of the pavilions,' she pointed out in answer to Neil's protests.

'If you see one, you'll want to see them all. They get you like that.'

'So what's the NASA one like?'

'I don't know. We didn't have time when I brought the kids.'

'Well let's find out,' said Lena decisively. 'You can show me what space is like.'

Neil laughed. 'It won't be anything like the real thing.'

He was wrong. The incredible special effects in the pavilion made it seem staggeringly like the real thing. Just as the British tourists had accepted the Rose and Crown as a genuine English pub, so Neil found himself accepting that the vision below was the real Earth viewed from a height of two hundred miles instead of very clever special effects that surpassed even the spectacle of Earth created in the shuttle flight simulators at Kennedy.

Looking around gave the vivid impression that the tiny open car

173

in which they were sitting was drifting in the awesome void surrounded by myriads of stars – a billion beacons of every conceivable colour shining out with an intensity never seen from the Earth's surface.

The car glided silently past giant satellites; huge, half-built space stations with seemingly life-size spacesuited figures working on their construction; and even a glass-sided replica of the orbital space hospital. So perfect were the details that it was possible to see surgeons at work in the micro-gravity operating theatre. The finale of the stunning journey was a beautiful moonrise: first a bulge in the great arc of the Earth's horizon and then the breathtakingly luminous glory of a crescent moon rising majestically against the stars – every detail stunningly perfect right down to the sunlight catching the peaks of the darkened mountains surrounding the mighty crater Clavius. The enchanted journey lasted twenty minutes. When it was over, when their car matched speed with the moving platform, Neil suddenly realized that Lena was gripping his hand tightly.

Both were silent as they walked out into the warm night.

'It was incredible,' Lena whispered as they walked back to the car park. 'Is space really like that?'

'Yes.'

'No wonder you're mad at them for what happened.'

Neil was silent for a moment. He put his arm around Lena's shoulders. 'Well, at least I'm going back now.'

On the drive back to Titusville Lena's conversation kept returning to the same subject. 'When I was looking down at the Earth – just a little ball of warmth and light – I kept thinking how stupid it is, having lots of different countries all fighting and quarrelling.'

Neil gave her a sharp, sidelong glance. 'It affects most astronauts like that.'

'Including you?'

There was a slight hesitation before Neil replied, which Lena noticed. 'Even me,' he admitted.

'Is it only that?'

Another hesitation. 'No.'

'Do you want to tell me?' Lena asked, sensing that she was venturing on to a sensitive topic.

Neil drove in silence for a while. 'With me it's a sort of defeatism.
174

Most of the time I feel that I just can't be bothered to argue and fight because everything seems so pointless. In some ways it's even worse than that. Going regularly into space makes some astronauts unable to cope with everyday problems. And the more they find that they can't cope, the more they need to go into space.'

'Is that why your marriage broke up?'

'One of the reasons. Yes, I suppose it was the main reason. I couldn't even be bothered to fight Helen when maybe the occasional row would've cleared the air. Later I let her lawyers walk all over me.'

Neil turned off the Beeline. He was about to head north when Lena suddenly said: 'It's a beautiful night for a walk. Let's go to the beach.'

'You're the boss,' said Neil, driving south.

He parked the camper at the edge of the coast road overlooking a lonely stretch of Satellite Beach. Together they walked along the sand stumbling occasionally over ruts carved by beach buggies. The wind had dropped. The night was hot and still and the only sound was the rollers booming themselves to a foam-white destruction.

Lena stopped in her tracks and started unbuttoning her blouse. 'Come on,' she ordered. 'We're going for a swim.'

'What?'

'Swimming. I'm the boss.'

The white blouse dropped to the sand. Neil had a tantalizing glimpse of her breasts as she turned away from him and unfastened her skirt. And then her body was a dark, almost invisible shape disappearing towards the ocean. 'Come on, chicken!' her voice yelled from the darkness.

Neil was out of his clothes in seconds and streaking after her. 'Hey, Lena!' he yelled splashing into the surf and nearly losing his balance when a wave crashed around him. 'Where are you? Lena!'

He spent some moments chasing after shadows and realized that when it came to a naked white guy racing around in the darkness after a naked black girl, the odds were in the girl's favour.

'Lena, where in hell are you!'

A giggle behind him, clearly audible above the rollers. He spun round. A pair of arms snaked around his neck, a pair of breasts flattened against his chest and Lena's lips fastened themselves to

175

his. He overbalanced and dragged her down with him. They clung to each other in the warm, surging tide, Lena moaning softly and arching her body against his caressing hand.

There is an old wives' tale about seventh waves. Neil didn't know or care whether it was a seventh wave, a seventieth wave, or even a sevenhundredth wave that had decided to pick on him. All he knew was that, at the precise moment he eased himself over Lena's willing body, it hit him in the small of the back like an express train and catapulted him, arms and legs flailing, over Lena and four yards further up the beach. Not content with depositing him on his head, the malevolent wall of water's encore at the end of its six thousand-mile journey was to fill his mouth with a mixture of sand and seawater. The same wave rolled Lena over several times but spared her much of the indignities it had heaped on Neil. She rose to her knees and promptly doubled-up with laughter at the sight of him of choking, spluttering and cursing.

'This never happened to Burt Lancaster and Deborah Kerr,' he moaned, wiping his mouth on his forearm as Lena hauled him to his feet.

'And what did they do?'

'Made love in the sea. An old movie I saw last week.' He grimaced and spat out some more grains of sand.

Lena pulled him close. 'I'm the boss – so show me.'

Neil's answe. was to pick her up and carry her towards the camper where there was a large, comfortable bed and where the rollers couldn't get at them.

58 Sarcha wasn't sure if he preferred the bleak, icy wind that whipped down the dark south London street to the warmer climes of Florida, but one thing he did know: he did not like having a gun jabbed into his ribs or, rather, jabbed into the fat that covered his ribs. Nor did he like the sound of the Irish accents belonging to the two heavies who were doing the jabbing. And he took an instant dislike to the beaten-up old Ford that the Irish accents were suggesting he and Heinlein enter.

'For Chrissake, Sarcha,' Heinlein muttered, tightening his grip on his briefcase. 'Just get in and stop making a fuss.'

Sarcha sighed and stooped to enter the car. And then he achieved the incredible for a man of his bulk: his movements became a blur as he twisted his body sideways and lashed out with a foot. The man immediately behind him collapsed to the ground in gasping agony as if a cannonball had been fired into his groin, and the man behind Heinlein groaned and went reeling backwards from a sledgehammer blow to the jaw that he never saw. Sarcha darted forward and seized the automatic that had fallen from the first man's fingers. His foot stamped down hard on the second man's wrist. The man yelped and let go of his gun.

Heinlein gave a groan of despair. 'Sarcha – for Chrissake –'

'They were supposed to meet us in the pub and they didn't show up,' Sarcha countered, levelling the automatic at the two men and giving Heinlein the second gun. 'So how do we know these two are the right guys?'

'We've hardly had a chance to find out, and they've not had a chance to show us.'

'So now we give them the chance. But on our terms,' said Sarcha. He jerked the automatic towards the car. 'OK, you two in the front.'

With a respectful glance at Sarcha and the gun that was trained unwaveringly on him, the second man helped his stricken companion into the car's front passenger seat before sliding behind the steering wheel.

'Seat belts,' Sarcha reminded.

The man snapped the buckles shut. Heinlein and Sarcha climbed into the rear seats. Sarcha pressed the automatic against the back of the man's neck and looked enquiringly at Heinlein.

'How does the old saying go?' he queried. '"Take me to your leader" isn't it?'

'Something like that,' Heinlein muttered.

Jack Farley carefully counted the bundles of used fifty-pound notes into neat heaps on his desk while Heinlein and Sarcha looked on. The heavies that Sarcha had dealt with were sitting in wooden chairs, nursing their wounds and glowering at Sarcha. Their expressions suggested that they were not grateful for the lesson in martial arts that the rotund little Englishman had given them.

The five men were in Farley's pin-up-festooned office inside his warehouse in London's dockland. The only respectable document

177

on the walls amid the display of female flesh was a calendar from a firm of shipping and forwarding agents.

'Two hundred grand,' Farley announced, feeling the texture of the notes. 'Nice.' He grinned. 'Of course, I could always insist on an increased down payment in view of the injuries to my assistants.'

'In future you should make certain they turn up at the right place, at the right time,' Heinlein replied. 'A third in advance is the agreed rate. And I think you know who that money belongs to.'

Farley chuckled. He had no intention of souring his profitable relations with the PLO. 'OK, squire. So what's the cargo?'

'That's our business.'

Farley nodded. 'Fair enough. But give me an idea of its size and weight and I can tell you what sort of shipping container you'll need.'

Heinlein glanced at the two heavies. Farley jerked his head and they left the office, the second one treating Sarcha to a particularly unfriendly scowl before closing the door behind him.

'We're talking about four cylindrical items,' said Heinlein. 'Thirty-three feet long by three feet maximum in diameter each. All up weight about eighty thousand pounds.'

Farley doodled absently on a notepad. 'Do these cylindrical items have stabilizing fins?' he asked casually.

'Does it matter?'

'I want to know what we can get away with crating them in, squire. Are the fins removable?'

'No.'

The two men could have been discussing the salient features of a new car. Farley jotted down some figures with the aid of a calculator.

'Port of lading?'

'Israel. So I suppose it'll have to be Haifa.'

'That's right. When?'

'March. April.'

Farley nodded and opened a looseleaf reference book issued by the Association of Fruit Importers. He looked up several tables and made some more notes. 'Be easier if you could make it early April. That way, we'd be working the fag-end of the orange season. Type 32 citrus fruit containers. Aluminium. Big bastards. Hermetically sealed and filled with nitrogen. Keeps the fruit fresh. All customs do is bleed some gas off and they're happy. Also, being sealed, they
178

can go as deck cargo. That way you can be certain of getting a sailing. Thirty-twos are greedy on hold space.'

'OK,' said Heinlein. 'Early April it is.'

After another five minutes finalizing a number of details, Heinlein and Sarcha shook hands with Farley. The less injured of the two heavies drove the two visitors back to the Park Lane NCP car park where Sarcha had left the Rolls.

'No real problems there,' Sarcha commented when he and Heinlein were heading south, away from London down the A3 towards Guildford. 'Money can buy anything.'

'It won't buy four Massada missiles,' said Heinlein curtly. 'Getting hold of them is going to be a real bastard of an operation.'

Sarcha chuckled. 'David, me lad. You're a lousy operator – letting those hoods get the upper hand – but I do have implicit faith in your planning.'

For once Heinlein wished he had Sarcha's confidence in his own abilities. That night, back at Thursley Hall, worrying about the forthcoming operation prevented him from dropping off to sleep. When all was quiet in the mansion he made a long-distance phone call. It was an hour before dawn before he finally drifted off to sleep.

59 Neil checked that the appropriate lights on panel R-13 were at green, indicating that all thirty-two catches on the orbiter's cargo bay doors were secured, and reported to Jim Bayliss who was sitting in the commander's seat.

'OK, that's fine, Neil,' said the instructor. He crossed the last items off his checklist and hitched himself out of the pilot's seat. 'Can't see the point of further payload deployment simulations until Surrey University tell us how they want the payload deployed.'

Neil stepped down off the aft crew station platform and savoured the evocative smell of hydraulic oil that pervaded even the shuttle simulators. The two hours had taxed his powers of concentration to the point of exhaustion, but he didn't care – he was back at NASA, working with his old colleagues.

Bayliss clapped Neil on the back as they left the flight deck.

'Nice going, Neil. I'll ask Earl if I can fly your payload. Be great to be together again, eh?'

Neil laughingly agreed and followed Bayliss out of the shuttle simulator. A technician called out to Neil that he was wanted on the telephone. It was Hackett.

'How'd the flight go, Neil?'

'No problems, Earl. We can't finalize the simulation programme until we know exactly what we're handling. I'm going to the UK next week, so I'll be chasing Surrey for dimensional and mass configurations of *Cyclops* for the simulator.'

'That's fine,' said Hackett. 'We've got four provisional launch dates pencilled in for the May schedule. Heinlein favours the May tenth launch but wants to keep some options open on alternative dates. Anyway, we can firm-up on the date next week. Drop by my office so we can finalize the scheduling.'

'OK, Earl.'

'Your boss, Heinlein, he wants to go on the mission. No reason why he shouldn't, but he'll have to go through the medical hoop and the emergency drill-training session. You know the procedure. So get some dates out of him and confirm them with Frank.'

Neil was intrigued. 'Heinlein wants to go on the mission?'

'Sure.'

'What as?'

Hackett laughed. 'Just for the ride, I guess. No reason why he shouldn't fly as an observer. Can't say I blame the guy. He's paying and you'll be flying a basic crew so there'll be plenty of room. Just tell him we need those medical checks and that training session. OK?'

'I'll tell him,' Neil promised and replaced the receiver.

60 'We've weathered the storm, such as it was, over the use of a tactical nuclear warhead,' Michael Greer argued at the morning meeting of the Emergency Defence Committee. 'I agree that the method of deploying the Massada was crude, but –'

'The only reason we've weathered the storm is because Maken has refused to acknowledge that we destroyed three of his aircraft,'

Ben Irving interrupted. 'Downing them was a tremendous morale booster for us, but that's as far as it goes. It was a fluke that won't happen again. Therefore I say that bringing in the Massada as an operational weapon before its booster is ready is a mistake.'

'How do you know it won't happen again?' Rymann asked.

The *Chel Ha'Avir* Commander-in-Chief clasped his stubby fingers together on the rosewood table and leaned forward. 'We know Maken's got an operational research unit and we know it's good. They wouldn't have to burn out too many computers working out that we used World War Two flight-predictor and proximity-fuze airburst tactics to down those aircraft. On the next raid, they'll change altitude and course after they've activated their ECM equipment and we'll be right back to square one. Bringing in the Massada as a front-line system is a waste of our manpower and resources. There's a hell of a difference between sending a few Massada transporters to one or two selected bases and bringing it in as an operational weapon with full backup facilities.'

The argument dragged on for another thirty minutes and ended with Rymann stating that he wanted the Massada to go into service. He ruled that that would be the recommendation of the Emergency Defence Committee to the Cabinet.

Rymann turned to his Foreign Minister. 'What's the situation on my visit to Washington?'

Samuel Kuttner cleared his throat. 'The US State Department agree in principle to a two-day visit.'

'OK. So they agree. When?'

'They'd rather wait until the spring. May or June.'

Rymann looked questioningly at Greer. The head of Mossad gave a slight nod and said to Kuttner: 'I suggest we go back to them for a May finalization. It's January; about now they'll be starting to grab their share of the presidential diary allocations for May.'

Rymann spotted Kuttner's resentment at the suggestion coming from Greer and moved in quickly to prevent an argument developing. 'Make it around the first two weeks in May so that I can be back for the Independence Day celebrations on the fourteenth,' he suggested. He grinned across the table at Greer. 'Be nice to have something extra to celebrate, eh, Michael?'

61 Heinlein and Sarcha expected problems at Ben Gurion Airport because their last departure from Israel at night by inflatable boat was, naturally enough, not recorded in their passports. Luckily the girl manning the control desk merely checked that the passports were valid, asked a few casual questions about their visit and allowed them through. They took a taxi to Tel Aviv, checked in at the Plaza Hotel and hired a car from Sun Tours.

'We'll be in a fine mess if one of those diamond merchants happens to recognize us,' Sarcha commented when he and Heinlein were reclining by the hotel's swimming-pool.

Heinlein chuckled and waved his drink at a gaggle of bikini-clad girls enjoying the warm February sunshine. 'There's no chance of that while they're around – which is twelve months of the year here.'

'Lest an eyeful of boob arouses their lustful passions?'

'That's right. They won't come within a mile of this place. Anyway, there's not been a whisper about the diamonds in the press.'

'True,' Sarcha admitted. 'So when and how do we plan our shipment of oranges, David, me lad?'

'The "when" is within the next five weeks,' said Heinlein. 'The "how" is a major problem that I'm still brooding on.'

'Brood on, oh ship of state,' said Sarcha contentedly, sipping his drink and having no religious scruples about allowing the nearest bikini-clad figure to arouse his lustful passions.

'All we have to go on is the telephone number of Jack Farley's contact in Haifa – Harry Laffin.'

Sarcha snorted. 'He won't be able to tell us where to find oranges.'

'I was pointing out the problems. But don't forget I used to be in the uniformed side of the orange business.'

Sarcha heaved his bulk on to his side and regarded Heinlein. 'David, me lad. Let me tell you something. There's a world of a difference between dealing with a load of respectable diamond merchants on a tour bus and making a killing on the fruit market. For one thing, we'll be up against a whole shebang of professional

182

operators behind wire fences, armed to the teeth with God knows what. Any killing made is likely to be in the sense that I'm not too keen on thinking about.'

Heinlein stood up. 'Come on, Sarcha. We might as well start work now. Let's go for a drive.'

Sarcha gave the girls a sorrowful last look and heaved his bulk off the sunbed. The two men returned to their adjoining rooms and changed into sober business suits.

'Have you ever heard of Ta'as?' Heinlein asked, driving south along the Herbert Samuel Esplanade.

'You mean the Soviet news agency?'

'No. Ta'as is a group of government-owned factories throughout Israel – Israel Military Industries. They make everything under the sun that goes bang, from tanks to percussion caps.'

'And they also make Massadas?'

'That's right.' Heinlein turned left past the Tel Aviv Dolphinarium and headed through the suburbs towards the railway station. 'But they're not made in one place. The electronics are made by Tadiran. Nose cones are made by a milk churn plant in Eliat. Fuel tanks are made in that plant coming up on the right. Don't make it obvious that you're looking at it.'

Sarcha's eyes swivelled right and took in a scruffy little plant crouching behind a rusty chainlink fence. 'Doesn't look very prosperous,' he commented.

Heinlein slowed at some crossroads. 'None of them do around here. They're not meant to look like the key plants in a missile production programme.' He accelerated. 'On the left is another Ta'as plant. But they don't make anything.'

Sarcha glanced briefly at the windowless bunker-like building. According to the sign outside it was a paint warehouse.

'So what do they do?'

'They store Massada warheads until they're ready to be moved to that plant straight ahead. Take a good look at it when I stop.'

Heinlein halted at the junction. The road was busy. He had to wait about two minutes for a gap in the traffic which gave Sarcha an opportunity for a close study of the Israel Precious Metals Company. To the inexperienced eye there was nothing unusual about the appearance of the modern, single-story industrial building except that it was set well back from the road in its own undulating, landscaped grounds. Sarcha's eye was not inexperienced and he immediately picked out a number of curious features.

'Notice anything?' queried Heinlein when the car was moving again.

'It's surrounded by nice lawns. The approach road snakes about. And the pretty, decorative rocks lining the road would make a fast getaway from the place impossible, especially as those rustic oak gates look as if they could stop a tank. Also the angle of the landscaped slopes around the place would deflect bomb blasts upwards. And the covered tennis court dome on the roof probably hides radar gear and anti-aircraft guns rather than a tennis court. Oh yes, the top section of the chainlink is electrified. I spotted the cables. Other than that, it's just another grotty little factory.'

Heinlein laughed. 'You're on the nose, Sarcha.'

'It would also be a pig of a place to take on. If you're thinking along those lines, I'd much rather watch.'

'We won't have to take it on,' said Heinlein, driving on until they came to an area where office blocks predominated. He pulled up outside an imposing but deserted tower block.

'So what do Israel Precious Metals make officially?' Sarcha asked.

'Ring blanks for the jewellery industry. Gold chains. That sort of thing.'

'A neat cover for lots of tight security,' Sarcha observed.

'That's right. They employ about two hundred people on normal production work but there's another fifty who work in the special products department. Their job is assembling Massadas.'

'Complete with warheads?'

'Complete with nuclear warheads,' Heinlein confirmed.

Sarcha whistled.

'They've got to be built somewhere,' said Heinlein. 'The main nuclear ordnance plant is too well known so Ta'as set up that place.'

'What's their production rate?'

'It used to be four a month but that may have been stepped-up. They're collected by an army flat-top low-loader. Four missiles at a time already mounted on their own launch platform.'

'How many men?'

'Just the driver and co-driver. Anything more than that might attract attention. The legitimate employees might start talking.'

Sarcha was puzzled. 'How do you know all this?'

'I was involved in the security set-up of the entire operation.'

With that, Heinlein got out of the car and stared up at the twenty-storey, empty tower block. Originally the entire area had been intended as an overspill zone to meet the enormous demand for office accommodation and plant space in Tel Aviv. The War of Attrition and the virtual halt of foreign investment in Israel had been more effective in ending the demand for offices and now the tower block and several neighbouring blocks stood empty. The floor-to-ceiling windows of the ground floor suggested that originally the downstairs had been planned as a large supermarket.

'What do you think?' asked Heinlein.

Sarcha looked up at the block. 'What am I supposed to think?'

'Why not think about the view from the top floor?'

Sarcha thought. He walked into the middle of the road and looked back in the direction they had just driven from. A grin spread across his face. 'Should have a nice view of Israel Precious Metals' front entrance.'

'On the nose, Sarcha.'

The two men strolled around the back of the block. They surveyed the spacious car park, surrounded by high walls, and paced the width of each of the giant roller doors that obviously led to enclosed loading and unloading bays for heavy goods vehicles.

'Ideal,' Heinlein murmured, noting down the name of real estate agency managing the property.

'You're not thinking of buying this place, are you,' said Sarcha in alarm.

Heinlein looked surprised. 'Heavens, no. Let's try for a lease.'

A letter typed on Stavolos Trust notepaper by a Plaza hotel secretary and sent by messenger to the Hayarkon Street office of the Anglo-Saxon Real Estate Agency produced a phone call from the agency within two hours. Heinlein fixed an appointment for that afternoon and returned at 3 p.m. twirling a huge bunch of keys which he tossed on the table beside Sarcha who was watching television.

'A six-month lease,' Heinlein announced. 'No problems.' He looked at his watch. 'You've got just enough time to go out and buy the biggest telescope in Tel Aviv.'

Heinlein applied his eye to the eyepiece of the biggest telescope in Tel Aviv and scowled.

'Everything's upside down.'

'That's because it's an astronomical telescope,' said Sarcha diffidently. 'But fantastic magnification, don't you think? I mean, just looking through that eyepiece makes you think you're standing right outside the gates of that factory.'

'As I've never stood on my head outside a plant main entrance, I wouldn't know.' Heinlein pushed his chair away from the telescope and glanced around the empty acreage of office space. Sarcha had set up the telescope on its tripod well away from the windows so that there was no likelihood of it being seen from outside. 'Those Palestinians you recruited for the diamond job. They were good.'

Sarcha grinned. 'Alef and his brother and friends? Of course they're good. I trained them myself. They're old buddies.'

'Could you find them again?'

'Same pay?'

'Double.'

'No problem. Give me a day.'

'You've got it,' said Heinlein. 'Bring them here. And there's a wrecker plus a few bits of artillery we're going to need. I'd rather not write out a shopping list. You can start now.'

Sarcha looked dismayed. 'Now?'

Heinlein's brow furrowed. 'Doesn't the word "now" mean "right this minute"? Yes, I'm sure it does, unless my old English teacher was lying.'

'But I'd arranged some entertainment for this evening.'

'Would this "entertainment" have involved having members of the fair sex in our rooms?'

'There was nothing fair about the fees they were charging,' said Sarcha glumly. 'And I paid them some money on account.'

'Life can be devastatingly cruel,' Heinlein observed.

First thing the following morning, Heinlein paid cash for a black, one-year-old Mercedes saloon which he purchased from a Tel Aviv main agent. He selected black because that was the current colour the army was using for senior *Zahal* officers' staff cars.

A fast two-hour test drive to Jerusalem and back along the M1 motorway proved the car to be sound. On his return to Tel Aviv he visited a large yacht chandler's and examined the store's display of ship-to-shore radio transceivers. A large and expensive twelve-volt Yaesu caught his eye, not because of its price but because it covered the one-metre band.

'Three thousand dollars,' said the helpful assistant respectfully, having examined Heinlein's business card. 'But I'm afraid the set doesn't cover all the bands. The one-metre VHF band converter has been removed. Defence regulations.'

Heinlein frowned. 'That's a nuisance. We may need the one-metre band to talk to the US coastguards when our yacht is in American waters.'

'I'm very sorry, sir. But we're not allowed to sell transceivers that can operate on the military's VHF frequencies.' The assistant cleared his throat. 'However, there's nothing in the regulations to say that we can't sell you the converter that we removed. It's just that we can't sell sets capable of operating on one-metre. The converter's easy enough to plug in. Take the back off the set and you'll see the empty socket.'

Heinlein grinned. 'Sometimes I think our rules and regulations are drawn-up by cretins.'

'Precisely, sir.'

Heinlein made a few more purchases and the assistant helped him carry the Yaesu to the Mercedes. He drove back to the office block and spent three hours behind the closed doors of a loading bay wiring the Yaesu to the car's electrical system. Returning the missing converter to its socket was simple enough; the trickiest task was teasing the Mercedes' headlining back into place after he had taped the wire-loop antenna to the inside of its roof.

With the Yaesu hidden under a blanket and switched to maximum power output, and with the microphone tucked between the seats, he drove into the centre of Tel Aviv, and surreptitiously keyed the microphone as he was passing a television shop. The VHF carrier wave from the transmitter effectively splattered out all the television pictures, turning them into crazy dancing patterns of zig-zagging colours for as long as he kept the microphone keyed. He tried the same again a few minutes later while waiting at some traffic lights. The Yaesu's carrier wave annihilated the heavy beat crashing out of the twin speakers of a car waiting beside him.

Heinlein returned to the office block well pleased with his day's work. There was no doubt that the Yaesu coupled to its mismatched antenna behaved as an effective broad-band jammer that could prevent the transmission or reception of radio signals within a wide radius – probably as much as half a mile.

He made another of his long distance telephone calls and returned to the office block. It was dark when he settled down at the telescope to keep Israel Precious Metals' inverted front entrance under observation. He was helped by a fortuitously positioned street light. A few cars came and went during the next two hours, their drivers occasionally exchanging brief chats with the men manning the gatehouse. Sarcha returned at 9 p.m. just as Heinlein was beginning to wonder if watching the inverted scene would permanently scramble his brain.

He shook hands with the four grinning Palestinians.

'And we've purchased all the necessary hardware,' said Sarcha, beaming broadly.

The party trooped down to the loading bays where Heinlein examined the breakdown recovery vehicle that Sarcha had obtained. It was a General Motors wrecker of the same type used by the Israeli army except that it was emblazoned with the name of a Narbus garage and it bore Arab licence plates. Sarcha demonstrated that its thirty-tonne hydraulic hoist was in working order.

'Alef is a dab hand with masking tape and a spray gun,' Sarcha claimed.

'Is that right, Alef?' Heinlein questioned.

The Palestinian nodded. 'It was my trade,' he replied. 'About two days' work and you won't know it from an army wrecker.'

Heinlein showed Alef the Mercedes. 'Also I want this dressed up with army plates and General Headquarters pennants.'

The Palestinian looked pleased. 'I know exactly where to steal them.'

Tunny's yard outside Tel Aviv consisted of six acres of commercial vehicles ranging from small delivery vans to thirty-tonne refrigerated trucks. At least one acre was occupied by a vast assortment of fruit containers and prime movers, all in varying states of condition ranging from pristine, bankrupt stock vehicles, to trucks and tugs that looked as if they had spent their working lives being used as blast shields by dynamite-happy quarry workers.

'Type 32 containers?' Tunny kept muttering to himself as he picked his way past a welding gang who were cutting up an old truck. 'Aluminium they are made of. Pressurized. Aluminium prices at the moment you would not believe. Strategic war material regulations.'

Sarcha squeezed his bulk between two slab-sided containers. 'OK,' he said. 'If you don't want to sell one of yours, maybe you know someone who does?'

Tunny slapped the side of the giant container which was at least fifty feet long. It was mounted on a low-loader chassis that was hitched to a Volvo tug.

'There we are, sir. By craftsman they are made. Top-loading. End-loading. For citrus there is nothing better. Her pressure she will hold for a century. A year old. Forty thousand kilometres on her clock is all the tug has.'

Sarcha spent thirty minutes checking the vehicle and the gigantic container while ignoring Tunny's running commentary on their virtues. For once in his career, the trader was being truthful – the Volvo and the container were in excellent condition.

'How much?'

Tunny looked uninterested. 'Shekels or dollars?'

'Dollars. Cash.'

'She's yours for thirty-five if a VAT receipt you don't want. Without a receipt, she will still run like a sewing machine.'

'I want a receipt,' said Sarcha firmly. 'Everything's got to be legal and above board.'

Tunny shrugged and reflected that the standard of his customers was going down. Above board indeed. Where was it all going to end? 'Then thirty-nine I have to say,' he declared.

'Thirty-seven.'

'Thirty-eight and she's yours.'

'Done.'

After seven days Heinlein began to worry about the effect that the long vigil was having on the group's nerves. Even the normally placid Sarcha was beginning to snap at the slightest irritation and on one occasion an argument between the four Palestinians suddenly turned unpleasant. A flick-knife was produced and only some adroit footwork from Sarcha, when he kicked the weapon from the belligerent's hand, prevented the dispute developing.

The trouble was that Heinlein had no reliable information on the movements of Massada missiles. The transport officers responsible

189

for the movements of the weapons issued the orders for their collection only on the day. This meant that all six of those waiting on the top floor of the office block had to while away the time in a constant state of readiness.

On the eighth afternoon Alef was taking a turn at the telescope when he gave a warning whistle. Heinlein skidded to his side. One glance at the inverted army low-loader with its tarpaulin-shrouded cargo leaving Israel Precious Metals' premises was enough.

'That's it!' he yelled.

The rehearsals paid off. The wooden blocks that held the lift doors permanently open were knocked aside and within two minutes all six men raced out of the tower block's rear entrance and piled into their respective vehicles.

Heinlein, dressed in the uniform of a *Segan-Aluf* – a Lieutenant-Colonel in the 7th Israeli Armoured Brigade – jumped into the back of the Mercedes while Sarcha, uniformed as his driver, dived behind the wheel and fired the turbine. Alef and his three fellow-Palestinians were wearing Armour Corps fatigues. They piled into the wrecker and followed the Mercedes as it drove at a normal speed out of the car park.

Once clear of the industrial estate, Sarcha accelerated hard to catch up with the heavy low-loader. The vehicle was out of sight but they knew the route it would be taking. Heinlein reached down and switched on the Yaesu. He pushed the microphone on to the passenger seat beside Sarcha where Sarcha could key it when he gave the word.

From then on everything started to go disastrously wrong. Sarcha weaved through the back streets, using short cuts that would be too narrow for the low-loader. Heinlein hung on to the passenger straps. Sarcha swung on to Route 44 – the main highway that punched south-east across the plain towards the old crusader city of Ramla – but there was no sign of the low-loader ahead.

'For Chrissake!' Sarcha shouted. 'They can't have got that far in front!'

'They've *got* to head for the Ramla depot,' said Heinlein. 'Put your foot down.'

'We'll get done for speeding!'

'Not in this car.'

Sarcha accelerated and passed several cars obeying the speed limit. After two miles the road widened into a dual carriageway.

190

'Alef won't come this far,' Sarcha argued. 'He'll think we've aborted and turn back.'

'He'll go on to the Rishon turn-off,' said Heinlein, cursing the operating conditions that made it too dangerous for them to risk using two-way radios. At that moment he and Sarcha saw the low-loader about a mile ahead.

'Christ, he's shifting.'

'Just get after it!' Heinlein snarled, yanking his pistol from its holster and spinning the silencer on to the end of its barrel.

The sound of the Mercedes' turbine rose to a muted howl. After five minutes Sarcha closed up behind the low-loader. It was charging along the fast lane – the tarpaulin covering its load flapping wildly – threatening to tear free from its lashings.

'Get beside it! And get ready to key the mike!'

'For Chrissake,' Sarcha shouted over his shoulder. 'You take out a tyre at this speed and you'll have the whole bloody caboose overturned!'

'Don't argue! Get beside it!'

Sarcha blasted the horn several times. The vehicle stuck doggedly in the fast lane. Obviously the army driver was delighted at the opportunity to obstruct what he thought was a staff car.

Cursing roundly, Sarcha hooked into the centre lane and passed the vehicle on the inside. Heinlein lowered his offside window. The slipstream howled into the car. Gradually the Mercedes drew level with the low-loader's rear end.

Sarcha hung grimly on to the steering wheel, fighting to counter the buffeting from the turbulence created by the big vehicle's proximity and speed.

'Key the mike on the count of three!' Heinlein yelled. One . . . !'

Sarcha grabbed the microphone.

'Come on! Faster! Two . . . !'

The Mercedes edged forward. The low-loader's bulbous tyres were screaming banshees pounding the highway within a few feet of Heinlein. The hurricane blasting into the car made it virtually impossible for him to control his aim. In desperation, he jammed the gun against the side of the door pillar. It no longer mattered if the low-loader's co-driver spotted the barrel.

'Three!'

Sarcha keyed the Yaesu's microphone at the same moment that Heinlein pumped six rounds into the low-loader's nearside rear tyres. At first nothing happened apart from Sarcha's braking to allow the army vehicle to surge ahead.

'Bloody hell! Self-sealing sodding tyres!' Sarcha snarled, keeping the microphone keyed.

Heinlein slammed another clip into his pistol.

Suddenly the low-loader slewed drunkenly across to the nearside lane and lost speed, forcing Sarcha to brake even harder. And then the heavy vehicle was snaking to the left and right, it's rear brake lights flashing on and off, a witness to the driver's self-control and skill in his fight to bring his crippled charge under control. With his speed dropping rapidly, he won the battle and succeeded in steering the low-loader on to the shoulder and bringing it to a standstill.

Several cars and trucks hurtled past towards Ramla, their drivers unaware that anything was amiss. Sarcha stopped the Mercedes some yards beyond the low-loader. He had the presence of mind to remember to open the passenger door for Heinlein.

Heinlein and Sarcha walked towards the sergeant and the corporal. The two soldiers had jumped down from their cab and were examining the shredded rear tyres. The sergeant was holding his assault rifle. The low-loader's bulk obscured the scene from oncoming vehicles. Both soldiers straightened up and watched Heinlein's and Sarcha's approach. Heinlein's uniform had no effect on them; they made no attempt to come to attention and salute.

'Trouble,' Sarcha muttered under his breath. He slipped his hand casually into the side pocket of his uniform jacket and released the safety catch on his Walther.

'Hey, what the hell do you guys mean, shooting our tyres out?' demanded the sergeant, levelling his rifle at the two men.

'I think you're mistaken, Sergeant,' said Heinlein pleasantly. 'We saw your blow-out so I ordered my driver –'

'Crap. I saw the shots in the mirror.'

Sarcha saw the sergeant's finger tighten on the trigger. He thrust Heinlein to one side and dived at the ground, whipping out his automatic and loosing off two shots at the same time. The range was less than three yards but it was a remarkable piece of shooting; even before their bodies started to crumple the corporal and sergeant were dead – both shot between the eyes.

Without wasting a second talking to each other, Sarcha and Heinlein quickly rolled the bodies into the undergrowth lining the road. Heinlein climbed into the low-loader's cab and listened to the signals' traffic on the transceiver. A flick through all the channels revealed nothing out of the ordinary. It was an immense relief. Either the Yaesu had done its job or the two soldiers had not used their transmitter. He reckoned that the men had been speeding to give themselves time for an unscheduled long stop-off. They would have been allowed an hour to get to Ramla. After being overdue an hour, a military police patrol would be sent out to check the roadside pull-ins and snack bars along the route. That would take another hour. After two hours, the alarm would be raised.

'They're coming!' Sarcha called out.

Heinlein scrambled down from the cab and waved to the approaching wrecker. Both Sarcha and Heinlein agreed that Alef's grinning face looking down at them as he pulled on to the shoulder was the most welcome sight they had ever witnessed.

Alef waited for a gap in the traffic and reversed the wrecker up behind the low-loader. His colleagues coupled the lifting gear and winched the army vehicle's rear axle clear of the road. Because the low-loader would have to be towed backwards, they close-coupled it to the wrecker with staybars to ensure its stability. The entire operation took a nerve-racking fifteen minutes. When all was ready Heinlein and two of the Palestinians held up the traffic while Alef manoeuvred the wrecker and low-loader through a hundred and eighty degrees so that they could continue in the same direction along the dual carriageway.

'Bloody hell,' Sarcha remarked a few minutes later at the wheel of the Mercedes as he followed the wrecker and low-loader off the highway and on to the little-used Rishon road. 'We only just stopped the bastard in time. Another mile and he would've been past the turn-off.'

'I miscalculated the speed he would drive at,' Heinlein confessed.

Sarcha chuckled and glanced in his mirror to make certain they weren't being followed. 'Army drivers – same all over the world.'

The wrecker swung on to a dirt road that weaved past some Arab-owned settlements. The road narrowed and skirted some low hills whose terraces were planted with olive trees. After another three miles it degenerated into a hard, rutted track and then ended abruptly in a dreary, chicken-infested farmyard that was over-looked by some squalid concrete bungalows with corrugated iron roofs. At the far end of the farmyard was a rusting Nissen hut that looked as if it dated from the days of the British Mandate. Outside the huge hut were a number of ancient agricultural machines and even a rusting, steam-driven thresher. About six Arab women clattered out of the bungalows and exchanged raucous greetings with Alef and the other Palestinians in the wrecker.

'They're smashing people,' said Sarcha with genuine affection, cutting the Mercedes' power. 'Salt of the earth. Those women spent two days clearing out that Nissen hut.'

Two of the women dragged open a pair of creaking barn doors that were set into the end of the hemispherical hut. Parked inside, close to one side of the curving roof, was a Volvo articulated truck coupled to the largest fruit container Heinlein had ever seen. Alef gunned the wrecker's engine and eased it forward into the hut to an accompaniment of arm-waving and shouted instructions from his colleagues. There was only just enough room to accommodate the wrecker and the low-loader alongside the Volvo.

Heinlein got out of the car. As he straightened, he suddenly realized just how much the strain of the last three hours had exhausted him. He yawned and stretched.

'Well,' said Sarcha, standing beside him. 'We've got the fruit container. And now we've got the oranges, I'm dying to take a look at them.'

They entered the hut. One of the Palestinians closed the rickety doors. Alef jumped nimbly on to the low-loader and unknotted the tarpaulin's lashing. All four Palestinians grabbed hold of the heavy canvas and hauled it aside. Their laughter and chatter was suddenly silenced by the sight that confronted them.

Resting side by side on shaped timber cradles were four ten-metre lengths of evilly gleaming, needle-nosed ugliness. For a few moments the four men contemplated the missiles. Sarcha reached out a hand and touched a stabilizer. 'Jesus bloody Christ,' he breathed. 'Did you ever see anything so obviously designed to cause lots of grief and misery?'

Even the phlegmatic Heinlein was momentarily lost for words.

'Do they have nuclear or conventional warheads?' asked Sarcha, not taking his eyes off the missiles.

Heinlein climbed aboard the low-loader and knelt down to examine the warheads. Etched beneath the access panel on each weapon was a serial number that was prefixed with the letter 'D'.

'Ten-kilotonne nuclear,' said Heinlein simply.

Sarcha swore softly to himself.

194

Heinlein untied a small crate that was packed between the weapons. 'And this,' he said, holding the crate aloft, 'is certain to be the fire control panel.'

He jumped down and Alef handed him a bulky envelope. 'Found this under the driver's seat.'

Heinlein opened the envelope. Inside was a looseleaf Ta'as servicing manual. Taped to an inside cover was a smaller envelope which he also opened. He removed a single sheet of paper that bore a column of typed numbers. He studied it for a moment and gave a mirthless smile.

'What is it?' asked Sarcha.

'The combinations for arming the warheads.'

Sarcha blinked and could think of nothing constructive to say.

62 Ben Irving brought his fist down on the table with a crash that nearly upset Rymann's water carafe.

'Stupifying, incompetent bungling!' he shouted across the table. 'Four of our most closely guarded weapons disappear into thin air! I simply refuse to believe that such a thing could have happened!'

'The latest information we have is that a police car on Route 44 reported seeing an army recovery vehicle hitching up to a low-loader that had broken down at the spot where the bodies were found,' said Greer calmly in response to Irving's outburst. 'They didn't investigate because they were travelling in the opposite direction and –'

'Then by God, we'll have their jobs!'

Rymann intervened. 'They didn't investigate because the vehicles were off the highway and everything seemed to be under control. Army wreckers hitching up to military vehicles which have broken down is a common enough sight.'

'But how could it have happened!' Irving demanded. 'Why didn't the men use their radio? How did whoever hijacked the missiles know about their movements? Why wasn't there an armed guard?'

'Two armed soldiers was considered sufficient. Anything more would've attracted attention – especially around the assembly plant.'

'Well the assembly plant's cover is well and truly blown now,' said

Irving sarcastically. 'So what's happening about finding the missiles?'

'I've got all my best operatives in the field now,' Greer assured.

Irving looked contemptuous. 'The institute is dealing with it?'

'Yes.'

Irving's expression hardened. 'With due respect to Mossad, they're hardly the best organization'

'They will find the Massadas,' said Greer curtly. 'Four missiles weighing nearly ten thousand kilos each can't be made to disappear. We've alerted all ports, airports and frontier posts to be on the lookout for suspicious –'

'You mean you haven't told customs and the police precisely what has been stolen!' Irving exploded.

'No,' said Rymann firmly. 'If the news leaked out, there might be a panic –'

'If the Goddamn missiles are fired there'll be a bloody holocaust. No "might" about it,' Irving retorted angrily.

Rymann remained unruffled. 'The warheads can't be armed without their launchers,' he pointed out.

'For God's sake, Rymann! The missiles are supplied on their launchers – all ready for firing. All right, so they haven't got the arming combinations. But we're not dealing with a bunch of terrorists without sophisticated resources. The enemy has got workshops –'

'Only *if* they can get them out of the country,' Rymann interrupted. 'And moving that sort of load out of the country is going to be impossible.' He looked at his watch. 'We've been discussing the matter for thirty minutes. Any more talk along these lines won't help get the Massadas back, nor will it help with an explanation for the Cabinet. Also I'm seeing the President in an hour.'

Rymann's wristwatch pager bleeped. He picked up the nearest telephone and listened. 'OK, fine. Send him in right now.'

Samuel Kuttner entered the room. It was obvious from his expression that he knew a row was in progress. 'If you'd prefer me to wait, Prime –'

'No. No, Sam. Come in and sit down. Do you have anything for me?'

'Yes. We've just received a message from Washington. Two

hours ago His Excellency Yaarcov Efrat was summoned to the State Department for –'

'Spare me the details,' said Rymann testily

'They've agreed to our proposed dates for talks. May 10th and 11th. Walter Swift will see me, and you if you wish, for three hours on the 10th. And the following day you will meet President Harding for an informal two-hour talk at the White House.'

Rymann gave a sigh of relief. 'Well done, Sam. At least that's a crumb of good news for the Cabinet and the President.'

The meeting ended thirty minutes later. The members trooped out, leaving Rymann and Greer alone.

'May 10th and 11th,' Rymann remarked thoughtfully.

'I'll see that the information reaches the right quarters,' Greer promised.

63 For an extra four thousand dollars Alef willingly undertook the hazardous task of driving the fruit container containing the four Massada missiles to Haifa. As a bonus, Heinlein had assigned him ownership of the Volvo. As Alef threaded his way through the outskirts of the ancient city, he was already making mental plans for the day when he would own a whole fleet of trucks operating the length and breadth of Palestine.

His timing was perfect; the heavy truck rumbled over the Giborim Bridge at 12.50 p.m. He drove through the Zevulun industrial zone and, at 1 p.m. precisely, parked the Volvo in a marshalling lane outside the freight office of the All-Israel Fruit Shipping Corporation at Kishon Harbour. The company belied its prestigious name; it was the smallest concern operating out of the port of Haifa. Its owner, chief shipping clerk, switchboard operator and receptionist was Harry Laffin, a former London fruit merchant who had fled from England some years before because of his beliefs, his main belief being that Israel was an ideal place to hide to avoid paying a very large income tax debt. He had maintained his London contacts, particularly with Jack Farley, who had put a useful amount of business his way. This latest deal looked like being the most lucrative of all.

Harry darted to the window as soon as he heard the Volvo draw

197

up outside. It was the right truck with the right licence plate. In fiction there is a regrettable tendency for some characters to give little dances of joy when confronted with good news. They have even been known to hug themselves with glee. Harry came perilously close to fulfilling both those clichés when he saw the truck. And why not? Another delicious ten thousand dollars was as good as his. He had a welcoming smile fixed in place by the time Alef entered his office.

'Ah. You must be Mr Heinlein's driver?'

Alef agreed that he was.

'Yes, Mr Heinlein and me finalized the details last night,' said Harry, barely managing to suppress his excitement. 'Charming man. All the paperwork's ready. The *Calder Castle*'s sailing in an hour, but I've managed to fix up some late-lading deck cargo space. Shouldn't be any problems. She'll be docking at Southampton in six days. She's got one port of call at Valencia. Last of the season's Jaffas. Mr Farley and Mr Heinlein should make a fortune. You've no idea what British housewives are paying for Jaffas this year.' Harry kept up a constant stream of chatter while hunting through a sheaf of documents. He found one and handed it to Alef. 'Lane eight. Give that into the clerk's office and the mobile crane will unload you. I'll see to the rest.'

Alef thanked Harry and turned to leave. 'One thing,' Harry called out. 'You will inform Mr Heinlein that everything went off OK, won't you?'

'When I see that the container has sailed,' Alef replied.

Harry gave a casual laugh. 'It's just that half my commission's still owing. Wouldn't like to lose out on it.'

'You'll be paid when the oranges have sailed,' Alef reiterated.

Once the mobile crane had straddled the Volvo and hoisted the container on to a loading pallet, Alef drove through Haifa's city centre and took the steep road that wound its way up Mount Carmel to the pleasant tree-lined suburb of Neve-Shaanan. He pulled up in a truckers' rest area which had a magnificent view across the Bay of Haifa. Laid out below him on the azure sheen of the Mediterranean was the entire harbour complex with its rows of silos, lofty cranes and dozens of toy-like ships lying within the protective embrace of the outer harbour wall. He unwrapped his kebabs and settled down to a late lunch. At 2.15 p.m. a scruffy merchantship being nudged by tugs into the centre of the harbour basin caught his eye. He focused his binoculars on it. The tugs moved clear and the water began to churn white under the ship's stern. It was the *Calder Castle*. Alef's binoculars traversed the length of the ship and came to rest on a number of assorted containers lashed down to the aft deck. One of them – the largest – was a Type 32. Alef steadied the binoculars so that he could read the serial number stencilled on the side of the container. It was the right one.

He drove on until he found a public telephone where he called Haifa's Dan Carmel Hotel and asked to be put through to Heinlein's suite.

Sarcha turned down the television's volume when the telephone rang.

Heinlein answered it. 'Heinlein.' He listened for a few moments and said: 'Thank you, Alef. Excellent news. I'll see that he's paid.' He returned the handset to its cradle and stared thoughtfully at the carpet.

'Well?' Sarcha enquired, wishing that for once, just for once, he could read Heinlein's mind.

'The oranges are on their way.'

Sarcha stared at Heinlein, his cherubic expression a mixture of wonder and disbelief. 'So we've done it,' he breathed. 'We've actually done it.'

64 Lena answered the telephone.

The caller cut short her polite identification. 'Lena, this is Heinlein. I'm calling from the project office at Surrey University. Is Neil there?'

'Mr Heinlein. I've been trying to get in touch with you for three days –'

'Is Neil there,' Heinlein repeated impatiently.

'No, Mr Heinlein. He's at a meeting at KSC. They've confirmed launch date as May 10th, as you requested, and they've selected the crew. NASA are now pressing for a date for them to fly over the pallet sections and the palletization team.'

'God, what an ugly word.'

'They also want you to confirm that you will make yourself

available for two days for your medical check-up and emergency drill instruction.'

'OK, Lena, we've got your messages here. Tell Hackett that we require only two more days' work on *Cyclops*. He can send the pallet sections and his team over whenever he's ready. I'll be at Kennedy three days before the launch. I want Neil over here on the next flight. How's he fixed for the next few days?'

Lena glanced through Neil's schedule. 'He's completed all the payload deployment simulations. All the contract details are finalized and there's no more coordination conferences until *Cyclops* is freighted over. He looks clear.'

'OK. Book him in on an SST to Heathrow and a seat for yourself on the same flight.'

Thinking she had misheard Heinlein, Lena asked him to repeat his last sentence.

'You can come with Neil too.'

Lena could scarcely believe what she was hearing. 'But –'

'Don't you want to visit the UK?'

'Well – yes,' her mind raced. 'But there's the office and –'

'The Florida bureau can look after itself for a few days. Tell NASA to liaise direct with this office. After all the work you've put in, you've earned yourself a trip. Get yourself and Neil over here on the five o'clock Miami flight. First class. Tell him to bring the complete mission schedule and *all* the information he has on the orbiter's emergency landing procedures and sites. Have you got that?'

Hardly able to contain her excitement at the prospect of a trip to Europe, Lena stumbled over her instructions. Heinlein made her repeat them – especially the request for data on the shuttle's emergency landing procedures and sites. He gave a grunt of satisfaction when she got them right and added, 'OK, fine. Sarcha will meet you both at Heathrow.'

'I don't know how to thank you, Mr Heinlein,' said Lena delightedly. 'This is a real –'

The line went dead before she could complete the sentence. After a few moments pondering the conversation, she called Pan Am and booked two first-class SST seats to London on the evening flight. She was sitting debating what clothes to pack when Neil walked in.

'Hi, honey. What are you looking so pleased about?'

'Heinlein's just called.' she said, returning his kiss.

'About time he surfaced. We've finished everything we can do at this end.'

Lena repeated her conversation with Heinlein. Neil was frowning by the time she finished. 'Hey!' she said indignantly, ruffling his hair. 'Why the long face? Don't you want my company?'

'It's not that, hon,' he said absently. 'I'll tell Earl to get the pallet sections and crew moving. But why in the world does he want the emergency landing procedures?'

Lena laughed. 'Maybe he's nervous about his first space flight and wants to know all the drills?'

Neil kissed her. 'Heinlein nervous? Are you kidding?'

65 It was 3 a.m. local time when Lena and Neil cleared Heathrow customs. Lena was dressed in white, eye-catching silk pants and a matching blouse that had endeared her to a number of bleary-eyed customs officials when she passed through their domain.

Sarcha was waiting for them outside the terminal. His moonlike face was a huge, welcoming smile. He threw his arms around Lena, gave her a passionate kiss and held her at arms' length to admire her. 'Lena, my angel! You look more beautiful than ever! And that outfit! Wow!'

The chubby little Englishman shook hands warmly with Neil and maintained a continuous flow of gossip while he carried their baggage to the Rolls-Royce. His patter never flagged as he drove along the deserted motorway and picked up the southbound A3.

'So neither of you have been to England before?' he quizzed over his shoulder. 'Well there's nothing much to see at this time of night. And this route out to Guildford is the London to Portsmouth road – it misses all the sights. Never mind, there'll be plenty of time for that.'

Despite the lack of anything interesting to see, Lena kept her nose pressed against the window for most of the journey. She was intrigued by traffic driving on the wrong side of the road and by Guildford's cobbled High Street, which Sarcha detoured through for her benefit. He kept the driving mirror tipped down slightly during the journey. The sight of Lena's and Neil's hands tightly entwined was gratifying.

Thursley Hall was wreathed in shadows and silence when they arrived. Lena and Neil said that they needed sleep more than food so Sarcha showed them to separate but adjoining bedrooms and explained that Heinlein was asleep and would welcome them in the morning. 'The housekeeper will be serving breakfast at 11 a.m.,' he said, bidding them goodnight. 'Just so that you can sleep in if you wish.'

Heinlein listened intently on the earphone while Sarcha held the amplifier's microphone pressed against the wall. He listened for no longer than was necessary to establish that the sounds coming from the next bedroom were those of Lena and Neil making love.

'Excellent,' Heinlein murmured with satisfaction. He returned the earphone to Sarcha. 'Exactly what I was hoping for. I doubt if Mr O'Hara will give us any trouble.'

66 Sir Max Flinders was in fine form. His rich voice boomed his congratulations through his face mask at the university technicians who had succeeded in closing the four sections of the cylindrical dummy pallet around *Cyclops* so that the giant satellite was completely enclosed.

'OK – that's fine,' Neil reported, when he had finished checking that all the pallet's electric latches were secure.

'How do you get it out of the shuttle's cargo bay?' asked Lena, standing close to the dummy pallet and staring up at it. 'It's huge.'

'It's not difficult, hon,' Neil answered. 'Just before payload deployment, we orientate the orbiter to a nose-down attitude in relation to the Earth. Then a few squirts with the orbiter's thrusters to speed it up slightly, and the entire pallet slides out of the hold.'

'You make it sound simple,' Heinlein commented as he joined them.

'Works every time.'

The five watched the technicians for a few more minutes and then returned to the project office where they climbed out of their sterilized coveralls and removed their masks. They spent thirty

minutes discussing details of the mission, including accommodation for the NASA palletizing team and the chartering from
Military Airlift Command of a C-5A Lockheed Galaxy to fly the
loaded pallet to the Kennedy Space Center.

'Aren't the C-5As a bit old?' queried Sarcha.

'Old but reliable,' said Flinders. 'And they've got the hold
capacity. That pallet's sixty feet long by fifteen feet in diameter.
We've got the necessary clearances to use the British Aerospace
aerodrome at Dunsfold, which is only about seven miles from here.
Either that or we use the Royal Aircraft Establishment at
Farnborough.'

Heinlein spread a map of Surrey on the table and asked Flinders
to point out the two airfields. 'Which is the most convenient?' he
enquired.

'Dunsfold is buried out in the sticks. It's a much quieter route.
As it'll be an abnormal load we'll have to have a police escort.'

Heinlein traced both routes with his finger. 'We'll use Dunsfold,'
he decided.

'Dunsfold it is,' Flinders agreed. 'Of course, we will have to
notify the local Customs and Excise office so that they can come out
and seal the pallet before it's shipped. It's a routine procedure and
the Guildford office are always very helpful. Then there's the
question of road transport. Pickfords are the obvious choice –'

'That's no problem,' Heinlein interrupted. 'I happen to know of
a specialist freight company who will transport the pallet from here
to Dunsfold.'

Flinders looked surprised. He was about to make a comment but
Lena spoke first.

'Give me their number and I'll fix it up,' she volunteered.

'That won't be necessary, Lena,' said Heinlein. 'The managing
director is an old friend. I owe him a call.' He looked at his watch.
'I think that's all for the time being. Neil, as you and I are going
into space together, there's a few things I'd like to talk over with
you.' He looked pointedly at the others. 'It won't take long.'

Flinders, Lena and Sarcha took the hint and stood. 'Come,
Lena,' said Flinders, draping an affectionate arm around her
shoulders. 'If you're interested, I'll show you the rest of the
complex.'

As soon as they were alone Heinlein said to Neil: 'You brought
the emergency landing procedures?'

'Yes. Sure.' Neil opened a briefcase and handed Heinlein a bulky looseleaf manual. 'Not that you need worry. The chances of anything going wrong are almost nil.'

Heinlein leafed through the manual. It was a mass of approach diagrams and lists of tables for various airbases throughout the world. 'What about the shuttle that made a forced landing at Nairobi last year?'

'And there was the Cairo landing,' Neil reminded him. 'So what? If something happens that prevents a Kennedy landing, then our second option will be Vandenberg. And if not Vandenberg, then there's Andrews, Edwards – a whole string of alternative landing facilities.'

'Which you could find? With no power?'

Neil sighed. 'The landing site is selected before the deorbit burn, that is, before atmospheric entry.'

Heinlein still looked unconvinced and Neil went into greater detail. 'If you look in that manual you'll see that there are four classifications of landing facility. Class A are the primary sites such as Kennedy and Vandenberg which have facilities specifically designed for the orbiter. Then there's Class B: major abort landing facilities such as Dryden; Rota in Spain; Okinawa and so on. They're usually AFBs with four to five thousand yards of concrete runway. The class also includes a few civilian airports. OK?'

'What about Class D facilities?'

Neil laughed. 'You've gotta be in one hell of a hole to go for a Class D option. There's a list of about fifteen sites in that manual. Saltflats. Lake beds. Stretches of bush. No one's ever had to use one and no one wants to. Landing without ground navigation aids? Jesus, no. Just because a site is listed doesn't mean it's safe. There could be holes, animals, anthills. It doesn't take much to bust an orbiter touching down at one hundred and eighty knots. The nearest I ever got to a Class D landing facility was on the simulator when I set down on Bonneville Saltflats.'

Heinlein mustered a smile to match Neil's amusement. 'How did you make out.'

'Pretty good. A quarter of a mile bounce but I stopped her. *And* the Goddamned simulator threw potholes at me.'

They spent another ten minutes discussing emergency landing procedures for the orbiter.

'OK, Neil. Thanks for setting my mind at rest. Can I keep this book?'

'Be my guest.'

Heinlein produced an envelope and handed it to Neil. 'For you and Lena. As you've not had a chance to visit London yet, I thought that maybe you'd both like the rest of the day off.'

Neil opened the envelope. Inside were two tickets for the show at the London Palladium, valid for that evening.

At 8 p.m. that evening only one light was burning in Thursley Hall in the small ground-floor study that Heinlein used as an office. Even the housekeeper's flat was in darkness because Heinlein had provided her with a ticket for the play at Guildford's Yvonne Arnaud theatre.

'I've decided on a landing site for the orbiter,' said Heinlein, spreading a large map of South Africa out on the desk and moving his finger down the border that ran from north to south between Mozambique and South Africa. 'The Kruger National Park.'

Sarcha stared aghast, first at the map and then at Heinlein. 'South Africa! You're crazy! Absolutely stark raving!'

'We're not talking about an ordinary game reserve,' said Heinlein, unpertubed by Sarcha's outburst. 'The Kruger National Park is bigger than Israel. Ten thousand square miles of flat bushland and scrub policed by a handful of rangers. The border with Mozambique is guarded by a two hundred-mile-long veterinary fence, designed to keep the game in and the Mozambican poachers and terrorists out.' He opened the NASA manual at a pull-out large-scale map of the park and pointed out an area in the north between the Letaba River and the Shingwedzi River that bore an east-west dotted line. 'That's one of NASA's dire emergency landing sites for the orbiter. It's a stretch of flat bushland.'

Sarcha bent over the map. He tried to work out the meaning of the complex tables of navigational computer-way loading coordinates printed down the side of the map and gave up.

'Check the scale,' Heinlein suggested.

Sarcha did so and commented on the fact that the dotted line landing site was within thirty miles of the Mozambique border.

'Precisely,' said Heinlein. 'Seven minutes' flying time for a Westland Werewolf helicopter such as those operated by the Mozambique Air Force.'

205

Suddenly Heinlein's choice of landing site began to make sense to Sarcha. 'Does Maken have contacts with Mozambique?' he queried.

Heinlein nodded. 'A fifteen-minute round trip to pull us out from the Kruger National Park will repay about one per cent of the favours that Mozambique owes Maken.'

'Us?'

'You'll be there waiting for us . . . with the black girl. And with all the necessary communication equipment to talk to the shuttle. Just in case O'Hara gives us problems.'

The front doorbell rang. Heinlein glanced at his watch. It was 8.15. 'Dead on time,' he observed.

Jack Farley was standing in the porch. He was wearing tatty jeans and a donkey jacket. He grinned aimiably at Sarcha who had opened the door. 'Evening, squire. I hope you gentlemen like oranges.'

Farley shook hands with Sarcha and Heinlein and jerked his thumb at the giant Type 32 container and its transporter that was parked in the wide drive. 'Thought I'd best collect it myself from Southampton. Being as how you're such valued cash customers.'

'Any troubles?' asked Heinlein as the three men walked across to the container.

'Nothing that a few readies couldn't buy us out of, squire. Got somewhere to unhitch it?'

Sarcha directed Farley around the side of the mansion to the barn. He switched on the outside lights and opened the barn's large double doors. Farley was a skilled driver and managed to reverse the articulated vehicle into the barn without undue difficulty so that the conta:..er was positioned to one side but with plenty of working space all around. Sarcha lowered the jacks and helped Farley unhitch the transporter. Once it was driven clear, Heinlein closed the barn doors and locked them.

'I take it you've got the balance?' Farley asked, jumping down from the driver's cab.

'It's in the house,' said Heinlein. 'And if you're interested, I've got some more work in mind for you and a few of your lads. Same terms – cash.'

Farley gave a knowing grin. 'Always interested in those sort of terms, squire.'

Lena and Neil returned to Thursley Hall shortly after 2 a.m. Neil parted with a small fortune to pay off the taxi driver who had driven them the fifty miles from London. The couple entered the silent, gloomy mansion and groped their way upstairs in the darkness with much giggling and stumbling about. Neil started singing one of the songs from the show they had just seen, obliging Lena to attempt a swift gagging operation with an evening glove. Her efforts ended with them collapsing in a heap of helpless laughter on Neil's bed. He circled his arms around her and pulled her close.

'No, Neil, not tonight, you've got to get up in the morning.'

Neil made a suitably coarse reply that had them both in hysterics. He started to unzip her dress. Lena suddenly became tense and pushed Neil's hand away.

'Listen!' she hissed.

'Whaa?'

'Not here. Not in this place any more.'

Neil nuzzled her between her breasts. 'OK. Just here then? Whatever turns you on, hon.'

Lena stuffed a sheet into her mouth to stifle her laughter. 'Not in the house any more.'

''S too cold in the yard.'

'Not in *this* house. It gives me the spooks. I keep getting this feeling that we're being watched all the time.'

'Who? Deedletum and Weedledee?'

Neil's Spoonerism sent Lena into a renewed paroxysm of laughter. 'Idiot,' she choked. 'Now listen. I'm the boss, right?'

'Definitely the boss,' mumbled Neil, nibbling a nipple.

'So you take yourself off to your room. You've got to meet those guys from Kennedy tomorrow.' She cradled his face and kissed him long and hard. 'Now beat it.'

'Will you marry me?'

'Yes. Now for Chrissake go.'

'Yes, ma'am.' Neil climbed unsteadily to his feet and tottered from the room. After five minutes sprawled on the bed in the adjoining room, he realized that Lena had evicted him from his own bedroom. Also he had a vague idea that either he or she had said something important. But sleep intervened before he could make up his mind what to do about both matters.

207

67　　In Jerusalem preparations for Rymann's visit to the United States forged ahead. Most of the detailed planning was handled by senior civil servants in the Israeli Foreign Ministry who dealt direct with the US Embassy in Israel, with the Israeli Country Desk Officer in the US State Department, Washington reporting directly to the Under Secretary of State for Political Affairs.

Daily progress reports were filtered through to Rymann. The only occasion when he interfered was his vetoing of a proposal to fly him and his retinue to Washington by a USAF B9 bomber.

'Prime Minister, you must take advantage of the US proposal,' Samuel Kuttner protested.

'When I leave Israel, it will be by an El Al civil aircraft,' said Rymann firmly.

'Which the PLO will shoot down over the Mediterranean,' Kuttner retorted. 'We're planning a joint announcement of your visit for next week, therefore it won't be secret. But Maken won't and can't touch a USAF B9.'

'Israeli heads of state use the state airline,' Rymann declared, eyeing a new secretary and assessing his chances with her. 'For me to do otherwise would be a break with tradition.'

'And having you shot down would be a break with tradition,' Kuttner replied, being uncharacteristically blunt. 'And besides, you really think it fair to place the other members of the party at risk?'

Rymann considered and eventually nodded. He knew when to yield and decided that this was such a moment. 'You're right, Sam. We'll fly by B9.' He chuckled and added. 'Will the United States bill us for its use?'

'I doubt it. The offer came personally from President Harding.'

'Well, if it's free, that's a better reason for accepting Harding's offer than the guarding of your neck I reckon.'

Kuttner did not appreciate the joke.

68 Neil and Lena went to Gatwick Airport on 15 April to welcome the arrival of the three-man NASA palletizing team. They met them with the Rolls-Royce while Jack Farley drove a flat-top truck to the cargo handling area to collect the dismantled sections of the pallet when they were unloaded from the Boeing's freight hold.

The NASA technicians were required at Vandenberg Air Force Base to prepare a military payload for a shuttle launch so they were anxious not to waste time. After spending two hours unwinding at the Angel Hotel in Guildford where they had been booked in, they called their chauffeur-driven car to take them to the University of Surrey.

Leader of the team was Paul Quincy, a wiry New Yorker who had been with NASA since the first shuttle flight in 1981. He and Neil knew each other well.

'Beautiful. Beautiful,' he said briskly to Flinders and Neil during his initial examination of *Cyclops* resting on its cradles in the clean room. 'As smart a payload as I've seen, Sir Max.'

Flinders beamed his pleasure. 'She's the result of many years' hard work, Mr Quincy.'

Quincy looked questioningly at Neil. 'Any problems during the dummy palletizing?'

'None at all,' Neil replied. 'The sections closed up around her as neat as you could wish.'

The team spent two hours laying out the pallet sections on the clean room floor and checking that everything was in order.

'OK,' said Quincy when they had finished. 'Now's the last chance you'll have for your final checkouts, Sir Max, because at eight tomorrow morning we start assembling the pallet around her.'

The NASA team returned to their hotel. For the rest of that night scientists and technicians in the university's *Cyclops* Control Centre put the giant orbital observatory through its paces, testing all its facilities. Power for the trials was provided by banks of Xenon lights that shone down from the roof of the clean room, their rays trained on the outstretched solar panels to simulate the energy that the observatory would be receiving from the sun when it was in orbit. A few faults were found during the night but they had been rectified by the time Paul Quincy and his two assistants were ready to start work the following morning.

'Sarcha and I would like to watch,' said Heinlein.

'No reason why not, fellers,' said Quincy affably, walking around the two men to ensure that they were correctly sealed into their sterile coveralls. 'OK, be our guests.'

With *Cyclops* suspended from an overhead gantry, the NASA men first folded the solar panels against the sides of the satellite and then fitted the lower curved panels of the pallet into place. Heinlein and Sarcha followed their every move, not speaking unless they were spoken to.

By lunchtime *Cyclops* resembled a monster crouching in a square-ended open boat.

From time to time throughout the rest of the day, Flinders, Neil and Lena would visit the project office overlooking the clean room to watch the progress below.

Two customs and excise officers arrived at 3 p.m. They climbed into sterile coveralls, gave the satellite a careful check-over and sat beside Heinlein and Sarcha to watch, fascinated, as the NASA technicians fitted the payload assist modules into position on *Cyclops*. The PAMs, as they were called, were solid-fuel rocket motors designed to boost satellites up to orbital heights that the orbiter could not attain. By 5 p.m. the remaining pallet sections had been fitted into place so that the orbital observatory was completely enclosed in a huge aluminium cylinder.

'A neat operation, Mr Quincy,' Heinlein congratulated.

'Thanks – but there's nothing particularly difficult about it,' Quincy acknowledged, pulling off his surgical gloves and removing his coveralls. 'It's just that we have to be sure that everything's A-OK.' He turned to the customs officers. 'Okay fellers. She's all yours.'

The two officials wound short lengths of toughened steel wire around all the pallet latches and crimped their official lead seals to the ends of the wires.

'Don't break the seals until after the pallet has cleared US Customs,' the official warned Quincy before he and his partner left.

'Don't worry,' said the NASA technician, sinking into a chair. 'Everyone knows the procedures.'

Flinders sailed into the clean room with a science undergraduate in tow who was bearing a tray laden with magnums of champagne and several glasses. Neil and Lena brought up the rear. 'We're going to celebrate,' Flinders announced, his booming voice echoing around the clean room's interior. 'Mr Quincy, is that pallet strong enough to withstand a bottle of champagne?'

'More than strong enough,' said Quincy. 'But I'm not so sure about us.'

It was the end of a long, arduous day. *Cyclops* – the product of thousands of manhours spent by the best brains in Europe and the expenditure of millions of dollars – was ready to begin a voyage into space that would take it to a geostationary orbit where it would be poised 22,500 miles above the equator. A voyage that it was destined not to make.

69   Heinlein and Lena saw the NASA team off from Gatwick Airport on 17 April. Heinlein had made certain that Neil would be busy because he wanted to talk to Lena alone.

'Well, Lena, that's another important phase behind us,' he commented as he drove the Rolls-Royce back to Guildford.

'But not the most important phase,' said Lena.

'The most important from the trust's point of view,' said Heinlein. 'There's not a great deal more we can do at this end now. We have to plan our next project.'

Lena was curious. 'And what's that?'

'A major TV documentary series about the effect of satellite information on Third World countries. The monitoring of crops to provide early warning of the onset of diseases. Wildlife movement for conservation. That sort of thing.'

'Sounds interesting.'

Heinlein slowed down to drive through the little Surrey town of Horsham. He gave Lena a sidelong glance. 'I want you and Sarcha to get the initial planning under way. Visit video locations and so on.'

Lena looked worried. 'I'd love to, Mr Heinlein. But I know nothing about making videos.'

'You didn't know anything about space satellites, but you managed very well. It's administrative ability that counts.'

'It's nice of you to say so,' said Lena, flattered. 'But –'

'I want you to start the day after tomorrow. You and Sarcha can fly to South Africa and take a look around some locations.'

Lena looked thunderstruck. 'The day after tomorrow?'

'That's right. The 19th. Why? Don't you want the job?'

'Well yes. I'd love it. Will I be back in time to see the launch?'

'I doubt it. You'll have at least a month's work in southern Africa. Why?'

'I did want to see this launch. After all, you and Neil will be on board.'

'Lena, you've done all you can on the project. It's time to move on, time to think ahead. Don't you agree?'

'Well – yes – I suppose so,' Lena agreed sounding unconvinced.

Neil looked dismayed when Lena broke the news to him that evening when they were sharing Lena's bed at Thursley Hall. 'A month?' he echoed. 'A whole month without you? I might die.'

Lena punched him playfully. 'Maybe it'll do us both good. Anyway, we'll both be much too busy to think of each other – you in your shuttle and me chasing around native villages.'

Neil took her in his arms and kissed her on the tip of her nose. 'When you get back to Florida, we'll look for a house.'

'Not on a condo,' Lena declared. 'Not on a condo. I'd go insane.'

'Condos are out,' Neil agreed. 'We'll have enough money for Delray or Boca Raton. My contract with the trust ends on landing. I could set up as a payload consultant.'

'Ah, but would you get the work?'

'I'll have a word with Earl when I'm back at Kennedy. There's another fifty shuttles going into production for the orbital hotel. There's going to be a helluva lot of work floating around.'

They sat without speaking for some moments, each wrapped up in their own thoughts.

'There's only one thing that worries me,' said Neil, breaking the silence. 'I don't like the idea of you jaunting off to Africa with Tweedledee.'

Lena smiled. 'I can look after myself.'

'Where are those two?'

'They seem to spend most of their time with their heads together in the project office – scheming.'

'Fiddling their expense accounts?'

'Funnily enough,' said Lena, 'I don't think they do. But

212

somehow I can't help this feeling that they're up to something. The way they stop talking when I enter the room. And all that interest they took in *Cyclops* being palletized. That was odd.'

Neil cradled one of her breasts. 'Everyone stops talking when you enter a room.'

Lena suddenly pulled him close. 'Oh God, Neil – I'm going to miss you.' She was nearer to tears than at any time since her childhood.

'And I'm going to miss you, hon.' He pushed her away gently and chucked her under the chin. 'I'll look out for you when I'm passing over Africa.'

70 Lena spent most of 18 April in London preparing for her trip to South Africa. Among her purchases were three smart but hard-wearing safari outfits and a pair of top-quality leather boots. That evening she drove Neil to Heathrow Airport for his return flight to Miami. She hated 'goodbyes'. She clung to him in a long, wordless embrace outside the terminal building and walked back to the short-term car park without a backward glance.

Almost twenty-four hours later she was back at the airport, waiting in the departure lounge for her flight to Johannesburg to be called. The original arrangement had been that Sarcha would accompany her. 'Heinlein wants me to stay in the UK another day to straighten out one or two things,' he had explained to Lena. 'Still, there's no point in wasting a ticket. You check in at the Jan Smuts Holiday Inn – it's right opposite the airport – and I'll fly out tomorrow.'

Although mystified by Sarcha's vagueness over exactly what it was that he had to 'straighten out', she had made no objections because she had not been looking forward to spending the long flight in Sarcha's company anyway. The jovial little Englishman scared her and she had never rid herself of the suspicion that he had spied on her and Neil making love.

A PA announcement broke in on her thoughts. Passengers were rising and moving *en masse* to one of the exits. Her flight was being called. She gathered up her belongings and joined the exodus. Two white South African army officers broke off their conversation in what she assumed to be Afrikaans to admire her. Their approving glances did nothing to ease the knot in her stomach. Despite her calm, self-assured demeanour, Lena was scared at the reception that white South Africa would accord her black skin.

71 April 21. Watching the agonizingly slow process of winching the giant pallet on to Jack Farley's low-loader was such a nerve-racking business that in the end Flinders made a despairing gesture and retired to his office with a request that he be summoned when his beloved satellite was safely loaded.

'Best out the bleedin' way anyway,' muttered the biggest of the men in Farley's five-man team as they heaved another wooden cradle into position for the pallet to slide on to.

Heinlein looked anxiously at his watch. 'How much longer, Jack?'

''Bout another hour, squire. OK, lads, take a breather.'

The fifty or so students who were helping guide the pallet relaxed while Farley and his gang lashed temporary restraints into place so that there was no danger of the huge cylinder sliding backwards down the loading ramp.

Two police cars rolled up. The sergeant in charge of the escort eyed the half-loaded pallet apprehensively.

'Aren't you ready yet then?'

Farley operated the winch motor and rolled his eyes to heaven. 'Jesus Christ, aren't our policemen marvellous? Does it look like we're ready?'

The sergeant was unmoved by the snide comment. 'Be dark in three hours,' he observed. 'No way will we let you shift this lot on to the A3 after 3 p.m.

'Bloody hell, mate, Dunsfold's only about ten miles away.'

'I don't care if it's ten bloody yards – it's going to take an hour to get there – which means we can't escort you after 3 p.m. Savvy?'

'For Chrissake get a move on and stop arguing,' Heinlein growled.

The pallet was loaded and secured to the satisfaction of the police sergeant twenty minutes inside his deadline. Farley climbed behind the low-loader's wheel and started the engine. His five heavies piled into the rear of the cab. There was no time for Flinder's speech and no one would have heard it anyway above the uproar as the entire university population turned out to cheer the low-loader as it rumbled slowly through the campus grounds. The sergeant's car led the way while the second police car followed the low-loader. Heinlein brought up the rear with the Rolls-Royce. Flinders sat beside him and Sarcha spread his bulk across the back seat.

'It's on its way,' Flinders kept repeating to himself. 'I don't believe it! I simply don't believe it!'

The convoy filtered on to the southbound carriageway of the A3. The police cars switched on their flashing blue lights and the convoy began the one-mile slog up Stag Hill. The route plan the police had agreed called for the low-loader to travel six miles south along the A3 and turn off towards Dunsfold at the Milford intersection. All went uneventfully until the convoy ground to a standstill just before the Milford intersection traffic lights. Traffic began building-up. No horns sounded because most of the drivers in the snarl-up were inhibited by the sight of the flashing blue lights. Flinders began to fret.

'I'll go and see what's happened,' said Heinlein, getting out of the Rolls. He was back ten minutes later. 'Farley says he's got a leaking air-brake reservoir.'

Flinders gave a loud groan. 'I knew something like this would happen,' he complained. 'How long will it take to repair?'

'He's called up his depot on the radio-telephone. They're bringing out a new reservoir now. Farley has suggested that he continues on along the A3 and lays up in the big truck park just before the Thursley turn-off.'

'But that's another four miles. Is it safe?'

'Yes,' said Heinlein, starting the car as the convoy started moving again. 'It's fairly level all the way to the truck park, but it's not safe to take the pallet along those narrow roads to Dunsfold. It'll have to wait until morning.'

Flinders looked aghast. 'But that's impossible! Why can't the loader be repaired now and moved now?'

Heinlein concentrated on negotiating the complex mass of traffic lights. 'Because it's going to take another three to four hours to fit a new reservoir and the police refuse to allow the loader to be moved at night.'

'But –'

'Listen, Sir Max,' said Heinlein patiently. 'That load can't be moved without a police escort. Farley's right – the best thing to do now is for him and his men to lay up for the night in the Thursley truck park where they can replace the reservoir. The sergeant has been very reasonable and has agreed to send the escort out again at 9 a.m. tomorrow. The Galaxy isn't due to take off until noon so that still leaves us plenty of time to get the pallet over to Dunsfold. OK?'

'It's deserted along that stretch. Will the satellite be safe? You never know what can happen these –'

'I don't think anyone will try to put anything over on Farley and his lads,' Sarcha remarked wryly.

'You should've allowed for this in your planning,' the scientist grumbled.

'I did allow for some sort of unforeseen eventuality,' Heinlein said calmly. 'Why do you think I arranged for the pallet to be moved on the day before its flight?'

Just before midnight that night there was a long-awaited lull in traffic on the A3. From his vantage point on the Gibbet overlooking the trunk route – one of the highest points in the south of England – Sarcha could see no sign in either direction of approaching vehicle lights. He flashed his torch five times and ran down the footpath to his car. Heinlein saw the signal and flashed his headlights across the entrance to the lorry park. The low-loader's engine burst into life. A minute later the vehicle and its monstrous load emerged from the lorry park, swung on to the lonely stretch of the A3, and headed south, its only escort being Heinlein following in the Rolls-Royce.

Everything went smoothly. After a mile Heinlein overtook the low-loader and the two vehicles left the dual carriageway at the Thursley turn-off. Farley had to drive at a crawl along the crown of the unlit country lane, following Heinlein's lights while keeping a wary eye on overhanging branches that he may have missed during his reconnoitres of the route. The only difficult moment was the tight turn into Thursley Hall's drive. Heinlein parked his car clear of the low-loader and opened the barn doors. The container had gone. Stacked up against one wall of the barn were several hundred

216

bales of straw. In front of the straw was a tarpaulin shroud. Farley was carefully reversing the pallet under the beam hoist he had rigged when Sarcha arrived.

'What about these?' queried Heinlein, examining the pallet's customs and excise seals.

Farley climbed down from his cab. 'No problem, squire,' he said, grinning impishly and pulling a crimping tool from his pocket. 'Got me own do-it-yourself kit.'

'OK,' said Heinlein, dragging back the tarpaulin and exposing the four Massada missiles. 'We've only got six hours before dawn – so let's get started.'

72 Lena was pleasantly surprised by her reception in Johannesburg. She was treated with great courtesy when she checked in at the Jan Smuts Holiday Inn. She showered, slept for three hours and took the lift up to the carvery restaurant on the top floor which was packed with airline crews of every conceiveable nationality. During the course of her meal she got into conversation with a party of female Qantas flight attendants who drank such vast quantities of beer and who roared with laughter at each other's incredibly crude jokes that she found herself wondering what Qantas male flight attendants were like.

'Don't go screwing white guys in the middle of Pioneer Park,' answered one of the Australian girls in answer to Lena's question about a black man and a white girl smooching at a corner table. 'The morality laws are there right enough but I've never heard of anyone getting busted any more.'

Lena made her excuses and left. She called the office in Florida and left a message for Neil with the answering service.

73 April 22. A few minutes before 9 a.m. two police cars drove into the lorry park and pulled up beside the low-loader. The vehicle, with the giant pallet in place, was parked in exactly the same position as the previous evening when the police had left it.

'Ready, lads?' the sergeant called out. Several bleary-eyed, unshaven faces appeared at the cab's windows. He laughed. 'Christ, you lot look knackered.'

'Bloody owls kept us awake all night, didn't they?' Farley growled.

'Brakes all fixed up, are they?'

'We're ready.'

'OK. Let's get this lot moving.'

Fifty minutes later, the slow-moving convoy arrived at Dunsfold Aerodrome, buried deep in the Surrey hills. Aerodrome was an old-fashioned word but the name had stuck; there was nothing old-fashioned about the sleek, third-generation Harrier jump jets that were undergoing various tests and pre-flight checks on the airfield. Dunsfold Aerodrome was the birthplace of over four hundred of the vertical take-off fighters. And giant Lockheed Galaxys, such as the one waiting on the perimeter near the beginning of the runway, were frequent visitors to the airfield to collect the Harriers ordered by the United States Air Force and the US Marine Corps.

After the security checks the convoy followed a fire tender around the perimeter track to the waiting Galaxy. They were joined by Heinlein, Sarcha and Flinders in the Rolls-Royce.

'Incredible,' Flinders muttered, gazing up at the Galaxy's vast cavern of a hold that was coming into view as the giant freight aircraft's nose section swung upwards like the visor on a medieval knight's helmet. 'It's impossible to believe that such a monster can even move, let alone fly.'

There was a brief conference between the Galaxy's payload master and Farley that ended with Farley reversing the low-loader towards the freighter. He stopped on a shouted command from the loadmaster. A truckload of helpers arrived on the scene and stood by as the Galaxy slowly retracted its twenty-eight undercarriage wheels into their pods so that the aircraft 'kneeled' to facilitate loading. The helpers attached extending roller ramps to the low-loader's tail and released the pallet's lashings. Winch cables were dragged from the depths of the Galaxy's hold and attached to the pallet's grapple points. A hydraulic motor whined, the cables tightened and the huge pallet began sliding along the ramps and into the freight aircraft's hold. The process had to be stopped several times so that the team of helpers could reposition the pallet. It was a tight fit in the hold: there was only just enough clearance to enable the payload master to worm his way between the pallet and the inside of the fuselage on his frequent inspections. The tricky operation took an hour to complete. When the pallet was secured to the floor to the payload master's satisfaction, the ramps were slid back into their housings. Farley's low-loader and rest of the vehicles were driven clear. The two police cars remained on the aerodrome because the sergeant wanted to see if the Galaxy really was capable of flight.

At noon precisely the mighty aircraft warmed up its four turbofan engines and taxied to the end of the runway, its drooping wings flexing alarmingly as its wheels encountered seams in the concrete. The pilot received take-off clearance at 12.10 p.m. The engines opened up to a shuddering roar that had the knot of watchers clapping their hands over their ears. The Galaxy began rolling. Its pace seemed unhurried at first, almost leisurely. And then it was accelerating rapidly as the thundering turbofans asserted their authority. There was a quarter of the runway left and very little of the watchers' nerves when the silvery leviathan finally lumbered into the air and heaved its bulk over the treetops.

Sarcha glanced at Flinders. The scientist's eyes were fixed on the dwindling Galaxy. The Englishman experienced a fleeting feeling of remorse at the thought of Flinder's beloved *Cyclops* resting on wooden trestles in the barn a few miles away at Thursley Hall instead of winging its way to the Kennedy Space Center.

Heinlein took Jack Farley to one side and slipped him an envelope. 'It's all there, Jack. Plus an extra five hundred each for your lads. They were bloody good.'

Farley palmed the offering into an inside pocket. 'Nice to do business with you, Mr Heinlein. I suppose we'll be learning all about this little adventure of yours on the telly in the next few days?'

'Maybe,' Heinlein admitted. 'But I hope not. Not if everything goes according to plan.'

The sound of the Galaxy's engines faded away and the party dispersed.

Heinlein and Sarcha spent the next two days tidying up their affairs at the University of Surrey.

'We'll be back for the first meeting of the board of trustees,' Heinlein told Flinders when he called at the vice-chancellor's office to say goodbye.

Flinders pumped Heinlein's hand. 'Thank you for everything, Heinlein,' he boomed heartily. 'Enjoy your trip into space. Maybe we'll get a chance to speak when the *Cyclops*' Control Centre is patched through to the shuttle?'

'Maybe,' Heinlein muttered. 'Maybe.'

The following morning, 25 April, Heinlein and Sarcha sat in the study at Thursley Hall going carefully over the details of their plans, making doubly certain that nothing had been omitted.

'The only thing that worries me is the helicopter,' said Sarcha. 'If it doesn't turn up, or if the South Africans get to us first, then we're right up Shit Creek.'

'It'll be there,' Heinlein assured him.

'I don't know anything about the Mozambicans. What I don't know about, I don't trust.'

'You trust Maken?'

'With my life.'

'He's given me his personal guarantee that Mozambique won't let us down.'

'Let's hope so, David, me lad.'

Heinlein looked at his watch. 'Time we made a move.'

They drove the Rolls-Royce to London, returned it to the hire company in Park Lane and took a taxi to Heathrow Airport. They purchased two tickets: one for Sarcha's trip to Johannesburg and the other for Heinlein's return to Florida.

'See you in South Africa,' was Heinlein's final remark when the two men shook hands and parted company.

'Or in hell if it all goes wrong.'

Heinlein gave a humourless smile. He looked at his watch. There was plenty of time before his flight was called for a long-distance telephone call.

74 Neil was at the Kennedy Space Center with Earl Hackett to watch the Lockheed Galaxy's touchdown on the giant runway that was normally used for orbiters returning from space missions.

'We'll be monitoring this particular mission with great interest,' Earl Hackett commented as the pallet was unloaded, winched out of the airfreighter and loaded on to a trailer.

'Why's that, Earl?'

'We haven't lifted that many full-size pallets into orbit. Once the orbital hotel project gets under way, we'll be launching nothing else. Be interesting to see how you make out if you're serious about setting up as a payload specialist.'

The next day Neil spent an hour in one of the giant hangars in the Orbiter Processing Facility watching a team of engineers lowering the giant cylinder into the cargo bay of orbiter vehicle OV-141 – *Dominator* – coincidentally, the same orbiter that was used for his last, ill-fated mission.

'Freighting-up' *Dominator* took a little over five hours. When it was complete the orbiter was towed into the Vehicle Assembly Building where giant cranes lifted the entire spacecraft into a vertical position and lowered it on to a mobile launch platform. Once the orbiter was secured to the service structure tower and the access gantries had been swung into place, work started on assembling the solid-fuel boosters and external fuel tank to the orbiter.

The digits on a large illuminated board at the side of the service bay indicated the hours, minutes and seconds of the countdown.

It was 25 April. Another fifteen days to lift-off.

75 On that same day the PLO launched their most ambitious air attack on Israel. The three Tupolev bombers refuelled over the Mediterranean which gave them the necessary range to rain down bombs on the *Chel Ha'Avir*

221

airbases at Hatzerim, Hatzor and Herzlia from a height of one hundred and sixty thousand feet. Ten Sharav fighters at Herzlia were destroyed in their underground bunkers by the concrete-piercing, gravimeter-guided bombs, and there was a serious loss of life at Hatzor when a bomb exploded in an underground communications room.

'Maken gambled right,' was Rymann's comment to Greer when news of the raid reached them. 'He knew damn well that we wouldn't dare use another nuclear airburst Massada against his aircraft within two weeks of my US visit. It would give Harding just the excuse he needs to call it off.'

'Have all the details been finalized?' asked Greer.

'A B9 is flying into Ben Gurion to collect us on May 10th and will fly us direct to Andrews Air Force Base. We're to be flown back on the 11th – right after my meeting with Harding. I now see why Harding offered the B9 – we're in and out of the country before we have a chance to draw breath. OK, what's this news you have on the Massada booster?'

Greer handed Rymann a report that was, as usual, typed on a single sheet of paper. 'My original estimate of three years to bring the booster into production was correct,' he explained. 'That analysis has been prepared by Professor Yarikon; she's the head of the new development team. She requires seventy weeks for development and tooling up, and sixty-five weeks to produce a prototype. Production of three pre-production boosters for test-firing will take fifty weeks; and the balance of the period will be required for the production of six operational boosters. At the end of three years we will have the means of obliterating Bakal.'

'Or even Moscow,' Rymann added as an afterthought.

Greer's gaunt features were harder than usual. 'If we have to – we will. Do you still agree with that, Hendrik?'

Rymann replied without hesitation: 'The decision I took that day when we went to Mount Massada hasn't changed. Nor will it change during the next two weeks. You have my solemn word on that, Michael.'

Greer permitted himself a rare smile. 'What Israel needs now is not promises, but time . . . . Three years, Hendrik. Three years . . . .'

76 'I don't know what to do, Neil,' said Lena miserably, lying back on her bed while holding the telephone. 'I don't even know if I'm allowed out at night.'

'Hon, of course you can go out.'

'There was something on the news last night about some blacks being arrested for being in a white area after 9 p.m.'

'Sweetheart, for Chrissake! You're an American citizen! Can't you ask someone? Call the American Embassy or something?'

'Neil, you don't understand. I'm too embarrassed to ask them.'

'Hey, what's happened to my tough, no-nonsense little Lena?'

'Christ knows, Neil. It's just that this country frightens me.'

'OK, shall I call the US Embassy for you and call you back?'

'Oh, Neil. Would you?'

'You know I'd do anything for you, hon. What time is it there?'

Lena looked at her watch. 'Quarter after three in the afternoon.' She suddenly realised how irrationally she was behaving. 'No – it's OK, Neil. I'll call them. I suppose it's being so lonely and missing you which is playing havoc with my self-confidence.'

Neil chuckled. 'I wouldn't mind playing havoc with you right now, hon.'

'Just hearing your voice is making me feel better already,' Lena admitted.

'OK, hon. I'll call you back in thirty minutes and see how you made out. Now don't you worry any more. Heinlein says that Sarcha should be with you any time now.'

'It's just that I've been so bored. I can't even go for a walk – this place is surrounded by freeways.'

'OK, hon. You take care and I'll call you right back.'

The line went dead. She replaced the handset. The phone buzzed immediately. It was Sarcha calling from the hotel lobby. He had just arrived in South Africa.

'You promised you'd be coming out the next day!' she stormed at him when he entered her room. 'I've been stuck in this

223

Goddamn hotel, not knowing what the hell to do and being bored to tears.'

Sarcha's moonlike face mirrored his alarm. He blinked sheepishly and explained: 'I'm sorry, my angel. But there was a problem at Nairobi –'

'Don't you "angel" me! I've had a miserable time, stuck out here. Mind-crashingly bored I've been with nothing to do but watch the worst television in the whole Goddamn world!'

For a moment Sarcha looked as if he was going to back off towards the door. 'Lena, I'm sorry. We start work tomorrow. You'll find it fascinating – I promise.'

Sarcha was as good as his word. The following morning he met Lena in the hotel's self-service restaurant where they had a hurried breakfast. They spent several hours in the company of a garrulous Zulu and his taxi who took them on a tour of every motor camper dealer in and around Johannesburg. It was late afternoon when Sarcha found a robust Chieftain fitted with heavy-duty suspension and tyres. It was a year old and had been well looked after. He paid cash the following day and drove it with Lena to a specialist communications company who agreed to fit it out with radio and television equipment in accordance with the specification he outlined.

'The work will take several days, Mr Sarcha,' the chief engineer stated once the details had been agreed. 'Retractable tracking dishes require a lot of installation. Their tracking gear alone –'

'How long?'

'At least six to seven days.'

'Can you work through the weekend?'

'We could. But fitting the navigation equipment –'

'Time is more important than money,' said Sarcha cryptically. 'Work through the weekend.'

The chief engineer promised to make an immediate start.

'Why do we need such complex communications gear?' Lena asked in the taxi on their way back to the Holiday Inn.

'The camper will have to serve as a base station for all the units once filming gets under way,' Sarcha replied.

'And when will that be?'

Sarcha shrugged. 'Let's see how our first recce goes, eh, sweetheart?'

224

77 As soon as the launch pad abort alarm shrieked, Heinlein scrambled through the orbiter's hatch and ran along the access arm's narrow corridor and into the white room. On the far side of the room was a row of two-man wire baskets attached to overhead slidewires. The nearest basket swayed and bounced frighteningly as he hopped into it. He experienced a fleeting sensation of vertigo when he glanced down just before he released the brake lever. With an anguished howl from the pulleys above his head, the basket screamed down the slidewire. Heinlein closed his eyes for a moment and preferred not to think about the ground that was hurtling up to meet him. In the army he had often used slidewires, but never from a height of two hundred and fifty feet in a basket that resembled a hypermarket trolley. There was a sudden deceleration as the basket hit the arresting net, followed by a loud twang from the break link as it absorbed the basket's momentum. Heinlein vaulted out of the basket before it bit into the sand. He staggered, recovered his balance and dived into the nearest blast bunker like a hunted rabbit going down a burrow.

'Weird, huh?' enquired the instructor, thumbing his stopwatch.

'Weird,' Heinlein agreed.

'Fifty-five seconds. Not bad, but wait for the basket to stop. There's no point in breaking a leg and not being able to get into the bunker in time before the big bang.'

Heinlein followed the instructor out of the bunker. He craned his neck up at the dummy service structure tower and the nose section of the orbiter he had just abandoned. 'Not again, surely?'

'Not unless you want to do it for the hell of it?'

'Thanks – no. So what's next?'

The instructor checked his list. 'You've had your medical; you've completed the emergency transfer drill. I guess that's it. You have now been rendered sufficiently insane to be fit for a shuttle ride.'

During the afternoon, Neil and Heinlein drove to the Vehicle Assembly Building to watch a shuttle roll-out.

The mighty door sections lifted open and a giant land crawler emerged, a vast platform moving at one mile per hour. Perched on

225

top of the platform – almost entirely hidden by the service structure and solid fuel booster motors, and dwarfed by the external fuel tank – was the *Dominator*.

It was May 1. Labor Day.

T minus ten days and counting.

78 Like gnarled, rotting teeth in lacerated gums, the ugly crags of the Drakensberg Mountains rose out of the red soil of the high veldt. The spectacle aroused Lena from her torpor, but soon they were through the mountains and the camper was once again speeding along the unending monotony of Route 4.

The communications company had transformed the Chieftain's rear saloon. Gone was the berth across the width of the vehicle. In its place was a swivel chair in front of a small but complex radio console. To the right of the console was a television screen set into a mixer panel for two portable TV cameras that were clipped to the bulkhead. Even the roof had been altered to accommodate a retractable Ultra High Frequency dish antenna. There was even an expensive inertial navigation unit beside the steering wheel.

One crumb of comfort for Lena was that at least the central partition was unaltered so that she could be assured of some privacy at night. Sarcha had agreed to sleep on a campbed at the rear while she had the single berth behind the driver's seat. Another consolation was that, although Sarcha never bothered to conceal his admiring looks during their sojourn in South Africa, at least he had never tried to touch her.

A change in the camper's motion broke in on her thoughts.

'You can take a turn at the wheel,' said Sarcha, pulling into a picnic area.

Lena was glad of something to occupy her mind. By 3 p.m. she was threading the Chieftain through the market town of Nelspruit. The flamboyant tropical trees lining the streets and the smells from the citrus warehouses reminded her of Florida. She was miserable with homesickness but she was careful not to show her emotions to Sarcha. She missed her father and the rundown little filling station, she missed the lagoons and waterways of Florida, the humped

226

bridges, the palmettos, and even the humidity. Most of all she missed Neil.

Sarcha took over the driving when they reached Komatipoort, an uninteresting tin-roofed village near the Mozambique border. They turned north on to a narrow tarred road and drove on to the Crocodile River Bridge that marked the southernmost border of the Kruger National Park. Sarcha stopped in the middle of the bridge and used the map references to set the inertial navigation unit. From now on the instrument would maintain a running fix on the vehicle's position with an accuracy of less than a yard.

'The Kruger National Park,' Sarcha announced as he drove the camper off the bridge. 'Doesn't look much, does it? Know what Heinlein once told me? This place is bigger than Israel.'

A ranger waved them down outside his house. He addressed them in nasal Afrikaans and switched to English when Sarcha apologized for not understanding him.

'Have you people got CB fitted?' the ranger asked, eyeing Lena. She stared coldly back at him.

'No, but we can drop on to any frequency,' Sarcha replied. 'Why?'

'Had some reports of infiltrators crossing the fence from 'Bique. Maybe poachers. Maybe not. If you see anything suspicious, give us a shout. We monitor two-six point nine-six-five on FM.'

Sarcha noted down the frequency. 'OK. We'll call you if we see anything.'

The ranger nodded. His eyes strayed back to Lena for a moment. 'Nothing like the Kruger for peace and quiet when breaking the law. Enjoy your trip, sir.'

'Bastard,' Lena spat after they had moved off.

They drove on into the depths of the bush.

'When the hell are you planning to stop for the night?' Lena complained some miles later.

Sarcha held the map across the steering wheel and consulted it and the navigation unit while driving. There was little danger – the road was nothing more than an untarred grassless strip across a flat plain. 'Just north of Lower Sabie,' he said.

In Lena's estimation, just north of Lower Sabie turned out to be the loneliest place on earth. An unending vista of thornbushes and stunted grass stretching away into the dusk. The grass was obviously suffering the effect of the particularly hot summer it had

227

just endured. There was no sign of the Kruger National Park's much-vaunted wildlife apart from the occasional languid shadow of an eagle keeping an eye on the camper for possible scraps.

'According to the guidebook, the big game's further north,' said Sarcha while Lena cooked a meal. 'Let's see if we can find something worth watching on the world's television. The chubby little Englishman sat in the swivel chair and operated the touch controls that deployed the dish antenna. 'Ah,' he said a moment later. 'Something that looks a cut above SABC's offerings.'

Lena glanced up from the steaks she was grilling. A boxing match supported by a French commentary was in progress. The status strip above the screen identified the programme's DBS source satellite and the originating earth station. Sarcha touched out '44' – the international request code for English – and the commentary switched language.

Lena groaned and dumped a plate of steak and mushrooms beside Sarcha. 'I'm not going to have to watch sport all night am I?'

Sarcha smiled and flicked through the controls. From the hundreds of channels available, he picked out a brain operation that was being broadcast in three-D. 'How about that?' he enquired mischievously.

'Not when we're about to eat.'

'It's coming from the space hospital.'

Lena suddenly remembered the evening at EPCOT with Neil when they had seen the space hospital in the NASA pavilion. She looked at the screen with interest. The technical nature of the commentary suggested that the broadcast was not intended for a wide audience. 'Can that equipment pick up any satellite?' she asked.

Sarcha started wolfing down his meal. 'That's right, sweetheart.'

'What about a shuttle?'

'If we've got a window on one, we'll be able to hear it – and see it if they're transmitting TV pictures.' Sarcha pulled a manual from a drawer and waded through tables of frequencies. He spent a few moments with the auto-scanner and was only able to pick-up some Russian voices from a manned satellite who were playing chess with their ground controllers. 'Sorry, sweetheart. That's the best I can do.'

Lena became excited. 'Neil and Mr Heinlein lift-off tomorrow. Will we be able to tune into them?'

'Sure. But we won't be able to speak to them – our transmissions have to be encoded unless they switch their receivers to clear.'

'Oh, I wouldn't want to talk to Neil, but it would be wonderful to hear him.'

Sarcha gave her an odd look. 'We'll have to see what we can do, sweetheart.'

After supper they watched a science-fiction movie screened by the BBC World Service. Shortly after 10 p.m., Lena announced that she was tired. She left Sarcha watching yet another movie and was about to draw the curtains at her end of the camper and close the partition when she saw a face leering at her through the window.

Lena screamed in terror and pointed. A Luger seemed to appear in Sarcha's hand from nowhere. Even before Lena had a chance to draw a breath after her scream, Sarcha, moving with incredible speed for his weight, yanked the camper's door open and plunged into the darkness. Lena darted to the door and locked it. She glanced fearfully around at all the windows to make sure that they were all fastened. Gradually her heartbeat returned to normal. She listened. Voices outside. Sarcha's laughter. Footsteps approaching the door.

'It's all right, sweetheart. Open up.'

Lena picked up a carving knife and slipped the latch on the door. She held the knife up in a defensive position and relaxed when Sarcha's cherubic face appeared.

'A friend,' he said cheerily, entering the camper. 'And he's very sorry he frightened you. Say sorry to the lady, Joss.'

An ebony giant of bone and muscle followed Sarcha into the camper. He had to twist his head to one side because he was too tall to stand upright in the camper. He wore faded denim shorts and a filthy T-shirt. A long sheaf knife hung from his left hip and a short but murderous-looking whip made from a rhino's tail was jammed in his belt. His features had the finely chiselled appearance that Lena had come to recognize as those of the Zulu. He was aged about twenty-five. He smiled at her, showing two rows of perfectly formed teeth.

'Sorry miss. Didna mean to fright you.'

'Lena, this is Joss, our guide.'

Lena stared at Joss and then at Sarcha. 'Guide? You didn't say anything about a guide.' She dropped the knife on her bed.

Sarcha chuckled. 'He wasn't supposed to show up until tomorrow. Joss is a tracker. A poacher really but he's left his poaching gear at home. Joss can lead us to places where there's game a long way from the water holes around the rest camps. The real game that the tourists don't see. He'll save us a lot of time. That's right, eh, Joss?'

Joss nodded his head as best he could. His long fingers toyed with the tufted tip of the rhino whip while his hungry dark eyes feasted on Lena. 'Thas right, Massa Sarch. Thas right.'

The Zulu's voice had a curious intonation that hinted at a Spanish accent. Like many Floridians Lena could speak good Spanish. What she was not familiar with was a Portuguese accent. She was embarrassed and frightened by the undisguised lust in the muscular Zulu's stare.

'When did you arrange for him to meet us?' she demanded.

'Oh, a few phone calls around my contacts in Jo'burg,' said Sarcha dismissively.

'Where's he going to sleep? There's no room for him in here.'

'Don't worry your pretty little head about Joss, sweetheart,' said Sarcha in a condescending tone that increased Lena's dislike of him. 'He'll sleep outside.' He jerked his thumb at the door. 'OK, Joss – outside.'

As Lena pulled the partition shut, her last image was of the giant Zulu gazing at her breasts. She could hear him moving about outside so she made absolutely sure that there were no chinks around the blinds for him to peer through. To make doubly certain she even undressed in the dark in case her silhouette was thrown on the blinds. She nearly cut herself on the knife when climbing into bed and was about to return it to the galley when she changed her mind and concealed it down the side of the mattress.

The thought of the slumbering giant only a few inches away from her on the far side of the camper's flimsy outer skin prevented her from falling asleep until well after midnight.

79 The B9 bomber touched down at Andrews Air Force Base at 10.15 a.m. local time. Once the steps were in position and the red carpet rolled out, the fleet of Cadillacs swept out to meet the Israeli delegation. Secret servicemen fanned out around the aircraft and the knot of newsmen pressed forward against the barrier with their portable TV cameras and microphones at the ready.

The microphones were wasted because there were no bands and no welcoming speeches. Walter Swift, accompanied by Deputy Under-Secretary of State, Gunter Schulke, and the Under-Secretary of State for Foreign Affairs, shook hands with Hendrik Rymann and the other members of the Israeli party which included Sam Kuttner, Ben Irving and Michael Greer.

Within ten minutes everyone was closeted in their respective cars and speeding towards Washington.

Two USAF servicemen proceeded to roll up the red carpet and a tug hauled the B9 to a hangar for checking out in readiness for its return flight to Israel the following day.

80 At 10.30 a.m. on that same day Jim Bayliss, Mike Pepper, Neil O'Hara and David Heinlein entered the white room in the service structure at Launch Complex 39A. All four men were wearing lightweight inflight coveralls. The personal effects pocket on Heinlein's left thigh carried a number of extra items – namely, a six-millimetre automatic plus two clips of 'varmit' rounds – soft-nosed slugs that spread on impact. The one thing Heinlein did not want was bullets passing right through a man's body and endangering the orbiter.

'Have yourselves an uneventful flight, gentlemen,' said the head of the handover/ingress team when she had completed the handover checks with Bayliss. The ground crewmen had spent several hours in the shuttle, taking the vehicle through its countdown to within forty minutes of lift-off. Improvements in computer monitoring

231

and control systems since the first shuttle flights meant that flight crews no longer had to board the shuttle two hours before the launch.

A ground crewman pulled aside the sliding door at the end of the gantry that exposed *Dominator's* circular hatch.

Bayliss entered *Dominator* first. He was followed by Pepper and then Neil. Heinlein entered last. Neil's heart had started beating faster from the moment they had entered the white room. It was really happening! He was going back into space again! And then the familiar smells as he entered the mid-deck area cleared his mind and he concentrated on the awkward task of crawling 'up' from the mid-deck on to the flight deck along a ladder that was on its side. The perpendicular attitude of the shuttle on the launch pad turned bulkheads into floors and floors into bulkheads. Bayliss and Pepper were already seated above him when he hauled himself into his own seat and turned to help Heinlein.

'You guys OK,' said Bayliss, glancing over his right shoulder.

'Fine, Jim,' said Neil, making sure that Heinlein had fastened his harness correctly. He pulled on his headset, wormed himself comfortably against his headrest and gazed up through the forward windows at the strip of clear blue sky.

Pepper, sitting in the pilot's seat on the right, reached up to operate his communications panel. 'Launch Control. This is *Dominator*. Radio check, over.'

Launch Control acknowledged. After a few checks, Launch Control confirmed that all the channels were working satisfactorily. Similar checks were carried out with Earl Hackett, the capcom in the mission control room.

Although it did not concern him, Neil could not help occasionally watching the computer screens in front of Bayliss and Pepper. The displays maintained a continuous confirmation that the countdown was proceeding satisfactorily.

The event timer indicated thirty minutes to lift-off.

'*Dominator*, this is Launch Control. Side hatch is secured.'

'Roger, we copy,' Pepper acknowledged.

The pre-launch checks continued at an unhurried pace. They consisted of orders from Launch Control which either Bayliss or Pepper would acknowledge and carry out.

Pepper keyed the controls on a central panel and the shuttle's planned flight trajectory appeared as a line on a CRT. 'Launch Control. This is *Dominator*. Flight plan is loaded, over.'

At seven minutes before lift-off the crew access arm was retracted. Neil glanced sideways at Heinlein and, like so many before him, wondered what was going through the inscrutable Israeli's mind.

A crucial stage was reached two minutes before lift-off with the closing of the vents on the giant external liquid hydrogen tank followed by the shuttle's switch-over to internal power.

'*Dominator*, this is Launch Control, APU start is go. You are on your on-board computers, over.'

'Roger, out,' Bayliss replied.

The seconds to lift-off winked away on the event timer: thirty, twenty-nine, twenty-eight . . . .

'Break a leg, you guys,' said Launch Control.

A row of green lights appeared.

'First, second and third SSME ignition,' said Bayliss as the shuttle's three main engines started to burn.

Ten, nine, eight . . . .

There was a dull sigh that seemed too distant to be anything to do with *Dominator*. The sigh became a roar and suddenly the orbiter did its 'twang', a heart-stopping, drunken sway in the direction of the external tank. Then the entire flight deck began to vibrate as the shuttle rocked back to its vertical position.

Flame and smoke roared from the shuttle's main engines.

'Five . . . . Four . . . .' reported the casual voice of Launch Control. 'We have main engine start. Two . . . . One . . . . Zero.'

The solid-fuel rocket boosters attached to the side of the external fuel tank suddenly spewed two solid columns of hell, adding their energies to the one and a half million pounds of thrust being developed by the main engines. A total thrust of nearly seven million pounds was needed to ram the shuttle into space.

'SRB ignition – lift-off.'

The launch controller's phlegmatic voice was nearly lost in the great tide of sound that filled the flight deck. At first there was little sensation of movement, and there was nothing to see out of the windows to suggest that anything was happening.

'*Dominator*, you've cleared the tower. All engines OK. You're looking as sweet as a month's vacation.'

Heinlein felt the mounting pressure on his back as the

233

acceleration gently pushed his body into the seat cushions. He also experienced some vision distortion caused by his eyeballs being pressed into their sockets. He had been warned about the sensation and it did not cause him any discomfort.

'*Dominator*, this is Control. Instituting roll manoeuvre,' advised Earl Hackett's voice as he took over from Launch Control.

At that moment the bodies of all four men began shifting sideways in their seats, caused by the shuttle beginning to twist. By the time the manoeuvre had been completed, the four men were nearly hanging from their harnesses. Heinlein was completely disorientated, no longer sure which way was 'up'.

'Roll manoeuvre completed, *Dominator*. You're looking good.'

'Roger, Control.'

The passing seconds were drowned in the sustained roar from the engines and boosters. Heinlein was watching the computer displays when Neil touched him on the arm and pointed at the two small windows above their heads. The visual effects created in the shuttle simulator in no way prepared Heinlein for the shock of seeing the Atlantic Ocean thirty miles 'above' him.

'Control,' said Pepper. 'This is *Dominator*. We have SRB burnout. Separation is on auto.'

'Roger, out,' Hackett replied.

Dominator was two minutes into her flight when a series of jolts from the exploding bolts heralded the separation of the solid-fuel boosters. These would parachute back into the Atlantic for recovery by two NASA ships waiting on station.

The spacecraft continued its spectacular climb, powered now by the orbiter's three main engines. The inverted spacecraft was clinging to the giant external tank like a winged parasite, greedily draining its dwindling supply of liquid hydrogen and oxygen. The acceleration rate was sustained so that at seven minutes into the flight *Dominator* had reached a height of eighty miles and was travelling at Mach 16. By now its flight path had virtually flattened out so that the Atlantic was visible through the forward windows. The flight computers automatically throttled back the main engines. Bayliss and Pepper adjusted the volume of Earl Hackett's voice to a more comfortable level.

'Control,' said Bayliss. 'This is *Dominator*. We have main engine throttle down, over.'

'Roger, out,' Hackett answered.

Deprived of forty per cent of its power, the shuttle began a long, shallow dive that would take it from a height of ninety miles down to eighty. The spacecraft's velocity mounted. Heinlein thought he saw a ship through the lacework of clouds above. Or was it below? He experienced a sensation of nausea and closed his eyes.

'*Dominator*. This is Control. You are go for main engine cut-off.'

Suddenly the roar of the main engines stopped. The silence was almost shattering in its intensity. Heinlein opened his eyes. He felt curiously comfortable in his seat. Neil grinned at him.

'I know how you feel,' Neil remarked quietly. 'That's the worst bit over. 'We're now going to jettison the external tank. We're nearly into orbit. Watch.' Neil held up the cue card and released it. Instead of falling 'up' to the floor or 'down' towards the roof, the card hung in mid-air.

'Hell,' Heinlein muttered, half to himself. He closed his eyes again when a renewed wave of nausea hit him. Another jolt forced them open again and he saw the huge external tank moving ahead of the shuttle like a departing airship.

'Control, this is *Dominator*. We have ET separation. Initiating minus Zee translation, over.'

'*Dominator*, this is Control. You are go for your OMS ascent burn.'

'Roger, Control, out.'

Bayliss entered the necessary commands on the digital autopilot panel. The small orbital manoeuvring system engines fired. The noise they made was barely audible on the flight deck and their thrust was gentle. The OMS engines burned steadily for twenty minutes – pushing *Dominator* up to her orbital height of two hundred miles. Heinlein's nausea passed and he began to enjoy the curious sensation of his weightless body sinking into his cushions and slowly bouncing back against the restraint harness.

There was a brief cut-off of the OMS engines during which Bayliss and Pepper performed several functions to prepare *Dominator* for orbit.

'*Dominator*, this is Control. You are go for your OMS insertion burn,' Hackett advised when the two astronauts had reported that all was well.

The small engines fired again and were closed down after ten minutes.

'Control, this is *Dominator*. OMS insertion burn cut-off,' Bayliss advised. 'We have achieved orbit.' He turned around in his chair. 'Welcome to space. Mr Heinlein. We are in orbit.'

81 In Bakal Joseph Maken entered his office and unlocked his desk. He removed his facsimile pad from a drawer and picked up the pad's electronic pen. He sat in deep thought. After months of anticipation the wording of the notes eluded him. He toyed with the pen and eventually wrote in Hebrew 'To Prime Minister Hendrik Rymann' at the top of the display. The pad's tiny computer faithfully conveyed the characteristics of Maken's handwriting into its memory, recording every sweep and flourish and even the slight variations in the pen's pressure. When received on a similar pad there would be no doubt that the text was in his handwriting. He stared at what he had written and, without further deliberation, wrote three separate notes to Rymann and signed them.

Maken read through what he had written. The sentences lacked his customary elegance but they were short and to the point. He made a few corrections and touched the appropriate keys to set the pad's memory so that the notes would be transmitted automatically at the preset times. The final operation was to key-in Rymann's personal facsimile number in the address field. It didn't matter that Rymann was in Washington – the notes would arrive on his personal pad no matter where he was in the world.

82 'Bloody hell!' Sarcha yelled and slammed on the brakes. The wheels locked. The camper slewed to a standstill and was enveloped in a cloud of dust kicked up by the skid.

Lena gave a yelp and was thrown forward across Joss. The big Zulu encircled his arms around her to prevent her falling to the floor of the saloon. Fingers, like a bunch of bananas, slipped momentarily inside her safari jacket. The powerful hand closed around her breast and squeezed it roughly. She pushed herself angrily away from the grinning Zulu and joined Sarcha who was staring in astonishment at the herd of elephants crossing in front of the camper. A towering old bull with a broken tusk was confronting the Chieftain, its head lowered menacingly, ears flared, as if it was challenging the vehicle to make the slightest move forward while his wives and offspring were passing by. Eventually the old bull swung his great bulk around and trudged silently in the wake of the last cow. Sarcha watched the jostling herd until it was a safe distance away. He gave a sigh of relief.

'What happened?' Lena demanded.

Sarcha looked sheepish. 'I can't tell a lie. I dozed off.' He chuckled and waved a hand at the departing elephants. 'Christ knows where they popped up from. You'd think it would be safe enough to set the cruise control and go for a pee, eh?'

Lena gazed across the veldt. It was exactly the same scene that they had looked upon at dawn when they had set off and when they had stopped for breakfast. Mile after mile of flat nothingness with the odd anthill and thornbush here and there to ease the monotony. She found it hard to believe that it was possible to drive for five hours with so little change in the terrain. 'Maybe I'd better drive for a while,' she suggested.

Sarcha checked the reading on the inertial navigation unit against the figures written down the side of the map. 'No. It's only another five miles now.' He released the handbrake and the Chieftain began moving again.

'*What* is only another five miles?' Lena enquired.

'The first recce spot.'

Lena glanced back at Joss who returned her look with a grin. He parted his knees and scratched his crotch. She looked away in disgust. 'Sarcha, why have we got him when we've got that navigation system?'

'Local knowledge, sweetheart.'

'Don't give me that bullshit. He's no more local than we are.'

Sarcha chuckled and continued driving. Lena noticed that the coordinates on the navigation unit were beginning to match the first of the two groups of numbers scribbled on the map. After five minutes' driving all the display's digits matched with the exception of the final number. Sarcha slowed down and drove in a circle, stopping when the match was perfect. 'This is the first spot,' he announced.

Lena stared around them. If anything the place was even flatter and there was less grass. 'What spot?'

Sarcha opened the driver's door and the midday heat leapt into the camper like a ravening beast. He jumped down from the cab. From underneath the vehicle he withdrew a six-foot pole that was topped with a white marker board. 'Knock this in here, Joss,' he instructed.

'Sure, Massa Sarch.'

The Zulu pushed the rhino whip into his belt. He removed a club hammer from the camper's tool compartment and proceeded to drive the pole upright into the baked soil. His exertions produced a glistening sheen on his black torso.

'OK, Joss, that's far enough.'

'Will you *please* tell me what the hell's going on!' Lena demanded.

'You'll see, sweetie. All aboard.'

Sarcha checked his bearings with a compass and drove in a straight line across the veldt. There was something hypnotic about the way the long grass disappeared beneath the front bumper. Sarcha swerved to avoid the odd thornbush and occasionally the vehicle lurched as its wheels encountered an anthill. All the time Sarcha kept glancing down at the navigation unit. The digits started matching-in with the second group of numbers on the map. Sarcha stopped when he had a perfect match. Lena saw that he had driven five kilometres from the marker – about three miles.

The process with the marker pole was repeated. Lena watched Joss driving it into the ground and turned to Sarcha. 'Now do you mind telling me what this is all about?'

'Simple, sweetheart,' said Sarcha, mopping the sweat from his forehead. 'Once filming is under way, we're going to need an airstrip to ferry in supplies.' He paused and levelled his binoculars at the first marker. 'This will be our airstrip.'

'Three miles long? What sort of transports will we be flying in here for heaven's sake? SSTs?'

Sarcha laughed. 'We've got the space so we might as well make use of it and be on the safe side.' He opened the tool compartment and removed two spades and a machete. 'OK, sweetheart. You and me will level the anthills and Joss can cut down the thornbushes.'

Lena stared at the Englishman. 'In this heat? You're crazy!'

Sarcha draped a chubby arm across her shoulders. 'Come on, sweetheart. The ground's flat as a pancake anyway. It won't take us more than a couple of hours.'

It took four hours; four hours of back-breaking work under a merciless sun before Sarcha, after a final high-speed drive between the two markers, declared that he was satisfied. As soon as he had parked, Lena shut herself in the shower cubicle and spent ten minutes soaping the dust and sweat from her body.

Joss fastened his hungry eyes on her from where he was sprawled when she emerged from the cubicle. She was wearing a clean safari suit. 'Is nice, Miss Lena,' he observed. 'Very nice.'

'Sarcha!' Lena shouted angrily. 'If you two creeps want an evening meal, you can Goddamn well fix it yourselves. I've had enough of the pair of you.'

The Englishman looked reproachfully at Lena from where he was sitting hunched over the communications console. Open in front of him was a large NASA communications manual containing radio frequency charts, operating modes, and instructions. He pushed his headset clear of one ear. 'Lena, my angel. What a way to speak to your Uncle Sarcha after he's gone to such trouble to prepare a little surprise for you.'

'Surprise? What surprise?' Lena queried suspiciously.

Sarcha touched a tape-recorder key. A faint voice crackled out of the speaker.

'Control. This is *Dominator* payload specialist requesting voice-check. Over.'

Lena's heart leapt. Neil's voice!

The answering voice from the speaker was too faint to distinguish what was said.

'Sorry, I can't do better, sweetheart,' Sarcha apologized. 'We can just hear Kennedy coming through on the TDRS-East repeater satellite. And we're only hearing *Dominator* because I'm pulling in her signal with the pre-amps.' He touched another control. 'OK, let's go live, see what's happening.'

'Roger, Control,' said a voice that Lena did not recognize. 'Neil's lifted the pallet clear with the Canada. She came out real easy without OMS translations. Over.'

'Roger, *Dominator* . . . .'

'That's Earl Hackett's voice,' said Lena excitedly.

'Glad to hear it,' Hackett continued. 'Time you guys grabbed your scheduled four hours' horizontal. We're about to do the same down here. Over.'

'Roger, Control. Sleep tight. Out.'

'They lifted off two hours ago,' said Sarcha. 'Sounds like everything's going OK for them.'

Lena nodded and gave a happy smile.

It had been a long time since she had last smiled.

83 Rymann sat in gloomy silence in the conference room at the Israeli Embassy in Washington and listened to Sam Kuttner's bleak account of his meeting with Walter Swift. Michael Greer was writing some notes and made no contribution to the discussion.

'We would have been better off in Swift's office,' Kuttner concluded. 'The Benjamin Franklin State Dining Room is hardly the place for an informal talk. Not with him on one side of that damn great table and me on the other.'

'OK, Sam. Well, let's hope I have more luck with Harding tomorrow.'

'Somehow I don't think you will,' said Kuttner as he left the room. 'They haven't the will or the interest to help us.'

When they were alone Greer rose from his chair and handed Rymann the notes – as was usual with every document prepared for Rymann, it was a single sheet of paper. 'I don't think there's any point in writing any more drafts,' said Greer. 'It now says everything you have to say to Harding and as concisely as possible.'

Rymann read through the paper and agreed with his friend's view. Of all the statements that had ever been read out to an American President, this one was certain to be the most electrifying in history.

Assuming it was ever chronicled in the history books.

84 Heinlein's leg cracked painfully against the side of the hatch when he hauled himself up the ladder from *Dominator*'s mid-deck to the flight deck.

Moving about in a weightless condition was not as easy as he had supposed. For one thing, without the damping effect of gravity, there was a tendency for limbs, especially legs, to flail about. Indeed, legs were a liability in space because progress around the interior of the orbiter was best achieved with the aid of the hands, either for pushing away from something or to prevent collisions.

Even more disconcerting was the micro-gravity toilet – waste-collection system in NASA jargon – located below on the mid-deck that he had just had to use in a hurry. To make body wastes move in the direction that they should and not float inconveniently about the orbiter's interior, a fan buried deep in the lavatory pan's complex innards sucked a hurricane of air past the toilet user. It was an uncomfortable sensation, unloved by two generations of crewmen and women, but still in use after twenty-five years because no one had come up with a better design.

Heinlein anchored his Velcro overshoes to the platform where Neil was working at the aft crew station. He peered through a window at the cargo bay. The gaping doors had been opened shortly after orbit stabilization to prevent the build-up of the sun's heat within the cargo pallet. Since then Neil had secured the Canada manipulator arm to the pallet's central grapple point and had succeeded in teasing the giant cylinder clear of the cargo bay.

'Looks neat,' Heinlein commented. 'Well done.'

'I was asked to try using the arm instead of an OMS burn. It just needs patience.'

'You won't try opening the pallet ahead of schedule, will you?'

'No. Not during a sleep period. If something went wrong, we might have to go on an EVA. Anyway, it's not possible to go outside in a hurry.'

Heinlein was interested. 'Oh? Why not?'

'The atmosphere in here is normal: normal pressure and the normal mixture of eighty per cent nitrogen and twenty per cent oxygen. The EVA mobility units can't be pressurized to the same extent, therefore you have to breath pure oxygen in them. That means breathing pure oxygen for two hours before an EVA to purge all the nitrogen from your bloodstream. Go into space with nitrogen in your blood and it froths up in your arteries.'

'Like the "bends"?'

'That's right.'

'Was that why you couldn't go after Al Benyon?'

Neil looked levelly at the Israeli. 'That was one of the reasons,' he said coldly.

Heinlein pressed his head against the window to look down at the Earth and could not find it.

'It's that way,' said Neil jabbing a finger at the roof.

Heinlein gazed up at the glorious crescent of blue and white that was suspended above them. 'Do we have to fly upside down all the time?'

Neil shrugged. 'There's no such thing as "up" or "down".'

'That's what my stomach is complaining about.'

'You'd better get some sleep,' said Neil, smiling.

Heinlein went head first through the hatch and banged his leg again when he entered the mid-deck. Bayliss slid aside his privacy panel when he heard Heinlein's curse. The astronaut was lying in his sleep restraint bag on his bunk, or sleep station as NASA called it. There were four of the berths on the right-hand side of the mid-deck opposite the galley. Three were tiered and the fourth one was upright. Bayliss was in the centre bunk.

'How are you making out, Dave?' Bayliss spoke quietly to avoid waking Pepper who was sleeping in the lower bunk with his privacy panel closed.

Heinlein turned his back on the astronaut and pretended to massage a bruise on his leg while opening the pocket on his coveralls and removing the automatic. 'So, so, Jim, but I still keep colliding with everything. And don't talk about my stomach.'

Bayliss chuckled. 'By the time you get used to it, we'll be starting our deorbit burn.'

Heinlein moved to his personal effects locker and took out a towel which he used to conceal the automatic. He turned around to face Bayliss and took a step towards him as though he was going to use the top bunk. 'How many missions have you been on, Jim?'

The astronaut did not have a chance to reply because Heinlein thrust the folded towel in his face and shot him at point-blank range. Heinlein grabbed a handhold to prevent the reaction from the bullet pushing him backwards. Bayliss' face collapsed inwards into a red and white pulp of bone and tissue. His body rocked in the sleep restraint bag and a gout of blood erupted slowly towards Heinlein from the terrible wound. In the weightless conditions the stream formed into obscene crimson globules that gyrated and twisted as if possessed of their own demonic life. Heinlein slammed the panel shut before any of the blood could escape.

Pepper yanked his bunk panel open. 'What in hell –'

A second shot pulverized Pepper's face in the same way. Heinlein thrust the dead astronaut's body back into his bunk and closed the panel. He levelled the automatic at Neil's face that had appeared at the top of the ladder that led to the flight deck. 'Neil! Get down here! Move, unless you want your head blown off too!'

Neil stared at the automatic and opened his mouth to speak.

'I said, move!'

The former astronaut pulled himself down the ladder and turned his body so that he was the same way up as Heinlein. He looked in bewilderment at the closed panels and at a floating globule of blood that had escaped before Heinlein closed the bunk panels.

'They're dead,' said Heinlein curtly. 'And so will you be unless you do exactly as I say. Over against the lockers.'

Without taking his eyes off the automatic, Neil moved to the bank of personal effects lockers. 'You killed Jim and Mike? I don't understand. Why?'

Heinlein used his free hand to pull himself up the ladder to the flight deck. 'You will. Now follow me – but keep your distance.'

Neil did as he was told and watched Heinlein move to the aft crew station.

'OK,' said Heinlein evenly. 'Now sit in the commander's seat . . . . That's right. OK. You've got a microwave ground link antenna for secure, narrow-beam TV and audio communications with Earth stations. Don't deny it because I know as much about this orbiter's communications systems as you do. I want you to lock the beam on to the Kruger National Park in South Africa.' Heinlein indicated the computer screen that showed the outline of the continents below that would be visible from the orbiter's windows. 'The radio "window" on South Africa has just come up, so don't say you can't do it.'

'For Chrissake, Heinlein, just what the hell is all this –'

'Do as I say!' Heinlein snarled, tightening his grip on the automatic and moving nearer to Neil.

Neil stared first at the Israeli and then at the automatic. His hand shook as he reached up to the commander's communication panel and operated the controls. 'I don't know the coordinates,' he said dully.

'Look them up. They'll be the same as those for the D6 emergency landing site.'

Neil requested the information from the computer's read only

243

memory and transferred the readings that appeared on the CRT screen to the antenna autolock. 'OK. We're locked on.'

'Fine,' said Heinlein, plugging his headset into the nearest audio terminal unit and setting the control on his belt to external communication. 'Now select channel 22 on your UHF S band.'

'That's a wide-band TV channel.'

'So? It can carry sound, can't it? Select it.'

Neil did as he was told. Heinlein heard the soft hiss of white noise in his headset. He adjusted the volume control and pressed the PTT button. 'Delta Hotel to Papa Sierra. Do you copy?'

Sarcha's voice answered immediately. It was faint but perfectly recognizable. 'Roger, Delta Hotel! This is Papa Sierra. We copy. A radio two signal. Give me a count so we can autolock the antenna on to you. Over.'

Heinlein counted slowly up to twenty and unkeyed the transmit button. Sarcha's voice when he answered had gained in strength. 'Delta Hotel, we've got you loud and clear.'

Phase one accomplished,' said Heinlein. 'We're standing by for phase two from you in ten minutes.'

'Roger, Delta Hotel. We'll be back in ten minutes. Over and out.'

Lena gave a shrill scream of terror when Joss grabbed her. He threw her down on the camper's bed and sat astride her hips, pinning her wrists to the mattress with one hand and wrenching her jacket open with the other. She screamed again and slammed her knees ineffectually into the Zulu's hard, unyielding back. She might just as well have tried to dislodge a fully grown gorilla. Joss yanked her jacket down over her arms so that they were pinioned to her side.

'OK,' said Sarcha. 'Roll her over.'

Lena's screams became muffled in the mattress as Joss turned her roughly on to her stomach and held her down while Sarcha wound a length of cord around her wrists.

'Scream all you like, sweetheart,' said Sarcha. 'No one's going to hear you out here. OK, Joss – strip her off.'

Lena twisted, squirmed and tried to bite but to no avail. Her trousers and briefs were torn off. Her screams gave way to panic-stricken sobs when she felt cords tighten around her ankles. The bonds prevented her from lashing out with her feet when she felt a hand gliding over her thigh.

'Nice,' said the Zulu appreciatively. 'Joss likes.'

'For Chrissake, you randy black bastard!' Sarcha snarled. 'Do you want to lose your bonus? Do you want to throw away all that money? What we're paying you will buy you enough pussy for a lifetime. But you won't see a penny if you bugger this up. Understand?'

Joss understood and took his hand away. He helped Sarcha tie Lena down to the bunk so that she finished up lying half-naked on her back with her legs held brutally apart by the cords. Tears rolled down her cheeks at the bitter humiliation and embarrassment of being so grossly exposed.

Sarcha picked up one of the portable television cameras and connected it to the communications panel. He switched on the monitor and trained the camera on Lena's face. He sharpened the picture with the focus control and panned the camera over her magnificent body, returning to her face and zooming slowly in so that her wide, terrified eyes filled the monitor screen.

'OK, that's fine,' said Sarcha glancing at his watch. 'Right, Joss me lad, do your stuff.'

Joss gave a broad grin and stood where Lena could see him. He drew the rhino whip from his belt. His powerful fingers toyed lovingly with its elaborately decorated haft.

'Joss comes from a long line of *nKwama*,' said Sarcha chattily. 'Guardians of the king's most prized cattle. His fathers looked after Shaka's cattle, right, Joss?'

Joss's grin widened. 'Das right, Massa Sarch. Shaka, the Great Elephant. An' Cetewayo.'

'Of course. And Cetewayo,' Sarcha agreed, noting with satisfaction that Lena's eyes were riveted on the whip's dangling tip. 'The *nKwama* were famed for their ability with the long whip. An *nKwama* with such a whip could kill a leech or a fly or any parasite on the king's cattle at a distance of thirty paces.' He nodded to the rhino whip. 'And what did the *nKwama* use that sort of whip for, Joss?'

'King's wives,' said Joss simply. 'When day bad girls.'

'Well she hasn't been a bad girl yet, Joss. But give her just a tiny, little taste of what the *nKwama* could do.'

'No. Please, no,' Lena whimpered.

Without acknowledging his order the Zulu suddenly flexed his arm. Before Lena could flinch, there were two sharp cracks that sounded like pistol shots. She felt a stinging sensation between her

245

breasts but that was all. Joss chuckled and spiralled the whip's thong around his wrist.

'Neat,' Sarcha murmured admiringly. 'Take a look, sweetheart.'

Lena opened her eyes and looked down. At first fear made it difficult for her to focus her eyes. And then she saw the neat cross that had been etched between her breasts. It consisted of two one-inch-long weals that were slowly puckering on her skin. A tiny bead of blood welled up where they crossed.

'Talented lad, isn't he sweetheart?' Sarcha observed. 'Of course, whether he uses such a talent on you rather depends on lover boy in the sky above.'

He lifted the television camera and looked through the viewfinder.

Heinlein looked up from his watch. 'Switch on,' he ordered.

Mystified Neil flipped on the receiver. Without any preliminary flicker, a steady colour picture appeared on the central screen between the commander's seat and the pilot's seat. The picture was a close-up of a woman's face.

'Lena . . . .' Neil whispered.

'Key your mike and talk to her,' Heinlein ordered.

Neil did as he was told. 'Lena? Lena – what's –'

Lena heard his voice. 'Neil!' she cried out. 'Neil! They're going to –' She got no further because a hand clamped over her mouth.

Neil twisted around and stared wildly at Heinlein. 'What's happened to her! What have you done to her!' He half rose in the seat but pushed himself down again when Heinlein made a menacing move towards him.

Heinlein adjusted the microphone on his headset. 'OK, Sarcha. Show him the rest of her.'

The picture zoomed out, revealing the rest of Lena and the obscene position in which she was held by the cords around her body. The camera closed in on Joss and tilted down to the whip's tufted tip. The Zulu brushed the tip over Lena's thigh, causing her to cry out in terror. Neil stared at the screen, dumb with horror as the tip moved away and danced enticingly on the ugly weal between her breasts. He tore his eyes away from the ghastly spectacle and looked as if he was about to launch himself at Heinlein.

'One word from me and she's finished,' Heinlein warned. 'And she's finished anyway unless you do exactly what I tell you. If
246

anything happens to me, if Sarcha doesn't hear my voice on every orbit, then your lovely Lena is going to be whipped to the point of death. The black is a Zulu. Believe me, he knows how to use that whip – both ends of it. And if that doesn't kill her, then she'll be tied down on a termite hill and left in the sun. Do you understand?'

Neil made no reply.

'*Do you understand!*'

Neil continued to stare at Heinlein, his eyes burning with a murderous hatred.

'Look at the screen,' Heinlein ordered. 'Look at it! . . . all right then. If that's what you want for her. Sarcha!'

Lena's scream and the double crack of the whip merged as one sound that shrieked from the spacecraft's speakers. A fresh cross appeared on Lena's body. This time it was larger and deeper – the weals were cuts that produced two streaks of blood. And they intersected at Lena's navel. Neil turned his head to the screen and involuntarily shut his eyes. 'All right! All right!' he suddenly shouted. 'Leave her alone, Goddamn you! Tell me what you want me to do and I'll do it, only leave her alone!'

Heinlein relaxed and gave a nod of satisfaction. 'OK, Sarcha. That's enough. We're going to the next phase.' He smiled at Neil. 'OK. Let's get started.'

Sarcha switched the camera off. 'Well done, Joss. Well done,' he complimented. 'Admirable self-control.'

'Thanks, Massa Sarch. Me pretty clever feller, uh?'

'Oh, undoubtedly,' Sarcha agreed, cocking his head on one side and looking thoughtfully at Lena. He reached forward and ran his hand over her flawless thighs. The girl whimpered and tried to shrink away from his touch. 'Very nice,' he murmured. 'So nice that one can't help half hoping that lover boy up there will do something silly.'

The manipulator arm released the last latch on the pallet and the section came free.

'Get rid of it,' said Heinlein.

'They have to be stowed for re-use.'

'Just get rid of it!'

Neil flexed the arm and released its grip on the pallet section. It

247

drifted away from the spacecraft in a slow tumble. He gaped in astonishment at the bales of straw that were packed into the pallet.

'What are they?'

'Bales of straw. What do they look like? Get rid of them too.'

Neil spent the next twenty minutes plucking the bales of straw out of the pallet with the Canada arm and discarding them – a tricky operation because the removal of each bale caused a shift in the pallet's centre of mass. He had to stop work at frequent intervals and use the Canada arm to prevent the pallet developing a dangerous tumble. His skilled use of his left hand to work the arm's pistol-grip controller and his right hand to operate the T-shaped handle that controlled the orbiter, gradually exposed four missiles. They were secured side by side to a launch platform.

'Pull them clear,' Heinlein instructed.

'What are they?'

'What do they look like?'

'They're missiles,' said Neil angrily. 'What sort of missiles?'

'*Dominator*,' said a voice. 'This is Control. Over.'

'Just think about what will happen to Lena,' Heinlein advised softly.

Neil hesitated. He looked through the window at the Massadas and then at Heinlein before keying his microphone. 'Roger, Control. This is *Dominator*. We copy. Over.'

'Hourly check, *Dominator*. Over.'

'Roger, Control. Nothing to report. Over and out.'

'Good,' murmured Heinlein. 'Now pull the missiles clear.'

Neil locked the manipulator arm on to the Massadas' launch platform and eased the cluster of missiles clear of the pallet. He noticed a control box of an unusual type attached to the side of the missile platform. He followed Heinlein's instructions and latched the entire launch platform to the edge of one of the cargo bay doors, using adjustable hooks that were fitted to the platform. When he had finished the four pencil-like shapes of the Massadas were trained at the Earth.

'OK, that's fine,' said Heinlein, inspecting the missiles with the aid of the television camera on the end of the Canada arm. 'Now you can get ready for an EVA.'

'Not until I know what all this is about.'

248

'You'll find out in good time.' Heinlein jerked his automatic at the mid-deck hatch. 'Now move.'

Neil spent the next two hours wearing a portable oxygen system and breathing pure oxygen instead of the orbiter's cabin atmosphere. During the purging period he had to acknowledge two radio checks from mission control.

Heinlein looked at his watch. 'OK, into your EMU,' he ordered.

Neil entered the airlock that was set into the mid-deck bulkhead between the bunks and galley. He slid the door closed and operated the controls that purged the nitrogen from the tiny compartment that was barely large enough for two crewmen. When the control panel indicated that the airlock's atmosphere was pure oxygen, he removed his breathing set and unhooked his spacesuit from its storage frame.

Heinlein watched him through the window in the airlock's cabin door. Donning the spacesuit took Neil ten minutes. After putting on the liquid cooling undergarment, he stepped into the bulky trousers garment and hitched it up. Getting into the upper torso with its built-in life-support system involved positioning it in mid-air and diving his head and arms into it in one smart movement. He pulled on his 'Snoopy' hat and adjusted the position of its microphones before using the controls on his chest to regulate the flow of oxygen. He plugged his intercom cable into a terminal.

'Voice check,' he requested.

'I copy you,' Heinlein's voice answered.

Heinlein watched carefully as the former astronaut pulled on his gloves, snapped them home on to their locking rings and lowered his space helmet into position.

'OK. I'm depressurizing the airlock now,' said Neil when he had checked that his spacesuit was functioning correctly.

As soon as the atmospheric pressure reached zero Neil opened the hatch in the side of the airlock and eased himself into space.

Heinlein returned to the aft crew station. There was a worrying two-minute interval during which Neil was out of sight. And then Neil's ungainly figure appeared, groping its way to the Massadas' launch platform by means of handholds set into the orbiter's fuselage. He reached the missiles and plugged his intercom cable into a socket on the cargo door.

'Listen carefully,' said Heinlein. 'There's a small T-shaped key clipped to the top of the control box. Can you see it?'

Neil positioned his body above the control box. 'I see it.'

'That's the key you'll need to open the access panels on the missiles. They're picked out in yellow.'

'I can see them.'

'Open the panels. But keep yourself clear of my line of sight from the camera. I want to see everything that's going on.'

Neil moved cautiously towards the panels and used the key to unlock them in turn while Heinlein swung the Canada arm to bring the television camera into position. The Israeli zoomed the camera in on the first panel and checked the monitor screen to make sure the close-up of the six-digit combination display behind the panel was in sharp focus.

'OK that's fine,' said Heinlein. 'You see the wheel that alters the combination's last digit? The thumbwheel on the right of the display?'

'I see it.'

'Reset it to read a "9".'

Neil did so. 'OK.'

'Get your mitt out of the way.'

Neil moved his hand out of camera shot.

Heinlein studied the combination. 'OK. That's fine. Close the panel and set the combination on the second panel so that the last digit reads a "3".'

It took five minutes for Neil to reset all four combinations to Heinlein's satisfaction. When he had finished, Heinlein said: 'Excellent, Neil. Well done. Now unclip that control box and bring it into the orbiter.'

'Roger,' Neil acknowledged.

Heinlein rarely allowed his emotions to show, but on this occasion – alone on the flight deck – he permitted himself a smile of satisfaction. Everything was going perfectly to plan: all four nuclear warheads on the Massada missiles were now armed and ready for firing.

85 Despite the forty-eight hours' notice no one was absent; the letter Joseph Maken had sent out to the sixteen members of the PLO Supreme Council summoning them to Bakal had ended with the terse command: 'It is essential that you attend this meeting. No excuses will be tolerated.'

Consequently there was an air of hushed expectancy in the conference room when Maken opened the meeting at 8 a.m. local time. There was no agenda and no pressing matters to deal with other than what was on his mind. He came straight to the point.

'You will recall the meeting a few months ago when I outlined a bold plan to bring about a quick end to the War of Attrition,' he began. 'All of you have at one time or another asked for reports on the progress of the operation and I have remained silent. I apologize for that. My silence has been necessary to ensure the success of the operation. That success is now in sight. The space shuttle *Dominator* is now in orbit and is under the command of the PLO.' Maken glanced at his watch. '*Dominator* has programmed and deployed her four Massadas. The missiles are armed with nuclear warheads and poised to strike against selected targets in our country.'

He paused. No one moved or spoke. Sixteen pairs of eyes were locked unblinkingly on Maken. The only sound in the room was the faint hum of the air-conditioning.

'At noon today,' Maken continued, 'my ultimatum will be delivered to the Israelis requiring their immediate unconditional surrender. The ultimatum spells out what we have done and the consequences of failure to comply with our demands. The Israelis will, of course, reject the ultimatum out of hand. At 2 p.m. we will launch the first Massada. I cannot tell you what the target will be other than that it will be an Israeli township with a population of approximately two hundred thousand. We will then deliver a second ultimatum. That too will be rejected. The second target will be a city. I bitterly regret that so many of our brother Palestinians will be sacrificing their lives in our glorious cause, but it is the one cause that any true Palestinian would willingly give his or her life for.'

251

The sweeping generalization passed unchallenged. Maken pressed on with his statement.

'With the obliteration of the second target and the annihilation of one million Israelis, we believe that the Jerusalem regime, which has occupied our beloved country for nearly three-quarters of a century, will collapse. If it doesn't, then our third target, following my third and final ultimatum, will be Tel Aviv followed by Jerusalem itself. If we have to use all four Massadas, then we will not shirk from doing so. Nor will we shirk from the awesome task of having to rebuild our country in the aftermath of the holocaust. For it will be *our* country once again. Just as it was the land of our fathers, so it shall become the land of our children and their children. And its name shall be Palestine.'

The stillness that followed the end of Maken's statement was broken by one of the council members clapping his hands. It was an unprecedented response to a speech and for some seconds he applauded alone. A second member joined in. One by one all of those at the table rose to their feet, clapping vigorously. They gathered around Maken and laughingly shook hands with him and each other.

86 Sarcha rolled Lena on to her side and untied the cords that bound her.

'OK, sweetheart. Five minutes in the toilet and then we eat.'

Lena was so stiff that Sarcha had to help her into a sitting position. She made an ineffectual gesture of resistance but the sheer fatigue and misery induced by being trussed-up for so long had drained her of the ability and will to fight. The thousand questions that had been crowding her mind over her cruel treatment were banished by the sound of Joss's deep chuckle. The Zulu had paused in his task of fishing steaks out of the camper's microwave oven and was watching her intently. The sight of the evil-looking rhino whip jammed in his belt jolted her senses and she tried to cover herself with a cushion.

Neither of the men made a move to stop her when she went into the toilet and locked the door. The tiny compartment started to spin. She held her head over the hand basin until the sensation of nausea passed. A hot shower soothed away the aches caused by the cords. The two crosses that Joss had cut on her body with the whip were still stinging. She examined them in the mirror and decided that there would be no permanent marks. The shallowness of the cuts was a stark reminder of the Zulu's skill with the whip. It was during that moment that she steadfastly resolved that she would deny her captors the pleasure of seeing her fear. She found her bathrobe hanging on a hook and thankfully pulled it on. Her courage nearly deserted her when she unlocked the door and stepped into the saloon. Sarcha unfolded the table which she sat at without saying a word as Joss served up three plates heaped with steak and peas.

'Now then, sweetheart,' said Sarcha affably, cramming food into his mouth. 'If you go along with us, we won't tie you up. But if you fight and scream . . . .' He finished the sentence with a shrug.

Lena flinched as Joss sat beside her but apart from that she sat still and did her best not to show her feelings. The Zulu took no notice of her and started tearing meat off his T-bone with his fingers. She picked up her fork and toyed with her food. She was torn between hunger and a feeling of revulsion at the thought that the meal had been cooked by the animal sitting beside her. She edged further along the berth. As she did so, her fingers encountered the carving knife that she had dropped on the bed the night before. It had slipped down between the mattress and the backrest. Whilst pretending to tighten her bathrobe, she pushed the knife well out of sight down the side of the mattress.

'So what's it to be, sweetheart?' Sarcha prompted.

Lena forced down some peas to give herself time to think. 'I don't know why you're doing this,' she said, 'or what it has to do with Neil. But I'd rather kill myself than cooperate with you.'

Sarcha nodded in agreement. 'Fair enough, sweetheart. I understand. I daresay having you trussed up looks that much more frightening to lover boy anyway.'

'That's if I don't kill you both first.'

Sarcha was taken aback by Lena's sudden show of spirit. He grinned and chewed noisily on his steak. 'Just as you wish, angel. Just as you wish.'

87 When Neil had recovered the Massada fire control box for Heinlein and brought it back into the *Dominator* there had been a few minutes before he had entered the airlock when he had been out of Heinlein's sight. He had used those precious few minutes to discover exactly what the box was, so he was not surprised by the sight of the miniature visual display screen when Heinlein Velcro'd the box to his knee and opened its lid. The gun was hanging in mid-air in front of Heinlein where he could quickly grab it if Neil tried to make a sudden move towards him.

'You know what this little gadget is?' Heinlein enquired.

'I'm not interested,' Neil replied from his position by the aft crew station where Heinlein insisted he should remain.

'You should be,' said Heinlein, touching the control box's keyboard and bringing the screen to life. He turned the unit sideways so that Neil had a better view of the screen. It bore a high-resolution outline of the North American continent which the shuttle was passing over at that time. The picture was an uncannily accurate duplicate of the image on the flight deck's central CRT display. 'That picture is being generated by the Massadas' celestial/inertial navigation computers,' Heinlein explained. 'Amazing, isn't it? They know exactly where they are in relation to their targets.'

Neil turned his head and looked through the aft window at the four Massadas that were poised on their launcher like a cluster of menacing black darts. 'What targets?'

'You'll find out in three hours.'

'You're crazy, Heinlein. When the motors burn on those rockets, the thrust will take them into a higher orbit.'

Heinlein's face twisted into a mocking smile. 'Not so, Neil. They're designed to operate in space. Once launched, they'll automatically orientate themselves so that their thrust cancels their orbital velocity and they fall earthwards. A deorbit burn I think you call it. As I said, those missiles know exactly where they are and what manoeuvres they'll have to make to hit their targets.'

'Who are you working for? Who planned all this?'

'You wouldn't believe me if I told you.'

88 The air-conditioning was unable to cope with the reek of strong, black coffee and every horizontal surface in the listening room adjoining the satellite communications room was hidden under a speckled sea of white plastic cups. The members of the PLO Supreme Council were sprawled in low chairs; some were chatting animatedly in small groups, some were having a serious discussion with Maken on the future administrative structure of Palestine and some were watching the battery of monitor screens that were displaying Israel's ten television broadcast channels.

Maken clapped his hands for silence. Everyone stopped talking and watched expectantly as a radio engineer sat at a control panel and tuned a complex receiver to 1.429 megahertz, the frequency of Israel's external services transmitter at Refidim. It was the frequency that Maken had specified in his ultimatum for the Israeli government to use when announcing its capitulation. The engineer flipped on the speakers. The sound of a concert from Tel Aviv briefly flooded the room until the engineer hurriedly adjusted the volume to a comfortable level. His last task was to preset a UHF transceiver so that Maken could talk directly to Heinlein in the *Dominator*. But the most important piece of equipment in the room was a blue telephone that could enable Hendrik Rymann to speak personally to Maken.

Maken looked at the wall clock that was displaying Eastern Standard Time. 'Comrades. Brothers,' he announced. 'In ninety minutes the State of Israel will have ceased to exist.'

89 Washington. The photocall for the benefit of the newsmen ended at 11.05 a.m. local time. Five minutes later President Harding and Hendrik Rymann were alone in the White House's high-ceilinged Oval Office. Rymann sat with his back to the bank of three-D confervision screens that kept the President in close touch with his senior aides and advisors. Both men made the maximum use of the preliminary polite exchanges to size each other up. Both were impressed. Harding was a tall, soft-spoken greying man, with aristocratic good looks and an air of relaxed authority. After two minutes in his presence Rymann sensed that here was a man who commanded respect because of his ability to see right to the heart of a problem with minimal briefing. Harding's other talents included the rare mixture of being a good listener and an attention-commanding speaker. Harding, Rymann instinctively sensed, was one of those born leaders who would later distinguish himself by his attention to detail.

Harding in turn, was impressed by Rymann's candour and directness, as was evidenced by the Israeli leader's opening remarks.

'Mr President. Thank you very much for seeing me. I have only an hour of your time, therefore I intend making full use of it. You know why I have come and I know that you are fully aware of the grave peril facing my country at the moment. I feel that any reiteration of our circumstances would be a waste of time.'

Harding regarded his visitor steadily. 'Your approach makes for a refreshingly welcome change, Mr Prime Minister. You are correct – I understand the situation in your country perfectly.'

'We have submitted to your administration two lists detailing materials' increases in the supply of military aid to Israel. The first list is one that we are prepared to make public and which you clearly cannot agree to. The requirements in the second list are much more modest but they represent the minimum level of military support that we need in order to guarantee our survival for at least another three years.'

'I studied the two lists with great interest,' said Harding, making a note on his memory pad. 'The principal request on the first list is for the supply of two hundred B9 fighter-interceptor-bombers. The second list requests a hundred B9s.'

'I'll be frank with you, Mr President,' said Rymann. 'The B9 is essential to us and the absolute minimum we require is seventy-five, plus a three-year spares and ground-support facility.'

'Why three years?'

'Because by then we will have developed a weapon that will make us independent of external aid.'

'Can you give me more details?'

'Can you say whether or not you are prepared to supply us with a hundred B9s?' Rymann countered. 'Forgive me, Mr President, I mean no disrespect, but I would appreciate a straightforward yes or no answer.'

'You deserve one. The answer has to be no.'

Rymann decided that there was no point in disguising his disappointment. He was silent for a moment – seemingly at a loss for words. When he finally spoke, his voice was strangely calm. 'I don't mean to sound melodramatic, but your words have sounded the death knell of my country.'

'I doubt it,' Harding observed cryptically. 'For many years I have admired the courage and resourcefulness of the Israeli people. I have every confidence in your ability to come up with something.'

Rymann touched the fingerprint recognition pad on his brief-case. The lid clicked open. 'Would it surprise you if I told you that we already have come up with something, Mr President?'

The icy note in Rymann's voice put Harding on his guard although he was careful not to show it. 'I'm not sure I follow you, Mr Prime Minister.'

'Your refusal to supply us with B9s means that we have no choice but to put into operation a plan that will give us the three-year breathing space we require.'

'Is this meeting the place to discuss your strategic planning?'

Rymann gave the impression of choosing his words carefully, when in fact he had already worked out with Greer what he would say to President Harding. 'Mr President. Yesterday one of NASA's shuttles – the *Dominator* – lifted off from the Kennedy Space Center. Stowed in its cargo bay were several of our intermediate-range Massada missiles armed with nuclear warheads. The shuttle is now under the command of an officer in the Israeli army who has instructions to launch the missiles against selected targets in the Soviet Union unless he hears to the contrary from me. You see, Mr President, we have decided that if the world wants Israel destroyed, and I'm sorry if I'm sounding melodramatic again, then Israel will destroy the world. We will exact an ultimate eye for an ultimate tooth.'

Not a muscle moved on Harding's face although his electric pencil stopped making notes on his memory pad.

Rymann produced a sheaf of documents and placed them before Harding. 'Those are detailed specifications of the Massada missiles with particular reference to their celestial/inertial navigation

257

systems. Your experts are free to study them. When they have done so, they will confirm that we do indeed have the ability to carry out our threat. Historically, my country has a track record of not uttering threats unless we have every intention of carrying them out. Whether or not we carry out this particular threat is entirely up to you.'

90 'Dominator, this is Control. Over.'
It was Earl Hackett's voice, sounding uncharacteristically strained. His check call was fifteen minutes early.

Heinlein was still sitting in the commander's seat with the Massada control box Velcro'd to his knee. He looked at his watch and gestured with the automatic to the pilot's seat. 'Acknowledge him. On PTT, not VOX.'

'Roger, Control,' Neil answered when he had pushed himself down into the pilot's seat. 'This is Dominator. We copy. Over.'

'Roger, Dominator. Go to conference secure channel group 13 USB.'

'Is that a scrambled channel group?' Heinlein queried when he saw Neil release his PTT – press to talk key.

'Yes.'

'OK. Go ahead.'

Neil reached up to the communications panel and spun the thumbwheels to a new setting. 'Control, this is Dominator. Over.'

'We copy Dominator. What in hell's going on up there?'

Heinlein keyed his microphone. 'Control. This is Lieutenant David Heinlein of the IDF. Do you hear me?'

There was a flat, unemotional tone in Hackett's voice when he replied, as if the substance of a bad dream had been confirmed. 'Roger, Heinlein. We copy you.'

'How secure is this channel?'

'One hundred per cent, Dominator. You're on microwave line-of-sight link to various ground stations along your track. Switching is automatic. Stand by.'

For an instant before Hackett unkeyed his microphone, Heinlein heard someone talking in the background to the ground controller.
258

He waited while keeping a wary eye on Neil. Hackett's voice came back a few seconds later.

'*Dominator*, we understand you have deployed an unauthorized cargo. Can you confirm?'

'Roger, Control, we confirm.'

Another long pause, then: 'What has happened to Jim Bayliss and Mike Pepper?'

Heinlein nodded to Neil to reply. 'Control, this is *Dominator*,' Neil answered. 'Jim and Mike have been shot. They're dead.' He snapped the words out and braced himself, half expecting a slug to tear into his body but Heinlein appeared unconcerned by the directness of the reply.

'Roger, *Dominator*,' Hackett intoned woodenly. 'We understand your problems. We would like a picture of your cargo.'

Heinlein keyed his microphone. 'Hackett, this is Heinlein. The Canada camera is already trained on the cargo. We'll give you a fifteen-second slow-scan picture on this band starting from now.' He unkeyed and said to Neil: 'OK, go ahead. Give them a fifteen-second eyeball of the Massadas.'

Neil touched out the controls necessary to activate the manipulator arm's television camera. A picture of the four missiles appeared on the flight deck's monitor screen. He thumbed the external transmit key for fifteen seconds and released it.

'Roger, *Dominator*. We copied that.' Hackett's voice was misleadingly calm.

Heinlein keyed his microphone. 'Hackett, do you hear me?'

'We copy you, *Dominator*. Go ahead, Heinlein.'

Heinlein checked the lapsed time indicator on the Massada firing control box. 'I shall be launching the first cargo unit in one hour – that's at 2.30 p.m. EST. But if our meteoroid proximity radar warns us of the approach of any missiles, or if you use any form of ECM radar jamming against us, then I shall launch my cargo immediately. Is that clearly understood?'

'Roger, Heinlein. Understood.'

91 At that moment President Harding, with Walter Swift at his side, was locked in confervision with Professor Anton Horovitz, Director of the Defence Intelligence Agency at the Pentagon. At thirty-five years old, the professor was President Harding's most trusted and respected advisor on military affairs. The matter was so urgent that there was not even enough time for him to go to the White House.

'I'm looking at the specifications now,' said Horovitz, speaking from one of the bank of monitor screens in the Oval Office. The professor was studying a screen that was out of the fixed camera's field of view. 'Some typical Litton celestial-fixing logic circuitry . . . I'm not sure what that does . . . Ah yes, that would be the reorientation buffer store. Circuit diagram thirty-six clearly shows –'

'Professor,' Harding broke in. 'I know you've had only a few minutes to study the information. But from what you've seen, do you think the Massadas are capable of striking at principle targets on Earth?'

Horovitz looked up at the camera so that he appeared to be looking directly at the two men. 'Yes, Mr President. The design concepts are excellent.'

'What targets can the missiles threaten?'

Horovitz did some hurried calculations. 'In one hour the *Dominator*'s orbital position will provide it with a favourable window on Soviet targets lying between fifty and sixty degrees north.'

Harding's brain wrestled with his knowledge of Eastern hemisphere geography. 'What cities does that include?'

'Leningrad, Kazan, Gorki, Moscow –'

'Thank you, Professor,' Harding interrupted. 'Remain on standby.' He thumbed the desk key to isolate his voice for a second. 'Holy shit.'

'General Hastings is standing by,' said Swift who was listening on an earphone to another conversation.

'I'm going back to Pelham first.' Harding pressed another key on the panel that was set into his desktop. Jason Pelham's gaunt
260

features appeared on one of the confervision monitors. The NASA executive's face registered nothing of the shock he had experienced when he had learned an hour earlier that his *Dominator* had been seized by Heinlein.

'Pelham, go ahead,' Harding ordered.

'The earliest we can launch a shuttle is thirty hours, Mr President. We cannot begin a roll-out until –'

There was no time for explanations. Harding cut Pelham off in mid-sentence, telling him to press on with the crash programme preparations to launch a shuttle. 'General Hastings, go ahead.'

General Theodore Hastings of the recently formed Space Defence Command at Vandenburg had been about to sink a putt on the eighth hole when his wristwatch alarm had sounded, summoning him to the confervision terminal in his mobile command centre. He was wearing his golfing cap and sweating slightly as he faced the camera. It was the first time he had ever spoken to President Harding. 'Mr President, all my staff officers are assessing the situation now. We require four hours to reorientate the PHOTON 6 gas-laser killer satellites. As you know, the PHOTON satellite chain was designed to destroy terrestrially launched missiles. They cannot –'

'What other means do we have of destroying the *Dominator*?'

'Sure. There's a thousand and one ways. But no way of doing it quickly enough. We can launch an AMS20 anti-satellite missile but the *Dominator* will have it in sight for three minutes during its approach –'

'That's useless,' Harding broke in. 'Isn't there any way of knocking out that Goddamn shuttle without it knowing about it?'

'No, Mr President. It's impossible to approach an orbital vehicle by stealth.'

'OK. Standby. Horovitz, go ahead.'

'A private word Mr President.'

Harding isolated the channels so that none of the others present at the conference could hear or see himself and the professor. 'OK, Professor, go ahead.'

'We've got fifty minutes. Number one priority is to persuade Rymann to give us more time.'

'We've tried,' said Swift. 'He says that Heinlein will accept only one order from him and that's to abort the attack.'

'No politician would narrow his manoeuvring room to that

extent,' Horovitz reasoned. 'We've got to press Rymann for more time.'

Harding gave a bitter laugh. 'It's not his manoeuvring room that he's narrowed – it's ours. His view is that the time he has given us is long enough for us to come to a decision. He said that asking us to agree to military aid on the scale that he wants does not require a reversal of our arms supply policy, but merely a reinstatement of our previous policy. The question right now is, do we warn Dranski?'

'No.'

'Why not? If the Soviet beam weapons could zap that shuttle –'

'There's several reasons why we shouldn't tip off the Soviets just yet,' said Horovitz. 'One reason is that they won't believe us. They're going to think it's a neat little scheme we dreamed up to test the effectiveness of their particle-beam systems.'

'For Chrissake!' Harding expostulated. 'Surely they're not going to think that we would sacrifice the lives of our astronauts so that we could learn about their defence systems?'

'How do they know we've got astronauts on that shuttle?' Horovitz pointed out. 'NASA experimented last year by launching an unmanned supply shuttle up to the space hospital. For all the Soviets know, we could have faked the voices of the *Dominator*'s crew.'

'Let's look at the possibility of telling Dranski the truth,' Harding suggested.

Horovitz frowned. 'I've thought about that. OK – so we tell him his country is being threatened by missiles launched from a US spacecraft? Walter Swift knows him well enough to know how he would react.'

Harding looked enquiringly at Swift. It was a question that was already uppermost in the Secretary of State's mind. He nodded. 'Dranski would smell monumental treachery and would threaten us with retaliatory strikes. And they wouldn't be empty threats. Once Soviet radar picked up the Massadas leaving the shuttle and on course for entry into their airspace, they would launch counter-strikes against us.'

The Georgian mantel clock in the elegant office ticked through several seconds of silence before anyone spoke.

'I've got a suggestion,' Horovitz ventured. 'Leave Rymann to sweat for another twenty minutes. Then call him in and begin
262

negotiations. Within fifteen minutes of his deadline, let the negotiations start swinging in his favour. Ten minutes before the deadline, give him some ground, not to much but just enough for him to realize that he needs more time. If you get an hour out of him, you can get two hours, and then maybe six hours. With six hours to play with, General Hastings might be able to come up with something.'

'Dangerous,' Harding commented, seeing Swift nod in agreement.

'Sure it's dangerous,' Horovitz agreed. 'But without some time on our side, we don't have a choice. The sonofabitch has gotten us over a barrel with our hands and feet tied to the floor. We've got fifteen minutes before you call Rymann in. Let's use it to make some checks.'

92 After a five-minute flight from Aldershot, the British Army Cougar helicopter dropped towards the undulating lawns of the University of Surrey and hovered with its undercarriage skids suspended a few inches above the grass.

Sir Max Flinders instinctively ducked as he dashed under the spinning rotors. A door swung open. Two soldiers in full combat dress reached out and hoisted the scientist aboard. The machine was lifting away and swinging south even before the door was slammed shut.

'Sir Max Flinders? Brigadier Austin Scott. Garrison Commander, Aldershot. I'm sorry about the suddenness of all this.'

Baffled, Flinders shook hands with the middle-aged officer. He noticed that there were ten soldiers sitting on the helicopter's floor. 'My secretary took your call, Brigadier. What is this all about?'

'Ten minutes ago I received a signal direct from the Prime Minister's office. Do you know Thursley Hall?'

'David Heinlein's residence. Yes, of course I know it.'

'That's where we're going.'

Flinders glanced out of a window. The machine was flying very low and very fast. He assumed that the main road, whose general direction they were following, was the A3. 'Why, Brigadier?'

The garrison commander shrugged. 'I'm as baffled as you, Sir

Max. My instructions are to fly you to Thursley Hall for you to identify any property on the premises that belongs to your university.'

The scientist gaped at the senior officer. 'Stolen property? But I still don't understand. Surely stolen property is a police matter. And David Heinlein can't possibly be involved in –'

'Landing area in sight, saar!' an NCO reported.

Brigadier Scott acknowledged and gestured to the radio transceiver and pin microphone that was clipped to his lapel. 'All I know, Sir Max, is that the Prime Minister himself is waiting at the end of this link for my report.'

The stately gabled rooftops of Thursley Hall appeared straight ahead. The door opened. The wash from the rotors blasted into the helicopter's interior. The machine lost height and stirred up a hurricane of movement among the trees surrounding the broad lawn as it settled on its skids. A barked command from the NCO and the soldiers tumbled on to the grass. With rifles at the ready they quickly fanned out and converged on the house. The housekeeper appeared and gaped in astonishment. She promptly thrust her hands into the air when ordered to do so by a soldier.

The next few minutes passed in a bewildering whirl for Flinders as shouting soldiers ushered him from room to room. 'What the hell am I supposed to be looking for?' he wailed plaintively to Brigadier Scott when the dining-room doors were kicked open for his benefit.

'Saar!' the NCO bawled out. 'Large locked barn outside. We're going to use ring charges on the doors!'

A minute later Flinders witnessed circles of small explosive charges obliterate the locks and hinges on the doors of Thursley Hall's oversized barn. The great doors toppled outwards and fell with a mighty crash like the walls of Jericho. The NCO dived into the barn and threw himself flat as though he were expecting a horde of guerillas to open fire on him. For a few minutes he lay prone on the floor just inside the entrance. He stood and turned to the watchers. He spoke quietly in his natural voice.

'I think we've found something interesting, sir.'

Flinders followed Brigadier Scott into the barn. He saw nothing at first because the light was behind him and his eyes had still to adjust to the gloomy interior. There was a click and the barn filled with light. A soldier swore and sucked in his breath at the sight of the colossal apparition with its single staring eye that was sitting squat and ugly in the centre of the barn's floor.

A paralysis seemed to have seized Flinders. He stared for endless seconds at the mighty satellite. 'Sir Max,' a distant voice kept repeating at his side. 'Do you recognize this machine?'

'What?' he heard himself say.

'This machine,' said the brigadier. 'Is it yours?'

'Yes,' said the voice.

'What is it?'

There was no reply and the army officer had to repeat his question. He looked in concern at the scientist and wondered if he was about to suffer a heart attack. 'Sir Max, are you all right?'

Flinders moved his lips. 'Yes, I'm sorry.'

'What is this machine?'

'*Cyclops* – an orbital observatory.' The words were a whisper.

'What is it doing here?'

A long pause. 'I don't know. It should be in Earth orbit. I wondered why we hadn't had confirmation . . . ' The scientist was unable to finish the sentence.

Brigadier Scott nodded and fingered the touch key on his miniature radio.

As Flinders gazed upon his beloved satellite, he found himself wishing that he were a weaker man so that he might weep.

93 Heinlein pushed the automatic into his breast pocket, forcing Neil to abandon the idea of launching himself across the flight deck and grabbing the weapon. The two men had remained silent for the past thirty minutes. That both of them looked momentarily startled when the speakers came to life was an indication of the state their nerves were in.

'*Dominator*, this is Control. Copy?'

'OK, answer him,' Heinlein ordered, dropping a warning hand on to the automatic's butt.

'Roger, Control. This is *Dominator*. We copy you.'

'How are you doing up there, Neil?'

'Nothing to report,' Neil replied noncommittally.

'We've fixed up a patch through to a Washington office. We need a voice check from you. Over.'

'Roger, Control. Go ahead.'

'OK, *Dominator*. Go ahead, Washington.'

'*Dominator*, this is Washington. Can you hear me OK?' The voice was vaguely familiar to Neil. Heinlein appeared to recognize the voice because he suddenly became tense. He looked expectantly at the nearest speaker.

'Roger, Washington,' Neil acknowledged, wondering who the voice belonged to. 'This is *Dominator*. We copy you.'

Earl Hackett's voice broke in. 'OK, Neil. That's fine. Remain on standby.'

Heinlein chuckled. 'Know who that was?'

'It's a voice I've heard before.'

The Israeli gave a mirthless laugh and ran his fingers through his dark hair. 'Of course you've heard it before. That was President Harding. It looks like we've got a direct line to the White House.'

'Who are you, Heinlein?'

'Lieutenant David Heinlein, Special Parachute Brigade of the Israeli IDF.'

Neil nodded. 'And you're going to use those missiles against the PLO base at Bakal?'

Heinlein stared Neil straight in the eye. 'One Massada is set for Bakal.'

'And the other targets?'

'The Soviet Union. Two on Moscow and one on Leningrad.'

Neil focused his eyes on the instrument panel before him. The familiarity of the controls helped him maintain a grip on reality. 'Why?'

Heinlein was silent for a while, as if marshalling his thoughts. When he finally spoke there was a curiously intense quality about his voice. He was no longer the inscrutable Israeli whose innermost thoughts one could only guess at. 'Have you ever heard of Massada?' he asked, looking past Neil through the forward windows.

Neil searched his memory. The name meant something. 'Wasn't there an old film about it? About some Jews who committed suicide?'

Heinlein nodded. 'Years ago, when I first joined the army, I was taken to Massada. It's now a ruined mountain fortress in the Judean

266

Desert. It's where a thousand of my people killed themselves rather than allow themselves to be captured by the Romans. I was taken to Massada with about twenty other newly commissioned officers. It was night. Do you know what the Judean Desert is like at night? You can almost feel the ghosts of Abraham, David, Solomon, reaching out and touching you, guiding you up the snake path to the summit of Mount Massada. It's a strange feeling. At no other time have I ever felt the strength of the bond between me and my country. Does that sound silly to you?'

Neil could think of nothing to say.

Heinlein smiled. 'It must do. You have no idea what it's like to have five thousand years of history prodding you in the back. Anyway, we climbed Massada in the darkness, stumbling about, terrified of falling. We arrived at the top with bleeding fingers and aching feet. Then there was a torchlight procession that ended at the terrace where the Romans came upon the bodies of my people. A thousand men, women, and children. That's where we stood in a circle and took our oath: that Massada would never fall again; that never again would the enemy set foot in Israel. Every detail of that scene, and its meaning, will remain with me for the rest of my life. We also swore that if the opportunity ever arose for us to destroy the enemies of Israel, even if it meant destroying ourselves and our land, then we would seize that opportunity.' Heinlein's dark eyes settled on Neil. 'Either that or we would create the opportunity – which is why we're here now.'

'The Soviet Union is not threatening your country with nuclear missiles,' Neil observed pointedly.

Heinlein shrugged and ran his finger around the firing keys on the control box. 'The Soviets are using methods to destroy us that suit them. Politically they're more likely to get away with slowly bleeding us to death from a thousand cuts administered by their PLO friends than they would with a quick death from one sword thrust. Unfortunately their slow death is dangerously fast for us, therefore we need time. That's why I'm here – to win time for my country – not to fire the missiles. But if I have to, then I won't hesitate.'

'And how do you hope to win time? By blackmailing my country into supplying your country with arms?'

Heinlein chuckled. 'More by demonstrating to your country just how dangerous a cornered rat can become.'

The atmosphere in the listening room was electric. The chatter had died away and all those present were staring at the UHF transceiver, waiting for it to burst into life as Maken had assured them it would. Maken picked up a telephone and requested, for the third time in an hour, for an engineer to check the equipment.

The digital clock on President Harding's desk was indicating 2.05 p.m. – twenty-five minutes before Rymann's deadline – when the Israeli Prime Minister was shown back into the Oval Office to face President Harding alone. The first thing that Rymann noticed was that Harding was wearing a tiny earphone radio in his right ear. He wondered how many people on the President's staff were listening in to every word that would be spoken in the office.

'Before we go any further,' said Harding coldly, 'I have to know what targets the Massadas are programmed for.' He turned the digital clock around slightly so that Rymann could see it. 'You have twenty-four minutes, Mr Prime Minister.'

Rymann's expression was one of surprised innocence. 'Surely your experts have calculated the likely targets that the Massadas will have a window on in twenty-four minutes' time, Mr President?'

'Bakal is one of them?'

'Of course.'

'And the other targets?'

Rymann's smile was that of a man who knows he has the upper hand. 'Let us hope that that worry does not arise, Mr President.' His gaze dropped to the coloured telephones on the President's desk. 'I take it we now have a communications link from this office to the *Dominator*?'

'The blue phone,' Harding replied. 'I want you to use it now to tell Heinlein to delay by an hour any action that he may be planning.'

Rymann shook his head. 'As I have already explained, Lieutenant Heinlein's orders are to proceed at 2.30 p.m. The only instruction he will accept from me is the order to abort the operation. And that can only come if you agree to step-up your military aid. As leader of a country that has lost so many of its young on foreign battlegrounds, you of all people must applaud the fact that we, unlike so many other countries, are not asking for your blood – only your bludgeons.'

'I appreciate that,' said Harding curtly. 'What I don't appreciate
268

is why a responsible statesman should give himself so little room for manoeuvre. We need more time.'

Rymann gestured to the digital clock. 'We now have twenty-two minutes, Mr President.'

Harding's expression hardened. 'We do not continue with this meeting until you've told Heinlein to hold off for another hour.'

Rymann gave a little bow. 'Very well then, Mr President. Thank you for seeing me. I shall wait outside in case you wish to resume the meeting.'

To Harding's amazement, the Israeli politician turned on his heel and walked out of the office.

'Walter!' Harding snapped, appearing to talk to an empty office. 'Keep him talking!'

A thin voice replied in Harding's ear. 'He's taken a seat outside and is just sitting there. The guy's nuts!'

Harding glanced at his watch. Twenty minutes. Christ. 'OK, Walter, leave him. No one is to talk to him. If he wants a trial of nerves, we'll give him one. Clear the ante-room. If he wants to talk to me, he can come back in here by himself.'

Harding slouched back in his high-back swivel chair and removed the earpiece radio. He thought deeply for a minute and then thumbed the control that gave him a wide-angle television picture of the ante-room. It was deserted except for Hendrik Rymann. The Israeli statesman was sitting perfectly relaxed in one of the chairs. He was reading a copy of the *Washington Post* as though waiting for a flight to be called.

Two more minutes ticked by. Eighteen to go.

Harding worked the zoom control. Rymann's unconcerned face filled the picture. The politician appeared to be concentrating on the paper and yet his eyes were not following the lines of newsprint. A rapidly pulsing vein on Rymann's neck caught Harding's eye. The US President spent one minute of the precious eighteen counting the pulses. One hundred and sixty.

The Georgian clock whirred quietly to itself and chimed a quarter after two.

Fifteen minutes.

There was a rustling from the ante-room. Unbelievably, Rymann had turned to another newspaper and was chuckling to himself at the comic section. Nevertheless, the Israeli's heartbeat had risen to one hundred and eighty per minute. Despite that Harding found himself admiring the man's brilliant act and the country that could produce such men. His thoughts turned to the days when Israel and the United States had shared a close relationship.

Twelve minutes.

Two telephone lights started flashing and the earpiece radio was making frantic squawking noises. Harding pushed it back into his ear and listened. 'IT'S OK, Walter. I know exactly what I'm doing.' He pulled out the earpiece and tossed it on his desk. He looked up at the television screen and resumed his study of Hendrik Rymann.

Ten minutes.

Harding was rewarded by the sight of Rymann slowly twisting his wrist so that he could look at his watch. A hand went up and covered the furiously pounding vein. Harding smiled to himself.

Eight minutes.

The lonely Chieftain camper was aiming a lengthening shadow away from the sun across the African bush when Sarcha tuned into the frequency he had been using to talk to Heinlein in the shuttle.

'Papa Sierra to Delta Hotel, do you copy?'

There was no answer.

Sarcha frowned and double-checked the frequency his transceiver was tuned to. 'Papa Sierra to Delta Hotel. Call?'

Again no answer. He switched on the monitoring receiver and called out again. He heard his own voice loud and clear in his headphones. It was being picked up by the monitoring receiver, so there was no doubt that the transmitter was working and that he was calling on the correct frequency.

As he unkeyed the microphone the signal meter suddenly indicated a carrier wave. 'Base to Papa Sierra. Do you copy?' Sarcha recognized the voice immediately. It was Joseph Maken.

'Roger,' he acknowledged. 'This is Papa Sierra.'

'Peter? What's happening?'

'I'm sorry, sir. I don't know.'

'He should have called fifteen minutes ago.' There was an accusing note in Maken's voice.

'There must be a communication problem, sir. Maybe some intense Sporadic E which is blocking his signals. Such atmospheric conditions don't last and they won't interfere with the

270

operation. It would be better if we kept the frequency clear in case he's trying to get through.'

'We're listening out,' Maken grunted.

'Wassa matter, Massa Sarch?' asked Joss.

Sarcha slid the headphones off his ears and switched over to the speaker. He shook his head, perplexed. 'I don't know, Joss,' he said slowly.

The Zulu gestured to Lena who was regarding the two men calmly.

'You want maybe I should . . . ?'

'No. Leave her alone for the moment.'

In the *Dominator* Heinlein steadied the control box on his knee and flipped up the guards that covered the four press buttons. A warning light winked frantically. He turned the arming key and a second warning light joined in. The Massadas were ready for launching. All that was required now was four jabs with his finger. He wanted to close his eyes and offer up a silent prayer, but Neil was watching his every move with cat-like intentness.

Neil sized up the risks involved in getting the control box from Heinlein. After all, what was his life against the lives of the millions below? And then there was Lena. It was the thought of what might happen to her that forced him to think rationally and calmly. Perhaps he should get Heinlein talking again, just in case an opportunity presented itself. He cleared his throat and asked: 'Did you plan all this yourself?'

Heinlein looked surprised. 'Of course not.'

'Then who did?'

'I don't know. He was just a voice on the phone. Someone very high up. I used to call him practically every day to let him know how things were proceeding and to receive my orders.'

Neil remembered Lena commenting on Heinlein's frequent long-distance calls. 'Then if you don't know who you are working for, how did you get involved in all this in the first place?'

Heinlein toyed thoughtfully with the control box but kept his eyes on Neil. 'Well, I don't suppose it'll hurt to tell you now. He sprang me from prison.'

The look of surprise on Neil's face caused Heinlein to smile tiredly. 'Sounds strange, doesn't it? Well – it's the truth. I was serving a prison sentence on a trumped-up court martial charge

271

when suddenly I received a note from him telling me that I was pardoned and that I was wanted to carry out some work for the government.'

'And you agreed?' Neil prompted, this time out of genuine curiosity rather than a desire to keep Heinlein talking.

'Yes – once I'd called my new employer's number and found out what he wanted me to do.' Heinlein's face hardened. 'Even if I was committed to prison through no fault of mine, I was still an Israeli – through and through. I took my oath at Massada, just like every other Israeli soldier. If Israel goes down, then, by my God, I'll see that the rest of the world goes down with her.'

There was an embarrassed silence.

'So where does Sarcha fit into all this?'

The burst of laughter from Heinlein was as sudden as it was unexpected. 'That's the biggest joke of all. Sarcha is a Palestinian mercenary. All along he and his PLO friends have fondly believed that I've been working for them. My employer even fixed up for me to be on the wrong end of an assassination attempt in New York, just so that I'd look good to the PLO. Right now Joseph Maken is sitting in a radio room at Bakal waiting for the capitulation of the Israeli government because he thinks that I shall be launching the missiles against Haifa, Tel Aviv and Jerusalem.'

There were six minutes left before Rymann's deadline when Harding opened the door that led to the ante-room.

Rymann slowly lowered his newspaper and looked questioningly at the US President.

'Mr Rymann,' said Harding quietly, holding the door open in a gesture of invitation. 'I think we should resume our discussion.'

The movements of the two men were deliberately unhurried. Harding returned to his desk and held out his hand to a seat. Rymann sat down. The digital clock was showing 2.25 p.m.

'The few minutes we have left are ample for what I have to say,' said Harding. 'I spent a few moments thinking about the predicament facing your country. I have put myself in your shoes and asked myself what I would do if I was you.' Harding gave a wry smile. 'You know, I would have done the same thing, Prime Minister. That is, assuming I had the men and women to put such a brilliant scheme into operation. You shall have your military aid. There's no reason why an airlift of supplies should not start next week.'

Suddenly the strain of the past months – and the past thirty minutes in particular – caught up with Rymann. His good-humoured face crumpled. He opened his mouth to speak but he found that the words would not come.

Harding looked at the Israeli – in concern at first and then in near panic. Christ! Just when the Israeli's voice was the only thing that could prevent a holocaust he had to go and have a coronary! 'Prime Minister, are you OK?'

Rymann took a deep breath in an effort to rid himself of the curious sense of detachment from his body that had assailed him. 'Yes, Mr President, I'm fine.' He chuckled. 'It would be typical of my good timing to pick this moment for a heart attack, eh?'

The digital clock was registering 2.27 p.m. and Harding failed to see anything to joke about. He rested his hand on the blue telephone. 'Two conditions, Prime Minister. You want extensive military aid for three years. You shall have it. But I shall still be in office in three years and I reserve the right to cut off all aid to Israel at the end of the three-year period.'

'Agreed,' said Rymann. 'And the second condition?'

'My guess is that your plans are for the shuttle to land outside the United States. It must return to Kennedy so that Lieutenant Heinlein can stand trial for the murder of astronauts Pepper and Bayliss.'

2.28 p.m. on the digital clock. Two minutes. *Two minutes!* A bead of sweat appeared on Rymann's forehead. 'I cannot agree to that, Mr President.'

One minute, fifty seconds.

'Why not?'

'I would be betraying a member of the IDF who has risked everything to –'

Harding kept his hand resting on the blue telephone. 'You would be betraying a murderer. You will order Heinlein to land the shuttle at Kennedy – otherwise there can be no deal.'

One minute, thirty seconds screamed the clock.

For the first time Rymann had to make a visible effort to retain his composure. 'I cannot give Heinlein that order, Mr President.'

'What are the Massadas' targets?'

'One missile on Bakal, two on Moscow, and the fourth on Leningrad.'

One minute, fifteen seconds.

'If they're launched, the last order I shall give will be for the

273

destruction of Israel.' Harding's words were clipped out like splinters flying from beneath the blows of an icepick.

Rymann's calm began slipping away. 'Don't you understand why we have done this?' he choked out. 'Israel is finished anyway!'

'One man facing trial for murder weighed against the lives of millions?' There was a deadly calm about Harding's voice. 'Is that the sort of equation you want to spend an eternity in hell trying to work out?'

Rymann found himself being hypnotized by the digital clock. *One minute! One minute! One minute!* 'I cannot betray Lieutenant Heinlein.' It was someone else speaking. Someone using his voice.

Fifty-five seconds . . . . Fifty-four . . . . Fifty-three . . . .

Rymann felt a steel hand closing around his heart. The blue telephone was moving towards him. It was swelling. Above it was Harding's face, a grotesque mask that was mocking him with a savage, taunting smile. To one side was the digital clock, hammering out the seconds with an awful ferocity that made the electrons coursing through its circuits audible.

Forty . . . . Thirty-nine . . . . Thirty-eight . . . .

The face. The telephone. The clock. All three were spinning round. And behind them was the voice. Detached –calm – indifferent.

The *Dominator* must land at Kennedy . . . . At Kennedy . . . . Kennedy . . . . Twenty-five . . . . At Kennedy . . . . Twenty-four . . . . *At Kennedy!* Twenty-three . . . . *At Kennedy!*

Twenty . . . . Nineteen . . . .

Almighty God! In the name of Zion! Make time stand still! AT KENNEDY!

Fifteen . . . . Fourteen . . . .

Rymann saw a pair of hands in front of him.

Thirteen . . . . Twelve . . . . Eleven . . . .

The hands were groping blindly. Colliding with objects as they reached for the hideous blue telephone. They were his hands, searching frantically. Discovering cold plastic. Struggling to lift a handset that was weighed down with five thousand years of history.

Nine . . . . Eight . . . . Seven . . . .

The face before him continued to mock him.

The smooth handset tried to escape from his sweat-soaked palms. He clung to it like a drowning man grasping at a lifebelt.

Six . . . . Five . . . . Four . . . .

A clock whirring somewhere as though it was about to chime.

274

'Heinlein! Heinlein! Do you recognize my voice?'
Oh, God! I'm holding it the wrong way round!
A clock chiming.
Three . . . . Two . . . .
'Heinlein! Abort! Abort!'

94 Heinlein's finger was actually touching the first key when Hendrik Rymann's distraught voice burst out of the shuttle's speakers. The Israeli froze. It was Rymann's voice. There was no doubt about that because he had spent several hours listening to recordings of the Israeli leader.

'Lieutenant Heinlein! Can you hear me?'

'I can hear you, sir.'

An immense sigh of relief bridged the gulf between Washington and the *Dominator*. 'Thank God for that. The operation has been a success. A tremendous success.'

Heinlein closed the control box's cover. 'I'm pleased to hear that, sir.'

'You can jettison the Massadas and return to Earth. But you must return to the Kennedy Space Center.'

Heinlein frowned. 'That's not part of the plan, sir.'

'I know that, Lieutenant. But under the terms of the agreement with the US government, the *Dominator* must return to Kennedy.'

'You've agreed an amnesty for my safe conduct out of the United States?' Heinlein queried.

The pause before Rymann spoke answered Heinlein's question. 'That has not been possible. We will, of course, provide you with the best lawyers. We can apply for extradition to answer charges at home.'

'I'm to be sacrificed?'

'Heinlein, it's not like that.'

A quiet rage began to simmer in Heinlein. 'Then what is it like? An electric chair in Orlando? You know Florida has reinstated the death penalty?'

Another pause. 'I'm sorry, Heinlein. I didn't know that.'

'So what are your orders now, sir?' The 'sir' was a sneer.

'The *Dominator* must return to Kennedy,' said Rymann flatly.

The rage suddenly welled up like an erupting geyser. Neil was forgotten. 'So I *am* to be sacrificed! I'm sorry, sir, but I refuse to accept that.'

'You've got to accept it!'

The brutal betrayal caused Heinlein to lose his icy self-control. Rage spasmed his face. 'I don't have to accept anything! What you have to accept is that I have the Massadas and I propose launching them! Now!'

'No, Heinlein! No!'

Heinlein opened the control box. At that moment the unit was knocked from his knee as Neil's weight crashed into him. The former astronaut yanked the automatic out of the front of Heinlein's coveralls and slipped the safety catch. Heinlein's body cannoned into the forward observation windows. He lashed out with his feet and the thrust sent him careering towards Neil. A shot crashed out. The tumbling control box suddenly lashed sideways like a hooked marlin and vomited a jet of shattered innards across the flight deck.

'Bastard!' screamed Heinlein. Before Neil could react, he was thrown sideways. One hand closed like a vice around the wrist that was holding the automatic and the other went for his throat. Neil was fit and strong but he was no match for the battle-hardened Heinlein whose fury was such that it doubled his strength. The automatic was wrenched painfully from his fingers. The two struggling men tumbled and turned in the micro gravity, their flailing bodies colliding first with the floor and then the roof. Heinlein managed to thrust Neil away. By a lucky chance the automatic drifted by in front of the Israeli enabling him to grab it. He pointed it at Neil. 'One move,' he panted. 'One move, O'Hara. That's all I need.'

'You kill me, Heinlein, and you're a dead man anyway. You couldn't land this bird by yourself,' spat Neil. He was clinging to the back of the commander's seat, his chest heaving, blood trickling into his eyes from a cut forehead.

Heinlein was in much the same state; a hank of bloody hair was hanging off his scalp and his face was badly bruised. His eyes were still blazing their fury and his knuckles were white where they were gripping the automatic, but Neil could see that his words had sunk in.

Heinlein hauled himself up to one side and jerked the gun at the aft crew station. 'Get down there. You can dump the

276

Massadas and close the cargo bay doors. Then we're going to land.'

'Something's wrong,' Sarcha declared abruptly. He reached for one of the television cameras. 'Joss! We're going to send them a picture just in case they can receive us.'

This time Lena did not scream out but she was unable to suppress a whimper of terror when the giant Zulu seized her and tossed her down on the bed.

'Don't bother with tying her up!' Sarcha snapped, aiming the camera at Lena. 'There isn't time. Just get on with it!'

Joss pinioned Lena down on the mattress by planting his foot between her breasts. He then yanked the rhino whip from his belt.

The first blow slashed across her kicking thighs, causing her to scream out in agony and to stop kicking. Joss rolled her on to her stomach and brought the thong down across her buttocks, slicing through her clothes.

'Jesus Christ,' Sarcha muttered, winding back the audio level on the camera so that Lena's screams did not cause signal distortion.

Another blow slashed across Lena's buttocks. She screamed out. The murderous pain dominated her consciousness and yet a fragment of reason retained sufficient control over her body for her to send questing fingers down the side of the mattress to seek the hidden carving knife.

95 'You're crazy,' Neil protested. 'We've *got* to land at Kennedy. I can't bring this bird down in the African bush!'

Heinlein's deadly calm had returned. He was sitting behind Neil in the mission specialist's seat. 'We're talking about one of NASA's designated emergency landing areas. That's where Sarcha is with Lena. They've checked and cleared the site of obstructions. Now, either you land there or we fail to send a report to Sarcha. We've already missed one report. If we miss another, Lena's as good as dead. So what is it to be?'

'I'll need mission control's assistance,' said Neil, reaching up to the communication panel.

'No! We won't be making contact with them again. The orbiter's on-board computers can provide you with all the assistance you need. And don't tell me they can't because I know Goddamn well they can.'

Neil made no reply. He dialled into the mass store. A high-resolution graphic of the Earth's continents appeared on the central display screen. All the landing facilities appeared as flashing points of light. Underneath was a list of code-names. He touched out KRUGER. The screen cleared and was replaced by a picture of the southern African continent. A second set of codes appeared at the foot of the screen. Neil called up the code for a computer-controlled landing. There was a pause while the computer carried out a software check to ensure that it was capable of controlling a landing. He touched a key again. Several columns of figures scrolled on to the screen.

'When do you want to land? We're over the Atlantic at the moment which will give us a window on Kruger within the next ten minutes on this orbit. That'll give us a landing an hour before sunset. Either that or we have to wait until the morning. We can't land in the dark.'

'We'll go on this orbit.'

Neil touched out the appropriate codes and sat back to wait.

'Call up Sarcha,' Heinlein instructed. 'Sound only.'

Neil set the channel selector to 22 and switched on audio receive. Heinlein pressed his PTT button. 'Papa Sierra. This is Delta Hotel. Do you copy?'

'Roger, Delta Hotel,' replied Sarcha's voice. 'We copy you.'

'We've run into problems. The control box to deploy the cargo doesn't work.'

'Oh, for Christ's sake!' Sarcha exploded. 'I don't believe it!'

'Nor did I at first, but it happens to be true. I can't launch the Massadas.'

Maken's voice broke in. '*Dominator!* Do you copy me?'

'Roger,' Heinlein replied. 'We copy.'

'What's happened?' The PLO leader's voice was unnaturally calm.

'I'm sorry, sir. But there's a serious problem with the control box.'

'Can't you repair it?'

'No, sir. Whatever the fault is, I can't trace it.'

'But you've got to fire those missiles! You've got to!'

Heinlein wished that he had a vision channel to Bakal so that he could see the PLO leader's face. For the time being just hearing the

278

note of hysteria that was creeping into Maken's voice would have to suffice.

'There is no way that we can fire the missiles without a functioning control box,' said Heinlein calmly, keeping a wary eye on Neil. 'Now, if you would clear the channel please, sir. We have to begin preparations for landing . . . . Sarcha?'

'I copy,' answered Sarcha's disappointed voice.

'We're ready for entry and landing.'

'Christ, isn't there anything you can do to launch them? Going out in a spacesuit or something?'

'I'm sorry, Sarcha. There's nothing. I've tried everything. Have you started your little party with Lena?'

'She's had a little taster just in case you want your trusty pilot to see her.'

Heinlein glanced at Neil who was staring fixedly at the blank screen. 'No, that won't be necessary, Sarcha. Stand by on this frequency.'

'Standing by,' Sarcha acknowledged.

Heinlein wondered how Sarcha would react when he learned that for several months he had been working for the Israeli government and not his favourite customers – the PLO. He guessed that Sarcha would be mad. Extremely mad and therefore extremely dangerous. For that reason Heinlein had decided that he had little choice but to kill Sarcha at the earliest opportunity after landing. But for the time being he needed the fat little Englishman's help.

'OK, Neil,' Heinlein ordered. 'Go ahead with the re-entry.'

'You'd better fasten your restraint harness,' said Neil, touching the computer controls. For the next few minutes he was sufficiently busy to be able to shut Lena out of his mind. His thoughts returned automatically to her while he waited for the computers to initiate the next phase of the landing procedure.

Five minutes passed without the two men speaking to each other. Neil watched the computer screen intently. The waiting merely tightened the knot in his stomach at the thought of landing the orbiter without any ground landing aids whatsoever. When instructed to do so by the computers, he operated the DAP controls to rotate the *Dominator* through one hundred and eighty degrees so that it finished up travelling tail-first along its flight path. Five minutes later the OMS engines fired for three minutes in a breaking burn that slowed the orbiter by two hundred mph and caused it to begin its ten thousand mile spiralling fall towards Earth.

After fifteen minutes he rotated the spacecraft again so it was pointing in the right direction. The nose lifted automatically so that the spacecraft was presenting its heatshield to the Earth's atmosphere. The orbiter began to shake.

'What's happening?' Heinlein demanded.

'Entry interface,' said Neil calmly, watching the central screen. 'Atmospheric buffeting, We're re-entering at seventeen thousand miles per hour. It'll get worse.'

The buffeting rose to a thunderous roar. Heinlein tried not to think about the pummelling the orbiter's airframe was receiving. His body swung from side to side as the *Dominator* performed a series of automatic 'S' turns. Unlike during the lift-off, the vehicle was the right way up in relation to the Earth, therefore there was nothing to see out of the forward windows except the blackness of space. And then the buffeting got steadily worse. The first moanings of the tenuous atmosphere rose steadily in volume to become the sound of a thousand demented banshees, howling and clawing at the windows. For ten, seemingly endless minutes the uproar continued. It died away. The incandescent colours that had burned around the windows faded and were replaced by sky – sky seen from below. Sky that had a definite tinge of blue about it.

'OK, we're through,' said Neil, resting his hands on the control column for the first time.

'Is the radio blackout over?'

'Sure.' He checked the screen to satisfy himself that all was well. 'We're in the autoland phase. Touchdown in five minutes.'

Heinlein looked out of the side window and saw the great yellow-red stain of the African continent. He pressed his PTT button. 'Sarcha! You'll have us in sight in about four minutes!'

'OK, Joss!' Sarcha snapped. 'You can leave her alone now.'

The Zulu still had his foot bearing down on the back of Lena's neck. He looked up at Sarcha, disappointment written across his chiselled features. 'You gotta let me mark her, Massa Sarch.'

'What?'

'My special mark. Mark of my family. Juss a few little tickles.'

Sarcha grunted. 'Suit yourself,' He watched Joss roll Lena on to her back and stand astride her, then stumped out of the camper and stood blinking at the reddening sun that was hanging above the western horizon. He stayed near the entrance so that he was in easy reach of the microphone when the *Dominator* called him.

As soon as Sarcha was out of sight, Joss grinned down at Lena and started unbuttoning his shorts. What he had in mind did not require the use of the whip so he dropped it on the floor along with the shorts.

A distant movement caught Sarcha's eye. He lifted his binoculars and focused them on the strange patterns of light and shade. It was some minutes before he realized what it was he was looking at.

Elephants! Jesus bloody Christ! A herd of fucking elephants heading his way! As he dived into the camper to grab a rifle, he heard a shrill, ear-numbing scream. Sarcha's eyes widened in astonishment. Joss was rising to his feet; his eyeballs were bulging and he was clutching both his hands over his groin from which the haft of a knife was protruding. Blood was pumping between his fingers, flowing from around the haft in great gouts that streamed down on to Lena's still form. Sarcha had witnessed more than his share of blood and violence but he had never seen the equal of what was before him now. It was Joss screaming – not Lena; Lena had fainted. The shredded remains of the Zulu's scrotum were hanging beneath his fingers.

'Massa!' he croaked. 'Massa – she . . .'

Sarcha didn't hear the rest of the Zulu's words – in that moment he heard the angry trumpeting of a bull elephant.

'Sarcha!' yelled Heinlein's voice from the speaker. 'We've got you in sight!'

Without power, the *Dominator* had the flying characteristics of an airborne brickyard. As it dropped earthwards, its automatic landing computers behaved beautifully. They locked on to their landing site and steered the orbiter down towards the Kruger National Park with a precision that required only the occasional correction from Neil. The 'head-up' display figures projected on to the window in front of Neil kept him continuously informed on the flight's status.

The terrain below resolved itself into grassland. After preflare Neil risked tilting the nose down for a few seconds so that he could have a sight of whatever it was he was supposed to be landing on. At thirty seconds to touchdown the scattered trees and thornbushes were not an encouraging sight.

'There's the camper!' Heinlein called out, pointing. 'And there are the markers!'

Neil saw the markers at the same time as Heinlein. They were in

281

exactly the right place, one marking the beginning of the landing strip and one marking the end, with the camper parked just beyond the last one. It was then that he saw the herd of elephants.

There was no time for Sarcha to deal with Lena or see to Joss – with that wound the Zulu was as good as dead anyway. He ran towards the herd clutching a rifle. The leader was the aggressive, one-tusked bull he had nearly driven into the previous day. He fired his rifle into the air. The old bull knew the sound of rifle fire and stopped. It raised its trunk, trumpeted angrily and then did something extraordinary: it turned around and started running backwards towards Sarcha. Only when he had emptied an entire magazine into the elephant's rump without the rounds having any noticeable effect did Sarcha begin to appreciate the finer points of the cunning old bull's strategy for dealing with poachers armed with rifles.

'I can't do anything about it!' Neil yelled, switching the autolanding computers off-line and taking over control. 'Elephants or no elephants, we're committed to a landing!' He nursed the control column like a mother holding a child and thumbed the button that lowered the main-gear wheels. He stared down through the side windows at the grass that was racing up to meet him. Without the usual friendly voices calling out his rapidly diminishing height, every second waiting for wheel contact with the ground was a single, isolated nightmare of its own.

Ten feet advised the ground-proximity radar on the head-up display.

The elephants were four miles away. Almost dead ahead and swarming towards the camper and the area between the two markers.

Eight feet, said the ground-proximity radar.

'For Chrissake – what's Sarcha doing!' Heinlein snarled. 'I'll kill the bastard!'

'Four feet! Christ! I've got the nose too high!'

Ground contact, when it finally came, was a massive deceleration and a series of hammerblows that seemed certain to tear the *Dominator* apart. Both men were thrown violently forward against their seat harnesses. The nose dropped and the nosewheel added a third furrow to the two that the charging orbiter was already ripping across the African landscape. The elephants were now a mile off and were spread right across the *Dominator*'s path. Neil crammed on the brakes when the ground-speed indicator was reading a lethal ninety knots. He was not sure what happened next because he had never experienced a landing spin. Miraculously the *Dominator*'s undercarriage stood up to the punishment: the entire spacecraft slewed sideways, throwing up a huge cloud of dust. The landscape seemed to tilt and spin in front of Neil at the same time so that the elephants suddenly whipped past the side windows and disappeared from sight. Then they reappeared. Nearer. Less than four hundred yards away. He had no control over the orbiter now. The shocks caused by the landing wheels smashing into obstructions were of such force and frequency that it was impossible to make his hands do what he wanted them do to.

And then all was still.

It was the final miracle. *Dominator* had performed a three hundred and sixty-degree spin on landing and yet had come to a standstill in one piece.

Sarcha gave a scream of terror as the bull wheeled round and charged him. He dropped the rifle and ran blindly. Out of the corner of his eye he saw what he first thought was another elephant. It was not an animal – it was *Dominator* – spinning sideways towards him – towing a huge cloud of dust in its wake. Again he ran but this time he wasn't fast enough. The nosewheel smashed into him and then rode over his mangled body as if it had never been there in the first place.

The electronic clanging of the flight deck smoke alarms sounding off provided all the impetus that Neil needed. He unfastened his harness and hurled himself at Heinlein, driving a fist straight into the Israeli's face.

Without stopping to see if he had knocked Heinlein unconscious, or even attempting to recover the automatic, Neil jumped through the floor hatch to the mid-deck. He released the emergency catches on the ingress/egress hatch so that it swung downwards to the horizontal position. He swung out the drop bar, clung to it for a second until his body stopped swinging, and dropped the ten feet to the ground.

Heinlein was after him immediately. Neil had destroyed the Massada fire control box; three months of planning; the lives that had been lost; the huge sum of money that had been spent – all that

283

had come to nothing because of O'Hara. And for that the American would pay with his life. Heinlein scrambled down to the mid-deck and allowed himself to drop to the ground from the open hatch. At first he thought the swirling dust had been thrown up by the orbiter's landing.

'O'Hara!' he bellowed.

An angry trumpet answered him. Heinlein suddenly realized that he was surrounded by elephants. They were pressing forward and then shying away when they sensed the tremendous heat that the *Dominator* was still radiating from its heatshield.

'O'Hara!'

Heinlein yanked the automatic from his pocket and fired a shot into the air. From the depths of the dust cloud the old bull heard the report. He lifted his trunk and bellowed for his herd to retreat. Heinlein fired two more shots. The ground shook as the elephants circled away from the orbiter.

'O'Hara!'

The great beasts lumbered away across the plain towards the setting sun that was just visible through the dust. Heinlein spotted a shape heading towards the camper. It was Neil. There was no cover and the grass was not long enough to hide him if he tried to lie low.

'Stop, or I'll shoot!'

Neil ignored the command.

A shot rang out. Neil felt a shock in the leg. He tried to keep running but his leg buckled under him. It was a flesh wound. Luckily the slug had missed the bone but the damage it had done to the muscle meant that he was forced to crawl. He heard running footsteps drawing near.

'That's far enough, O'Hara.'

Neil looked up. Heinlein was standing over him, his face contorted with hatred. The primitive savagery in those eyes told Neil that he could expect no mercy. Heinlein raised the automatic, pointed it at Neil's head and tightened his finger on the trigger.

A single shot crashed out. It was not the sound made by an automatic. Heinlein lowered the gun and turned to face the new sound. There was a puzzled expression on his face. Another shot crashed out. Heinlein staggered and straightened up. But not for long. He staggered again and then pitched forward in a lifeless heap.

Neil pushed himself up on his elbows. What he saw next

convinced him that he was suffering from some sort of hallucination, probably brought about by the loss of blood from his leg. Running towards him was a blood-splattered apparition clutching a rifle.

As she drew near, she cried out to him. It was a voice that he knew and loved.

'Neil! Neil!' Sobbing, Lena threw herself down beside him and cradled his head in her arms.

'Hey,' he said weakly. 'You're breaking my neck, hon.'

Sergeant Eugene de Kock of the South African police swore as the vibration from his elderly Scout helicopter threatened to shake the binoculars from his fingers. The radio was squawking something but he had long given up trying to make out what it said. How many times had he complained about the lousy headset? Christ, it was as old as the clapped-out chopper that he was struggling to keep airborne and on course. He slowed to a hover at a height of five hundred feet and had another go at sweeping the darkening terrain ahead. Despite the hammering his eyeballs received whenever he attempted to peer through the eyepieces, he eventually managed to focus them on the tailplane of a large aircraft that was sitting on the veldt about six miles ahead. The setting sun was shining straight on the fuselage, making it impossible for him to distinguish any markings. He grunted to himself; the SAAF radar station at Messina was right – someone had made an unauthorized landing in the Kruger. It was an unusually large aircraft. Parked near it was a camper. No sign of life. They had to be poachers. Poachers! Christ! They were now flying in freighters to steal bloody elephants!

As de Kock neared the offending tailplane, it slowly dawned on him that there was something distinctly odd and yet vaguely familiar about the aircraft. Leading away from it for a distance of about two miles were three swerving furrows cut deeply into the red soil. Probably caused by a rotten landing. Good – at least they could be busted for disturbing the topsoil – that would do for the first charge.

The headphones made more noises. He yanked the jack-plug out of the transceiver in disgust and tossed the headset out of the door. It was time the bastards bought him a new radio anyway. And a new helicopter. His mood was such that he dropped the machine down somewhat heavily a few yards from the camper. He cut the turbine, climbed out and stood, surveying the scene, while unfastening his holster. Christ, it was a weird aircraft. Where had he seen it before?

He approached the camper with great caution, pistol in hand, and called out a couple of times. No one answered. Pity the door was open – he liked kicking down doors. There was a sound from the camper's interior. Sergeant de Kock leaned into the vehicle and regarded the scene before him with sorrowful eyes that spoke of the reams of reports that he would be obliged to write. A blood-splattered black girl was holding a crude torniquet around a white man's leg who appeared to be unconscious. At the same time she was desperately trying to staunch the flow of blood from an ugly wound in the man's leg. She looked up when de Kock's bulk filled the doorway, obscuring the setting sun.

'Please!' the black girl pleaded. 'We've got to get him to a hospital before he loses any more blood. *Please*! You must get help.'

Eugene de Kock's idea of offering practical help was to advise the woman and the unconscious man that they were both under arrest.

On the fourth day of her solitary confinement in Pretoria's Central Prison, Lena was taken from her cell and ushered into an interrogation room. It was the same room where she had spent several hours after her arrival answering the same questions over and over again that had been fired at her by relays of interrogators.

This time the interrogator was a thin, balding man whom she had not seen before. He gave her a frosty stare and indicated that she should sit opposite him at the table. She did so. Several minutes slipped by while the interrogator studied some documents.

'Can you tell me how Neil is please?' she asked.

The man ignored her. She repeated her query but still he ignored her. Eventually he deigned to look up at her.

'Miss Jackson. You will sign this document please.' He passed Lena a pen and printed document.

'I suppose I'm allowed to read it first?'

'Go ahead,' said the man uninterestedly. 'It's an extract from the transcript of your questioning.'

Lena read through the document. It was simply a statement saying that she had shot and killed a David Heinlein five days previously, and, on the same day, that she had stabbed an unidentified black to death.

'I can't sign this,' Lena declared.

The man looked irritated. 'It's the truth, isn't it?'

'Basically – yes. But –'

'Then sign it.'

'Look, I can't sign this. My God – the way it's phrased – you'd think I was in serious trouble.'

'You are in serious trouble, Miss Jackson,' the interrogator warned. 'And believe me, you'll be in even more serious trouble if you don't sign it.'

Lena tried to out-stare the interrogator and lost her nerve. She signed the statement and returned it. The man stood.

'Follow me, please.'

Lena was taken to another room and handed over to a female orderly. To her surprise, her clothes from the camper were returned to her.

'Get dressed,' the orderly commanded.

Unable even to guess what was going to happen to her next, Lena climbed thankfully into her clean clothes. The woman removed a brown envelope from a drawer and handed it to Lena. Inside was her passport, driving licence, and various other documents which she was obliged to sign for.

'OK,' said the woman, nodding to the door. 'You can go now.'

'What?'

'You may leave. Go through that door and turn right at the end of the corridor. The warders will let you through. Stay out of trouble in future.'

In a daze Lena followed the woman's directions. Warders unlocked doors for her on her route and slammed them shut behind her. When the last door crashed behind her, she discovered that she was standing in a busy street.

'Lena!' a voice cried out. 'Lena! It's me!'

She spun round. Earl Hackett was walking towards her, a wide smile of welcome on his face. Beyond him a car was parked at the kerb. Neil's face was grinning at her from the rear passenger window. He waved frantically.

'Hallo, Lena,' said Earl Hackett, shaking her warmly by the hand and leading her to the car. 'We're all booked out on a flight to Washington that's leaving Jan Smuts in ninety minutes. We haven't got much time.'

The quiet luxury of the Boeing SST's cocktail bar was a million miles from the bleakness of Pretoria's Central Prison and from the blistering heat of the Kruger National Park with its harsh memories of Joss and his rhino whip.

Lena sipped her drink and listened attentively as Earl Hackett outlined what had happened since her arrest. While he was talking her hand maintained a fierce grip on Neil, as if she were afraid of letting him out of sight for an instant.

'*Dominator*'s in remarkably good shape,' Hackett was enthusing. 'Amazing really. We're working on a method of rigging up a mate/demate facility and hoisting it on to a truck so we can transport it to an SAAF airbase. The South African government are doing all they can to help.'

'Then why did they make me sign that statement?' Lena demanded.

Neil looked embarrassed. 'Red tape, hon. You killed those two on their soil therefore they wanted their paperwork nice and straight.' He lifted her hand to his lips and kissed her fingertips one by one. 'It's all over now, hon.'

'I've got some great news,' Hackett chimed in. 'Pelham's resigned and I've been appointed acting director of the Kennedy Space Center. The betting is that the appointment will be made permanent. Anyway, I'm making good use of it while I can: I've given Neil his old job back. It's more than his old job – he'll be the fleet captain of the orbital hotel construction and service fleet.'

That news alone called for another celebratory round of drinks. Later the conversation turned to Heinlein.

'What exactly did Israel hope to gain by the operation?' Lena asked.

'Three years. And that's exactly what they got.'

Lena frowned. 'Three years? What possible use can three years be to them?'

Hackett laughed. 'You can achieve a helluva lot in three years. That's about the time Neil should have the orbital hotel finished. It's gonna be a lot of hard work, eh, Neil?'

Neil encircled his arm around Lena's waist and drew her close. 'And a lot of fun, Earl.'